JOURNEY IN THE DARK

Journey in the Dark

By Martin Flavin

———————

GROSSET & DUNLAP
PUBLISHERS NEW YORK
By arrangement with Harper & Brothers

To

Flavia, Martin, and Sean

JOURNEY IN THE DARK

I

SAM BRADEN NEVER TALKED ABOUT HIS FATHER. IF HE SPOKE OF HIS family it was always of his mother, and always with affection and respect. A portrait of her hung in the library at Glencoe across the room from the portrait of his wife. It had been made long years after her death from a daguerreotype taken when she was a bride, and it showed a very lovely face, thoughtful and gentle, with soft dark hair and sober, questioning eyes. The painter had idealized his subject, and yet had captured something from the cracked and faded glass—a sense of quality and honesty. When visitors looked at it—

"My mother," Sam would say. "She was a Hathaway—old colonial stock." And this was true.

If they asked about his father—

"My father was a lawyer," Sam would answer and then would change the subject. And this was only partly true—not true at all in fact.

Jim Braden's antecedents were obscure. He *had* studied law somewhere in New York, and had hung out a shingle in a little upstate town, and had stayed there long enough to marry Sarah Hathaway. And then he had moved on, in search of something else, to some place in Ohio where two children had been born a year or two apart—Madge and Tom. This was in the seventies. But no record of this period exists beyond the fact that they were very poor, and if he practiced law it was probably pure practice—without clients.

He was tall and handsome, rough and uncouth, but with a certain dignity. He had something of the air of an adventurer which women find intriguing and which may have stimulated Sarah's fancy. But this was a deception. He was in reality a lazy, shiftless, discontented man—the kind of a man who, if he had been there when the Indians sold Manhattan for a pair of leather boots, and had had a pair of boots which wouldn't have been likely—well, he would not have bought the island. He would have winked his eye and grinned—too shrewd to be taken in by anything so obvious. He would have figured out in his thick handsome head that somewhere up the river in the neighborhood of Nyack would be a better bet. But he would not have purchased even then because he would not have had the boots. He was saved from bad investments all his life by no greater virtue than his indigence.

In the early eighties they went on—Jim Braden and his wife, and little Madge and Tom. And they probably went right through Chicago, a bustling, growing city, alive with opportunity. But Jim was too smart to be fooled by things like that. He had it figured out that the big lakes had no future; the Mississippi River was the place where things would happen. There may have been some nostalgia in the idea, for he had grown up close to the Hudson. In any case they rode the steamcars on across the state to the bank of the big river. And here there is a record of legend in the matter—

Their money was exhausted; two dollars and a half was the total of their resources. But Jim was determined to go on. The town in which they had alighted from the cars was not what he had pictured, and the muddy, swollen river was a bitter disappointment. Madge, who was four or five, retained throughout her life a memory of the scene: the yellow river in a drizzling rain, muddy, unpaved streets and unpainted ugly houses; her tall and handsome father and her slender little mother, looking serious and frail, with the baby in her arms; and the baggage piled about them—tied up boxes and valises which contained their few possessions.

"I ain't aiming to stay here," Jim Braden said.

The baggageman came out of the depot and spat tobacco juice across the platform. He had come from somewhere else and he agreed with Jim that the town was devoid of opportunity—"Deader than a mackerel," as he put it. He pointed down the street to the stack of a steamboat tied up against the levee. "That's the 'Mary Queen'," he said. "She'll be pulling out in a few minutes now. And my advice to you folks is to go on down the river."

"Will things be any better down there?" Sarah asked.

"They won't be any worse, ma'am," the baggageman assured her.

"Humph!" Jim Braden grunted. It was then he had searched his leather pocketbook and spilled out the contents in his hand—two silver dollars and a half.

"Is that all we've got left, Jim?" his wife had asked.

"That's all."

"But we can't go anywhere with that."

"We can get out of here," he said.

He called a negro boy to help him with the baggage and they hurried down the hill to the levee where the "Mary Queen" was tied—not a big boat to be sure, for the big boats stopped at Memphis, but with two high smokestacks side by side, and a big stern paddle with her name in bright gold letters—the first boat Madge had ever seen.

"Where to?" the ticket agent questioned.

"As far as this'll go," Jim said and shoved his money underneath the wicket.

"You ain't particular," the man grinned, checking the family with his eye.

"I ain't particular."

"For a dollar more you could go to Burlington."

"I'll go where that'll take me."

"Yeh, well—Wyattville, I guess, is the closest I can make it." He handed out two tickets and pushed back four silver dimes, one of which Jim gave to the waiting negro boy.

And in Wyattville Jim Braden spent the long balance of his lazy, worthless life.

It was not very far—a few miles down the river on the Iowa side, south of Muscatine—a sleepy river town of about a thousand people, with a main street crawling up the bank above the levee, and a few brick store fronts on it with wooden canopies built out across the crazy wooden sidewalks which were lined with hitching rails and were high above the unpaved, muddy street. At the foot of the street was the hotel—the Wyatt House, a two-story wooden building with a porch which looked out across the river. Beyond it was a big brick building which had been a warehouse—abandoned now, for the river of the sixties was already dead. Its busy traffic had gradually succumbed to the railroads which were pushing here and there in all directions, presuming even to parallel its banks. Beyond the warehouse, farther down along the levee, was a cluster of ramshackle negro cabins—stevedores who persisted. At the top of the street the town spread out along the bank into a decent village of modest wooden houses with gardens, trees, and grass, and a pleasant rolling country at its back.

The weather had cleared and the warm June day was drawing to a close when the "Mary Queen" sidled up against the levee and made fast, straining at her stern line, for the current ran swiftly near the bank. The Iowa shore must have been a pretty sight in its early summer dress, with the sunlight slanting down across the wooded hills and sifting through the cottonwoods that lined the bluff. Madge never forgot her first impression of it. She was tired with excitement but not hungry, for they had had their dinner on the boat, included in the passage money.

And she remembered that—all the things they had to eat, ending up with chocolate cake and apple pie.

There were no other passengers for Wyattville, and indeed, except for an occasional drummer, there rarely were, though George Wyatt always came out on the porch of the hotel to make certain of the fact. The town was full of Wyatts, descendants of the founder. It was George who saw them first, standing on the levee in the way of the negroes who were busy with the cargo—standing doubtfully, he thought, as if uncertain what came next. He called his wife who was busy in the kitchen and sent his negro boy to fetch the baggage, and waited on the porch with his thumbs in his suspenders—a fat, good-natured man, never much concerned whether travelers came or not, but friendly and curious and helpful. He watched them come, picking their way around the mudholes, Jim Braden in the lead—a tall, big, handsome fellow, not far from forty then, and the frail little woman at his heels with a baby in her arms and a child of four or five tugging at her hand—ten years younger than her husband, not pretty any more, but with something in her face that you remembered—a kind of pride and quality. But let George Wyatt tell the story as he told it many times in after years—perhaps not exactly as it was, but close enough—

"Howdy," George had said, and "Howdy," Jim had answered. He took the proffered pen and signed the flyspecked register: "James Braden and wife—New York."

"New York, eh?" George was impressed. "You're quite a ways from home."

"Yeh, quite a ways."

"Business or pleasure?"

"Both." He gave the negro boy a dime; there were two more in his hand that he kept rolling in his fingers. His wife was standing with the baby in her arms and her back against the counter, looking up into his face.

"One room or two?" George asked.

"One'll do us."

"Well now, let's see—" He turned his back to fumble with the keys which hung on pegs below a row of empty pigeonholes. But he couldn't keep from asking questions. "Aiming to stay a while?"

"Yeh." Jim smiled and he had a pleasant smile. "I'm aiming to settle in this town."

"To settle here?" George stared. "In Wyattville?"

"That's right."

"Oh!—Might I ask what line you're in?"

"Attorney at law."

"Oh—Oh yes!"

"I guess a man could make a living here?"

"Well now—" George Wyatt hesitated. There were three lawyers in the town which was two more than it needed. Old Judge Nicolls was the only one who really had a practice. He was a bachelor and lived in the hotel—its only permanent guest. George handed out the key. "Why yes," he said, "I guess so."

It was then that Sarah Braden spoke for the first time, still leaning with her back against the counter, looking up into her husband's face. "You tell him, Jim," she said. Jim mumbled something underneath his breath. "You tell him, Jim." And when Jim shrugged and made no answer: "No," she cried and turned her back on him to face George Wyatt. "We haven't any money."

"What's that?" George said.

"We haven't anything to pay for board or lodging." And it wasn't an appeal, not tearful or defiant—just a statement of the fact.

"Oh—" George stared, twisting the key between his fingers. "Is—is that right, mister?"

"That's right." Jim grinned a little sheepishly, balancing the dimes on the thumbnails of his hands. "Two dimes, that's all—enough to buy a drink if you'd care to drink with me."

"Why, thanks—" George gulped, and he half turned around to hang the key back on its peg, not being sure yet just what he meant to do. But Mary Wyatt, who had gone behind the counter, took the key out of his hand. She was a comely, easygoing woman, with children of her own.

"You come with me," she said to Sarah. "Those children ought to be in bed."

"But we can't pay you." Sarah stood her ground.

"I understand."

"I'm handy with a needle. I could do some sewing for you."

"Don't you worry about that—leastways, not tonight."

"Oh, thank you—" Sarah said. The tears came to her eyes and she turned her face away. "I'm not crying; I'm just tired."

"Yes, I know." Mary Wyatt led her up the stairs, the baby in her arms, and the sleepy little girl still clinging tightly to her mother's hand.

"Dawgone it!" George would chuckle, when in after years he told the story. "I walked right in the bar and got a bottle off the shelf, and poured two drinks, and took the dimes and put 'em in the drawer. When the Judge came home to supper the bottle was half empty, and me and Braden were old friends."

But Jim Braden never practiced law in Wyattville.

Instead of that he was appointed to enforce it, with the title of Town Marshal. There is no record of exactly how it happened, but the office was vacant at the moment, the incumbent having died some days before. No doubt George Wyatt vouched for him, and probably Judge Nicolls was enlisted in his cause. Perhaps the town was flattered that a lawyer from New York State had selected it to live in, or possibly it chose the easy way out of an awkward situation, for folks could not be let to starve —or couldn't in that day in Wyattville.

At all events Jim Braden got the job, and held it for a quarter of a century. The pay was twenty dollars monthly and a house to live in. Years afterward he got a little more, but Sam figured out one time that the total compensation his father had received from the town of Wyattville, in the lifetime that he lived there, was about six thousand dollars —a quarter of what Sam was then earning in a year. And though such comparisons are devoid of positive value, still the fact remains that, even in that day in Wyattville, twenty dollars monthly was not much on which to raise a family. Indeed, without Sarah's needle, which was quickly recognized to be an expert one, and without her ceaseless vigilance and labor, it could not have been done. And despite this they were very poor.

The house was of course on the "wrong side of the tracks." There were no tracks in Wyattville but there was, none the less, a line of demarkation. At the top of Main Street on the bluff was a vacant piece of ground, known as the Square, but really just a pasture where cows grazed in the daytime, though it did have a cannon and a monument— a wooden one with the names of the boys who had gone from Wyattville to fight the Civil War. The more substantial citizens—retired farmers, tradesmen and the like—lived around this square and to the north of it in comfortable, unpretentious houses which were pretty much alike. They had porches, summer kitchens, sheds or barns, outdoor privies, hand-pumped wells, cisterns underneath them, and ample ground around them with trees and shrubs and flowers, but not lawns or formal gardens. They were not quite urban, not quite rural, but in an intermediate stage—half farm, half town. Two of the three churches were on this side of the Square—the Baptist and the Methodist.

South of the Square there was a swale—a shallow ravine at right angles to the bluff, and this was the *wrong side* of the tracks. It was plainly less desirable for residence—boggy in wet weather and hotter in the summer; and it had been shunned by the elite. The houses were smaller and most of them unpainted. The Catholic church, a very small affair, stood in the bottom of the swale, surrounded by communicants who were known as "shanty Irish"—ordinary laboring people, wagon drivers, livery stable fellows, pick and shovel men, whose women took in washing and did other menial things, and a few store clerks and other minor gentry. There was one negro family in the section—King Cole, a bandy-legged paper hanger who, though black, was much respected for his industry and habits, and his young wife, Cora Lee, light of skin and pretty, and an infant daughter named Acacia but called Cassie.

The house allotted to Jim Braden was across the swale on the south edge of the town. It was shabby and unpainted, of typical design, built like a T turned on its side, two stories at the end, divided into four small rooms. The upper ones, cramped beneath the shingles of the narrow gable, were bitter cold in winter and blistering in the summer. The shaft of the T, one story high, was sitting room and kitchen, though there was a summer kitchen tacked against its side. The small room in the front was called the parlor, and it was rarely used; indeed, for several years it had no furnishings. There was a narrow porch along the front—the long line of the T; and at the back there was a shed, big enough to keep a cow.

The place had been unoccupied for a long time, so that it was in pretty desperate shape—broken windows and loose boards and leaky shingles. But it had some compensations. The house stood on ground near an acre in extent—King Cole's whitewashed picket fence was a hundred yards away—and there were fine shade trees on it, and an enormous apple tree right outside the kitchen door; and in front of the house, all along the porch, were lilac bushes which reached above the eaves. The view was something too, for the house stood near the bluff and looked out across the river to the low green shore of Illinois. Still, it was a poor and shabby place; excluding the negro cabins on the levee, perhaps the most dilapidated house in Wyattville.

In this house Jim Braden lived for more than thirty years—until, in 1914, Sam bought the Elliott Wyatt house on the north side of the Square and gave it, in joint ownership, to his father and his sister, Madge. Nelly was born here in the spring of '82, and Sam in October, '83—in the little, narrow room behind the parlor. And in this room Sarah died. . . .

Cora Lee was hanging out some washing in her yard on the day that the Bradens took possession. She saw them through the trees across the picket fence—a big man, and a woman with a baby in her arms and a child of four or five dragging at her skirt—and George Wyatt with a wagonload of furniture, broken and discarded odds and ends which Mary had collected from their attic and the attics of their friends. And she came around the fence, curious no doubt, but anxious to be helpful. George Wyatt introduced her.

"It'll be nice to have somebody living here again," Cora Lee said pleasantly. She spoke with a soft drawl but not like the levee negroes. "I think you'll like it once you're settled down."

"I'm sure that we will," Sarah agreed. She spoke as she would to anybody, black or white; she had little color prejudice. Madge had climbed onto the porch and was playing in the door, in the way of the men who were carrying in the furniture.

"Call the child away," Jim said. And Cora Lee ran up the steps to get her.

"If you'd let me take her, Mrs. Braden, and the baby too—" she said. "I'll put the baby down—I got one of my own about that age—and the little girl can play around the yard—"

"That's mighty kind of you."

" 'Taint nothing—" Cora Lee laughed softly. "But they'll be out of your way while you're getting things moved in." She took Tom in her arms and captured Madge's hand, but Madge was startled and held back. "Now you come along with me," Cora Lee persisted gently. "We got a dog at our house and five teeny weeny puppies, and your mama'll be right here when we get back." And so Madge went, looking back over her shoulder, not entirely reassured. "Don't you worry, Mrs. Braden. I'll see she gets her dinner. 'Tain't a mite of trouble. You just rest yourself of them until you want them back."

It was a friendly, helpful, democratic world, along the Mississippi in the eighties. The frontier had moved on not very long ago, and the memory and habits of it lingered. Folks were still accustomed to need a helping hand, and to give one freely without question.

Later in the day Annie Hogan came to call—a plump, plain, comfortable woman whose husband, Michael, drove the hack for Birney's Livery Stable. They were neighbors on the other side. Jim was busy in the back, nailing loose clapboards on the house, and she came up on the porch and looked in the open door.

"Anybody home?" she called, and then she saw Sarah in a corner of the room, scrubbing on her knees. "Oh! I guess you're Mrs. Braden?"

"Yes—" Sarah looked up, startled. "Yes, I am."

"My name is Annie Hogan. We're neighbors over yonder. I saw George Wyatt's wagon, and I heard you might be moving in today."

"Oh yes—" Sarah started to get up—to undo the scrap of sacking which was tied around her waist, but Annie checked her with a gesture.

"Don't bother now," she said. "I didn't come to chatter but to see what I could do."

"You're very kind," smiled Sarah, "but there really isn't anything."

"There's plenty, I should think." Annie peered around with an expression of dismay. "Glory be to God, but the place is in a mess! It'll wear you out entirely to clean it by yourself." She looked at Sarah anxiously. "And a little body too."

"Oh no!" Sarah assured her. "I'm strong and well. I can manage nicely."

"Maybe so," Annie agreed, "but the two of us can do it faster." And though Sarah protested, she hurried home to return in a few minutes with bucket, mop, and brush; and she worked like a Trojan through the afternoon—not chattering very much, but pausing once to ask: "I guess you're Catholic too?"

"No.—No, we're not."

"Oh—" Annie sighed. "Well, that's too bad." There was a pause. "I thought the name was Irish."

"It is," Jim Braden said, looking through a window from the porch. "Or anyway it was when my grandfather was born."

"Well—" Annie blinked her eyes. "—all the Irish that I ever knew were Catholic."

"I'm not Irish, Mrs. Hogan."

"You're not?—What are you then?"

"I'm American," Jim said.

"Oh sure, so am I—" And Annie laughed. "—like everybody else. But you're Irish all the same."

"No—" Jim shook his head. "Maybe a long way back—not any more. I'm American, that's all." And he went on nailing clapboards.

There was silence for a time and then Annie paused again—

"What Church do you belong to, Mrs. Braden?"

"Church?" Sarah wiped the sweat out of her eyes. "My family were Episcopal and I was raised that way."

"Episcopal—" Annie sighed again. "There ain't none in Wyattville."

"Yes, I know."

"There's the Baptist and the Methodist—on the other side of town."
A pause. "A person's got to have a church to go to."

"Yes," Sarah said.

"Well, which one will you be?"

"Which one?" Sarah thought about it. "I guess the Methodist would be closer to my own."

"Maybe so—" Annie shrugged with obvious disappointment. "But I'll tell you, Mrs. Braden: the Catholic church is the closest one to God. You better think it over."

"Yes," Sarah said, "I will." There was silence again for a long time—until, late in the day, Annie rose from her knees and looked out at the sun.

"There now—" she said. "I must run back home and get Mike's supper, but I'll come again tomorrow, Mrs. Braden."

"No, please—" Sarah protested. "You've done enough for me."

"It's nothing." Annie laughed, holding out her brawny arms and big rough hands. "Scrubbing floors is easy for me—" She winked a jovial eye. "—but I'm not so handy with a needle. I might be needing help—about a dress."

"Of course."

"Well now, we'll see when you get settled—" Glancing through the window she saw Jim coming from the shed. "Here comes your man and he'll be hungry too, so I better run along." She paused at the door. "A handsome man you've got, and kind and friendly too, or I'm no judge."

"Yes—" Sarah said.

"Folks will like him here in Wyattville."

"I hope so, Mrs. Hogan."

And people did like Jim. They discovered in the course of time that he was no-account, but by then they had accepted him—and by then they had learned to admire and respect his wife.

He was not a bad man. Occasionally he drank too much; not often. He was honest on the whole with everybody but himself. He was not ill-tempered then, not argumentative or quarrelsome; not excitable or talkative but reserved and rather silent—a silence which in time gave place to taciturnity. He was not without ambition but without the will to gratify it, and frustration finally soured his natural amiability. He was not wanting in courage, of the most obvious kind, and, on the few occasions when the duties of his office led him into danger, he behaved with decent valor. Perhaps he loved his wife, though he never spared her anything. But he did not love his children and never took the

« 10 »

trouble to try to understand them. He believed in God and regularly went to church, and he was a staunch Republican. The position of Town Marshall had been designed for him. It is hard to conceive of any other job which he could have successfully undertaken.

He wore a nickel-plated star inside his coat lapel, or pinned to his suspenders in the summer. He rose early in the morning but not until he smelled the coffee on the stove, and he went to bed at nine o'clock. He split and carried in the wood and did other household chores until the children were grown big enough to relieve him of these tasks. In time there was a cow to milk, and chickens to be fed, but the duties of them fell on Tom and Madge, and, in due course, on Sam and Nelly. He never owned a horse until, in later years, Sam gave him one; but he had an eye for horses and a shrewd sense of their values. At farm auctions he would stand around with a straw between his teeth, and there were many people who asked for his advice and deferred to his opinion.

After breakfast he would walk downtown—across the swale, through the Square, down Main Street—pausing to chat with people that he met, dependent on his mood and on the weather. Sometimes he would stop in Clem Wyatt's general store and join the group of loafers that was always to be found there; and sometimes he would stroll on to the Wyatt House and find an easy chair in the bar or on the porch. He made it a point to be on the levee when the "Mary Queen" came in— sitting on a barrel, whittling a stick, with a stern eye on the negroes who had great respect for him. He was always home for dinner prompt at twelve—coming up the swale this time, directly from the levee, through the heart of Shanty Town—completing a sort of watchman's beat.

After dinner he would take a nap, and then as a rule, unless the boat was coming in, he would putter around the house or in the yard till suppertime. In the evening he would sit in a big chair and roll his thumbs, seldom speaking to his wife or to the children—oblivious, it seemed, to what might be going on. He rarely read the paper, and Sam never saw him with a book. At nine o'clock he would take off his boots, wind the clock, and go to bed. But on Saturday nights, when the farmers were in town, he would be out and around until ten, or even later— watching out for city slickers and questionable characters; and once in a long while he would put someone in jail, usually a drunk—in the little brick house, known as the calaboose, behind Clem Wyatt's store. But these were events of rare occasion.

On the Fourth of July he was busy all day long, and on Decoration

Day he took charge of everything. He would march out to the cemetery with the G.A.R., leading the procession, though he was not one of them. Nobody quite knew why, since he was of proper age to be a veteran. If the question was raised he would answer with a smile, "No, I didn't get to go, but my brother, Tom, was killed at Shiloh." And this was true enough, if dubious explanation. A faded picture of the boy hung on the parlor wall beneath a forage cap and rusty saber.

Sometimes on Sunday he went fishing. He was a good shot with a gun and there was game around—prairie chicken, ducks and geese, quail and rabbits—but he liked fishing best; it was something that he could do sitting down.

He was not a bad or disagreeable man, and when Sam was a child he dearly loved his father, though he never felt he knew him very well. It was to his mother that he carried all his questions—his little needs and hurts, but he loved his father too—remotefully, worshipfully, like some legendary hero in a story. It was something, of course, to have a father who wore a shiny, nickel-plated star—to whom men called out in the street, "How are you, Marshal?" and passing negroes bobbed their heads and touched their caps; and from whom, on Halloween, his playmates fled in terror. Yes, that was something for a child. He was ten or twelve years old before his half-thought doubts began to crystallize—before he began to understand the kind of man his father really was.

Sam took care of the old man until he died in 1924. He remembered him best as he was then, in the last years of his life—sitting in a rocker on the side porch of the house, with an overcoat buttoned to his chin although the day was hot—gaunt, hollow-cheeked, with skin like faded parchment, his long white beard stained yellow at the lip—rolling his gnarled, arthritic thumbs—gazing at his son with complaining, rheumy eyes, and belching at him mournfully.

He had taken a day off to see his father, driving his new Marmon from Chicago, starting early in the summer Sunday morning. He crossed the river at Rock Island and came down the river road through Muscatine, as he had done many times before.

The town had not changed much since his childhood. The north side had expanded modestly: stucco bungalows without much ground around them—paved streets, of course, and sidewalks—electric light and sanitation. The barns and sheds were gone, replaced with small garages. He drove around the Square which had now the pretension of a park with lawn and benches and some beds of wilted looking flowers. The cannon was still there. They were building a new monument to the boys from Wyattville who had fought in the Great War.

He drove on slowly, past the Henry Wyatt place—the big brick house with its crazy cupola and iron fence—abandoned now and falling into ruin. As a child it had seemed to him like the palace of a king. But the place had bitter memories of injury and defeat. He paused at the bluff and looked down the empty street to the deserted levee. There were no steamboats any more. The Wyatt House was gone, had burned down long ago. There was another hotel halfway up the street, and some five and ten cent stores, and a moving picture theater. The old warehouse was still there, no more ruined than it had been. But the warehouse, too, had disconcerting memories.

He went on around the Square and stopped before the well-kept, comfortable house which, ten years ago, he had bought from Elliott Wyatt and given to his father and to Madge. A child on a velocipede pedaled to the curb, looking at the car—a chubby little boy with long blond curls, bare legs and socks, and trousers much too short—not the sort of thing you saw in Wyattville

"Hello, young man," he said as he got out of the car. "Do you want to buy a Marmon?"

"I would buy it," the child replied politely with a funny foreign accent, "but I haven't any money."

"Well, suppose we make a trade?"

"No, thank you very much. I don't think my mother'd like it."

"Okay—" He laughed.

He walked up the path and pulled the bell—waiting with a vague sense of discomfort and depression. Cassie Cole came to the door as he had thought she would. Still, it always made him feel uncomfortable at first.

"Oh, it's you," she said respectfully and surprised, smiling at him from the darkness of the hall. He had noticed that she never used his name if she could help it. She was light skinned like her mother, slender and still pretty.

"Hello, Cassie."—Madge had hired her, first asking his permission, and how could he object?—Damn it all, he thought, as he had thought many times, what difference does it make? Bygones are bygones.—He said, "How's Father?"

"About the same." There was barely a hint of negro accent in her speech. "You had your lunch?"

"I picked up a bite in Muscatine."

"Oh—" she nodded slowly. "You staying overnight?"

"No, I've got to get right back."

"Well—" She motioned toward the sitting room. "Your sister's sitting with him on the porch."

"Yes—" He started and then stopped. "Everything all right with you, Cassie?"

"Just fine," she smiled with level eyes.

"How's your mother?"

"She's doing fairly."

"Good," he said and went on across the room.—Damn it all, he thought, what utter nonsense!

"Why, Sam—" Madge got up to kiss him. She was tall and thin and plain, and she seemed old.—Poor old Madge, anchored here in Wyattville while the years had run away—"You didn't let me know—"

"I just thought I'd run out for the day." He sat down on a chair facing his father. "How are you, Father?"

"Eh?" The old man roused.

"It's Sam," Madge said.

"Oh—" Jim Braden nodded without interest.

"How you feeling, Father?"

"Poorly." He mumbled on about his symptoms for a time; nothing else concerned him.

Sam murmured sympathetically and tried to shift the subject, but in vain. The conversation languished and came to a dead end. It was always the same—like a stone wall—like something withdrawing in a shell, impossible of contact. He had been there half an hour and was itching with impatience to be gone.

"Well—" He glanced at his watch. "—I've got to run along."

"So soon?" Madge said, looking disappointed. It was a formula he knew by heart.

"It's a long drive, Madge."

"You could stay overnight—"

"I must be at the office in the morning."

"Well—" She stood up, sighing and resigned.

"Good-by, Father—" He leaned over the old man and took his hand. "Eh?"

"Sam's going now," Madge said.

"Oh—"

"Good-by, Father." There was no pressure in his hand; it was limp

« 14 »

and dry and cold. "I'll be up again soon, Father." No answer and no change in the expression of his face.

Madge went with him through the sitting room to the front door. Dr. Bentley had been in, she said, a day or two before. There was no change except, of course, that he was failing—

"Yes—" he said, pausing on the step. The child with the velocipede was still looking at the car.

"Oh!" she said, looking down the path. "You've got a new car, Sam."

"Yes, a Marmon. Would you like to take a drive, out past the cemetery?—I intended to run out there anyway."

"No—" She hesitated. "Not today, I guess. Some other time." But she kept him with her eyes. "Have you heard from Nelly lately?"

"No, not very lately, but she's all right, I think. I heard from Dr. Goldsmith a month or so ago. He seems encouraged, Madge."

"Oh, I'm so glad." She walked along beside him.

"He keeps a close eye on her."

"Yes, I know.—Your family's well, Sam?"

"Just fine."

"I've never seen your wife or boy. It seems funny in a way—"

"Yes—" He laughed uncomfortably. "I keep meaning to bring them—" —He had meant to bring them, too. But with Cassie Cole here now, coming to the door!—"And then something always interferes," he said. They were on the sidewalk now, and the child pedaled back out of their way.

"When I grow up," he said, "I will buy a car like that."

"I bet you will." Sam laughed. He kissed Madge on the cheek and got into the car.

"Oh Sam—" She leaned across the door.

"Yes, Madge?"

"I meant to tell you something—"

"What?" He was fumbling with the gears.

"I hope it won't upset you, but I think you ought to know—"

"Yes? What?" he said, curbing his impatience.

"Eileen Wyatt's here."

"Oh—" He nodded, startled. So that was it.

"She came last week."

"Not to live here?"

"I don't know. She's staying at the hotel with her parents. I don't suppose—"

"No, no, of course," he said. That would be absurd.

"That little boy—" She leaned closer to him, whispering, "—that's her boy, Sam."

"Oh—" He looked and immediately detected the resemblance. "Well—" he shrugged, shifting the gears, in a frenzy to be off.

"I thought I ought to tell you."

"Of course, but—it doesn't matter now."

"No, of course," she said. "Good-by, Sam."

"Good-by—" He drove off quickly, on around the Square, looking from the corner of his eye, despite himself, at the old house with the cupola.—No, it didn't matter now. But the truth was that it did. Everything mattered, and there was no end to it.

He turned off to the right across the swale, through Shanty Town— still a muddle of poor, unpainted houses—up the slope upon the other side, past the old Hogan place—past the house where he had been born. It was empty again. The shed had fallen down; the windows were broken and the porch was sagging. But the apple tree was there and the lilacs were in bloom. He drove by rapidly, on past the little house where Cora Lee still lived, and out the South road to the cemetery.

No one was there. He left the car and walked through deep grass to the gate. The Henry Wyatt mausoleum stood bleakly in the center, ugly and ornate, not imposing after all. He noticed that the marble was already checked and beginning to crumble at the edges. Eileen would be laid in there some day—or perhaps she wouldn't, not if she didn't choose.—There was Judge Nicolls' grave. George Wyatt's lot was just beyond.—The Bentleys, the Ballous, more Wyatts. There was Clem's. But the Elliott Wyatts did not come home to be buried, and some of them were deep in distant places—at the bottom of the sea and in strange lands.—He walked on across the grass to the far end which looked out across the river.

The lot which he had bought, marked with a modest monument, was neatly kept. He paid something every year to have it cared for. There was one grave with a decent headstone—his mother's. There was room for six—five more: his father and himself, and Madge and Tom and Nelly. But he did not think that he would ever lie there.—He stood for a while, thinking of the past, but mostly of his mother. And then he went back to the car and drove away, not going through the town, but skirting to the west around it.

It was a few days after this that he looked up from the letters on his desk, in his fine, big office high above Lake Michigan—

"Mike—" he said.

"Yes sir?" Mike Hogan came back to the desk—not the Mike who drove the hack for Birney's Livery, but his son—a square-faced man with thick black hair slicked down on his forehead, like a ward politician or a bartender. "Yes sir?" he repeated, standing waiting at the desk.

"Mike, when did you first discover you were poor?"

"Discover I was poor?" Mike looked startled.

"Yes, poor." Sam leaned back in his chair, smiling in a way he had when the matter was a personal one. "When did you find it out—that you were poor?—that you lived in Shanty Town, on the wrong side of the tracks?"

"Jesus!" Mike grinned. "I think I knew that, Sam, on the day that I was born." He never called him Sam unless they were alone, not even then unless there was something in Sam's eyes that invited him to do so.

"No. —No." Sam shook his head. "Little kids don't know those things —not for quite a while."

"Well, maybe not—" Mike scratched his head. "Maybe when we went to school—when we didn't get invited to the parties on the north side of the Square."

"Yeh—" Sam thought about it. "—along in there, I guess." He lit a cigarette and began to read the letters which were waiting to be signed. "Is that all?"

"That's all." He went on with his letters—reading them and signing them, but there were other things in the background of his thoughts. . . .

II

H E WAS NINE YEARS OLD AND DESPERATELY IN NEED OF A NEW SLED. The old one was the kind that little children have—short and high above the ground and flimsy—good enough to sit on and be pulled around, but not suitable for coasting.

Tom had a coaster—a long, low, sleek one, with shiny runners anchored to the frame. Tom was twelve—a big, rough boy, handsome like his father, and careless and strongheaded. Tom would not let him touch his sled, nor would he have thought to do so. The gap between them was much too wide for that—so wide, indeed, that it was never bridged. Sam was a slender, wiry child—thoughtful, rather gentle. He had freckles and a turned-up nose and a cowlick in his hair, and nice blue eyes—steady and inquiring. He took after his mother, people said. The two boys shared one of the narrow rooms beneath the gable, but they rarely spoke to one another. Sam was sick sometimes; he often had bronchitis in the winter, and he would cough at night. And Tom would wake, and roll and thresh about.

"Oh, shut up!" he would groan. "Shut up! Shut up! Shut up!"

And Sam would hide his head under the pillow, and almost strangle in his effort to comply.

Madge was all right. But she was fifteen and seemed quite grown up —like any other adult. She told him things to do and he was supposed to mind. Nelly was his friend and confidant. She was eighteen months older and a grade ahead in school, but she did not put on airs. She liked to play with him and he was devoted to her. She was pretty and gay, and sympathetic.

It was coming close to Christmas. The first snow of the winter had fallen in the night, and he was trudging home from school with Nelly. He wore a threadbare, cut-down suit of tight knee pants and jacket which had belonged to Tom, black stockings and a cap that pulled over his ears. His woolen underwear reached to his ankles and he had warm mittens, but his shoes were badly worn. He was not aware that he was poorly dressed. He had never thought about his clothes.

He was thinking of his sled, and had thought of little else since he woke up in the morning. It was no good for coasting. It would run a little way and then slow down and stop—or, if it did get going, lying on your face you couldn't steer it with your toe. It would whirl around and run into the bank. And anyway the top was loose; the board had split so you couldn't make it stay.

He trudged at Nelly's side, scuffing in the snow. Mike Hogan galloped past, streaking it for home.

"Hi, Sam!" he yelled. "Hurry up and get your sled."

But Sam pretended not to notice. Mike had a coaster—not as good a one as Tom's, but good enough. Mike was his friend and would no doubt let him ride a time or two, but what use was that? The only way to coast was belly-whopper, and you had to have a whole sled to yourself. Mitch Ballou and Grover Bentley came shouting, tearing past, each with a coaster at his heels. All the children in the town were converging on the swale, for in spite of its social limitations Shanty Town was a popular resort when snow lay on the ground. A narrow road wound through it to the levee—an ideal coasting run.

"Hurry, Sam!" urged Nelly. He was lagging behind her, kicking at the snow. "Aren't you going coasting?"

"No."

"Why not?"

"My old sled is no good."

"Oh!" she nodded sympathetically. "Christmas is coming soon. Maybe you'll get a new one." He mumbled doubtfully but hope sprang in his breast. "Come on—let's build a snow man in the yard."

"Well—all right."

They crossed the swale. Coasters were already speeding down. Tom came tearing by with a group of bigger boys. Some little children with ordinary sleds fled out of the way in response to warning shouts. Mitch and Grover raced past side by side. Sam trudged across the road as if he had not seen them. They climbed the slope and went through the yard to the back door. The snow was deep around the stoop.

"We could build it here," said Nelly.

"Yes." Sam felt his spirits mounting. "You get the shovel from the shed, and I'll get some buttons for his eyes." He went into the kitchen.

His mother was wrapping up a dress, and Madge was helping her to fold it. She was forty now but she looked older. Her hair had turned quite gray and there were many wrinkles in her face, and lately she had not been very well. She had finished the dress which was promised for today, hardly rising from her chair since early morning, and then had pressed it, keeping one eye on the stove, on which supper was cooking; and now she was folding it and Madge was helping her.

"Oh, Sam," she said, "will you do an errand for me?"

"An errand, Mom?" His heart sank. "I was going to build a snow man in the yard."

"I'm sorry, dear. I meant to have Tom do it, but he got in and out before I caught him."

"All right—" He winked the tears back.

"Nelly can go with you."

"Oh, I don't care. I'll go alone."

"It's this dress for Mrs. Henry Wyatt. It's just across the Square."

"I know—" But it couldn't have been worse, he thought. He had never been inside the iron fence; and the big brick house inspired him with terror. And suppose he should come face to face with Eileen Wyatt. She was in his class at school, and he was strangely fascinated by her, though he always pretended not to notice her. She had blonde curls and she was very pretty. And then there was her grandfather—that crochety old man. Suppose—

"You can take your sled," his mother said. "Madge, you get the basket."

He took the basket out and tied it on his sled. Nelly was already hard at work: the snow man had risen to his knees.

"Did you get the buttons, Sam?"

"No."

"Why not?"

"I have to go on an errand."

"Oh!— Well, hurry back."

"All right—" But he knew it would be dark by then.

He trudged across the swale with the silly little sled bobbing up and down behind him. Mike Hogan, belly-whopping down the road, yelled at him derisively, but he did not look around. He tramped on drearily, kicking at the snow—the first snow of the winter. Much good it was to him! He couldn't even build a snow man in the yard. It was hard to be the youngest. Everybody else did what they pleased, but he was always caught.

He came out on the bluff and cut across the Square. The snow had drifted and he picked the deepest spots which were almost to his knees, pretending for the moment that he was an explorer, jerking the poor old sled along behind him, and calling out instructions as if he had a dog team in the lead. But it wasn't any fun—a wretched substitute—and his feet were so cold, inside his broken shoes, that they were getting numb.

There was the iron fence, and— His heart sank like a lump of lead. There were children in the yard; he couldn't see them but he heard their voices. He crossed the street with lagging steps and peeked between the bars. It couldn't have been worse: Eileen Wyatt and a boy whom he had never seen. She had on leather leggings and a little red cap cupped around her flaxen curls, and the boy had sailor trousers and a short coat called a reefer. They were right there by the path to the front steps, putting the final touches on a snow man—a most imposing one. It had big black buttons for its eyes, and a pipe stuck in its mouth, and an old stovepipe hat cocked on its head. The unknown boy was arranging a broomstick for a staff, and Eileen was standing back and looking on. They were chattering and laughing like old friends.

He wanted to run away. Perhaps there was no other time in all the years that followed when the urge to run was stronger—nor when he had better reason. But he didn't run away; he was not the running kind. He found the gate and opened it, and went slowly up the path with his eyes fixed on the door. He knew that they had stopped what they were doing, that they were watching him. He heard the boy say in a lowered voice, "Who's that?" But he didn't hear her answer. He passed by so close he could have touched her with his hand, and climbed the wooden steps to the front door. They had been freshly swept, but he didn't notice that.

He was terribly embarrassed. Perhaps he would never again be so embarrassed in his life. At any rate, not thinking what he did, he dragged the old sled up the steps behind him. He was looking for a bell to pull when the door was thrown open and the terrible old man—Old Henry Wyatt—stood glaring at him, roaring in a terrifying voice:

"How dare you dirty up my steps?— What the devil do you want?" Sam stared at him without the breath to speak. "I won't have sleds dragged up my steps. Take it away." He saw the basket now and added furiously, "Go around to the back where you belong." And he shut the door with an appalling bang.

Sam turned and stumbled down the steps, the old sled bumping at his heels. At the bottom it ran into him and tripped him, and he went down flat, sprawling in the snow. He heard them laughing. When he scrambled to his feet two men were coming up the path, and he saw that one of them was Old Henry's son, Young Henry, the father of Eileen, but the other one he didn't know. This one, laughing not unkindly, set the sled back on the path.

"There now, son," he said, "no damage done." Sam shook his head. "Father's fussy about his steps," the man went on, "but his bark is a lot worse than his bite. What did you want?" But Sam would not trust himself to speak.

"It's the Braden boy," Young Henry said.

"Braden?" He started slightly, nodding to himself. "Oh yes!"

"His mother is a seamstress." Young Henry turned to Sam. "Something in the basket you wanted to deliver?— Well, take it around to the back door." He spoke not harshly, but not pleasantly. Sam backed away.

"Wait a moment, son—" The other man was feeling in his pocket. He took out something and put it in Sam's hand. "There now, don't feel badly. Everybody comes a cropper now and then."

Young Henry was standing on the steps. "Come on, Elliott," he said. And he called to the children who were looking on and giggling, "Eileen —you and Neill had better come in now. It's almost dark."

"Right around the corner, son—" Elliott Wyatt pointed with his walking stick. He did not look like his brother, nor like any man that Sam had ever seen. His clothes were different and his hair and the mustache on his lip, and the walking stick he carried which was very thin and shiny, and the way he walked and talked—

Sam fled around the corner of the house.

Cora Lee came to the door. She was helping in the kitchen for the Christmas holidays.

"Why, Sam—" she said. Then, looking at him closely, "What's the matter, honey?"

"Nothing—"

"You been crying.— Did you fall and hurt yourself?"

He nodded. It was easier to let it go at that. The depth of his distress was impossible to tell. "It's a dress—" He pointed to the basket. "—for Mrs. Henry Wyatt."

"Sure enough." Cora Lee took the dress out of the basket. "Now you come in and warm yourself."

"No—" He backed away. Suppose Old Henry should find him in the house.

"Yes sir." Cora Lee was firm about it. She took his hand and led him into the kitchen which was filled with pleasant odors. "Sit up there on that chair while I find a piece of cake."

"I don't want any cake—"

"Yes sir, you do." And Cora Lee disappeared into the pantry.

It was then for the first time that he became aware of something clutched tightly in his mittened hand—something flat and round, but he had not really seen it. He opened his hand and could not believe his eyes.—A half dollar.—There was no mistake about it. He had never had so much money in his life. It was a fortune. Cora Lee came bustling with the cake—

"My goodness, Sam, how come you got that money?" But he was speechless. "Young Mr. Henry give it to you?" He shook his head. "Then who?"

"The other man."

"What other man?"

"He had a shiny stick."

"A cane.—Mr. Elliott, I bet."

"Yes," Sam said, remembering to have heard the name.

"He's mighty nice—" Cora Lee turned to the stove. Sam put the coin deeply in his pocket and began to eat his cake.

"Is that—his boy?" he ventured.

"What boy?"

"The one—" Sam motioned toward his legs. "—with sailor pants."

"That's him." Cora Lee laughed gaily. "Neill Wyatt—about your age, I guess. There's another littler one named Wayne. Wayne Wyatt—" She rolled it on her tongue. "Ain't that a pretty name?"

"Yes—" he said without enthusiasm. "Are they going to stay here, Cora Lee?"

"Stay here?— My goodness, no! They live in Chicago. Mr. Elliott just came to spend Christmas with his pa."

"Oh—" Sam felt relieved.

It was dark when he got home, and the snow man was unfinished—had not in fact progressed above the knees. Well, it didn't matter. He had had enough of snow men for the day. He found Nelly in the kitchen and beckoned her into a far corner of the room; and he told her what had happened and showed her the half dollar.

"Sam!" Her eyes were big with wonder. "What will you do with it? Why, you could buy a coaster!"

"Maybe—" But he had a feeling that it would not be enough. "I'm going to buy Mom a Christmas present."

"You are?— But what about the coaster?"

"Well—" He turned the matter in his mind. "You said I'd get one Christmas."

"I didn't, Sam. I said you might."

"Oh—" He had thought perhaps she knew, and had shrewdly tried to trick her into an admission; and he was disappointed. "Well anyway, that's what I'm going to do."

At supper he was silent and detached, considering the matter from all angles. But Jim Braden, who seldom spoke at table, had something to relate: Elliott Wyatt had come home, all the way from Chicago, to spend Christmas with his father, and had brought his wife and children. The family hatchet had apparently been buried.

"What hatchet?" Madge inquired.

It was Sarah who explained: Elliott Wyatt, who was younger than Young Henry, had gone back East to school, to Harvard College; no doubt his own idea, since his brother had been satisfied to accept such education as the state university afforded. At all events Elliott had spent four years at Cambridge, and in Boston he had met the girl who was to be his wife. At the end of his last term he had married her and brought her back to Wyattville to live. Old Henry had accepted the matter with good grace—he had then been a widower for some years—and had even built a house for his younger son to live in and given it to him for a present—the comfortable white house on the north side of the Square, next door to Dr. Bentley.

"It still belongs to him," Jim said, "but it's been closed up for years."

Sarah went on: Elliott had gone into his father's bank—the only one in town—where Young Henry was already well installed. But then things hadn't worked; the brothers didn't get along. Elliott was full of new ideas while Henry, like his father, preferred to plod along in dull but steady fashion. And the wives agreed no better than their husbands; there was rivalry between them which flared up into quarrels. Daphne Wyatt who had come to her new home with sparkling expectations and trunks of city clothes, could not adapt herself to life in Wyattville any better than could Elliott. The thing just wouldn't work.

"But I don't see why," said Madge. "They had lots of money, didn't they?"

"I'll tell you why," her father answered, frowning to himself. "This poky little town wasn't big enough for them. They wanted to be some place where they could get along."

"Maybe—" Sarah sighed and then went on: Elliott who had always been, so people said, a harum-scarum boy, began to drink too much, and that made matters worse. And one day Daphne Wyatt, who did not lack for spirit, packed her pretty clothes and left—just walked out without a word. "That was just before we came here," Sarah said.

"And then what happened, Mom?"

"I'll tell you, Madge," her father interposed. "He was like a crazy fellow. He'd hitch up his team and drive to Muscatine or even Davenport; and he'd get drunk and leave his horses tied out in the street all day and night. Or he'd get aboard the "Mary Queen" and go down to St. Louis and be missing for a week. Or he'd set around the Wyatt House drinking whisky by himself until George Wyatt locked the door at night and took him home. He always acted like a gentleman no matter where he was, but he was young and headstrong—" Jim chuckled to himself. "I nearly had to lock him up one time—"

"Lock him up?" Tom stared, and Sam was listening now. "What had he done, Pa?"

"Nothing really bad . . ." Jim pushed back his chair. "He was down on the levee arguing with Mike Hogan. He wanted Mike should drive him to Chicago in Birney's livery hack."

"But that's two hundred miles, Pa."

"Yeh—" Jim grinned. "He didn't care. He said he'd buy the hack—he'd trade his house for it. 'I want to get out of here,' he shouted. 'I'm done with Wyattville.' He had hold of the horses so Mike couldn't drive away, and he was pretty noisy. The niggers on the levee were enjoying it a lot."

"What did you do?"

"Nothing much—" Jim chuckled. "I says to him, 'Elliott, I'm sick of this town too. I'll tell you what let's do: I'll go with you to Chicago.'—'You will?' he says. 'Are you serious about it?'—'I sure am,' I told him. 'I been waiting for the chance ever since I got here.' And I opened the door for him to get inside, and then I winked at Mike and jumped in the hack beside him."

"Did you really mean it, Pa?"

"Well, yes and no—" Jim said. "When we went by the Wyatt House I called to Mike to stop, and then I says to him: 'Elliott,' I says to him, as careless as I could, for I wasn't dead sure that it was going to work, 'suppose we have one farewell drink before we start.' He thought about it for a moment, and I was in a sweat, for if it didn't work I'd have to run him in. 'Jim,' he says, 'that's a very good idea.' And we got out of the hack and went in to the bar. George Wyatt looked at me as if I had gone crazy—" He chuckled at the memory.

"And then, Pa?"

"Well, of course, when we got back, Mike had driven off."

"Oh!— What did he say?"

"He said—" Jim paused to light his pipe. "Yeh, I remember what he said. He took hold of my arm and he was laughing—laughing so hard that he could hardly talk. 'That's a horse on me,' he says, 'and I won't forget it, Jim.' And he went on up the hill—back to his empty house."

"But he did go to Chicago."

"Yeh, he went soon after that, but not in Hogan's hack. He went all right, and that's where he was smart—" He sighed and pushed his chair still farther back, closer to the stove. "He's made a lot of money in ten years—on the Board of Trade or something of that kind. Some people say he's richer than his father—" He leaned back in his chair, the animation fading from his face.

"What's the Board of Trade, Pa?"

There was no answer.

"But what happened to his wife?" demanded Madge.

"Everything came out all right," her mother said. Daphne Wyatt had come back to her husband in Chicago, and the two boys had been born, and they were happy.

"Oh—" Madge nodded.

Tom edged toward the door and slipped away. But Sam was spellbound with his elbows on the table and his chin cupped in his hands. He helped to clear the table in a daze, and then while his mother and the girls were busy with the dishes, he sat on the little wooden stool which was his own, outside the lighted circle of the lamp, with his eyes upon his father—that big, strong, handsome man whose hair and beard were beginning to turn gray—with the sparkling silver star hidden out of sight on the inside of his coat—who could have, and almost had, locked up Old Henry's son, the kindly, smiling one whose half dollar he was clutching in his pocket—run him in and locked him up just like anybody else, in the calaboose behind Clem Wyatt's store. Yes, that was his father—

"Sam—" His mother roused him with her hand upon his head. "What are you puzzling now?"

"Nothing, Mom—"

"Shall I read you a chapter before you go to bed?"

"Please, Mom." He ran to get the book, a tattered volume of *Tom Sawyer,* and he found the place and sat on his stool against her knees beneath the lamp. Madge was sewing something, but Nelly came to listen. It was getting toward the end—the part where Tom and Becky were lost in the great cave. It was terribly exciting, and an agony to stop— "One more chapter, Mom," he begged.

"It's bedtime, Sam, so run along—and you too, Nelly."

He put the book away on the shelf beside the clock. "Good night, Pa," he said. But Jim Braden did not answer. He was rolling his thumbs, and his thoughts were far away in the midst of the things he had not done. "Will you come up, Mom?" He always asked the question when he started up the stairs, pausing to look back, pleading with his eyes that she would come, when he was in his nightgown, and listen to his prayers and tuck him into bed and answer something that was in his mind, or anyway just be there.

"Yes, Sam, I'll come." And presently she stood beside his bed while, kneeling in it with clasped hands, he hurried through the ritual: "Now I lay me down to sleep—" The candlelight was merciful; her workworn hands looked soft and white, and the wrinkles in her face were smoothed away. But she always seemed beautiful to him. She had kissed him and was reaching for the candle—

"Mom—"

"Yes, dear?"

"Could—" He hesitated. It was rather hard to say, and a lot of things depended on the answer.

"What, Sam?"

"Could Pa arrest—Old Henry Wyatt, Mom?"

"Arrest Mr. Wyatt?" She was startled. "But, sakes alive, what for?"

"But *could* he, Mom?"

"You mean, if Mr. Wyatt did something wrong and wicked?"

"Well, yes—"

"But he wouldn't do such things."

"Yes, but if he *did*."

"You mean, if Mr. Henry Wyatt broke the law, could your father arrest him?"

"*Old* Mr. Henry—yes, Mom."

"Why, I expect he could, Sam."

"Just like anybody else?"

"Just like anybody else."

"And lock him in the calaboose?"

"Yes, I guess he could."

"Oh—" He sighed with satisfaction.

"But what put such a notion in your head?"

"I—I was just wondering."

"Were you?" She drew the covers tight and tucked him in. "You're such a funny little boy—always wondering about things." She snuffed the candle out. "Good night, dear. Pleasant dreams."

"The same to you, Mom."

And his dreams were not unpleasant, though terribly mixed up and thrillingly exciting. He was lost in a great cave with a pretty little girl with flaxen curls. Her name was Becky Thatcher but she looked like Eileen Wyatt. And there was a buried treasure—a crumbling wooden box crammed full of bright half dollars, and a man named Injun Joe with a face just like Old Henry's. . . .

Next day after school he went with Nelly to Clem Wyatt's store, and Clem came to wait on them himself.

"Well, my young friends, what can I do for you?" He was a big, good-natured man like his brother, George—not resembling in the least his Uncle Henry.

"How much is a coaster?" Sam inquired, fingering the half dollar in his pocket.

« 27 »

But it turned out, as he had both feared and hoped, that a coaster was entirely out of reach: one like Tom's would cost four dollars, and a little one like Mike's was two dollars and a half. There was an awkward pause in the proceedings until Nelly mustered courage to step into the breach.

"We would like to buy a Christmas present."

"Oh, I see—" Clem looked around. "How much money do you want to spend?"

"This much," said Sam and displayed the precious coin.

"Hum—" Clem seemed impressed. "You want to spend all that?"

"Yes, all," Sam answered with grim determination.

"Well now, let's see.—But who is it going to be for?"

"For my mother."

"For your mother, eh?—Well sir, that's fine." Clem led the way to a glass case which was full of glittering jewels. "How about a brooch to pin her dress?"

"She's got a brooch," said Nelly, "and it's gold."

"Oh well—" Clem scratched his head. "There's lots of other things. Suppose you look and see—" They pressed their noses to the glass.

"There—" Sam pointed.

"Where?"

"It's a thimble—" It was in a red plush box and it had a band around it which sparkled beautifully.

"Why yes," said Clem, "the very thing." He got it out and flashed it in the light. It was more than fifty cents but he was a kindly man. "It's marked a dollar—"

"Oh—" Sam's heart sank.

"But I'll tell you what I'll do," Clem grinned. "Seeing that it's you, Sam, I'll let you have it for exactly fifty cents. And it's silver-plated too."

"Silver!" Nelly was ecstatic. "And those little things that sparkle— are they diamonds, Mr. Wyatt?"

"Diamonds?" Clem pretended to examine them. "Well now, I don't know if they are. I wouldn't guarantee them, but they sure look like diamonds. And things that look like diamonds are as good as diamonds, ain't they?"

"I'll take it," Sam said firmly. He relinquished the half dollar, and Clem Wyatt picked it up and dropped it in the drawer as if it had been nothing.

"I suppose—" he remarked, wrapping the little box with special care, "I suppose you two are going to the party."

"What party?" Nelly said.

"Eileen Wyatt's Christmas party. Her mother's been in here buying everything in sight—candy and the like, and those paper things you pull that snap like firecrackers. I had to send and get 'em from Chicago—" He saw from their faces that the subject was unfortunate and amended it as deftly as he could. "I just remember now that Mrs. Henry said the children hadn't been invited yet.—There you are, Sam." And he put the package in Sam's hand.

But they were not invited to Eileen's Christmas party which took place on the afternoon preceding Christmas day. And they knew that they would not be invited, which is not to say that they did not hope. But they knew in their hearts that hope was vain. Before the day was out they heard about the party from half a dozen children. But they did not mention it between themselves, nor speak of it at home, not even when they saw their mother making Eileen's party dress. And when Madge referred to it they pretended not to hear, but they saw their mother frown and shake her head.

There was no good reason why they should have been invited. They were not close friends of Eileen, and Sam, indeed, had pointedly avoided her—and the source of his behavior had no bearing on its outcome. Not all of the children in the town were invited to the party—not half of them in fact. And they had not been omitted from the list of fortunate ones because they were poor and lived in Shanty Town. Mrs. Henry Wyatt who taught in Sunday school and regarded herself, and justly too, as a kindly Christian woman, was incapable of such discrimination. Had the matter been called to her attention she would have said, "Good gracious, why I never thought of them!" And this would have been true.

They were not ignored or overlooked. Their names had not been considered and rejected; they had simply not been mentioned by anyone concerned. At the bottom of all this the fact remains that had the Bradens lived elsewhere than Shanty Town—had they lived, for example, on the north side of the Square, as did Mitch Ballou whose father, Mitchell J., job printer and owner of the Wyattville *Gazette*, was in debt to everybody and a drunken sot to boot—well, had they lived where Mitch lived; or had Jim Braden really been a lawyer with an office and a desk, regardless of whether he had clients; and had Sarah Braden, whom everyone respected, not made dresses for Mrs. Henry Wyatt and numerous other women; had one or more of these things been different, why then the chances are that someone would have said: "Oh yes, Eileen, and don't forget to ask Sam and Nelly Braden—" And no voice would have protested.

It was of course unfortunate that most of their close friends were among the favored ones: Mitch and Grover, George Wyatt's daughter, Jane, and Hub Baxter and his sister. Mike Hogan was almost the only one not included in the list. He and Sam and Nelly spent the afternoon in the woods beyond the town, climbing trees for mistletoe. The party was not mentioned except once when Mike shouted:

"Say, this is fun! I'd sooner be out here than going to a party."

"You bet!" Sam shouted in reply, but he didn't really mean it.

It was dark when they got home, loaded down with mistletoe, to the warm and cozy house which Sam had never known was poor and shabby. The long, low-ceilinged room seemed very bright and cheerful in contrast with the night. Madge had made some wreaths with Sarah's help, and Tom had felled and dragged home a Christmas tree—not a very big one like the one the Sunday school would have, but tall enough to touch the ceiling. It was standing in the corner, waiting to be trimmed. Party or no party, this was Christmas Eve—not a time to indulge in vain regret. In the morning there would be—well, probably a coaster. He had been watching for it, had peeked into the parlor and explored the shed; but nothing like a coaster had been anywhere in sight. Still, he knew from experience that this didn't mean a thing, and he was not discouraged.

After supper corn was popped to trim the tree and while the children strung it Sarah read to them—Dickens' *Christmas Carol* which they almost knew by heart, for it was always read on Christmas Eve. Jim had gone back to town—just to keep an eye on things. But Tom was at home and lent a hand to reach the higher branches. It was really very pretty all festooned in big white flakes—like a snowstorm in the house. And then there were the candles of many different colors, and when they had been lighted the big lamp was put out.—Yes, it was beautiful.

Sam and Nelly were permitted to come downstairs in their nightgowns, to hang up their stockings on a chair beside the stove. And after that, cuddled on the sofa, they listened to stories of Christmas in New York State when their mother was a girl—stories Sam had heard a hundred times but never wearied of:—the broad, wooded acres spread out above the Hudson with real mountains at their back, and the horses and the cattle, and the big brick house—Glencoe it was called—

"As big as Old Henry Wyatt's, Mom?"

"Yes, I think maybe."

"Bigger?" he insisted.

"Well, I don't know. About the same, I guess."

"And the kitchen fireplace—could you really stand inside it?"

"Yes, you could do that. The logs that it burned were as big around as you are, and the chimney was made for Santa Claus."

"Oh—" He sighed ecstatically. He knew of course that there was no Santa Claus, but there had been a time, not very long ago, when the narrow, crooked stovepipe had seemed fatal to his hopes.

"Mom—" Nelly stirred.

"Yes, dear?"

"Did you go to parties—when you were a little girl?"

"To parties?—Yes, sometimes—"

"Did you ever have a party—I mean, at Glencoe?"

"Yes, I expect so."

"A big one, Mom?—with lots of children and—and—"

"Those paper things," Sam said. "You pull them and they snap like firecrackers."

"No—" Sarah smiled. "I don't remember anything like that. Sometimes we pulled candy. But they weren't big parties, Nelly. Glencoe was in the country and there weren't many children round about."

"Yes—" Nelly nodded deep in thought. "Do you think we'll ever have a party, Mom?"

"Why, of course you will." She laughed, but it didn't sound to Sam just the way that laughing should. "You'll have them and you'll go to them. Don't you worry about that. And now it's time for both of you to run along to bed."

"Will you come up, Mom?" Sam asked from the stairs. And when she had come and tucked him in and kissed him. "Mom—"

"Yes, dear?"

"When you were a little girl—" He hesitated, fearful lest his question be revealing.

"When I was a little girl—yes, Sam?" she prompted.

"You used to hang your stocking up—"

"Every Christmas Eve."

"Well—" He squirmed deeper in the covers. He could feel the thimble box beneath his pillow. "—why don't you now?"

"Why?" She sat down on the bed, stroking back the stubborn lock of hair from the earnest freckled face. She loved all four of them but Sam was her favorite—the youngest and the last that she would have; and there were things about him that seemed strangely reminiscent of herself. "Grownups just don't, Sam."

"Well—" He was determined to keep the matter casual. ". . . I don't see why."

"Do you think I ought to, Sam?"

"Well—" He pretended to reflect. "—it can't do any harm."

"No, I suppose it can't," Sarah agreed.

"Of course, when you look, there might be nothing in it."

"Of course—" she nodded.

"But anyway, if you don't hang up your stocking—well then, there couldn't be."

"That's very true, Sam." She appeared to turn the question in her mind. "You know, I think I will. I'll just hang one up and see."

"You will, Mom?" But he instantly suppressed his exultation and added with a gloomy note of warning, "Of course it may be empty in the morning."

"Yes, I know, but it can't do any harm to try. Nothing ventured, nothing gained: that's what my father used to tell me." She pressed her lips against his cheek. "Good night, dear." She snuffed the candle and lingered for a moment at the door. "Don't you get out of bed until the fire's lighted."

"No, Mom, I won't."

But he was wide awake in the black night long, long before he heard his mother moving in the kitchen, and smelled the pitch pine burning in the stove. And then, not waking Tom, in a shivering jiffy he was into his clothes and down the stairs. It still dark; the lamp was lighted; and Nelly, who he had feared might get there first, had not appeared. There was no one but his mother, busy at the stove. The thimble box was in his pocket—

"Merry Christmas, Mom."

"Merry Christmas, Sam."

He glanced eagerly around. There were the stockings hanging on the chair, and two of them were bulging, but nothing like a coaster was anywhere in sight. His heart was thumping on his ribs.

"Don't forget to wash and comb your hair, Sam."

"Yes, Mom." He rushed to the sink and pumped into the basin.

"There's hot water on the stove."

"I don't care about it hot—" He plunged into the icy water. "Did you look, Mom?—in your stocking?"

"No, I waited for you, dear."

"Oh—" He stood on tiptoe at the mirror to comb his tousled hair. He could see in the mirror all around the room, and there was nothing like a coaster. Still, of course, you couldn't tell. "I'm ready, Mom." He ran to the chair, slid the box from his pocket and into the empty stocking. "But aren't you coming too?" His heart was pounding but he tried very hard to sound a melancholy note. "It looks awfully empty, Mom—"

"Yes, it does—" she sighed, standing close behind him. He was thankful that she couldn't see his face. "I guess it wasn't any use— maybe I'm too old—"

"But, Mom—look there!"

"Where?—what?"

"Down there in the toe. It looks like something, Mom."

"Why, I declare it does."

"Well, why don't you look and see?"

"I'm almost afraid to touch it." She pressed the stocking in her hand. "Why, Sam, there is!" He nodded breathlessly. And then she felt inside and drew it out. "A little box! Now what do you suppose—"

"Well—open it."

"Just let me get my breath—" She sank down in the chair to take the paper off. "Yes sir, it is a box."

"But open it," he begged.

"Well—" She hesitated. "You don't suppose it could be meant for someone else?"

"Oh no!" But then he caught himself. "It was in your stocking, Mom, and you've got a right to keep it."

"Yes, I guess I have." She raised the cover. "Oh!" she cried.—Yes, there it was—the precious thing in its bed of crimson plush.—"Sam!— A thimble!" But he was completely speechless. "My goodness! Well, I never!" She slipped it on her finger and turned it in the lamplight. "It's beautiful, it's wonderful, and the very thing I needed; my old one's worn thin. And see how it sparkles—just like diamonds, Sam."

"Yes, yes—" he stuttered. "Clem Wyatt wasn't sure, Mom. He said they might be diamonds, but anyway he said that they were just as good."

"Sam!—You don't mean— It's not from you; you didn't buy it for me?"

"Yes—" he nodded, almost overwhelmed. "Nelly went with me, but I bought it."

"Oh, Sam, Sam—" She drew him tight against her breast. There was something in her voice—and then he was conscious of teardrops on his cheek, and he looked up anxiously—

"But why are you crying, Mom?"

"Because I'm happy, dear."

"Oh—" He accepted the explanation; he was almost crying too.

And in all the years that followed he would not forget this moment, nor would there be another in his life which would quite equal this. There were many gifts that he would give, and among them would be diamonds—big and real ones; but he would not again experience the emotion of this moment, the wealth of its completeness—feeling his mother's tears against his cheek—and the tawdry little thimble with its chips of broken glass. . . .

There was no coaster. For quite a while he kept on hoping, unwilling to admit the fact, though he could plainly see there was nothing underneath the tree which could possibly resolve into a sled. Still, you couldn't be absolutely certain. Waiting for the others he explored his stocking with what enthusiasm he could muster, and with decent exclamations of delight designed to cover up his sinking heart. There was nothing in it that he really wanted:—a candy cane, an orange and some nuts, a whistle, a knife—but it had a broken blade, some marbles—of no use at all in winter.

Nelly came tearing down the stairs, then Tom and Madge. And in the subsequent confusion his despair was not observed. The important presents were underneath the tree: new dresses for the girls, pretty frocks that had been fashioned in the hours of the night after they had gone to bed; an air rifle for Tom—not a new one, which Jim had picked up somewhere; and for Sam there was a book—*David Copperfield*, and written on the flyleaf: "To Sam from his mother" and the date.

He got through his breakfast someway, gritting his teeth and winking back the tears which threatened to drip into his porridge. Had it not been for the thimble he would have broken down; he kept his eyes glued on it, sparkling in the sunshine beside his mother's plate—the center of attention and subject of stimulating comment. Long afterwards, remembering the expression on her face when she looked down at him, sitting at her side, he felt that she had known what was passing in his mind—had known and suffered with him. But at the time he did not understand: it was a tragedy without an explanation—

After breakfast he escaped into the shed where Nelly found him sitting on a box beside the empty manger. He jumped up quickly pretending to do something.

"What's the matter, Sam?"

"Nothing—"

"What are you doing?"

"Nothing much—"

"Let's go see Cassie Cole."

"No—" He shook his head.

"Why not?"

"You said—" He kept his face averted. "You said I'd get a coaster."

"I didn't, Sam. I said—you *might*."

"Well, anyway—"

"Maybe you'll get one yet."

"You know I won't."

"I do not—no such thing."

"Well—when?"

"Maybe this afternoon—"

"Yes—where?" he answered scornfully, but with a flash of hope.

"Maybe—" Nelly searched the empty sky and struck out boldly. "Maybe in Sunday school when they have the Christmas tree."

"No—" he said, frowning but considering, "—they don't have things like that in the old Sunday school."

"Well—they might, this time."

"No—" He kicked an empty box, but hope would not stay down. Perhaps she knew. Perhaps—

"Let's see what Mike got, Sam."

"Well—" he assented grudgingly.

The Hogan house was bedlam. There were six children in the family and Mike was in the middle. He had got a pair of skates and was clumping up and down the kitchen floor. Old Mike was beaming through the smoke of a cigar—a box of which he had from Dave Birney, his employer. There was of course a Christmas tree and Annie was busy stuffing a huge turkey. They had all been out to early mass.

"What did you get, Sam?"

"A book," Sam said almost defiantly.

But Mike was not attending. "Say, just watch me now—" He climbed on a chair and jumped crashing to the floor. "They're rockers, Sam. They won't come off or slip."

It was all very depressing. They ate some candy and then they departed and went back across the yard and climbed the picket fence into the Cole place.

"Skates!" Sam muttered as they approached the door. "Who cares about old skates!"

There was a Christmas tree—no bigger than their own but not just with popcorn on it. King Cole, a bandy-legged little black man, was sitting in his chair with his Bible laid open on his knees. He was very religious and a deacon in the colored Baptist church down on the levee. Cassie was eleven, slim and light and pretty, the picture of her mother. She had a lot of presents: a bright red coat, a real lace handkerchief, and a ring with a red stone which she told them was a ruby. Even Nelly was discouraged for a moment.

Peewee who was seven and ink black like his father, was pounding on a drum and dividing his attention with a train of wooden cars. Cora Lee was busy with the dinner which included a goose and an avalanche of things—cake and fruit and candy—left over from the party at the Henry Wyatt house. She filled a market basket for them to carry home, ignoring their polite but feeble protest.

"Now don't you young folks worry—" King Cole dismissed the matter with a gesture of benevolence, rolling out his words in his formal preacher voice—he had great dignity and quite a negro accent. "You jes' take that basket home to your ma and pa. Blessed is them that gives, and the duty of a Christian is to pass the good things on."

"Thank you very much," they said, and went racing home with the basket swung between them.

By dinnertime Sam felt revived. After all there might be something in this Sunday school idea, though nothing of the kind had happened in the past. But still you couldn't tell, and it might be that Nelly had some special information. He sat down at the table with a mildly shining face and a proper appetite. To be sure there was neither goose nor turkey, but there was a roast of pork, crisp and succulent, and a bowl of applesauce, and finally mince pie, topped off with the contents of the basket. When he got up from the table he was staggering with repletion.

The Sunday school party was prompt at three o'clock, and for this event he put on his other suit—a decent blue one, though getting pretty snug; and Madge and Nelly wore their fine new dresses. They all went except Jim who was stretched out on the sofa with the Wyattville *Gazette* spread across his eyes.

The Sunday school room was packed with boys and girls in their best suits and dresses, with shining hands and faces, and hair slicked down or done in careful braids. They were ranged on folding chairs the length of the big room, facing a huge, resplendent tree which occupied the center of the platform commonly reserved for Mr. Baxter. He was present at the moment, in earnest conversation with Mrs. Henry Wyatt and a lady whom Sam had never seen, and who was so smartly gowned that, had she been a Hottentot, her appearance could not have been more startling. In response to Madge's whispered question he heard his mother say: "That's Mrs. Elliott Wyatt."

He looked around; he knew everybody else—Mitch and Grover and the Baxters; he grinned and waved. There was Eileen—a row or two in front. She turned and caught his eye but he pretended to be looking past her. There was the boy in sailor pants sitting right beside her, and another smaller one in a suit just like his brother's—silly kind of clothes. They better go back home where they belonged. A boy in sailor pants —lost in a cave—would be pretty easy meat for a man like Injun Joe. He would not know how to find his way—would never even think about the kite string. . . .

Mr. Baxter stood up beside the tree and cleared his throat. "My dear young friends, members of the Sunday school of the Methodist Episcopal Church of Wyattville, welcome to our annual Christmas party—"

But Sam was not attending. He was looking at the tree and trying to determine if a coaster could be under it. It stood on a white sheet with cotton strewed around, and the branches were so low that it was hard to see, but there did not seem to be anything at all. He nudged Nelly with his elbow—

"I don't see anything—"

"What?"

"There's nothing under it—"

"Shh—don't—"

"You said there would be—"

"I didn't—no such thing. I just said—maybe."

"Well—" He relapsed to dismal silence. But he could not really see beneath the branches, and there was still a chance.

The Reverend Huntziger, pastor of the church, succeeded Mr. Baxter and delivered an address to which nobody listened. He was a flabby, smiling man with a chronically bad breath. He liked to hold your hand and draw you close to him and breathe into your face. Sam detested him. After this they sang two hymns, led by Lucy Hibbs who directed the choir and gave piano lessons. And then Mrs. Henry Wyatt took charge of the affair.

"Now children—" she began. Sam straightened up, gripping the edges of his chair. "—please come forward to the platform as your names are called. I shall need several monitors to help me distribute our little Christmas gifts." She consulted a list. "Madge Braden—Homer Gosford—"

"There's nothing under it—" Sam muttered to himself. And he was right.

The gifts were fastened to the branches just as they always were, and they weren't really gifts or anything that anybody wanted. The monitors untied them—or, if they were too high, Mr. Baxter reached for them, standing on a chair. And then the names were called and you had to go and get them. The whole thing was a sell. Sam got a cornucopia filled with jelly beans. He was so completely crushed that he did not say "thank you," and Mrs. Wyatt glanced at him with fleeting disapproval.

"I told you so," he said, trudging home at Nelly's side.

"Well—" she sighed, "I just said—maybe." There was silence for a time. "Sam—"

"What?"

"Why couldn't we fix that old sled?"

"Fix it?—How?"

"Well, take it all apart and make it over?"

"No—"

"I don't see why."

"No—" he said again, but he was thinking hard.

"All you want is for it to be flatter."

"It's busted."

"But if we made it flatter—"

"It's no good anyway."

"Well, I bet we could fix it so it's just as good as Mike's."

"Yes, how?" He was scornful but impressed.

"All we need is the hatchet and the saw."

"Shucks!" But the moment he got home he tore out to the shed with Nelly at his heels. It might be possible, he thought. If he sawed the frame in two—and could put it back again— He hoisted the sled into the sawbuck, studying the matter with a calculating eye while Nelly fetched the hatchet and the saw.

"You see, it's easy, Sam." She selected the manger as a post of observation, and climbed up and swung her legs.

"I don't know—"

"All you've got to do is make it half as high."

"Well—" He pried doubtfully at a runner with the blade of the hatchet, and it suddenly came off. "There now, you see!"

"That's what you wanted, isn't it?"

"But I can't put it back."

"Of course you can."

"No!" He flung away the hatchet. "It's just no good, I tell you—no good—no good. And now—" He sobbed; he had been close to it all day; he was only nine years old. "And now it's finished. I can't use it any more—not for anything." And he sat down on the ground, careless of his Sunday suit.

"Oh Sam—" She jumped down and ran to him. "Don't cry about it, Sam. We'll put it back again. Maybe Tom or Pa will help us—"

"No, they won't. And I don't care." He was crying out his heart, and he was angry too, seething with a sense of injury and abuse. "It isn't fair. I should have had a coaster just like everybody else. It isn't fair—it isn't fair—"

"Sam, don't—" Nelly was startled and distressed. "I guess they didn't know you wanted one."

"They did," he stormed. "They knew it all the time—the only thing I wanted, and not just an old book. They knew and they don't care."

"Sam!" Madge was standing in the door. "How can you say such things?"

"They did," he mumbled.

"You ought to be ashamed."

"I'm not."

"Suppose Mom heard you?"

"Well—" He dug his toe into the dirt, unyielding.

"Don't you know why you didn't get a coaster?"

"Because they didn't care."

"No, that's not the reason. Because we're poor—that's why."

"Poor?" He stared. He had never heard or thought the word in reference to himself. "What's that got to do with it?"

"Pa hasn't any money. We're poor, I tell you—poorer than the Hogans or the Coles—than most anybody in the town. And if Mom didn't sit up nights dressmaking, we'd maybe starve to death."

"Oh shucks—" he said, but the horrible idea was gripping tight and spreading.

"Yes, poor, that's why. And that's why you weren't invited to Eileen Wyatt's party—why your shoes are full of holes—why everybody else has turkey for their dinner—because we're poor. And don't you go thinking nasty things and saying them to Mom. It's not her fault. You didn't get a coaster because we've got no money—because we're poor, that's why." And she turned on her heel and went back to the house.

He sat there on the ground staring through the open door. It was getting dark. He could see the lighted windows of the kitchen—the old unpainted house, the apple tree with its bare, ghostly branches, the pump beside the door—the littered yard with broken, rusty things sticking up out of the snow. And he could see through the walls into the house—all the things he knew so well, become in a moment strange and unfamiliar—the sofa with its broken springs that stuck up through the cover; the coarse, thick dishes, cracked and chipped; the sugar bowl without a top; the rag carpet on the floor, worn through in spots; the sewing machine beside the window and his mother sitting at it, treadling with her foot—his bare little room with the two narrow beds and the holes in the shingles through which he sometimes caught brief glimpses of the stars. He had never seen these things before and would never see again the things that he had known—warm and comfortable things, satisfying and secure.

At last he said, not crying now, and almost to himself, "Pa could arrest Old Henry Wyatt."

"Could he?" Nelly danced around the shed; her feet were cold.

"Mom said he could."

"Well then, I guess he could."

"And lock him in the calaboose."

"Um—" she nodded. "Let's go in, Sam."

"Oh, all right—" He got up slowly, brushing wisps of straw from his stockings and his pants. "When I grow up—"

"What?" she prompted, but she was too cold to care.

"When I grow up I won't be poor," he said.

The year, drawing to its close, was 1892. Grover Cleveland, after sitting out one session, had been re-elected President of the United States. He had published a letter warning the nation that the silver policy must result in a crisis of great severity. This prediction had been amply confirmed and the country was now in the grip of a depression. Factories were closing down and men were unemployed. At Homestead, Pennsylvania, on a July day, Pinkerton guards and strikers had clashed in actual battle, and eighteen men had died. The militia had been called and the town and the steel mills put under martial law.—In Chicago The World's Columbian Exposition was in process of construction. It would open to the public on the first day of May, 1893; and many folks in Wyattville were expecting to attend. Young Henry was planning to take his wife and daughter and spend a week or two with his brother, Elliott. But Old Henry had no taste for such frivolity. He had been, and would be much too busy in the bank—studying his ledgers and poring over bundles of farm mortgages. The times were perilous—the kind of times when smart and careful bankers watched every move of things—like hawks, still in the wind with planing wings.

III

S AM WAS FIFTEEN WHEN HIS MOTHER DIED.
The intervening years were uneventful—at least until the summer that preceded Sarah's death. He was fourteen then and had graduated from eighth grade, receiving his diploma from the hand of old Judge Nicolls who commonly presided on occasions of this kind. His most intimate friends were in the graduating class—Grover Bentley, Mitch Ballou, and Mike; and so was Eileen Wyatt. But still he did not know her very well, for the barriers of childhood are not easily broken down.

Of course they met in many places now: at the Sunday school picnic in July, on hayrack rides, at parties—more than once he had been inside the big brick house, but he never felt at home there or quite comfortable. They were not allowed to dance, but they did play kissing games when they were about twelve—post office and the like. But when he had the chance he never called Eileen, though once she had called him—and kissed him on the lips. He had gone into the room where she was waiting for him, trembling in a sweat of joy and terror, and she had kissed him; and then without a word they had gone back into the other room. Nelly had been there and afterwards she said:

"Why don't you ever call Eileen?"

"Why should I?" he had mumbled.

"Well, she called you."

"She's not so much."

"Maybe she likes you."

"Aw shucks!" he shrugged. "She likes her cousin, Neill."

"Well—" Nelly mused, half to herself, "I don't blame her much."

"That sissy!" he had sneered, but he didn't really mean it.

"You're jealous, Sam."

"Aw shucks!" he said again.

But he tossed through half the night, remembering the feeling of her lips, moist and soft as velvet—filled with strange new longings which he did not understand, which would ebb and then flood back like liquid fire. . . .

Since the reconciliation the Elliott Wyatts had been coming every summer to occupy the house on the north side of the Square—Daphne and the two boys, Neill and Wayne. And Elliott would run out from Chicago for a few days at a time when he could get away. He was on the Board of Trade and making lots of money, people said. They brought a maid with them, but sometimes Cora Lee would be called in to help; and they hired a negro man to tend the flower garden, and kept a team of horses at Birney's Livery Stable. Daphne Wyatt drove them to a dog-cart, shipped out from Chicago; and often on a Sunday they would go prancing by, Elliott and Daphne in the front, and the two boys behind them facing back. In time they outgrew their sailor pants, and then they wore identical blue suits with broad, starched linen collars, and little peaked blue caps. But of course when they were playing they wore ordinary clothes much like everybody else, though they did not go barefoot as a rule.

It had been something for the good folk of Wyattville to face:—a gardener and a maid, and a woman who drove a team of horses!—drove them to a ridiculous contraption painted red, like something in a circus. And on Sunday too! For there were many women in the town who would not prepare a hot meal on the Sabbath, believing it to be a violation of God's will. Yes, Wyattville had gasped and then had settled down to acceptance of the facts. It knew Elliott of old, and despite his youthful wildness it had always liked him. And too, it is futile to be critical of people who are sure of themselves—who go on doing exactly as they please, not caring a hoot what anybody thinks. It gives you an idea that perhaps you may be wrong. People wondered what Old Henry thought about it, but whatever he thought he kept carefully to himself, and in the big brick house across the Square life continued to pursue the even tenor of its way. . . .

Neill Wyatt was no sissy, and Sam knew it. He was a slender, handsome, loose-jointed sort of boy with something almost birdlike in his face, and a careless, eager quality, reflected in a speech that sometimes stammered. He had brown eyes like his father, and his hair was reddish brown—not parted in the middle or the side like everybody else, but combed straight back from his forehead. You couldn't do it if you had a cowlick. Swimming in the river, when he came up from a dive it would be over his eyes and he would toss his head and flick it back with a gesture which Sam envied. The younger boy resembled him—same eyes and hair, same eager, restless manner. And they were very close and fond of one another, not usual among brothers whom Sam knew, and something he resented as being sissified.

But Neill Wyatt was no sissy. Sam had discovered that in the early days of their acquaintance. At the Sunday school picnic—the first one Neill attended—he had undertaken to confirm the theory which he had advertised to numerous friends. After several tentative, provocative remarks which discovered no determined opposition, and while Eileen and Mitch Ballou were looking on, he had selected a particularly squashy hunk of lemon pie and weighed it in his hand—

"Sailor pants—" he said with all the derision he could muster. "Just old sissy pants!" And he let fly the pie which caught Neill squarely in the face and splattered beautifully.

And Neill, when he could see, had charged at him and knocked him down. And there had been a fight which was certainly no better than a draw at the moment that the Reverend Huntziger arrived upon the scene and put an end to it. Indeed, at the moment of this timely interruption, Sam was not doing very well and was glad to be relieved of further effort.

On another occasion, playing on a log raft in the river where they had no right to be, he had slipped and fallen in, and in falling bumped his head hard enough to daze him. He had come up underneath a tangle of loose logs which were grinding together in the current, and it might have been disastrous. The other boys had scurried for the shore, including Mike—they were little fellows then, ten or eleven. But Neill Wyatt had come back and pulled him out, treading the rolling logs as if he didn't know that they were dangerous—or didn't care about it.

"You—you—you all right, Sam?" he stuttered, clinging to Sam's wrist and staring at the blood which was trickling from a cut above his eye.

Sam gulped and wriggled out onto a section of the raft where the logs were firmly lashed, and sat there for a moment sucking in his breath. "I could've made it by myself," he said ungraciously, but he was by no means sure that he could.

"I thought you might get carried underneath," Neill ventured, which was very nearly what had happened.

"Shucks! These old rafts—" Sam coughed and spit. "I could swim under water all the way."

"Your head is bleeding, Sam."

"Shucks! That's nothing—" But he felt for the blood with a pang of apprehension. "I fell off our roof one time."

"You did?"

"Higher than a tree," Sam said importantly. This was a gross exaggeration. He had fallen off the shed roof of the summer kitchen—a very modest plunge.

"Did you hurt yourself?"

"Um—" Sam nodded reminiscently. "They thought my leg was broken." But the truth was that no one had suggested such a thing.

Jim Braden came hurrying down the levee. He had been sitting on the porch of the Wyatt House, talking with George Wyatt, and a negro had run up and told him what had happened. The boys on the shore fled with warning yells.

"Sam!" Jim shouted from the levee. "You come on in here now."

"Who's that?" Neill asked.

"That's my father," Sam replied. "He's the Marshal of this town."

"Marshal?—what's that?"

"Shucks—" Sam said, disgusted and dismayed at such appalling ignorance. "He's got a star and a six-shooter too."

"What for?"

"He can arrest anyone he wants, and lock 'em in the calaboose—even your old grandfather."

"Oh—" Neill was impressed. "Will he be mad?"

"I don't know," Sam answered boldly but with a quaking heart. "And I don't care."

"Will he whip you?"

"Maybe—" They were crossing toward the bank. "Shucks, what's an old whipping anyway!"

Jim took him home, but he had not been whipped. His mother had interceded for him.

They got on better as the years wore on, but they were never friends —like Grover, Mitch, and Mike. And the happy expectations of the summer were always slightly clouded by the knowledge that Neill Wyatt would be coming back—coming with something new, if it were nothing more than a new slang word or a new kind of hat. It wasn't just

Eileen that stood between them, though certainly she did. There was something much more subtle, welling up from hidden places—something which had been born that winter day when he stumbled down Old Henry's steps and fell sprawling in the snow, tangled with his wretched sled—when he hadn't been invited to the party—when Madge had stood there in the doorway of the shed, upbraiding him— "Because we're poor," she said, "that's why."—things that Neill Wyatt was completely unaware of. He was a democratic boy which simply means that he was socially well adjusted; he had never had a reason to be anything else. He was unconscious of the fact that in America, as elsewhere in the world, there is a *caste of poverty*, hard to get out of to be sure—even when the poverty, itself, has been relieved; and not easy to get into unless you have been born to it.

Still, it should not be inferred that Sam's boyhood was a melancholy sequence of frustrations and defeats. On the whole he led a healthy, carefree life whose underprivileged aspects which, in some degree he shared with numerous other boys of his acquaintance, were seldom in his thought unless events demanded their consideration.

Mike and Mitch and Grover were his intimate friends, but Mike came first. Mike Hogan as a boy was a juvenile replica of Mike Hogan as a man. In short he always looked, even as an infant, like the popular conception of a ward politician or a bartender; and he always talked out of the corner of his mouth in a fine spray of saliva. He was not then, or later, bothered by the fact that his father drove the hack for Birney's Livery. He was not a sensitive person.

Mitch Ballou was a very different sort. To begin with he had lost an eye, and he sometimes took the glass one out and displayed it in his hand—a performance of no mean distinction. He had lost the eye when he was four—in a runaway accident in which his mother had been killed. His father, Mitchell J., had been responsible. He had been drunk and laid a whip across a fractious horse, and the beast had run away. The mother, with the child clasped in her arms, had jumped, and her head had struck a fence post; and a splinter from the post had put out Mitch's eye. Mitchell J. had not been really sober since. He ran the printing shop and edited the Wyattville *Gazette* in an alcoholic haze. A female relative kept house for him—if kept it could be called, and supervised young Mitch. He was a frail and high-strung boy with a quick and witty mind. The poorness and disorder of his life were cushioned by the fact that his father was regarded as a literary man.

Grover Bentley was the son of Dr. Bentley, the leading allopath.

There was nothing remarkable about him. He was a steady, sleepy sort of boy, disposed to plumpness. He expected to be a doctor like his father —and in due time he was.

There were no girls in Sam's life, aside from Nelly who was not like a girl but like a friend—except of course Eileen, and this was not a practical relationship. It was something to be thought about at night, cuddled warmly in your bed, when you were dropping off to sleep—or in the evening after supper, reading some story of adventure in which the heroine was in peril of her life. But in the daytime it took flight again. . . .

But there were all the seasons of the year and all the things that went with them: birds' nests in the hedges in the spring, when uncommon specimens were hunted and collected, though of course they never took more than one out of a nest; when marbles were exchanged, and bats and catchers' mitts recovered from the attic; when a canopy of blossoms decked the apple tree outside the kitchen door, and white and purple lilacs filled the house with fragrance; and then there was the river with its sand bars and its islands, a never-ending source of adventurous explorations; and hunting with their air guns, meadow larks and doves and rabbits, though they almost never managed to bring down any game; and farmers' berry vines and melon patches—exciting undertakings when the corn had grown high and they crept between the rows toward their objective; and thunderstorms on still, hot days—black monsters gathering swiftly and rushing through the sky to burst in jagged streaks with splitting, crashing sound—and they knew they must not run and stand under a tree, no matter how the rain poured down. . . .

There was one such thunderstorm he was never to forget. It was late in the summer of the year he graduated, when he was fourteen. He had been working all that summer for Clem Wyatt in the store—for a Pope-Toledo bicycle. He had made up his mind to get along without one. Neither Mitch nor Mike had bikes, and the one that Grover had was sadly out of date. But Eileen had a bicycle; and then in June the Wyatt boys arrived with Pope-Toledo Specials—robin's-egg blue, with ram's-horn handle bars, and sprocket wheels so huge that they could sail along and barely move their feet. It was more than he could bear and he hurried to the store to discuss a proposition with Clem Wyatt. He had worked for Clem before, occasional Saturdays when he needed a few cents for this or that, sweeping out the store, unpacking boxes and the like; but of course this was altogether different—

"Well now, let's see—" Clem said. He got out the catalogue, and then it developed that the whole vacation period was not nearly long enough to accomplish the result. "Shucks, that's too bad. . . ." He scratched his head, studying the disappointed, freckled face. "I'll tell you what I'll do, Sam: I'll sacrifice my profit."

"Gee!—You will, Mr. Wyatt?"

"Yep." Clem was figuring with a pencil. "We'll call it eight weeks, Sam. And that'll give you a week to ride around before school starts again."

"Gee!—Thank you, Mr. Wyatt."

"I'll have to order her from the factory back East, and it's likely she won't get here until around that time."

"Yes sir, Mr. Wyatt, that's all right," Sam said.

Young Henry Wyatt had been standing by the counter, waiting for something he had bought and he said, smiling with thin lips like his father's: "You won't get rich doing business that way, Clem."

"I ain't aiming to get rich," Clem Wyatt grinned with a little hint of malice in his voice. "I'm leaving that to your branch of the family." And he turned back to Sam who was edging toward the door. "Seven o'clock tomorrow morning, Sam."

"Yes sir, Mr. Wyatt, I'll be here."

And he had been there, day after day through the long summer—six days a week from seven in the morning until six o'clock at night, with half an hour off to tear home for his dinner—sweeping, packing and unpacking endless barrels, crates and boxes, running errands, filling orders, beginning, toward the end, to wait on customers—faithful and industrious, and dog-tired at the end of every day. But the long hard grind was drawing to a close. The Pope-Toledo had been shipped, was somewhere on the way, expected on the "Mary Queen" almost any trip now. And then there was that Sunday. . . .

Nelly had gone out, and Mike had not responded to his shouting. He had sat around a while and then had dug some bait and gone down to the levee by himself to fish for catfish. It was in the afternoon—a hot, still day. He had gone on past the old, abandoned warehouse to a place where the river cut in close against the bank—not seeing anyone he knew, or anyone at all when he passed around the bend, until he came on Cassie Cole and Peewee, crouching in the shadow of a broken end of piling. Peewee was fishing, and Cassie—she was sixteen then and a year ahead of Nelly in the high school—was lolling back against the piling with her slim brown legs spread widely in the water. She had on a thin print dress which clung against her slender, pretty figure—and not much else, it seemed.

"Hi, Sam!" she called, and beckoned languidly.

"Hello—" He came on slowly, watching her—her trim legs in the water, with something stirring in him which he did not want to recognize. "Hello, Peewee," he said. "Having any luck?"

"You betcha, Sam." The little black boy held up a string with three small bullheads on it. His eyes were sparkling.

Sam baited a hook and threw it in. It was not a spot he would have chosen; he knew a better place a little farther on, but it was too hot to matter, and he wanted to go on—looking at Cassie. He sat in the narrow fringe of shade against the piling. His knee touched hers but she did not draw back—lolling with her legs spread widely and her brown toes wriggling in the water.

"How come we never see you, Sam?" she said.

"I'm working for Clem Wyatt in the store." He drew up his knees and clamped the willow pole between them, leaning back against the piling; their shoulders touched.

She laughed. "You don't work nights or Sundays."

"Oh, I got chores to do around the house, and—Mom's been sick."

But the truth was that the color line had intervened between them, though a little while ago he had hardly been aware of it. He had grown up with Cassie, had known her almost as well as he knew Mike but more in the way that he knew Nelly. And then one day, some taunt or something—he could not remember when or what; or perhaps it had been nothing except the passing years. But anyway one day he was suddenly aware that Cassie Cole was black and he was white. And from that moment he had been self-conscious in her company—wondering what people thought, uncomfortable, afraid. Even now his eye strayed off along the path, alertly watchful. Suppose Eileen should suddenly appear—Eileen or Neill! But of course that wasn't likely. They would be sitting somewhere in the shade, on the porch or in a hammock, drinking lemonade—or they might be riding on their bicycles. But it was too hot for that—so hot that it was difficult to breathe; the air felt like a soggy blanket.

"It's sure hot," he said.

"I'll say. Look, Sam—" She pulled her dress down tight across her breasts—firm little breasts with the nipples sharply outlined in the flimsy cotton stuff which clung wetly to the flesh. "Just sitting still I'm sweating—"

"Me too—" He laughed with a sound that seemed unfamiliar to him, and quickly looked away, pretending that a fish had nibbled at his hook. Sweat broke on his back and spread upon his shirt which felt cold against his skin; his hands were trembling. He knew well enough the source of what he felt—the tightening of his breath and the pounding of his heart, the burning, surging torture of repression. He knew, and still knew nothing.

He knew what boys of fourteen knew in those days—those fine Victorian days of secrecy and prudery. He knew what he had learned from dirty rhymes and pictures scrawled on privy walls, and the distorted lore of sex which sifted down from older boys who bragged of their adventures in words half understood. There were stories of things that happened at the race track—the half-mile track on the west edge of the town behind the school, with its whitewashed judge's stand and shaky bleachers—where, for a few days in September, there were trotting races and a small town fair with gambling games and side shows, and which was deserted for the balance of the year. But things went on there —disorderly affairs, keg parties and the like, which Jim Braden was sometimes called on to disperse. And there were other purposes to which the place was put, for boys took girls out there on summer nights, or said they did, and told what they had done in the musty, cobwebbed shed beneath the judge's stand—in the long grass underneath the bleachers. . . .

Yes, he knew about sex—what an adolescent boy could learn in the school of the mid-nineties, a vicious jumble of misinformation without a redeeming implication, without a hint of nobility or beauty. And because he was a sensitive, imaginative boy, it took him half his life to overcome his introduction to the subject; perhaps he never did entirely. He knew of sex as something which had no decent mention, of which you were and ought to be ashamed, from which your sisters were in some strange way removed, which could not apply to a girl whom you respected, which you could not even think of in the presence of your mother.

Half what he was feeling at this moment was a sense of guilty shame, for Cassie Cole was almost like his sister even though she wasn't white; and to have such thoughts about her was horrible and wicked. It did not cross his mind that Cassie might be sharing in his wanton torment, that her slim, brown legs were not widely spread by chance, that the stretching of her dress across her breasts was an act of deliberate provocation. . . .

« 49 »

"That old fish got away," he muttered, jerking out the line. But the worm on the hook was still intact. He flipped it in again and leaned back against the piling, feeling for her shoulder, determined that he wouldn't—

"Look, Sam—" She pointed. A great black thunderhead loomed in the southern sky, its ragged edges billowing like white foam. It was traveling fast; you could see the shadow racing up the river.

"Shucks!" He laughed. "I never noticed that old storm sneaking up on us." The air was still and breathless—like a vacuum. Then distant thunder rumbled.

"Maybe we better go—" But she made no move to start. He was conscious of the pressure of her shoulder.

"Aw, what's the hurry, Cassie?"

"I'm not hurrying, Sam—" She chuckled softly—almost in his ear, he thought, but he dared not turn his head to look.

"Just an old thunderstorm—" His knee relaxed and rested against hers, and a tingling flash went through him; his mouth was dry and he could hardly breathe. "It may not rain at all—"

"May not—" she said, nodding languidly. He could feel her breath upon his neck.

Peewee caught another bullhead and jerked it, flapping, in their faces. He got it off the hook and on the string, and then the sun went out; the thunderhead eclipsed it in an instant; and the air began to stir with a low, moaning sound. The little boy had been intent upon his fishing, but now he looked up at the sky with a comic air of consternation—

"Hey, look, it's gonna storm—" They laughed at him, as older people laugh at children. He hastily wrapped his line around the pole and gathered up his fish. A jagged fork of lightning split the black cloud overhead, and a shattering peal of thunder shook the earth. "Cass, come on—" he cried.

"Peewee's scared," Sam said.

But the little boy was not disposed to argue. He was pulling at his sister's arm. "Come on, Cass, please—" Raindrops began to fall—big splashy ones. "Cass, I'm going home—"

"Well, go on home," she said. "There ain't nobody holding you." A zigzag streak of flame semed to dive into the river, and the thunder split so close you could feel it in your ears.

Peewee stared at them incredulously. "What for you want to stay here, Cass?"

"Wha' foah," she mocked with sudden irritation. They did not talk like ordinary negroes, but Peewee, when excited, sometimes slipped into his father's way of speech. "Go on home, you little pest," she added angrily.

"All right, Cass, I don't care. I'm going." And Peewee streaked away along the levee path with his pole across his shoulder and the string of bullheads dangling from his hand.

They watched him disappear around the bend.

Sam laughed. "Old Peewee's sure making time," he said.

A wave of cool fresh air came sweeping up the river and they sucked it in with sighing breaths. He felt the tightening pressure of her body —arm and thigh and leg, but he did not turn his head. What now, he thought in a tangle of uncertainty, what next? He gripped the fish pole in his hands, with his eyes upon the river where the raindrops splashed like bullets. He wished that he were safe at home. What was he waiting for—sitting in the rain?

"Maybe we ought to go," he said.

"Maybe—" She cuddled closer to him, turning partly on her side, nuzzling with her face against his shoulder, one slim brown leg flung over his, and her breast pressed tight against him. He could feel the pounding of her heart—or perhaps it was his own.

He pulled his line in slowly, pretending it was snagged—taking all the time he could. He kept saying to himself that of course it wasn't true; it was something he was making up out of his evil longings. Cassie was sixteen; she had known him all his life; she simply couldn't have such thoughts about him—couldn't have such thoughts at all. If she dreamed what he was thinking she would slap his face for him, and she would tell her mother. Still, he wasn't sure. His torment was exquisite.

"Sam—" Her groping hand slid underneath his shirt. He turned his head and suddenly her lips were glued upon his mouth—

And then the storm let loose. The wind came howling at them in a cloud of dust and trash; the yellow river riffled backward, furrowed like a mud flat. The belly of the thunderhead was webbed with streaks of flame, and one crashing peal of thunder blended with another in terrifying sound. As they scrambled to their feet lightning struck a cottonwood on the bluff above them. They heard it split and smelled the burning wood and sulphur fumes. And now the rain came in a drenching torrent.

"Gee!" Sam gasped. The bolt that struck the tree had almost blinded him. "Cassie! Where are you?"

"Come on!" she called, poised on the path for flight. "The warehouse, Sam." And she was off, running like a deer.

"All right," he shouted. "But I got to get this old line rolled up first." He wrapped it round the pole as quickly as he could and set out in pursuit. He was really scared. He had never seen a storm of greater fury, and it seemed as though the lightning was being aimed at him—perhaps in vengeance for his wickedness—

He came around the bend and saw her running far ahead. She looked back, waving him to hurry. It was dark as dusk and the rain was like a curtain; you could hardly see the river. The lightning kept on stabbing at him in blinding crooked flashes—missing him by inches, he imagined; and the thunder split and crashed against his ears. Another tree was struck and the top of it came splintering down the bank almost in his path.

"Gee—" he gulped, running with one arm held up to shield his face; he didn't want to see those crooked streaks come at him. Cassie had disappeared, and the old brick warehouse was looming close ahead. He ran along beside the wall, beneath the broken windows, and dodged through the gaping door—just escaping, he felt certain, a vicious fork of fire directed at his heels. The resulting clap of thunder rocked the building like an earthquake, and a pile of empty barrels tumbled clattering to the floor.

"Gee—" he said again, standing, drenched and panting, with his back against the wall.

The old warehouse was a gloomy place in any kind of weather; the rafters dripped with cobwebs and bats lived in the gable. The earthen floor was littered with barrels and great hogsheads—relics of some long-abandoned enterprise. And there was an odor in the place—from something, no doubt, that the barrels once had held—a musty, sour, sweetish smell, sickening in effect—of vinegar and sugar and some other unknown thing. It was not a place to linger—even in a storm.

He peered around but he did not see Cassie. There was another door in the farther wall, facing toward the bluff. Perhaps she had not waited for him. There was not much use of shelter when you were already soaked—shivering from the touch of your wet clothes. And the storm was letting up; the thunder was receding. Yes, she had gone, he thought; and he was relieved and glad. He had had enough of her, whatever she had meant, of all of it in fact. And then the memory of her lips came

surging back—the moist, hot velvet of her lips glued round his mouth—
the softness of her breast and her leg curled over his; and the torment
swelled up fresh as if it had been waiting—just waiting for the chance—

"Cassie—" he called.

"I'm here, Sam." Her voice was muffled and remote.

He caught his breath. "Here?—Where?"

"Back here—" She giggled softly. "Way back behind the barrels."

"Oh—" He stood still in the doorway, looking out. The rain had
almost stopped; there were patches of blue sky.

"Where are you, Sam?"

"Right here."

"Well, where?"

"By the door."

"What're you doing?"

"Nothing—" He waited for a moment, trembling again, not knowing what to say. "The old storm's over, Cassie."

"That's good." A pause. "Why don't you come back here?"

"Back where?"

"Where I am—here."

"What for?" His voice was thick and funny.

"Oh nothing—" And she laughed.

"Well—" He took a few slow steps, peering through the gloom
between the piles of barrels. "What're you doing back there?" He was
trying to sound careless.

"Me?—Well, come and see."

"All right—" He went on noisily, feeling his way, thumping the
hogsheads with his fish pole. "Gee! It's dark back here."

"Dark?" She chuckled and it sounded very close. "You can see when
you get used to it."

"I can't see a darn thing." He stopped, looking closely here and there.

"I can—" Her voice was almost whispering in his ear.

"Shucks now!" He rolled a barrel over with a kick. "Where are you
anyway?"

"I can see you," she said.

"You can?" He was no longer shivering with the cold, nor even conscious of his dripping clothes.

"Look, Sam—"

And as she spoke the sun broke through the scattering clouds and
shot a narrow beam through a window high up in the wall. And there
she stood revealed in the circle of the light, so close he could almost

« 53 »

reach his hand to touch her—brown like the color of the hogshead at her back, indistinguishable from it in the darkness. And she was naked. She had taken off her dress which was spread, as if to dry, across a barrel. There she stood, straight as an arrow, perfectly proportioned, like a figure carved in wood—not shrinking back nor fluttering with her hands to hide her charms, not guilty or ashamed but with a kind of daring in her eyes, as if, no matter how, what she was doing must be done—slim and brown, and beautiful, much more so than his frightened, inexperienced eyes could know, but a picture he was never to forget.

"Gee, Cassie—"

"My dress was soaking wet." She laughed. "I hung it up to dry."

"Oh—" He nodded stupidly.

"I guess you think I'm—bad?"

"No—I—" he mumbled with averted eyes, standing with his back against a barrel and the fish pole in his hand, inflamed and terrified, wishing that he dared to run away and yet not wanting to.

"You don't?" Again she laughed, and came to him across the slanting sunbeam. "Why don't you look at me?" He raised his eyes. "Don't you like me, Sam?"

"Gee, yes—" he gulped.

And then her arms were round him, her small hot hand tearing at his shirt, her soft lips feeling for his mouth. . . .

He had left her there, curled up on the earthen floor—waiting for her dress to dry, she said. He had wanted only one thing: to get out—to get away from the darkness and the cobwebs and that sickening musty odor—

"Why don't you go on home?" she had suggested.

"Well, maybe—" he agreed, fumbling with the buttons of his shirt; there was a gaping rip where she had torn it. He could not see her face, for the sunbeam had moved on, and he was glad that she could not see his.

"I guess you hate me now, Sam?"

"Aw shucks!" He laughed, but there was no laughter in him. He did not know what he felt. "Well, so long—"

He picked up his fish pole and went out onto the levee. The storm had vanished; it was hot and still again. His sticky, soggy clothes would dry quickly in the sun. The rip in his shirt reached nearly to the armpit; there was no way to conceal it—and her fingernails had scratched the skin—

He walked along with aimless steps. He did not want to go home, to meet his mother's eye. He was terribly confused: dejected and elated—a curious mixture of guilt and shame and pride. He had crossed a boundary line and he could not go back to the boy that he had been. He was still fourteen, of course, though he would be fifteen soon, but he felt years older than he had been that morning, older now by far than Mike or Mitch or Grover, who knew nothing of these mysteries—no more than he had known an hour ago. He had passed, in the twinkling of an eye, from the world of boys into the world of men—a strange, new world for which he was unready, in which he could not orient himself—

And the thing itself, what was it?—It was difficult to answer. But certainly not much, for all the talk about it—not anything that mattered like a Pope-Toledo bicycle, not anything that lasted or was really very much while it was going on. It had been over in a moment—a dizzy, tingling moment, to be sure, almost as sharp as pain; and then there had been nothing but emptiness and horror—

He passed some levee negroes squatting in the sun, loafing and fishing. They were calling to each other, cracking jokes and laughing in their lazy, careless way; and he hurried by them with averted eyes—

He wondered about Cassie. Was she feeling what he felt?—was she ashamed and sorry?—He didn't think she was. She would not have stayed there curled up on the floor, relaxed and half asleep, if she had felt as she did. Perhaps it had not been new to her. She had certainly known how to go about it. Yes, no doubt she had done the thing before, perhaps even there in the old warehouse. She had found her way around it pretty easily in the dark—and taking off her dress and then calling him to come, and—well, everything—as if she knew exactly what was bound to happen next.

But he was only partly right. She was not feeling what he felt, but not for the reason he imagined. She was outside the narrow, stifling pattern of his background; her emotions were not bound upon a torture rack; her morality was of another fiber. But she had not done the thing before; she was, in fact, a novice like himself. The difference was that her instinct had been truer, less obscured and warped by fear.

"Hi, Sam!"

He looked up with a start. He was opposite the Wyatt House. Neill Wyatt was calling to him from the porch, and there were other people, sitting in armchairs around a table. The dogcart was standing near the steps with its team hitched to the rail, and rubber aprons pulled across the seats.

"Hi, Neill!" He looked away, meaning to hurry on.

"Come on up and have a lemonade."

He didn't mean to go, but he found himself across the road and half-way up the steps, and then it was too late. His heart sank to his toes. The whole family was there, and, worst of all, Eileen. They made him welcome in their breezy, casual way, and he sat down in the only vacant place, next to Eileen. They had been on a picnic, Neill explained, up the narrow levee road, and the storm had come along. But they had not gotten very wet, crouching on the floor under the apron. It had really been a lot of fun—

"Shucks, what's a little rain—" Sam mumbled, trying hard to feel superior. But he felt a bitter pang, thinking of them cuddled in that snug and cozy place, while he had been—

"You should've seen the lightning," Wayne broke in. "Gee, it was fierce! It scared the horses and they tried to run away."

Elliott Wyatt laughed. "Not when your mother holds the reins," he said, and reached across the table to pat his wife's gloved hand.

Sam looked away. It was revolting: people in a family talking to each other in that silly, mushy way—patting each other's hands!

George Wyatt came out with a tray—bottled beer and lemonade. His daughter, Jane, was helping him. She was just Nelly's age and they were friends—a levelheaded girl, nice looking but not pretty.

"Why, hello, Sam," George said. "Looks like you been fishing?"

Sam shook his head; he could not think of anything to say. Daphne Wyatt asked about his mother.

"Oh, she's all right," he mumbled and then added, "Well, she has been kind of poorly." He put his fish pole down and took a glass of lemonade. He was completely miserable. His feet were bare, his ragged trousers rolled up to his knees, and his mussy torn shirt. He tried to keep his arm held down to hide the rip. He was looking at Eileen out of the corner of his eye. He thought that she was beautiful—more beautiful than anyone that he had ever seen, than the actresses whose pictures came in packs of cigarettes.

And she was a pretty girl, pink-skinned and blonde, in her dainty summer frock, with a ribbon in her hair—not mussed up in the least by the picnic or the storm. Her eyes, like her father's, were a shade too close together, and her chin was square and sharp, a little like Old Henry's; but she was pretty. The rest of them were chattering, but she was not joining in—just sitting there relaxed, looking out across the river. She had never much to say. It seemed to him he had rarely heard her speak except when she was called on to answer things in school. She was like

—well, like a goddess, untouchable, remote. And suppose she knew what he had done that afternoon!—He looked away, cringing from the thought.—Yes, that would be the end—perhaps it was already, for he was no longer fit to come into her presence, to think of her, or hope—

"Is it true, Eileen?" Jane asked.

"True?—What?"

"That you're not going back to school in Wyattville?"

His fingers tightened on his glass; his heart stood still.

"That's right," Neill said. "She's going back with us, to a boarding school on the North Shore, near Chicago."

He didn't bat an eye, or turn his head.

"She's coming to our house for Christmas," Wayne chimed in. "We'll go skating in the park, and to matinees and things."

"What fun!" Jane said. "You're a lucky girl, Eileen."

"Grandpa says its nonsense," Wayne went on. "But mother talked him into it."

"Now, Wayne," his mother cautioned. "Uncle Henry and Aunt Maud planned it long ago."

So that was it, he thought, a conspiracy among them—the whole darn family plotting things against him—sending her away so she could be near Neill—

"When are you going?" Jane was asking.

He held his breath.

"A week from tomorrow," Daphne said.

He breathed again. There would be another Sunday! He had still a full week to work for Clem, according to his contract. But if the Pope-Toledo came, there would be that one day before she went away—perhaps forever. He would ask her to go riding, just themselves, though he had never asked her anything like that. But now on that last day he would have the courage. And suppose she suggested that Neill and Wayne go with them?—Well, he would find some way to handle that. They could take some sandwiches and go down the river road, past the cemetery—down through Beaton's woods. And they would stop at last. when they were good and tired, and sit in the deep grass under a tree, and he would tell her then exactly what he felt—how wonderful and beautiful she was, and—and—

"Here comes the 'Mary Queen,'" George Wyatt said, sitting on the porch rail, pointing up the river.

Yes, there she was—a silver speck, growing bigger every minute, coming swiftly down the river, coasting on the current. The whistle blew far off.

"Say, Sam!" Neill was excited. "Your old bike might be on it."

"Might be—" he said, as if it didn't matter, but his heart was pounding.

"What say we go and see?"

"Well, I don't care—" He got up awkwardly, putting down his glass, wanting to thank someone and not knowing how to do it. "So long . . ." he muttered. Neill and Wayne were already down the steps.

"Come on, Eileen," Neill called.

He looked back. She was coming, slowly and unhurried, shaking out her skirt which was almost to her ankles. He waited for her in a kind of panic, wondering what he'd say when she was there beside him—

"Shucks—" George chuckled, watching her pick her way across the muddy road. "She'd step out on the river if Neill called her."

"What!" Daphne turned with a frown on her thin, aristocratic face. "Why, they're only children, George."

"Maybe—" He grinned, cutting some tobacco from a plug.

"She's not the only one," Jane murmured, smiling to herself.

"You see—" George tucked the tobacco in his cheek. "Neill's got a way with him. He's like his father was—"

"Good Lord!" Elliott Wyatt laughed. "Don't let him pull your leg, darling." He reached across the table to fill her empty glass. "No woman ever walked on water for me."

Daphne changed the subject. "Is Mrs. Braden very ill?" she asked.

"Yes," George said, "I guess she's dying." He went on to explain what he had heard from Dr. Bentley. She had not been well for a long time. It was probably a cancer. The doctor had wanted her to go to St. Louis for an operation, but— He shook his head.

"You mean, she wouldn't go?"

"They're poor folks, Daphne. They can't afford such luxuries."

"But—" Elliott looked up. "—surely they have friends."

"She has," George said. "But she won't take charity or things she can't pay back, and maybe—" He paused and winked his eye. "—well, maybe that's the reason that she's got 'em. She's a proud one, Elliott,—as proud as you, I guess. And she'll die in her own time, in her own way."

"Poor boy—" Daphne sighed, watching the ragged figure walking down the levee. "He always seems so self-conscious and uncomfortable."

"Don't worry about Sam." George spat tobacco juice into the road. "He'll get along all right, once he gets started. He's his mother's boy."

Neill and Wayne were far ahead. Sam walked along beside Eileen at the leisured pace she set, picking a way for her around the mudholes so she would not soil her shoes—conscious of his fish pole which kept getting in the way, and the rip in his shirt which he had to keep concealed. The "Mary Queen" came scooting by with a shrill blast on her whistle, already backing paddle for the landing, and the negroes on her deck standing ready with their lines. He had not said a single word—not yet, and the time was getting short—

"Oh say, Eileen—" he blurted. She glanced at him and smiled; her eyes were like blue flowers. "If my old bike should come—well, how about next Sunday? Suppose we took a ride—just the two of us, I mean."

"That would be nice," she said, politely and indifferently.

"You bet—" He caught his breath. "We could start early in the morning and take some sandwiches and—and go to Beaton's woods—" She nodded with her eyes upon the boat which the negroes on the shore were warping to the dock. "We could eat our lunch under the trees— just the two of us, Eileen—"

"Hurry up, Sam," Neill was calling.

"Would—would you like to go, Eileen?"

"I guess so—" She was waving back at Neill. ". . . if it isn't very hot."

"Oh, it won't be hot—" Sweat was trickling down his freckled cheeks. "Say, that's great, Eileen."

"Hi, Sam!" Neill was dancing with excitement. "I think I see it."

"Let's go," she said, and ran.

The Pope-Toledo had arrived. There was no mistake about it. It was coming off the boat, carried carefully by two negroes in a splendid wooden crate. You could see the color of it and the shiny nickel plate through the cracks between the boards. And there was a tag on it addressed to Clement Wyatt. Andy Bolt, the wharfinger, said that he could have it—right this minute if he wanted. Clem had left word about it.

"Oh, thanks—" he gasped. Neill and Wayne helped him unpack it. They borrowed Andy's hatchet. "Be careful," he pleaded. "Look out, don't scratch her, Neill."

"D-d-don't you worry," Neill stuttered in reply, more excited if possible than Sam. "Say, here's the lamp—" He undid it from its wrapping.

"Here's the handle bar—" Wayne pulled it out. "Ram's-horn—just like ours—"

"You bet," Sam gloated. "Good old ram's-horn—yep." He rubbed off imaginary dust.

They fixed the bar in place, and the saddle and the lamp. It was robin's-egg blue—like the sky and like her eyes.—God, it was beautiful! —The Rolls Royce that he would have one time in London was a poor old tarnished thing in comparison with it.

"It's a honey." Neill assured him. "Go on and try her, Sam."

"Well, gee, I guess I will. Here, keep my fish pole, Neill." He rode around the dock, thumbing the warning bell which tinkled musically. She was geared like a racer so you hardly moved your feet when you were going slow. "So long—" he yelled, starting up the hill. "So long, Eileen—"

Afterwards he thought: if only he had waited until tomorrow morning! —if he hadn't known about it, if he hadn't stopped to drink that lemonade, if Neill Wyatt hadn't called him from the porch!—Those Wyatt boys were always butting into things.—But, shucks, that wasn't fair.— Why had he been walking on the levee, not even really knowing where he was?—Well, that was Cassie's fault. If she'd just let him alone, if he'd gone on home with Peewee!—If—if—if— But it wasn't any use to try to pin it down.

He was very late for supper. He had stopped at Grover's house, and then at Mitch Ballou's, and finally at Mike's. They had all been much impressed, but Mike was nearly speechless.

"Well, holy smoke—" was all he found to say, sputtering damply from the corner of his mouth.

They were still at the table when he came into the kitchen—his mother sitting stiffly, very thin and white. But a boy doesn't notice things like that: people getting old or being sick. There was nothing in her face alarming to his eyes; she seemed to him as she had always been. And his father and the girls—

Old Madge was twenty now—tall and rather plain and very serious. But this was nothing new; she had always been that way, not a bit like Nelly who was pretty and gay and irresponsible. She had been away at Teachers' College and had gotten her certificate that spring—without help from anybody, doing housework for her board and making both ends meet; and already she had been accepted for a job in a rural school some miles away. She would be going soon and would live out in the country with a farmer's family; this had been arranged. She had been home all summer, but not having much vacation—helping her mother with the sewing and the house. A young man had come to see her once or twice—a boy whom she had met when she was away at school. He was tall and thin, and he wore glasses, looking like a teacher which he was. His name was Mr. Daniel Price. Once he had stayed to supper and afterwards the two of them had sat out on the porch for a long time. Sam had been cautioned not to bother them. He understood of course that Mr. Price was Madge's beau, but it seemed a little silly.

Tom was not home, but this was not unusual; he was often late or absent. The truth was, though Sam did not know much about it, that Tom had been giving trouble for some time. He had always been head-strong and sullen, careless of his schoolwork—playing hookey, and such things, and often being whipped with a stinging leather strap that hung behind the stove. But this had not happened lately; he was getting pretty big to be ordered to the woodshed where such punishment took place. He was seventeen that summer—a big, good-looking boy, silent and unfriendly. He had gone one year to high school and then he had quit and worked a while for Dave Birney at the stable, taking care of horses, feeding them and grooming them. But then Dave had let him go for some reason not explained, and he had not worked regularly since— just odd jobs now and then, but mostly loafing in the poolroom near the levee or with some rowdy fellows stabling trotters at the race track. Sam hardly knew him, for, though they still shared the narrow attic room, they almost never spoke to one another. Sometimes when Tom came home late at night Sam would be awakened, and would hear him fumbling in the dark and stumbling over things—and there would be a smell of beer or liquor. But of course he had not mentioned this or, indeed, thought much about it.

"Why, Sam," his mother said, "where have you been?"

"Wait, Mom," he begged, hiding something behind him in the door-way. "I've got something to show you. Just close your eyes a moment."

"What is it?" Nelly started to get up.

"Wait, Nelly, please—and keep your eyes closed too."

"All right, but hurry up."

"I will—you bet—just wait—" He wheeled it in and stood it grandly near the lamp. "Now look!"

"Oh, Sam!" Nelly jumped out of her chair and ran to touch it. "Mom! Isn't it wonderful!"

"Yes, it is," she said, smiling through the creases pain had etched into her face. "It's wonderful, Sam, and I'm very proud of you."

"Yes, Mom—" He was in such a fever of excitement, of pure joy. Cassie Cole had been forgotten—everything in fact. "Look, Nelly—" He displayed the ram's-horn bars, the tinkling bell, the lamp. Even Jim got up and looked.

« 61 »

"Come and eat your supper, Sam."

"But I'm not hungry, Mom."

"Well, you come and eat a little anyway."

Madge filled his plate. He was hungry after all, bolting down his food and talking very fast—about the Wyatt family sitting on the porch and inviting him to join them, and drinking lemonade—and how Neill and Wayne had helped him to unpack it from the crate—and, oh yes, Eileen Wyatt wasn't going to the high school. She was going back with them to a boarding school not far from Chicago. Neill and Wayne were going to take her skating in the park, and to matinees and things—

There was an interruption. A man came to the door—a farmer whose cornfield bordered on the race track. He had driven over in his buggy and he was hot and angry. A gang of hoodlums, he explained—they'd been there all afternoon with kegs of beer, drinking and carousing. He had heard them from his house, swearing at each other and shouting dirty language. And now they had a fire going right beside his fence. He had gone down to see about it—to warn them to be careful, and they had cursed at him, and thrown stones and clods. One had hit him in the shoulder. It was a disgrace, he said, to have such toughs around. He wanted them arrested and locked up.

"All right," Jim said, "I'll tend to them." He didn't take his gun which was kept locked in a drawer—just a heavy stick he carried, loaded at the end, a weapon adequate for bums and rowdies. And he went out with the man.

Sam and Nelly were still sitting at the table. She had been deep in thought, and she said, half to herself:

"I'd like to be in her shoes."

"Whose shoes?"

"Eileen's."

"You would?" He laughed. "Our old school's good enough."

"I don't mean that.—I'd like to go to matinees—and things."

"Well, maybe—" he admitted, but he had the Pope-Toledo and it didn't matter much.

"I wish my hair was blonde. I wish I looked like her."

"Aw, you look all right."

"Do I?" She smiled, then frowned. "I guess she'll marry Neill some day."

"Shucks!" he said. "I'll bet she don't." But he was startled.

"Sam," his mother spoke behind his chair, "however did you tear your shirt like that?"

"What, Mom?" he gasped, clapping tight his arm, the hot blood rushing to his face. "Oh, that old shirt!—Well, I don't know—" He got up quickly, backing out of range. "I got to take my bike out to the shed." He pushed it closer to the lamp and found some specks of mud. "I got to clean her up—"

"Well, go ahead," she smiled. "But Tom hasn't come home and you'll have to milk the cow."

"Yes, Mom," he groaned, "I will." He got the pail and went out to the shed and lit the lantern.—Darned old cow!—Someone had given Jim a sickly heifer, expecting it would die, but it had flourished.—"Get over, Boss," he said and started in to milk. "Darned old cow!" he kept repeating.—And what call did Nelly have to say a thing like that—just when everything seemed perfect?—"Soo, Boss—" He jabbed her with his knee.—Well, next Sunday, down in Beaton's woods— But he left the thought unfinished; he didn't know quite what.—And then there was his shirt! They had to notice that and remind him of his wickedness. —Darned old cow!—He shoved her so hard that she turned her head and looked at him reproachfully. "Well, I don't care—" he said.

He carried the pail into the house and got some rags and a cup of kerosene, and came back to the shed in a better frame of mind.—That old Pope-Toledo—well, she was really something! She wouldn't go away to school or marry anybody or get him into trouble or rip his shirt to pieces.—He put the lantern on the floor and set to work to polish her— every tiny speck of mud; he even washed the tires. And then there were the tools, suspended from the frame in a little leather case. He had not had time as yet to look them over carefully—the tire pump and wrenches and a lot of other things, beautiful and shiny. He wiped off every one before he put it back. And then he thought perhaps she ought to have a little oil, so he filled the tiny can and went over everything into which oil could be put. Last of all he filled the lamp from the cup of kerosene. There was simply nothing else that he could think to do. He left her propped against the wood block, and he stood for a long time in the doorway, before putting out the lantern—hardly able to tear himself away.

"Well, so long, old bike—" he said, and he went across the yard and through the kitchen door. And then he stood there, staring—feeling terrified and sick—

His brother, Tom, was standing in the middle of the room, sullen and defiant, looking at the floor, and not standing very straight or very steady, but swaying back and forth and shifting his feet to keep his balance. He was dirty, as if he had fallen in the mud. His father was standing with his back against the door that led onto the porch, breathing hard as if he had been walking fast, and looking—well, looking in a way that Sam had never seen him look before—much worse than angry. His mother and the girls were there, but he did not notice them, except that his mother was standing near the table. His father was speaking as he came into the room, and his voice was thick and different.

"Get me that strap." He was pointing at the strap which hung behind the stove.

"I'd let it be now, Jim," his mother said.

He understood the matter in the moment that he saw them: his father had gone out to the race track, and the gang had run and scattered the way they always did—all but Tom perhaps; or maybe his father had run after him and caught him—maybe that was when he fell down in the mud; and he had brought him home, walking very fast to keep him out of breath, holding his shirt sleeve pulled tight around his wrist and jerking him along. He had seen his father handle things like that. And Tom was drunk and was going to be whipped—

"Fetch me that strap." Tom stood there swaying, staring at the floor. "You hear me—what I say?"

"I'd let it be now, Jim," his mother said again.

"You never mind." He took a step or two. "Fetch me that strap."

"What for?" Tom answered suddenly.

"You know what for."

"You ain't going to whip me any more."

"Yes, by God, I am. I'm going to learn you something. No son of mine can be a dirty bum and bring disgrace on me."

"And what are you?" Tom shouted.

His heart stood still. He heard his mother's voice as if it came from somewhere far away, but he couldn't turn his head.

"Wait, Jim—" she said.

"You stay out of this." He took another step. "Go get that strap."

"I won't—" Tom lurched away, defiant but half crying. "I won't be whipped no more."

"Go get it now."

"I won't—I won't.— You leave me be—" Suddenly he straightened up and struck out at his father—a childish, drunken blow. Jim caught his arm and twisted it, and he went down on his knees, crying out with pain.

"Oh—" his mother moaned, and sank down in her chair with her arms spread on the table.

"Get up." Jim shoved him with his foot, and then jerked him to his feet, half ripping the collar from his shirt. "Go get that strap."

"I won't—I won't—" The boy was sobbing now, but he reached across the stove and took the strap.

"Give it to me." Tom held it out. "Now go on to the shed."

"I won't—I won't.—You can't whip me no more." But he went, lurching through the door, whimpering like a dog. Sam backed against the wall out of his path.

"You, Sam—" his father said. "You go to bed."

"Yes, Pa—"

He ran across the room and up the stairs, not glancing at his mother or the girls; and he tore off his clothes and huddled in his bed with the sheet across his face. Something new and terrible had come into his life; defiance of authority—his father and his brother almost fighting with their fists. He was sorry for them both, for everybody in the family—sorry and ashamed. He kept thinking of the Wyatts, of Elliott and Daphne—how the father had reached out to pat the mother's hand. It might be mushy, but such things wouldn't happen if people felt that way. He couldn't picture Elliott whipping someone with a strap—or Neill or Wayne being dragged home drunk and dirty. Why was his family different?—They were poor—yes, that was it; that must be the reason. Tears came to his eyes, and they were tears of shame—

He heard the girls come up—heard them talking through the wall, and Nelly crying, but he could not make out what they said; and he did not want to hear them, to hear anything at all. He hid his head under the pillow, just leaving room to breathe. But through the open window he heard the cracking strap, and could not shut it out—blow after blow, like the beating of a drum, but not any sound of crying or of protest. At last there was an end to it.

The kitchen door banged—banged again. And then he heard his brother coming up the stairs, stumbling in the dark and still whimpering like a dog—heard him grope his way across the room and sit down on his bed beside the window. Peeking with one eye he could discern his figure against the starlit sky—swaying back and forth and muttering to himself, but he could not tell what he was saying. He heard his father's footsteps in the kitchen, heard the winding of the clock, and his father's boots dropped heavily on the floor. And then he knew that Tom was moving in the room, cautiously in stocking feet—fumbling in the drawer

that held his things. He wondered why. He had a sudden urge to speak
—to say, "I'm sorry, Tom." But of course he didn't do it, didn't stir or
make a sound; and in the midst of this he fell asleep.

When he woke in the morning Tom was gone, and his bed had not
been slept in. But he hardly noticed that. He jumped into his clothes and
ran out to the shed. And then he stared and rubbed his eyes. It wasn't
there, where he had left it propped against the chopping block. It wasn't
anywhere in sight. He looked in the yard and then tore back to the
kitchen with something dreadful clutching at his heart—

"Mom, my bike—"

"What, dear?"

"It's gone."

"Oh no—" she said.

"It isn't there." Jim came out of the bedroom. "Pa, my bike . . ."

"Well, what?"

"It's gone." Suddenly he understood. "And Tom's gone too."

"What's that?"

"Oh, Sam—" His mother put her arms around him—thin, wasted
arms, trembling as they held him.

"It's gone," he said, "my brand new bike—"

"Wait now—" Jim scowled, pulling at his lip. "He'll bring it back."

"He won"t," Sam cried, pushing away his mother's arms. "He's gone.
He took his things. I heard him in the night."

"Jim—Jim—" she said.

"Quit now—" he answered angrily. "He'll come home fast enough
when he gets hungry."

"He won't—" Sam sobbed.

"He will, I tell you. Quit crying now. I'll get it back for you."

"No." Sam shook his head. "You won't. You never will. It's gone."
A kind of frenzy came into his voice. "I can't have anything—because
we're poor, that's why—"

The girls were there—Madge helping with the breakfast, and Nelly
coming in, tearfully sympathetic. They tried to comfort him. He'd get
it back, they said. But he couldn't talk about it; he jerked away from
them and went without his breakfast.

He had to tell Clem Wyatt. There was no way out of that.

"Damn!" Clem said. "Say, that's too bad. But I guess you'll get it
back."

"Yes sir—" He tried to smile, but he knew better. He would never
get it back—or if he did, it would be old and busted.

"Say, looky, Sam—" Clem liked the boy. "—suppose we call it square. this last week, eh?—I mean I'll let you off from working any more."

"Oh no, sir, Mr. Wyatt—"

"Well—" Clem scratched his head. "—suppose you take today off anyway."

"I—I'd sooner work," Sam said.

He did not tell anybody else, but the story got around. Mitch and Grover came into the store to commiserate his loss and inquire the details, and Mike came in the evening, sputtering sympathy. But he recognized the fact that they really didn't care—were perhaps a little glad, and he was tight-lipped and silent.

"Aw shucks," he said. And he walked away or spoke of something else. The hurt was too deep; he couldn't talk about it.

On Wednesday there was news: someone who had been in Muscatine, had seen Tom on the street there Monday morning, riding on a bicycle. Jim borrowed a rig from Birney's Livery and drove over the next day— a twelve-mile trip. It was late when he got home. He had found the Pope-Toledo.

"Now, Sam, you see—" cried Nelly.

"Go on, Pa," Sam said stonily.

And Jim went on: Tom had sold it to a man for twenty dollars. But there was no trace of Tom. He had made a careful search of the blind pigs and the poolrooms and in one had found a clue. Tom had been there and had said he was going to Chicago—to train horses at a race track. As for the Pope-Toledo—

"But where is it?" Nelly asked. "Did you leave it at the stable?"

"No—" Jim cleared his throat. "I didn't bring it, Nelly." The fact was that there wasn't any way to get it back unless they would declare it had been stolen. And that would mean that Tom would be a thief, and would have to be arrested if anyone could find him. The man who had the bicycle had bought it in good faith, and he wouldn't give it back—not even for the money he had paid. He leaned back in his chair and began to roll his thumbs.

"Yes—" Sam nodded, looking at his father with a new sense of contempt:—that big and handsome man whose hair was turning gray —with his nickel-plated star and gun and loaded stick. But he couldn't bring the Pope-Toledo back. His strength was a delusion, like a scarecrow stuffed with straw. Old Henry Wyatt, old and feeble though he was, wouldn't come home empty-handed; and Elliott Wyatt would get what he went after, in his smiling, easy way. Well, they were rich. And money was more powerful than nickel-plated stars and guns and loaded sticks.

"Good night, Mom." He stopped beside her chair and bent to kiss her.

"Good night, dear—" But she clung to him, searching his eyes. "You —you—"

"Shucks, Mom, I don't care. I knew we'd never get it back. I knew it all the time." And he had known it, so he hadn't been surprised or disappointed—at any rate not much. He had not had any hope about the matter. He went on up the stairs to bed. At least he had a room now to himself.

On Saturday Neill Wyatt came into the store. He brought the fish pole back, and asked for a can of deviled ham—for sandwiches, he mentioned. He knew of course about the Pope-Toledo.

"Gee, Sam," he said, "that's too bad about your bike." His sympathy was genuine; he already had a bike and no reason to be envious.

"Yep," Sam answered shortly, and got the can of ham.

"For a picnic," Neill explained. "Eileen and I—we thought we might ride down to Beaton's woods tomorrow."

"Oh, that old place—" He laughed, throwing the money in the drawer. He felt as though someone had stabbed him with a knife.

"Say, Sam—" Neill lingered, leaning on the counter. "—don't you want to go along? I mean, Wayne isn't going and you could take his bike."

"Naw—" He shook his head ungraciously. "I got a date tomorrow."

"Well, so long, Sam."

"So long."

Sunday was fine and not too hot, with great white drifting clouds. He loafed around the house, in the yard and in the shed. He didn't go to church and his mother didn't urge him. He read a while; the book was *Pickwick Papers*, but he couldn't keep his mind on it. After dinner Mike came over, but he got rid of him. He went out and dug some bait. Madge and his mother were sewing on the porch, and he stayed around behind out of their sight. He got his fish pole from the shed and strolled across the yard, along King Cole's white picket fence, looking through the currant bushes—hoping and fearing. He had not seen her all the week —had not wanted to see her, or thought he ever would, until today. She was lying in the hammock on the porch, one slim brown leg hanging down across the edge. His heart began to thump. He walked less cautiously, whistling a tune—as if he was just going by. She raised her head.

"Hello," she said, "that you, Sam?"

"Hello—" Already his mouth was getting dry.

"Where you going?"

"Fishing."

"Oh—" There was a pause. He waited, digging with his toe.

"You—want to go?" he said at last.

"Um—maybe—" Another pause.

"Well, I'll be waiting for you."

"Where?"

"Oh—" He seemed to turn the matter in his mind. "Down by the warehouse."

"Um—" She chuckled softly, swinging in the hammock, pushing with one brown foot on the porch.

"Well—" He went on down the road with the fish pole on his shoulder.

When he came home at evening he found the can of bait where he had left it in the yard; he had not missed it until then.

The days went by. On the following Sunday Mr. Daniel Price appeared, driving over in a buggy from the town in which he lived. He had come to call for Madge—to take her to the farm where she was to make her home. But Madge said she couldn't go, she had written to the school board to explain: her mother wasn't well and she felt she couldn't leave her. Sarah was in bed that day—just resting, so she said. Lately this had happened several times, and it had seemed very strange— coming downstairs in the morning, not to find her in the kitchen, not to see her the whole day unless, of course, you went into her room. And she would be lying there, so little and so thin that the bed looked almost empty. And you would say, "Good morning, Mom—" and ask her how she felt; and she would smile and answer you, "I'm all right, dear—just resting—" But despite this reassurance you felt somehow uncomfortable—

Mr. Price seemed badly disappointed. They went out on the porch and talked for quite a while, and once Sam heard him say:

"But Madge, dear, you really must think about yourself."

He couldn't hear her answer but he thought that she was crying; and shortly after this Mr. Daniel Price departed—driving off alone, looking very solemn.

School started, but Sam had no heart in it. There was no Eileen to look at—no thinking in the morning when he woke, that in a little while you would be sitting near her, watching the soft blonde hair clinging close around her neck and curling on her shoulders, listening for her voice when the teacher asked a question. It had gone on for years, and it left an awful emptiness.

He wrote a letter to her—a hundred in his mind, a dozen before he got one right enough to send. He began, "My dearest dear—" but the one that he sent was less emotional. "Dear Eileen," it started, and went on for several pages, getting pretty warm in spots when he spoke of the "old days" in Wyattville; but he let it go at last after hours of thought upon the closing line: "Yours forever—Sam." Jane Wyatt knew the address; he posted it himself.

The days and weeks went by. There was no answer. He was hurt and angry but, oddly enough, not angry with her. Neill Wyatt was the object of his wrath. "Old slicker Neill," he called him, talking to himself— butting into his affairs, taking her to matinees, going out to see her every week most likely. "Shucks, I don't care. Let her have him if she wants. She'll find out some day—" And he would kick a rock or stick lying in his path. He felt that he was getting hard and tough.

As for Cassie—*it* went on, with occasional good resolves which didn't last. Repetition is insidious and the way of the transgressor becomes smoother at each step. If you fail to heed the warning at the start, the whistle blows less loudly—less and less, until it is no more than a whisper in your ear. A consuming sense of guilt is not easy to maintain; in time you wear it out. This is not to say that he had reached such a point, that he did not suffer qualms of conscience—devastating hours of remorse and shame, but they came less frequently and they were less severe.

And the *thing* itself discovered values not discerned in its first quick, frightened aspects. It was soothing and relieving—immensely satisfying as they went on together, learning from each other, relying on her instinct until his own awakened. Sometimes in the warehouse—sometimes cozily hidden in a furrow between high rows of tasseled corn—in the woods in deep lush grass—beneath the stars. . . .

There was nothing strange about it. He was lonely and unhappy. Home was not the same; no one was cheerful, even Nelly was depressed. Saturdays and Sundays he would wander in and out, fuss around the yard or in the shed; and then he would find himself beside the picket fence, peering through the currant bushes—

"Hello—"

"That you, Sam?"

"What you doing?"

"Oh, nothing much—"

"Well—"

That was the way of it. And they were sly and cautious, arranging assignations in whispered words which sounded innocent enough unless you knew the code. They went and came alone; they had a dozen ways of getting rid of Peewee; at school they never glanced at one another.

October came—the warm, soft days of Indian summer. His birthday was at hand, and passed almost unnoticed. Nelly remembered and, of course, his mother. She was in bed that day but she had a present for him. When he went in to see her in the morning she got it out from underneath her pillow—a locket that she sometimes wore with her Sunday dress: it was gold and inside there was a tiny picture of her when she was a child, but it was badly faded. She said that when he grew to be a man he could wear it on his watch chain.

"Oh, thank you, Mom—" He tried to sound excited but a use for the locket seemed very far away.

It was that morning, standing on the porch, that Nelly said to him: "Sam, do you think that Mom could die?"

"Die?—Mom die?" He stared at her, shocked and limply angry. "You ought to be ashamed to think such things. You know she's only resting."

"But—she isn't getting any stronger."

"Well, shucks, just give her time—"

Dr. Bentley drove up at this moment in his buggy, and came swinging up the walk with his worn leather bag. He came nearly every day now —a portly, pleasant man who, regardless of the weather, always wore a long black coat like Judge Nicolls and the preacher.

"Well, my young friends—" he greeted them in his jovial, boisterous way. He had brought them both into the world.

"Good morning, Dr. Bentley," Nelly said, and dared to ask a question. "Is Mom all right?—I mean," she added hastily as he frowned and hesitated, "I mean, she's getting better?"

"Well now—" He hurried on across the porch, "we're doing what we can, Nelly."

"Yes, I know," she said and followed him a step. "She's just resting, isn't she?"

"Just resting—yep, that's right." He opened the door and put an end to it.

"You see!" Sam said, "I told you so."

But a dreadful doubt was born—or brought to light, for the possibility had already crossed his mind—on the day that Mr. Daniel Price had called, when he thought he heard Madge crying, and something in her face and in his father's. But he had thrust it back out of his thought. It was impossible to contemplate a world without his mother.

And there were other matters, more or less alarming. People were always coming in to call. Cora Lee and Annie Hogan came almost every day, bringing things to tempt the invalid's palate—a glass of jelly or a bowl of broth. But this did not seem strange; it was the others—people who had never been inside the house before, whom he hardly knew. Returning from school one afternoon he actually encountered Mrs. Henry Wyatt coming down the walk. When he recognized the large imposing figure it was too late to escape. She was charging down upon him in a purple dress whose long skirt swept the dusty ground; her sleeves rose from her shoulders like balloons, and her hat was adorned with nodding cherries. She was the daughter of a county judge and the social apex of the town.

"Why, Sam—" she smiled, holding out a soft plump hand. She explained that she had been to see his mother, and then went on to say that of late she had not seen his face in Sunday school. She shook her finger playfully. She hoped he would be coming soon again.

"Yes'm—" he mumbled, digging with his toe. He had never liked her, and being Eileen's mother had not helped the situation. Indeed he had wondered more than once, as many another had before him, how the object of his dreams could derive from such a mother. Old gabble-mouth, he called her in his thoughts—always sticking in her nose and asking silly questions. No wonder Eileen was rather silent; with a mother like that you would have no chance to talk—

Mrs. Henry chattered on: Eileen just loved her school—she had not been homesick once, if her letters could be trusted. The girls were all so nice, and many of them lived in Chicago or near by. There was one in particular whom Eileen called her chum. She had been to this girl's home to spend a week end, and there had been a party and her cousin Neill had been there. The girl's name was Rebecca but Eileen called her Becky—an odd name, wasn't it?

"Yes'm—" Sam admitted. He hated this Rebecca; he hated all of them.

It was a great advantage, she went on, being near her aunt and uncle. Every other week end she could go to visit them, and this was almost like being home, but probably more fun. Neill and Wayne had so many nice young friends, and they were always planning things to do. On Thanksgiving she would be with them and they were going to a comic opera. It was all such a wonderful experience for Eileen. Of course she missed her daughter, but— She paused for breath and sighed.

"Yes'm—" Sam agreed, but he was thinking darkly that Mrs. Henry Wyatt was a meddlesome old fool and had made a fatal blunder. Old Henry had been right: no good would come of it.

"Well, good-by, Sam. I hope your dear mother will soon be well again." She hurried down the walk in a little swirl of dust from the trailing purple dress. "And don't forget to come to Sunday school."

"No'm, I won't. Good-by—" And he added to himself, "Darned old gabble-mouth!"—Well, she'd find out sometime—when it was too late. And she'd be sorry then—they'd all be sorry.—He picked up a clod and threw it at a cat, and went on into the house.

The days dragged by. November came. It was beginning to be cold— too cold for comfort in the fields or woods, too cold in the old warehouse among the rotting casks. The cornstalks had been reaped and shocked in dry, harsh piles; the trees were bare of leaves; the grass was brown and scratchy. The cozy hidden places were bleak and uninviting, not hidden but exposed to prying eyes. And the days were getting short. He had begun to wonder what would happen when the winter really came, when the snow was on the ground—

And then one night he woke to find Madge standing by his bed.

"Sam—Sam—" She was calling him and pulling at his shoulder. He sat up yawning, rubbing at his eyes. "Mom wants to see you, Sam."

"Mom—wants to see me?" He thought he might be dreaming. "But it's the middle of the night."

"No," she said, "it's almost morning." She put the candle down. "Come quickly, Sam."

"Yes, Madge—" He was wide awake and shivering, suddenly afraid and quaking in his stomach as if he might be sick. He pulled on his pants and shoes and hurried down the stairs.—Mom wanted him—

The lamp was lighted. There was his father sitting in his chair, rolling his thumbs around—all dressed except his shoes. And there was Annie Hogan standing by the stove, poking at the fire. His father did not speak, but then he seldom did unless you asked him something— not always then. Annie spoke to him, but he did not think what she was saying.—Mom had sent for him—

"Wait," his father said.

"Mom wants to see me, Pa."

"I know."

He waited by the door. He could not face his fear; it was all unreal

—impossible. There was her sewing basket on the table by the lamp—just where it always was. The clock began to strike; he counted five. In a little while it would be daylight. Perhaps it was a dream—

Madge came out of the room with Nelly. She had her arm around her. Nelly was crying, sobbing; she did not look or see him. His heart stood still.

"You can go in now, Sam," Madge said.

"Yes, Madge—" he whispered, and went in on his tiptoes, as he had come to do when she was resting.

The lamp on the table by the bed was shaded with a piece of heavy paper. He could not see his mother's face. And then he was aware of Dr. Bentley standing by the window, motioning him to come—and even smiling at him, but not smiling humorously the way he always did. Yet he waited by the door.

"Mom wanted me," he whispered, "but—maybe she's resting now."

"No." Dr. Bentley spoke so loudly that she couldn't be asleep. "And she wants to see you, Sam." He came and put his arm across Sam's shoulders. "You go and speak to her."

"Yes sir—" He went—went closer. Why was it so hard to take those steps? "Mom—"

"Speak right out, Sam. She can't hear you very well."

"Yes sir—" He pressed his shaking knees against the bed. Just a little while ago he had said good night to her, and she had heard him then. She was awake; her eyes were open—looking at him. "Mom—" He thought she smiled. "You—wanted me?" He waited a long time. "What was it, Mom?" The doctor came and stood beside him.

"It's Sam," he said. "Remember?—you wanted Sam to come." Her eyes replied; her thin white hand was groping. "That's right," he said, and then to Sam, "You take her hand, my boy. I think that's what she wants."

"Yes sir—" He took her hand in his and knelt beside the bed. He could feel the little hard spots on her fingers, calloused from the needle. "Mom, you wanted me.—What is it, Mom?" Her lips moved but he could not understand. The doctor leaned across the bed.

"Now, Sarah, just a little louder. Try real hard." And he repeated what he heard. "She wants you to be a good man, Sam. Not great, but good, she says.—You understand that, Sam?"

"Yes sir—"

"She says, take care of Nelly—of Nelly, Sam."

"Yes sir—"

"Is that all, Sarah?" Suddenly he straightened up and drew her hand away, and took Sam's arm and led him toward the door, almost hurrying him but very gently. "I guess that's all. Now, son, you run along and ask your pa to come."

"Yes sir—" he said. He knew that he had seen his mother die. "Dr. Bentley wants you, Pa."

He stood beside the table. There was the sewing basket—the worn thimble with its band of broken glass which once he had believed might be real diamonds. He picked it up and held it tightly clasped. Annie Hogan came and put her arms around him. . . .

Sometime in that endless day a neighbor brought a letter from the post office—addressed to him in a sprawling schoolgirl hand. The flap of the envelope was modestly embossed: MISS MELVILLE'S SCHOOL FOR GIRLS—LAKE FOREST, ILLINOIS. He went out to the shed to open it.

Dear Sam,

You must forgive me for not answering your nice letter sooner, but I have been very busy with my school work. I like it very much here. It is a beautiful place right beside the lake. Of course it is too cold for swimming now, but the lake is clear and blue, not a bit like our old river.

Everyone has been lovely to me. My roommate and chum is named Rebecca Adams, but we call her Becky. Her father is a banker in Chicago and I have been to visit her. I am sure you would like her if you met her. Perhaps sometime she will come to visit me.

Uncle Elliott and Aunt Daphne are fine, and so are Neill and Wayne. I see them quite often, and we often talk about the old days (ha! ha!) in Wyattville, and all the fun we've had. Please write soon again and tell me all the news. I am writing in my study period and now the bell is ringing for a horrid class in French, so I must close.

Your friend
Eileen

His first love letter.—He read it many times, sitting on the wood block in the shed, shivering with the cold, with hot tears burning in his eyes—searching for and finding between the barren lines a warmth which was not there.—"Our river—" his and hers; "Old days in Wyattville—" something they shared; "The fun we've had—" and "Please write soon again—" It was nothing—less than nothing, a hasty scrawl, empty of emotion, even of interest—a polite impertinence actually. But the human heart is credulous, and the letter was from her. . . .

The church was crowded for the funeral. He stood by Nelly's side in the front pew—then Madge, and then his father. The girls were dressed in black—things hastily improvised for the occasion, and Madge had a long black veil. You couldn't see her face through it. He wore his Sunday suit, dark blue and much too small; it pinched under his arms, and the sleeves wouldn't cover the frayed cuffs of his shirt. He kept trying all the time to pull them down.

He had never seen so many flowers, not even in the summer, and it was almost winter now. The coffin was covered with big white chrysanthemums which he heard someone say had come from Davenport. You couldn't catch a glimpse of what was underneath them. The choir sang "Lead Kindly Light." And then the Reverend Huntziger stood up—

"Well done, thou good and faithful servant— "

That's how it began.

The year was 1898. William McKinley was President. Two years before, in a bitter and spectacular campaign, he had defeated William Jennings Bryan on the issue of free silver. Substantial people felt that the country was now safe—America was once more on the march. There had been a war with Spain. Nobody seemed to know what it was about. Our battleship, the "Maine," had blown up and sunk in the harbor at Havana; and most people thought that was enough. The thing only lasted a few months, and tended to confirm a popular idea: that one good American could lick a dozen foreigners. Some boys from Wyattville had gone and two or three had died of typhoid fever in the swamp of Chickamauga, but most of them came back none the worse for their experience.—A rich young man named Hearst was successfully promoting a new kind of journalism—big black headlines and cartoons, savagely attacking the most important people in the country, respected citizens like Mr. Rockefeller and Mr. Pierpont Morgan, and even the President in the White House. He was out to bust the Trusts and save the Working Man, or so he said. Old Henry Wyatt would not tolerate his paper in the house. But most folks didn't care what he thought or wrote; they laughed at the cartoons and let it go at that. They were busy with their own affairs.—Electricity had come to Wyattville. Naked light bulbs were suspended above street intersections—though not as yet across the swale in Shanty Town, and many families had installed them in their houses. There was much discussion of the matter: the convenience and expense, and whether or not it might be dangerous. The electric company had built a power plant. Old Henry had tried to sell them the abandoned warehouse on the levee, but they claimed he wanted too much money for it. At the moment he was occupied with something else. Elliott had written from Chicago that the Rock Island Railroad, he was reliably informed, was preparing to construct a branch line from Muscatine to Wyattville. And Old Henry had been busy looking into things. As a preliminary step he had recently foreclosed a mortgage on a piece of property where he figured the railroad might want to build a depot.

IV

HE DID NOT SEE CASSIE ANY MORE.

But one day in December just before the holidays, her father overtook him coming home across the swale. It was almost dark when he heard the little black man's voice behind him.

"Good evening, Sam." King Cole was returning from a job of paper hanging with his canvas sack of tools and he rested the sack for a moment on the ground while he spoke of this and that, inquiring of the family—how they all were getting on. And then he asked, pleasantly enough, "Would you kindly call to see me after supper?"

"After supper?" Sam repeated, startled and alarmed, not knowing what to say.

"After supper if convenient," the little man went on in his formal preacher way. "Jes' something that I'd like to speak with you about." Sam nodded; there was nothing else to do. "I'll be expecting you and— thank you kindly." He picked up his sack and hurried on across the swale.

Sam went home in a panic. Cassie had not been at school the last few days. She had written him a note which Peewee brought—just a line which said that she must see him, and to come out to the fence at an hour that she named. But he had not gone nor sent an answer. He had questioned Peewee who said that she was sick, but he did not know what was the matter with her. That was several days ago and nothing else had happened. He did not want to see Cassie any more—not in that way, or to be reminded of it. And now—and now—

"Why don't you eat your supper?" Nelly asked.

He mumbled that he wasn't hungry.—Just old beans, about all they ever had now!—He pushed back his plate and got up from the table.

"Where you going, Sam?"

"Just out—" he answered shortly.

He crossed the yard and scaled the picket fence.—What did that little black man want to talk to him about?—what?—*what?*—Well, shucks, perhaps it wasn't anything.—Should he go to the back door or the front? —The lamp was lighted in the parlor, perhaps to guide his steps. Yes, the front door would be best.—From the porch he could look into the room—a small, neat room with lace curtains at the window and gilt-encrusted wallpaper. There was the organ on which Cora Lee played hymns, and the hand-painted vases on the whatnot in the corner, and the carpet with the flowers, and the plush-covered chairs and little sofa, and the table with the Bible. And on the wall above it was the picture of King Cole in its big gold frame. He was wearing a funny looking hat with feathers in it, and a wide red sash wrapped around his waist, and carrying a sword. It was not a reassuring portrait and for a moment Sam was tempted to retreat. But uncertainty, he argued, might be even worse—

He pulled the bell which clanked with a melancholy sound. His heart was thumping.

King Cole came to the door, dressed in his preacher coat—and this was ominous. Through the narrow hall he caught a glimpse of Cora Lee busy in the kitchen with the supper dishes, and Peewee doing homework at the table, but there was no sign of Cassie.

"Come right in, Sam." He motioned toward the parlor. "Jes' step in and take a chair." He was smiling, but quite sadly, like a person at a funeral. "Kindly make yourself to home." He sat down by the table with his finger tips together—the way that preachers did before they started preaching.

Sam sat on the sofa—on the very edge of it. His hands were sweating and he rubbed them on his knees.

"You and me is old friends, Sam." The little man kept smiling, tapping his black fingers. "I've knowed you all your life, sence you was a tiny baby—before you learned to walk or talk or nothin'. You been running in and out here jes' like my own chil'ren."

Sam nodded, but with mounting apprehension.

"Your pa has been my friend. Also your blessed ma who rests safe in Jesus' arms. She loved you, Sam—loved you most of all, and she was mighty proud of you."

A lump rose in Sam's throat.

"Now wait—" King Cole held up his hand. "You been a good boy too, and she was justly proud. I know you loved your ma and how you miss her now—and Christmas time most here. Yes sir, I understand. But I felt I ought to talk to you, talk to you like a friend, like one of my own chil'ren—with no anger in my heart or bitterness or such. I felt your ma would want me to do that."

Sam bowed his head. He knew now what was coming.

"Wages of sin—" The fingers tapped again. "Ain't no way to escape 'em. They come home to roost like the chickens in the night." He paused; there was a tremor in his voice. "Sam, you and Cassie has done wrong—mighty, mighty wrong."

Sam gulped and winced.

"Wait now—" He motioned with his hand. "We is all tarred with the same brush. That's why Jesus died—to save us, Sam. And I ain't blaming you, poor sinner that I am. I ain't saying you led Cassie from the straight and narrow path. More likely she led you. But you yielded to temptation—to the devil and his works. Takes two to make a bargain, and you both done mighty wrong. Yes sir, that's what you done—a nasty, wicked thing." He paused.

Sam waited, staring at the flowers in the carpet.

"You brought great sorrow to me, but I forgive you both." Again he paused. "My little Cassie—seems only yesterday she was a baby in my arms—" His voice broke; he got up and paced across the room.

Sam watched him from the corner of his eye—the little black man in his preacher coat, but not a comic figure.

"Sam, I want to pray for you. I want to ask the Lord to help you both. Will you pray with me, Sam?"

Sam nodded. He was crying now from the tension—from sheer misery.

"We'll pray together, Sam. We'll ask the Lord to wash away the sin." He went to the door and opened it and called into the hall, "Cassie—"

Sam ground his knuckles in his eyes. He heard her moving in the room above, then coming down the stairs—

"Come in, my chile—"

And then he saw her standing in the door, barefooted, dressed in a flannel wrapper—as if she had been in bed. Her face looked almost white, but not as if she had been crying. She did not glance at him.

"Come in, my chile—"

« 79 »

He heard the closing of the door, and saw her slim, brown ankles below the flannel wrapper, but he did not raise his eyes again.

"We is gathered here to pray—you and me and Sam. Kneel down, my chile—" He took her hand in his. "Come, Sam, and kneel with us."

Sam went and knelt beside him. He kept looking straight ahead—at the table with the Bible, at the picture of King Cole with the feathers in his hat, and the red sash and the sword—

"Lord God and blessed Jesus—" His voice rose like a preacher's. "—we is come to ask forgiveness for these sinners—my little Cassie here, and this poor, lonely boy whose blessed ma is resting in your bosom—"

Sam sobbed aloud. He was thinking of his mother, of the grief that she must feel, looking down upon him from the shelter of God's arms. He could not follow closely what King Cole was saying. It went on and on and on—

And then at last it ended. "We ask you, Lord, for Jesus' sake. Amen." He rose and took Sam's hand and led him to the door. The tears were running down his cheeks. "God bless you, Sam," he said.

Cassie was still upon her knees. She turned her head and looked at him —a strangely searching glance. She was not crying. It even seemed she might be smiling. And then she looked away.

He stumbled through the door and fled across the yard. And of all the things he could have fancied, least likely would have seemed the one that was to be—that more than twenty years would pass away, that he would be a man with half his life behind him when he saw her again.

The days dragged by. Cassie Cole did not return to school and was nowhere to be seen. In response to guarded questions Peewee said she had gone with her mother on the "Mary Queen"—down the river to St. Louis to visit Grandma Cole. He didn't know how long they would be gone or why they went, and seemed unconcerned about it. When, weeks later, Cora Lee came home alone, there was nothing in her manner denoting any change—toward him or any of them. She said in her pleasant, drawling voice that Cassie might go to school down there—for the present anyway; Grandma Cole was getting old and needed someone. No other reason was assigned. Sam didn't know—and he was never to find out.

A few days before Christmas a letter came from Tom, addressed to Madge and written from New Orleans. He had heard from someone of his mother's death, and he spoke of her in childish, sentimental words and with a bitter reference to his father—that she had "slaved herself to death for a mean, no-account, hardhearted man who never done a thing for any of us." Jim had brought the letter home and Madge had to read it to him, but of course she skipped this part. He was working at the race track, Tom explained, learning how to train race horses, a steady job with money. He had come down to New Orleans with a stable from Chicago, and might spend the winter there. It was certainly a change from Wyattville. He was "sorry about taking the kid's bike," but he had been "driven to it." He made no suggestion of any restitution. "Merry Xmas," he concluded, "and I hope you all stay well. Will write again when I get time." It was written with a pencil, crudely phrased and badly spelled.

Christmas was terrible. There was no tree—no wreaths or mistletoe—indeed, not much to eat. No one gave any presents. There was literally no money in the house. Nelly wasn't home; she had gone to spend a few days with Jane Wyatt. And Jim was drinking, which he had not often done—not up to then. Someone had given him a jug which he kept under the bed. All Christmas day he kept going back and forth from the kitchen to the bedroom—sitting in his chair beside the stove, not saying anything, sodden and morose, rolling his thumbs.

In the afternoon Mr. Daniel Price arrived, bringing Madge a box of candy. He wanted her to go with him for a drive, but she thought it was too cold. They went into the parlor where they could be by themselves, and Sam made a fire for them in the parlor stove which was almost never lighted.

After that he went to Mike's house where he was always welcome. It wasn't so much fun—the Hogan Christmas tree, and looking at Mike's presents, but better being there than by himself, and he stayed on and had supper—cold turkey and plum pudding. The truth is he was hungry. When at last he started home the stars were shining brightly, and he was surprised to see Mr. Price's horse and buggy still hitched outside the gate. And then the door was opened and Mr. Price came out. Madge walked down the path beside him and it looked as though he had his arm around her. They stood talking for a while beside the buggy—

"Yes, dear, I understand—" Sam thought he heard him say in a kind of sighing voice. It seemed as though they kissed, and then Mr. Price got in his buggy and drove off, and Madge stood watching him—

He slid around the house and came in the kitchen door. His father wasn't there; his boots were standing by the stove, and he could hear him snoring in the bedroom. Then he heard Madge on the porch and started toward the stairs.

"Oh Sam!" He stopped. He saw she had been crying. "Sam, wait!" she said. "Please wait—" She began to cry again while she was speaking.

He waited, embarrassed and uncomfortable. He had never felt he knew Madge very well. She had always seemed to him completely grown up, and he thought of her now as approaching middle age—almost through with life in fact.

"I don't suppose you'll understand—" She sat down, sighing wearily, in her mother's chair beside the sewing basket. "But I have to talk to someone. I'm so unhappy, Sam—so terribly unhappy." And she told him in tired, disconnected phrases what he had long since suspected—they were in love, she and Mister Price—the best and kindest man she'd ever known, the only man she'd ever cared for, or had ever cared for her. He had asked to marry her, just now this afternoon, and—well, she had told him that she couldn't—

"I don't see why," Sam said. It was passing through his mind that love couldn't be important to Madge and Mr. Price, couldn't really matter as it would to someone younger—to himself and Eileen Wyatt, for example.

"You don't?" She smiled wanly through her tears. "No, I don't suppose you do, Sam." She explained that Mr. Price was poor, almost as poor as they were. He had to teach a country school so that he could save the money to continue on at college. He had a brilliant mind and some day in the future he would be a famous man, a professor probably in some great university—if nothing interfered to hold him back from the goal he had in sight. She paused and went on drearily. She had hoped to earn her living as a teacher, to help him and to go on at his side until the need for doing so was past. But now that was impossible.

"I don't see why," Sam said.

"You don't!—And who'd keep house for you and Pa and Nelly?"

"Well, shucks—" He scuffed his toe against the floor. "I guess we'd get along."

"How, Sam?—Just tell me how.—The cooking, and the sewing—" She pointed to the basket. "That's what we've lived on all our lives—the sewing that Mom did."

"Nelly—" he ventured doubtfully.

"Oh, Sam!" She shook her head reproachfully. "Nelly's like a child, and she hates to cook or sew. She can't even stitch a hem and keep it straight."

"Well, she could learn—" But he knew this was silly when he said it. Nelly would blithely undertake anything on earth, but that would be the end of it. She'd forget it in a moment in pursuit of something else.

"It wouldn't work—" Madge sighed. "I can't even keep up with it myself—can't do the things Mom did. Every woman in the town wanted her to make their dresses, but I'm not as good as she was and they know it."

"Aw, you're all right," he said.

"Sam, dear—" She hesitated. "I hate to burden you—to put things on your shoulders at your age, but I have to talk to someone and there's just nobody else—"

"Well, what?" he said.

"Things can't go on like this."

"Like what?"

"I can't make both ends meet. I just can't do it, Sam."

"Oh—" He stared at her, half comprehending.

"We haven't got a penny in the house—haven't got the food we need."

"Oh—" He was groping for an answer. "But we always got along before."

"While Mom was here."

"Well, Pa gets paid for being Marshal."

"Not enough to keep us, Sam."

"Oh—" He nodded dully.

"Mom worked and scrimped and saved—that's how we got along." She hurried on, explaining there were bills that had piled up while their mother had been ill—for food, and for medicines and such things —and Dr. Bentley's bill, though he never mentioned it, and quite likely didn't care how long he had to wait—and for the funeral too, that wasn't paid. No one was pressing them, and that was not the point. The bills were bad enough, but they could wait—though wait for what?—She spread her hands out helplessly. "But I can't make both ends meet— right now, from day to day."

"I guess—" He was thinking very hard. "I guess maybe Pa ought to get another job—one that would pay him better."

"Where, Sam?"

"Well, I don't know—" He could hear his father snoring in the bedroom, and he had no confidence in what he said. "Maybe if you talked to him about it—"

"I've done that, Sam."

"And he couldn't think of anything?"

She shook her head.

"Oh—" He was silent for a while, turning the problem in his mind. At last he said, "I guess I better quit going to school—"

"Oh, Sam!" She began to cry again. "Mom wouldn't want you to do that."

"No—well—" He was thinking suddenly that he would be glad to quit. He had had no heart in school since Eileen went away. "I guess Mom wouldn't mind. She'd understand about it."

"What would you do?"

"I'll go back to work for Clem."

"Oh, Sam!" She was remorseful and enormously relieved. "But you've only started high school."

"I'm fifteen," he asserted. "And high school's not so much. I can save a lot of time by quitting now." He was thinking to himself: when old Neill was finished school he'd be far ahead of him—maybe richer than the Wyatts. And he was calculating— "Clem's been paying me three dollars—that's the way we figured it, but perhaps he'd give me four— or three-fifty anyway. I'm more experienced now." He looked up anxiously. "Would—would that make both ends meet?"

"I think so—yes—" She nodded, struggling with a sense of guilt.

"Well, I guess that fixes it."

"But—I don't know if I ought to let you, Sam?—I don't know what to say?"

"Shucks, I don't mind." He laughed. "I'd sooner be at work and earning money."

"And maybe Pa won't like it?"

"Pa?" He turned the question in his mind. "Aw, he won't care. I'll go see Clem tomorrow." He started toward the stairs and paused. "Say, Madge—"

"Yes, Sam?"

"Will this fix it so you can—" He hesitated, scuffing with his toe.

"So I can what?"

"You know—I mean, so you can marry Mr. Price?"

"Oh!" She started, smiling wanly. "Sometime perhaps."

"But I mean—now," he urged. "That's what you want to do."

"We'll see about it, dear. Don't you worry about that."

"Well—good night, Madge."

"Good night, Sam."

And thus was a great decision made.

He went to work for Clem, six days a week, from seven in the morning until six o'clock at night—and often nine on Saturdays when the farmers were in town. And he started at four dollars—about six cents an hour—which was somewhat higher than the customary scale for young fellows starting out, but Clem said he was worth it.

Jim made no objection. Nelly was disturbed and then rather pleased about it. She quickly saw his point, that getting started now would put him way ahead of Mike and Mitch and Grover—even of Neill Wyatt. Her imagination galloped. She saw him already as a rich, successful man living in a mansion in a fabulous city like Chicago or New York, with a red painted dogcart always waiting at the door, and a coachman in a livery; and she saw herself arriving for a visit in a trailing purple dress and a hat with cherries on it, and possibly a muff of ermine or chinchilla, for by now of course she was rich and famous too, perhaps an opera singer—she had a pretty voice and was singing in the choir—or possibly an actress, like Mme. Modjeska whom she had read about, who could make you laugh and cry in the same breath. Her enthusiasm mounted; she confided the idea—

"Shucks!" Sam was shocked. "You'd never go and do a thing like that!"

"Why not?"

"Well, you ought to know what actresses are like."

"I don't. They're no such thing."

"Mom wouldn't want you to."

"Well—" She compromised. "—an opera singer then."

"Aw, shucks—" he said disgustedly. But he let it go at that. He was not quite sure of the opera's moral status.

Every Saturday night he gave four dollars to Madge, retaining nothing for himself. No other distribution of his earnings had occurred to him. He was working for the family; it was his responsibility to see that both ends met. If he needed a few cents for a skate strap or a knife, he would ask apologetically—

"But it's yours, Sam," Madge would say.

"I know—" And he would scuff his toe, subscribing to this fiction. "But—you sure you don't need it?"

At the store he was diligent and punctual, polite and competent. In no time at all he learned the stock—every item in its place on every shelf, no simple matter since Clem Wyatt's merchandise ranged from groceries to dry goods. "Oh, Sam—" Miss Murgatroyd would call, "where's that new lot of ladies' corsets?" Or Mr. Stahl would shout across the store, "Say, Sam, did those hack saws come in yet?" Even

Clem appealed for help from time to time. And he was good with customers; they liked him. "Where's Sam?" they would ask, looking around.

He had very little time for social matters. Evenings he would read until he went to bed, prompt at nine o'clock; he was up at half past five, for he had the cow to milk and chores to do. His mother had inspired and maintained his love for books, and his library card was rarely idle. On a shelf in his room were a few treasured volumes she had given him: *Tom Sawyer, Huckleberry Finn, David Copperfield, Great Expectations*—this last one was perhaps his favorite story.

He saw less of Mike and more of Mitch, and Grover hardly ever. Mitch was fond of books and he was working, too—after school and Saturdays, setting type for the Wyattville *Gazette*. Sam saw him frequently running over to the office with the copy for Clem's ad, or making changes in it; and if Mitchell J. was out, as was usually the case, he sometimes paused to talk—

"What're you working for?" Mitch said to him one day. He was always very positive and abrupt.

"Aw, I don't know—"

"I do. I'm saving up to go to college."

"You are?" Sam was impressed, but he spoke contemptuously. "Say, you wouldn't catch me dead in an old college."

"Why not?"

"I got no time to waste on stuff like that."

"Well—" Mitch cocked his one good eye. "—if you don't know what you're working for, I'd say you're wasting time."

"I'm working to make money—" Sam was annoyed. "—and plenty of it, too."

"Clerking for Clem Wyatt?" Mitch began to laugh.

"N-no—" Sam winced. He did have doubts about it. "I ain't aiming to be clerking all my life."

"You won't get rich in Wyattville."

"Old Henry Wyatt did."

"Oh him!" Mitch spat between his teeth. "Say, he ain't really rich. Nobody'd even notice him in Chicago or New York."

"He's rich enough for me."

"Oh, well—" Mitch shrugged. "—if that's the way you feel! But if I was aiming to be rich, I'd be like Rockefeller."

"Yeh?" Sam was getting angry. "Well, what are you aiming at?"

"I'm going to be a writer and an educated man. I'm going to write books—like my father used to do."

"Shucks, you won't get rich that way."

"I don't care if I don't. I'll be living in big cities—maybe London, maybe Paris. I'll be traveling everywhere, all around the world, seeing everything and writing stuff about it."

"Well, I may be traveling, too," Sam hinted loftily.

"I'll be a famous author. Everybody'll read my books."

"Maybe so," Sam sneered. "But you won't have any money. You'll be walking in the mud when I go by in my carriage with a coachman in a livery."

"You'll be clerking for Clem Wyatt," Mitch answered scornfully, "right here in Wyattville."

"I—I—" Sam stuttered furiously, "I'll just bet you a quarter on that, Mitch."

"I wouldn't take your money—"

Mitchell J. came in and banged the door—as drunk as usual but apparently no drunker. Sam hastily slid away. But the conversation and its varied implications rankled in his mind. He made an effort to discuss the thing with Mike, but no revealing light was shed upon the subject.

Mike was lethargic and depressed. He said, out of the corner of his mouth, that he did not know why he was going to school—he saw no good of it, and he did not know what he would do when he got out and had not thought much about it. He had an uncle in Chicago, a policeman, who sometimes came to visit with the family. He had heard this uncle say, winking his eye, that good money could be made around the City Hall if a fellow kept his eyes open. His uncle seemed well fixed, and the life of a policeman might not be a bad one. As for writing books—well, look at Mitchell J. who was just a drunken sot and owed everybody money. There was nothing very tempting in the picture he presented. Anyway he didn't think he would ever want to write as he never read a book if he could help it. Of the higher education he spoke contemptuously—college was a place for dudes and sissies, and his uncle thought so, too. He even disapproved of Mike's going to the high school and had said the previous summer in a very gloomy voice that if he kept on at school with a lot of dirty Protestants, he would certainly be damned. He was not so much concerned about the other children, but only about Mike who was his favorite nephew. He had written recently, offering Mike a home with him and promising to send him to a good parochial school where he would not be corrupted by heathenish ideas, and might possibly be saved a long stay in purgatory. His father and mother were considering the suggestion—

"But I mean—" Sam interrupted, "—don't you want to be rich, Mike?"

"Sure," Mike agreed. "I'd like to run a livery like Dave Birney."

"Shucks, I mean really rich—a millionaire."

"Aw, well—" Mike shrugged. His imagination would not function in this realm.

Sam dropped the subject.

It was toward the end of March that Clem raised him to five dollars. "Gee, thanks—" he said, and hurried home in an ecstasy of joy. He felt that at last he was really getting started.

He explained the thing to Madge, concluding awkwardly, "I think, if it's all right, I'll keep a dollar for myself."

"Of course, Sam," she agreed.

"A dollar every week—" He watched her anxiously. "You see, I ought to have another suit—"

He had been struggling with this problem: his Sunday suit was much too small and worn out—and he must have a new one by the time Eileen came back—something really stylish, like the Wyatt boys would wear. He had had his eye on such a suit and a pair of shoes to match, in Mr. Bergman's window, right across the street from Clem's. He had been afraid that somebody would buy it. It was yellowish with purple stripes, and the shoes were the color of ripe oranges. The cost of the outfit was exactly eighteen dollars—

"Yes, you should have a new suit," Madge assented heartily.

"Gee, thanks, Madge,—thanks—"

In his lunch hour on Monday he tried on the suit and shoes which, Mr. Bergman said, fitted to perfection—"like the paper on the wall." Looking in the mirror at his resplendent image he felt a surge of pride and satisfaction—he was surely getting somewhere. Old Neill Wyatt wouldn't have a suit like that—and this was true.

There existed for many years a record of this suit, from a tintype taken in September at the fair. It was loud and cheap and ugly, and at least a size too large. And the shoes, whose sunset glow could not be reproduced, had long pointed toes and big brass buckles. In the picture he was wearing a straw hat—a flat one with a narrow brim. It was very funny afterwards; it was funny even then.

Mr. Bergman prepared to wrap it up.

"Gee, no—" Sam shook his head. "No, I don't want it now."

"You better take it, Sam," Mr. Bergman urged.

"No, I haven't got the money."

"Your credit's good."

"I'd sooner pay a dollar every week, and you keep it till I want it."

"Just as you say, Sam."

"I'll maybe want it before I get it paid for."

"All you got to do is ask."

"Well, thanks, Mr. Bergman—"

It was too late for dinner and he hurried back to Clem's. The suit was off his mind. It would be there when he wanted it—when Eileen came back.

She had written, when his mother died, a formal note of condolence; and they had maintained a kind of correspondence: long letters which he wrote, and long-delayed replies, hasty and brief, ignoring everything that called for comment—like the tremendous fact that he had gone to work. But he read between the lines and detected hidden tenderness which, of course, existed only in his fancy. He assumed that a goddess couldn't speak out frankly. The anemic heroines in the books that he had read, were the soul of modesty; at the very thought of love they hid behind their fans or swooned away. This was ladylike and proper.

He had asked her to let him know when she was coming home, but she hadn't answered that. He hoped she would. He had visions of himself, in his new suit and shoes, standing on the levee when the "Mary Queen" came in—if it should be a Sunday—strolling on the dock while the negroes nudged each other and made admiring comments. But he would pretend not to notice them, just nodding carelessly to the people that he knew. If Young Henry and his wife were there, he would smile and greet them pleasantly. He would have in his hand a big bouquet of lilacs—if the lilacs were still blooming. She would see him from the deck, and smile and wave her hand, and come tripping down the gangplank. And then—and then—

But it happened otherwise—as such things do.

It was in June—a Saturday in fact, and the store was full of people. He was waiting on a fussy farmer woman, a Polack who was hard to understand, scooping sugar from a barrel with his eye upon the scale, when suddenly he was conscious of her presence—before he really saw her. And he didn't hear her voice; she didn't speak. He turned so quickly that he missed the paper sack, and the sugar in the scoop poured on the floor—

Yes, there she was—dressed all in white, with her golden hair like a nalo—like a crown. There was another girl standing at her side, but he didn't see at first what she was like.

"Gee—Eileen—"

She was smiling, nodding toward the other girl, introducing them, "This is Becky Adams, Sam."

"Oh, pleased to meet you—" He started to shake hands but he had the sugar scoop. The Becky girl was laughing. She was pretty, too, but in a different way—small and dark and pert looking, in a very fancy dress. "Well—gee—" The Polack woman was complaining, and Mr. Stahl was shouting something at him. Clem came along and took in the situation at a glance.

"Hello, Eileen," he said, and then to Sam, "I'll tend to this. You see what Eileen wants."

But she didn't want a thing. They were just passing by and had dropped in—

"Well, gee, I'm glad you did—" He wiped his sweating hands across his apron.

The Becky girl explained: she was being shown the sights of Wyattville. She kept watching him and laughing—not out loud.

"Well say, that's great—" But his eyes were on Eileen. "How's old Neill and Wayne?"

She nodded, smiling. She was never one to waste her words.

"I suppose they'll be along soon?"

No, they were not coming to Wyattville this summer. Uncle Elliott had taken a house at Lake Geneva—

"Right next to ours," the Becky girl cut in with the faintest hint of malice.

"Gee, that's too bad—" But he was thrilled.

Could he come, she was saying, to her house tomorrow evening—for supper about six?—If the weather was fine they might have it on the lawn—a kind of picnic supper—

"You bet.—Well say, that's fine—" His heart leaped high—he would wear his new suit for this occasion—

And would he ask Nelly, too?

"I sure will, Eileen—" They were standing in the doorway, and one of his good customers was fidgeting near by. He pretended not to see him. "Say, that's mighty nice of you—" The Becky girl was laughing as if there was a joke, though nothing the least funny had been said.

They mustn't keep him any longer from his work. She was edging through the open door—

"Well, so long, Eileen—" And then he remembered and quickly found his manners. "And I'm pleased to have met you, Miss—Miss—"

"Becky," she said pertly.

"Oh—oh yes—" he stammered.

They went on down the street, and judging from the way her shoulders shook, Becky was still laughing. He did not think much of her—she was the giggly kind.

That afternoon he called on Mr. Bergman.

Nelly said that he looked wonderful—that the suit was simply scrumptious. But her critical judgment was impaired by her excitement: she was going to a party—and a party at the Wyatts'—

"Do I look all right, Sam?"

"You bet—" But he didn't really notice.

As a matter of fact Nelly was a pretty girl, with brown eyes and soft brown hair and a dainty little figure. Above all she had a cheerful, enthusiastic spirit which, how often crushed, took flight again. She was wearing a new dress which Madge had made—a simple organdie, but not one to be ashamed of. And Madge was on her knees, adjusting something, when she looked up at Sam—

"Land sakes!" she gasped.

"Yep." He posed beside the door. Her exclamation could be construed as admiration. "Well, let's get going, Nelly." He was wriggling with impatience. "Please hurry, Madge. Do you want us to be late?"

"Just another minute, Sam."

Jim was sitting in his chair, rolling his thumbs. They did not ask him how they looked. They had reached a point where they rarely asked him anything. He was like the chair he sat on—just something in the house.

They walked quickly by the Hogans'. Mike was sitting on the porch.

"Hah, sassiety!" he hooted.

They ignored this pleasantry, correctly ascribing it to envy. And they hurried through the swale, across the Square—arriving hot and out of breath—and early. Nobody else had come yet. Mrs. Henry gabbled at them across the vast expanse of dim and musty parlor with its square rosewood piano—with bad paintings on the walls in massive gilded frames—and crowded, heavy furniture: highboys and lowboys, whatnots in the corners piled with curios and sea shells—and the statue of a naked boy standing on a pedestal, but he had a kind of apron spread across him—and thick, green curtains hanging at the windows, tied back on huge glass buttoms and festooned across the tops—antimacassared chairs and painted china vases—and the black clock on the mantel-

piece which ticked like doom and struck the plodding hours like a dirge
—and the chandelier for the new electric light, dripping crystal doo-
dads— A rich man's house! But it was pretty gloomy and depressing.

His heart sank.

Mrs. Henry said that the girls were getting dressed—they had been
to a tea party and had only just come back—so many things were
planned to entertain them, and Becky Adams was such a lovely girl—
they would be down in a moment.

But it had begun to sink when, through the cottonwoods, he had
glimpsed the big brick house with its lofty cupola and iron fence. And
this would always be, through all the years to come. He would never
climb those steps without that wretched sled dragging at his heels—
never wait outside the door without half expecting it would suddenly
fly open, that Old Henry would appear and shout furiously at him.
And it would be no different when Old Henry was dead, no different
when the house was falling into ruin—when the iron fence was red with
rust and broken—

Young Henry looked in at the door and greeted them with cold
politeness. He had no warmth. He was tall and spare and getting gray.
His eyes were close together, and his lips were thin and tight. He wore a
suit as colorless as he was, bought ready-made from Mr. Bergman. He
was a small-town, Midwest banker—he was completely that. He said
something to his wife relating to the party, and went away.

Mrs. Henry gabbled on. She said they would have supper on the
lawn—it was such a pleasant evening and would be a moonlight night
—there would be eight of them, young people, she meant; the adults of
the family would have supper in the house; Mr. Henry, of course, as
she called her husband's father, never stepped outdoors at night—

Sam felt glad of that. His shirt was so tight that it was choking him,
and the collar was frayed. Every time he turned his head it scratched
his neck.

Mrs. Henry went on to something else. She said Eileen was urging
them to have a tennis court, like the one that Becky Adams had at
Lake Geneva. There was a nice place for it at the side of the house
where the croquet wickets were, but she thought Mr. Henry would
object to the idea—he was always so conservative. Still, tennis was a
nice game—did they know how to play it?

They said they didn't.

The big, black clock made a groaning sound, and then struck six.
—Well, the old clock at home must have been wrong.—The girls came

down in swishing pink and white—calm and cool and comfortable. But no sooner had the Becky girl come into the room than she was overtaken with another giggling fit, and had to rush back into the hall. It was just too silly. She simply made him sick.

The other guests arrived: Mitch Ballou and Grover Bentley, and Hub Baxter and his sister. There were the usual painful introductions followed by an awkward pause until the boys slid away into a group. Mitch and Grover stared at Sam and made cracks about his suit, but Hub merely grinned and kept his mouth shut. He was wearing white duck pants and feared reprisal. Mitch inquired if the party was to be a masquerade—he hadn't known about it or he would have dressed accordingly. Grover felt the cloth and pointed out the purple stripes. He asked Sam how it felt to be a convict. They did not overlook the orange-colored shoes. Mitch pretended to believe they were on fire.

Sam took it in good part. He was sure of the suit and of the shoes —that young men of wealth and fashion were wearing just such things in Chicago and New York. Mr. Bergman had assured him this was true, but anyway you could see it for yourself. He felt certain that the cracks had their origin in envy; and he was partly right, for Mitch and Grover were not sure of themselves—not sufficiently informed to be certain he was wrong. They were presently united in attacking Hub's white pants.

Mrs. Henry, gabbling steadily, led the way out to the lawn. Two tables had been set on the croquet ground, and there were some paper lanterns strung between the trees. Young Henry was lighting them although it wasn't dark yet, and Cora Lee was helping him.

They stood around. They couldn't romp or pull each other's hair; they had gotten beyond that, but as yet no other where. They had nothing to say; they couldn't talk. They were in that dreadful period *between*—too old for play, too young for love, not children and not adults. The girls did better; they were more mature, more at their ease. But the boys were wretched.

"Each one must find his place," Mrs. Henry was explaining, "by the place card with his name—little cards beside each plate."

Well, this was sure doing things in style!—They walked around the tables, making jocular remarks. Sam found his card, but he thought for a moment that it must be a mistake: he was not at the table with Eileen, but with Mitch and Susie Baxter, and that awful Becky girl—

"Don't trip on the wickets," Mrs. Henry warned. She paused beside him and shook a playful finger. "Sam, I'm leaving it to you to entertain the guest of honor."

"Yes'm—" he mumbled weakly.

"When she gets back to Chicago I want her to remember our boys in Wyattville." She departed toward the house.

He sat down. The Becky girl was giggling—glancing up at him and giggling, and he quickly looked away. Mitch was pouring root beer from a bottle. The Baxter girl was colorless and shy; she hadn't said a thing. He could hear Nelly's voice, chattering and laughing, but not Eileen's. Perhaps she wished she were sitting here with him—Cora Lee began to serve: salad and creamed chicken and hot biscuits. She smiled and nodded at him, and this made him uncomfortable. He gulped a little root beer. That Becky girl was saying something to him. He jerked his head around and scratched his neck.

"I know you're disappointed, Mr. Braden—"

"Shucks—" He laughed. No one had ever called him that before, but it sounded kind of nice. "Sam's good enough," he said.

"Well, Sam, then—" She had a pretty voice—soft and sort of purring.

"Well, what?"

"I know you're disappointed—"

"Disappointed?—What about?"

"To find me sitting here—"

"Aw, I don't care." He meant to be magnanimous.

"You don't?—That's awfully sweet of you." She was giggling again. "You see, I asked to sit by you—"

"You did?" He felt relieved. Of course Eileen had to humor her request. "Well, why?" he asked.

"Oh, just because—" Now she was being coy.

"Because of what?"

"I've heard so much about you—"

"You have?" His heart began to thump. "A lot—" She nodded, nibbling at a biscuit.

"I hope it's good?" He was trying to sound careless.

"Maybe—" she admitted.

"Who told you?"

"Who do you think?"

"Well—" He pretended to consider. "Old Neill Wyatt, I suppose." She laughed and shook her head.

"Then who?"

"Eileen, silly."

"Oh!" He affected mild surprise. "What did she say?"

"Wouldn't you like to know?"

"Aw, I don't care." His heart was racing.

"You're an awful fibber, Sam." She was smiling, kind of flirting. "But perhaps I'll tell you—sometime."

"Well, go ahead."

"No, I don't believe I will." Now she was frowning at him. "You're supposed to entertain me." And she flounced around toward Mitch.

"Gee—" He was startled and confused. "I'm sorry if—"

"Never mind—" She was giggling again. "I'm only joking, Sam. You've been very entertaining." She turned to Mitch. "Now you entertain me for a while."

"Well say," Mitch laughed, "I've been waiting for a chance." He took out his eye and put it on the table. "No matter where I am, I'll be watching you," he said.

"What's that?" she gasped.

"That's the eye that never sleeps."

She screamed and grabbed Sam's arm.

"Shucks," he reassured her, "it's just his old glass eye."

"Take it away!"

"Just an old piece of glass—"

"I don't care. I don't like it."

"It can't hurt you—" He pushed it with his fork.

"I don't want it looking at me. It's horrible. It's dreadful." She was almost crying now. "Please put it back," she begged.

"Anything your little heart desires—" Mitch picked up the eye and put it back. "I'm just being entertaining—"

She watched this performance with horrified amazement.

"Now just turn your head a moment," he continued brightly, "and I'll take off a leg."

"No!" she said as if she thought he might.

"What's happening?" Nelly called.

"Just Mitch and his old eye."

"Oh well—" They were all laughing now.

It broke the ice. But Miss Rebecca Adams was subdued for quite a while—not having any giggling spells, or being coy or smart. Good old Mitch had put her in her place—even if she did come from Chicago and her father had a house at Lake Geneva with tennis courts and stuff —but of course he was equipped with a glass eye—

He began to eat his supper. The neckband of his shirt was choking him—every time he swallowed it was like being hanged; he was terribly afraid the button would pop off and drop into his plate. Susie Baxter was trying in her shy and mousy way to make herself agreeable—

she was saying something to him, but his mind was somewhere else. He could see Eileen from the corner of his eye, sitting like a goddess—not talking much or giggling or making any effort, but just accepting things as queens accepted homage.—What had she said to Becky about him?

Cora Lee removed the plates and brought ice cream and cake. It was beginning to be dark; the paper lanterns glowed, swinging to and fro like monstrous fireflies. The mosquitoes came to life and buzzed around, nipping at ankles underneath the table. It was not polite to slap at them, he thought. He rubbed his ankles, twisting them together.—Mitch and Becky seemed to hit it off all right. She was being smart again—tossing her head around and acting flirty. But Mitch could handle that. He gave her back just as good as she sent over, and she laughed as if she liked it. It appeared to work like that: if a fellow acted rough and snappy with them, they seemed to eat it up, as a cat would lap up cream. But of course that wouldn't work with a person like Eileen—not where your interest was really deep and serious—

"Why don't we have a picnic sometime, Sam?" Susie was asking him. "You and I, and Hub and Nelly—just the four of us sometime?—down at Beaton's woods, or on the island?"

"Say, that would be fine," he answered absently, "but I have to work, you know."

"Well, some Sunday?"

"Yep, you bet."

But his thought was somewhere else. What had Eileen said to Becky about him?—It was good, she had admitted. Yes, but how good? Could she have confided that she was in love with him? And, if it wasn't something of this sort, why would Becky act that way?—being so secretive and teasing him about it?—promising to tell him, and then saying that she wouldn't?—Well, he'd get her by herself later in the evening; he'd go at her good and rough—the way Mitch did; he'd find out exactly what she knew about it—

The rim of the moon rose out of the river; frogs began to croak. The night was still and warm, and languorous and romantic—

"Say, Sam—" Mitch leaned across the table. "—remember the time you soaked old Neill with a hunk of lemon pie?"

He grinned and nodded.

"Remember, Eileen?" Mitch called to her. "—at a Sunday school picnic? You were there."

"Yes, I remember, Mitch." She wasn't laughing.

"We were just kids," Sam said.

"Naughty little boy!" Becky frowned at him. "Whatever made you do such a horrid thing?"

"He had on sailor pants—"

"No," Mitch said, "that's not the reason."

"Then why?" she asked.

"Sam was jealous of him."

"Shucks—" Sam laughed, but he was embarrassed now. "We were just kids."

"Maybe so—" Mitch chuckled. "But you'll do it again if you ever get a chance."

"Sam Braden!" Becky shook her finger at him. "I'm ashamed of you."

"Aw, shucks—" he mumbled. But he wasn't sure that she didn't mean it—wasn't altogether sure about anything she said.

Eileen came to his rescue—strolling over like a goddess, leaning with her soft white arms on the back of Becky's chair—

"Darling," she said, "go and get your ukulele."

"Do you really think I should?" Becky tipped her head back. She was being coy again. "Well, darling, I simply can't resist you." She got up, shaking out her skirt. "Mr. Mitch, you come with me—" Now she was making eyes and being cute. "I'm afraid when it gets dark." She slipped her arm through his and went, edging close against him, toward the house.

"Mind the wickets," Eileen said, and sat down in Becky's chair.

"Yes, darling," Becky giggled, "and you mind your *p's* and *q's.*"

"Susie," Grover called, "I can turn a glass of water upside down and never spill a drop. Come over here and look."

Susie slid away and went to see.

They were alone.

The moon was up—yellow and enormous, like an incandescent cheese; the paper lanterns twinkled, dancing lightly up and down; the frogs croaked in a chorus, and the mosquitoes sang like tautly trembling wires.

It was too dark to see her face, and he was glad that she could not see his. He thought that he must look as foolish as he felt—all that silly stuff about the lemon pie; and he wasn't much to look at anyway, with that cowlick in his hair and all his freckles which, his mother had assured him, would disappear in time. But she had always laughed when he complained about them, insisting that she loved them—that they weren't the least bit ugly—

What was Mitch driving at with that last funny crack?—that he'd do it again if he ever had a chance: soak old Neill with a hunk of lemon pie. Well, of course he'd never do a thing like that again. But maybe Mitch meant something else entirely—that he and Neill would fight a battle to the death for the lady of their choice—not with lemon pieces but with weapons that could kill: guns and knives and poison. Well, maybe Mitch was right—

It sure had been slick—the way she changed the subject. She had done it like an empress—sending the Becky girl off about her business, and then sitting down beside him, just to show them that nobody could make funny cracks about him.—What was an ukulele anyway? Some new kind of game perhaps. But he wasn't going to ask and give himself away—

Gee, here they were alone and the minutes ticking by, and he hadn't said a thing. It was silly asking Becky when Eileen, herself, was here. All he had to do was put the question—just plump it right out straight: "Do you love me, Eileen?—Do you really care about me, more than Neill or anyone?—Will you marry me some day?—Oh, I'll have lots of money. Don't you worry about that.—Well say, don't you see, I've already got a start; I'm ahead of all those fellows wasting time with school. I'm as good a clerk right now as the others in the store. Clem says so, himself. And I'm only getting started. I'll be rich before you know it.—Just tell me if you love me—"

"Say, Eileen—" he blurted.

She turned her head. The moonlight made her blonde hair shine like gold. But already they were coming back across the lawn—Mitch and the Becky girl; and something was tinkling like a broken mandolin. It was too late.

"Aw, never mind—" he said.

"Don't trip on the wickets," Eileen warned.

"Or the wicked," Becky said and set them laughing.

So that was the ukulele!—that little tum-tum thing she was holding like a baby and strumming with her fingers. It sounded as silly as it looked—

They got cushions from the hammock and the swing, and sat in a circle on the grass beneath the paper lanterns. He was sharing a cushion with Eileen, but Grover was close by on her other side. The golden opportunity had vanished. The moon was climbing up the sky, getting white and smaller—no longer like a cheese. The frogs kept croaking, sounding very much like the ukulele; you had to listen closely to be sure which was which. The mosquitoes hummed around; you could slap at them now you were no longer at the table. Cora Lee was gathering up the dishes—

"Sing something, darling," Eileen said.

"Do you really think I should, darling?" Same old stuff again. "Well, I simply can't resist you—" And she began to sing, cuddled on a cushion, kind of leaning against Mitch—"My Old Kentucky Home."

He wished Eileen would lean against his shoulder, but of course she'd never do a thing like that. And it was pretty brazen, the way that Becky acted with a boy she'd only met an hour ago. It was funny Eileen liked her. Anyway she couldn't sing much—couldn't sing for sour apples!

"Come on," she paused to call. "Come on in, the water's fine."

Some of them joined in, but Nelly's high, sweet voice rang clear above them all. She was sitting by herself, leaning back against a tree, and she sang right out as if she were in church. Pretty soon the others stopped; she was singing all alone—

It was terribly embarrassing. He wished he were close enough to nudge her—to remind her that this wasn't choir practice, that she was at a party at Eileen's, and it was pretty raw to butt in and sing like that, drowning everybody out. Even Becky had quit now, but kept strumming on the thing just to be polite. His hands were sweating—

"Darling!" Becky cried when the song came to an end. "Darling, what a voice!"

He winced. Was this a crack?

"Oh, I can't really sing—" Nelly laughed excitedly.

"Oh, but you can!" It sounded like she meant it. "Sing something that you like and I'll try to pick it out."

"Well, mostly I know hymns—"

"Hymns!" Becky sniffed. "You should be singing opera."

That must be a crack, he thought.

"Carmen or Traviata—"

"Do you really think so, Becky?—that I could sing in opera?" Nelly, his own sister, lapping up that kind of stuff!

"If you had a little training in Paris or New York—"

"You mean—I really could?"

"You sing divinely, darling.—Doesn't she, Eileen?"

He held his breath. Eileen wouldn't say anything she didn't mean.

"Yes," Eileen said, "divinely."

"Oh, Eileen!" Nelly sounded almost tearful.

"Now that's settled," Mitch said dryly, "go ahead and sing, Nelly."

And Nelly sang—some hymns she knew, but they didn't go so well with the ukulele, and most of the time she had no accompaniment; and then the songs they all knew: "Annie Laurie," "Comin' Thro' the Rye," "Good Night Ladies"—

He was impressed. Maybe Nelly could sing. They kept begging her for more every time she stopped. Maybe she could sing opera—Carmen and that other one they mentioned—if she had a little training in Paris or New York. It couldn't be disgraceful to be an opera singer; they got paid a lot of money. Rich people went to see them—men in long tail coats with stovepipe hats, and ladies dressed in furs and decked with jewels. Maybe they would cheer when Nelly sang—stand up and clap their hands. And maybe he would be there, sitting in a box—he and Eileen; and perhaps they would have guests, and one of them would say, "Isn't she divine!" And he would smile and nod. "My sister—" he would answer, proud but modest.—Well, maybe— He wished he knew what Eileen had said to Becky; he must try to pin her down before he left. He wished that Nelly would quit singing so he could explore that other matter. He wished Eileen would turn her head and not keep watching Nelly all the time. It was past his usual bedtime and he was getting sleepy. He wished that he could skip the next few years—

Mrs. Henry came snooping from the house—a signal that the party was about to terminate. But Becky insisted that Nelly sing a final song for her. "Home Sweet Home," she wanted; and Nelly sang it. She really sang it, too. It made funny little feelings in your stomach and the tears come to your eyes—

"Lovely," Mrs. Henry chirped. "Simply lovely, Nelly."

"Couldn't she sing in opera, Mrs. Wyatt?" Becky asked.

"Why, I'm sure she could." Mrs. Henry spoke with confidence, never having been to the opera in her life.

"You see, darling!"

"Oh, thank you—" Nelly was in heaven, dancing on the clouds.

He got up. Now was the time and there might not be another. He would thank Mrs. Henry and get that over with, and then he'd tackle Becky and find out what was what. She was standing beside Mitch, strumming on that thing. Well, he'd get rid of Mitch; he'd be good and tough about it. He started briskly—too briskly perhaps; anyway his toe caught in a wicket and down he went, sprawling on his face, right at Mrs. Henry's feet. He heard the button pop—

There were screams and laughter.

"You can always count on Sam," he heard Mitch say.

"Why, Sam—" Mrs. Henry drew back in alarm as he scrambled to his feet. "You didn't hurt yourself?"

"No'm—" He was clutching at his throat. His necktie was the kind that fastens on the button, and of course it had come off; he was holding it in place. "I tripped on a wicket—"

From the corner of his eye he could see the Becky girl—giggling fit to bust, hanging onto Mitch's arm.

"You didn't hurt your neck?" Mrs. Henry persisted.

"No'm. Just my necktie that came off—"

"Oh, well—" Mrs. Henry smiled doubtfully.

"I've had a nice time. Thank you very much."

"I hope you'll come again, Sam."

"Yes'm, I will—" He turned his head. Eileen was watching him; she wasn't laughing. "Well, thanks, Eileen. So long—" He included the others, waving carelessly with the necktie in his hand. "Well, so long—" And he walked away across the lawn.

"Wait for me, Sam," Nelly called.

But he went on.—Dawgone it!—tripping on that wicket and falling on his face like a clown in a circus! And the button and the necktie! He shoved it in his pocket. And that giggling, smarty girl! He'd get square with her sometime; he'd get square with all of them. But Eileen hadn't laughed—

He was at the iron gate when Nelly overtook him.

"Sam, wait!" She was out of breath from hurrying. "Whatever made you run away like that?"

"I'm not running," he said glumly.

"You didn't even say good night to Becky."

"Why should I?"

"But the party was for her."

"I don't care. I don't like her."

"Why not? I think she's nice."

"Giggly smart aleck—"

"She's so gay and full of life—"

"She makes me sick."

There was silence for a while. They went on across the Square—through the moonlight and the shadows of the cottonwoods.

"Sam—"

"What?"

"Do you think I could ever sing in opera?"

"How should I know?"

"You heard what Becky said—"

"Becky!" he snorted. "I'd sure be a sucker to believe that kind of stuff."

"Oh well—" Nelly was hurt. "You're just mad because she thought your suit was funny—"

"Funny! My suit!" He stopped and stared.

"Well, it is—a little funny, Sam."

"You're crazy," he said scornfully, but his confidence was jarred. "It's the latest style of suit. Anybody but a hick would know it."

"Well, maybe—" Nelly was contrite. There was a pause. "I *can* sing, Sam—"

"Sure, you sing all right."

"If I could go to Paris or New York—"

"If cows could fly—" he muttered.

"Would it cost a lot of money?"

"What do you think?"

"Yes—" she sighed. They came out of the Square and turned toward Shanty Town.

"Maybe," he said, "when I get really started—well, maybe I could help you."

"Yes, but when, Sam?"

"Oh, I don't know—" He shrugged; it seemed terribly remote.

"Maybe I'll be too old then—"

No answer.

"I don't see how you'll ever earn enough—clerking for Clem Wyatt."

"I'm not going to be clerking there forever."

"Well, what are you going to do?"

"I don't know yet." He didn't know and it had begun to worry him.

"You ought to make your mind up pretty soon."

No answer. They were trudging through the swale, as they had trudged together, back and forth to school, so many, many times.

"Sam—"

"What?"

"Why do you care so much about—Eileen?"

"Why?" He was startled; she had never said a thing like that before.
"Because I do, that's all." He kept looking straight ahead.

"Because she's pretty?"

"No."

"Because she's rich?"

"What difference does that make?"

"I'm only asking you—just wondering what you see in her?"

No answer.

"She hardly ever talks—just sits there, looking pretty."

"Well, that's something anyway."

"She's never cared for anyone but Neill."

"That's what you think," he said angrily.

"Everybody knows it."

"I don't." A pause. They were climbing up the slope.

"She's so hard and—cold."

"She's not. You just don't know her."

"Do you, Sam?"

"Aw shucks—" he said. But he had a sneaking feeling that he didn't. They went past the Hogan house.

"There are other pretty girls in Wyattville—nice ones, too."

"Well, who?"

"You know as well as I do—" But she named some.

"Oh them!" he interrupted with a sneer. "They don't interest me."

"They might, if you'd give them half a chance—"

"No." He laughed and shook his head. "I guess I'll stick to Eileen."

"Well—" Nelly sighed. "I don't think she'll ever really care about you, Sam."

"Yeh?" He was sure getting things rubbed in. "A lot you know about it."

"I know what girls are like."

"All right. All right. You're pretty smart." They turned in at the gate; the house was dark.

"Oh dear!" She sighed again. "I wish I could go to Paris or New York—"

"I wish," he jeered. "I wish I had a million dollars."

"Well, if you did, then would you send me, Sam?—so I could sing in opera?"

"Yep. You bet," he said.

They went in quietly, so as not to wake their father.

V

IT TOOK SAM NEARLY THIRTY YEARS TO ACQUIRE HIS FIRST MILLION. There was nothing spectacular about it: hard work, eternal vigilance, and a kind of native shrewdness—these plus Lady Luck, who smiled at him at last, ultimately turned the trick. And the million, once acquired, quickly multiplied itself, for wealth breeds wealth, and even stupid people with a nest egg of this sort, are as likely as not to go on getting richer.

At the height of his success he was worth somewhere around six million dollars. He never knew exactly, for values are shifting every time the clock ticks, and even static things are impossible of accurate appraisement. For example: who could put a proper value upon Glencoe?—what the place had cost in money? (if one could determine that—the cost of reproduction? (if it could be reproduced)—what it would fetch at a forced sale? (certainly no more than a fraction of its worth)—or what some other rich man might be inclined to pay for a Colonial mansion with stables, barns and silos set in a park of rolling, timbered land (once known as Beaton's woods)—and level farming ground and broad, green meadows, two thousand acres in extent, with horses, blooded cattle, and fields of golden corn stretching far along the bluff above the river—a rich man's home or hobby. Who could say what it was worth to anyone but him?

However this may be, measured by the standards of the world in which he lived, Sam Braden did become a rich, successful man. But not any more than that; not what the press would describe as a tycoon—not powerful, not rich enough for that; capable at most of corrupting minor bureaucrats—far removed from the business of buying federal judges, subsidizing legislatures, and electing Presidents—from the realm of the tycoon.

He was practically unknown to the tycoons or the public; at no time in his life was he famous or notorious. He was rarely interviewed or quoted by the press; he took no part in politics. His commercial reputation was always of the highest; he was known to keep his word. He had excellent connections in the banking world—for example: Stanley Adams in Chicago, who was closely connected with the Morgans in

New York; and the Elliott Wyatt Company which had spread out everywhere across the country, doing general brokerage business and extensive underwriting in the field of high finance, really reaching tycoon class.

But Sam, himself, was not of tycoon caliber. He had too many qualities of the sort that endow or afflict the average man. He was, in fact, too human.

Mike said to him one day—it was in '28—sitting in the office, looking out across the lake—

"Jesus, Sam," he said, "if only you'd happened to get into oil or steel, instead of this penny-pushing business! Say, you'd be as rich as any of 'em."

"Yeh—" Sam grinned, but he knew better.

"You'd run circles round 'em, Sam." Mike believed in him, believed in him completely. But Mike Hogan was a very stupid man.

"Well, maybe—" Sam leaned back in his chair and lit a cigarette.

He had been telling Mike: on the Century, going to New York, he had run into Wayne Wyatt with some Oklahoma oilmen, big shots of the day. Someone had called his name as he was walking through the train from dinner, and there was Wayne, sitting in a drawing room with three big husky fellows—looking just the way he always did, as Neill had looked, slender and well dressed, with his hair brushed straight back, and that easy, careless, sure way about him.

"Hi, Sam!"

He had paused in the doorway. They were finishing their dinner and the waiter was clearing off the table—the remnants of thick steaks and empty highball glasses.

"Well, Sam, how are you?" They shook hands across the table, and Wayne had introduced him to the others whose names were front-page news—two of them at least—tycoons, in fact. But he had recognized them before he heard their names—big, broad-shouldered men, strong and tough, and hard. They had made him roughly welcome as a friend of Wayne's, had poured a drink for him, and one of them had said:

"Braden, eh?—Never ran across the name but once before. Fellow used to work for me, trained some horses for me once—Tom Braden was his name. No relation, I suppose?"

"Yes," Sam said, "my brother." Though if Wayne had not been there he might have let it go. He had wondered afterwards whether he would or not.

"Yeh? That right?" The man had paused to give an order to the porter who had come to the door in answer to the bell. "Fetch two decks of cards, George, and another round of setups. Step on it now." And then he had come back to the subject. "Good trainer, knew his business —trained some winners for me. But he couldn't let the booze alone. Haven't heard of him in years. What's become of him?"

"He's dead," Sam said.

"Yeh? Well, that's too bad. Smart fellow with a horse."

But he did not mention this episode to Mike. They had asked him if he cared to play a little poker, to while away the time; and he had said he wouldn't mind. He had wondered afterwards why he had accepted, why he hadn't gone on to his compartment and to bed. He had a book to read and he wasn't fond of cards and rarely played, and he was not a gambler—not with games. Perhaps he had wanted to be sociable; he was a lonely man. Or perhaps he was flattered by the idea of being in such company—with men who were really rich and powerful. Perhaps he had been curious about them—to find out what they were like, what made them drive ahead to the front of the procession in which he felt himself a humble marcher. Perhaps he had thought he might pick up some information—some tip that might come handy. He knew that Elliott Wyatt was involved with these fellows, marketing an issue of securities; he had read that in the papers; and that, of course, explained why Wayne was with them.

Anyway he had accepted. They had moved into another drawing room—it seemed that they had two, and two compartments—and had started in to play. The game was stud. He had not inquired anything about the stakes—

"Jesus!" Mike exclaimed "You were stepping into something."

"Up to my neck," Sam nodded. The man who was banking had handed him some chips—just an ordinary stack of red and blue and yellow, and had written down his name and after it had put—"Well, how much would you guess?"

"Five hundred bucks?" Mike ventured.

"Double that."

"A thousand? Holy Mother!"

"Yeh, that's right." But he had felt pretty sick; his hands had begun to sweat the way they used to do when he was a boy.

"How much did they take you for?"

"How much?" Sam grinned. "I won nine hundred dollars."

"By God, now think of that!" Mike beamed on his employer. "So you took those big shots for a ride!"

"Hell!" Sam laughed. "They're no different from anybody else." But he knew this wasn't true.

They had quit at four o'clock; he had won nine hundred dollars, playing close to his belly, but why not?—about what Wayne had lost. The heavy loser, the man for whom Tom Braden had trained horses, had finally called a halt; he had lost six thousand dollars to the other two—

"Christ!" he said, "I've had enough. It's time to go to bed." And he had scrawled the checks, paying what he owed—yawning while he did it.

They had kept the porter up—running back and forth for setups, for cigars and cigarettes, emptying ash trays, waiting on them. They had done it without caring or even thinking of it. They were not accustomed to think of things like that—a nigger more or less. They tossed him fifty dollars at the end—but tossed it, crumpled up, so the fellow must stoop down to pick it up.

In the course of the evening they consumed two quarts of Scotch— most of it themselves, for he and Wayne drank little. But at that they were not drunk, not careless in their playing, and neither gay nor quarrelsome. They were friendly enough, but cold as ice; there were walls behind their eyes which you could not penetrate. They had little to say, really nothing in the way of conversation but, between themselves, a kind of badinage, brusque and rough and second rate. They did not mention business.

"Did you see 'em in the morning?" Mike inquired.

"Only for a moment on the platform at Grand Central."

They had gone striding past him, with Wayne like a stripling among giants, with redcaps at their heels—two hundred million dollars worth of men—clean shaved, pink cheeked, clear eyed, while he felt dopey, half awake, with a thick taste in his mouth—wishing he had gone to bed at a reasonable hour, dreading the work he must get through that day. Yet no trace of dissipation lingered on them. Their minds were fresh and keen; no one would trip them up. They had grinned and nodded to him, and Wayne had waved and called:

"Come in and see us, Sam—" The Elliott Wyatt company had long since removed headquarters from Chicago to New York; and Elliott was playing with the crowd that ran the country, really going places now— with a town house in New York and a big place on Long Island and another at Palm Beach—and a beautiful new wife—

"Yeh, I'll do that, Wayne." He had walked on slowly, not wanting

« 107 »

to catch up with them, or to seem to want to do so, thinking to himself: what was it that they had?

It was then that Mike had said, sputtering damply from the corner of his mouth: "Jesus, Sam, if only you'd happened to get into oil or steel, instead of this penny-pushing business!"

But he knew better. In oil or steel or motors he would have been a flop. In the days when men built railroads he would have gotten nowhere; he could not have held his own with Gould and Hill and Harriman; he didn't have the stuff. It was lucky for him, this penny-pushing business which was fitted to his talents, not too big and not too small—not big enough to tempt the big-shot fellows. And lucky for him, too, that he knew his limitations. But what was it that they had?

"Well—" Mike stood up. "—if there's nothing else, I guess I'll toddle home, Sam." It was after six o'clock.

"No, nothing else—"

"Well then, good night—"

"Oh, Mike!" His voice had changed.

"Yes sir?" Mike stood waiting at the door.

"I want those raw stock contracts figured out tomorrow."

"Yes sir."

"I don't want long commitments. It's a runaway market, but it can't go up forever."

"Yes sir."

"Don't forget—tomorrow."

"No sir, I won't. Good night—"

He sat there for some time after Mike had gone.

What was it that they had?—They were big, strong, healthy fellows; they had physical machines that would stand a lot of wear, but of course that wasn't all. They had very simple minds, focused clearly on one point, not deflected by any doubts or scruples; they were sure of themselves. Their job was making money, that was all. But with money came power; that's what they were making, though perhaps they never thought of it that way. And with power came contempt for the rights of other people less fortunate than themselves. They were ruthless; they were hard. No doubt they loved their wives and children, and would grieve if they died—or went away. But it wouldn't get them down or turn them off their course. They would go on making money—making power; every other thing in life was subordinate to that. Yes, they were *hard.* Perhaps that was the difference, the fundamental one: the quality of hardness—of hardness getting harder and harder with success.

He would never be like them, and never rich like that. Nor would he ever be like Elliott or Wayne, as Neill had been. That was another formula, but one you must be born to, which could never be acquired. To appreciate money you must have been without it, must have felt the teeth of poverty. It was Mitch Ballou who had made that clear to him —Mitch who hated what he called the "predatory rich," who would have hated those fellows in the drawing room, would have turned his back on them—

"The Wyatts!" he had sneered. "They're not really dangerous." It was several years ago when the penny-pushing business was still small but growing fast. "They've had money all their lives. They don't care enough about it to constitute a menace—no more than they do about a set of tennis or a horse race. There's a sporting element about the things they do; they can win or lose without getting off their balance. And they care for other things—not only money: their pride, their moral character, their souls perhaps—"

"So what?" he had prompted. They were sitting in the bar of the old Stratford Hotel and Mitch was a little drunk.

"Watch your step, Sam! Watch your step!" He had drained his glass and thumped on the table for another. "I don't care how much you make if you don't corrupt yourself—if you don't quit thinking straight."

He smiled now to himself remembering it—Well, it wasn't likely he'd corrupt himself or anybody else, not likely he'd be dangerous and a menace to the country—a little businessman with a paltry million dollars, trying to make money like everybody else—trying to get along.

Good thing he hadn't gotten into oil or steel. This penny-pushing business was plenty big enough. It had made a million for him, and now that its stock was quoted on the curb—Elliott Wyatt had talked him into that—by shrewd manipulation it might make a couple more—or three or four—

Funny how he had got into it—how one thing led to another—

He scarcely saw Eileen again that summer, and didn't tell or ask her anything. In a week or two she went back to visit Becky at her Lake Geneva house. And then Young Henry and his wife went on a vacation to Chicago. Old Henry had composed a deal with the Rock Island Railroad, selling them the site on which to build a depot, accepting annual passes for himself and family, as part consideration. And Young Henry had to travel, people said. However that might be, Eileen went back to school without coming home again. Their correspondence lan-guished and then died. A letter that he wrote remained unanswered.

Elliott came now and then to see his father, but the house across the Square remained unoccupied—for fifteen years in fact. The Elliott Wyatts came to Wyattville no more. It had been all right while the boys were children, though it couldn't have been chosen by Elliott or Daphne as a place to spend the summer—a sweltering little town, with nothing to be done but driving in a dogcart or sitting on the porch, drinking lemonade. They had come very faithfully for six or seven years, and no doubt had done enough toward patching up the past, and now that it was patched were content to let it be. The boys were growing up and had interests of their own, and Daphne was involved with social under-takings, and Elliott was busy getting on with big affairs. The chance to rent a place adjoining the estate of Stanley Adams, whose acquaintance had been formed through Becky and Eileen, presented no alternative; and the Lake Geneva summer was a prelude to the end. Probably Old Henry was content to have it so; he was getting rather feeble and more crotchety than ever, and was less and less disposed to have his house upset, to have young people running in and out. He had not looked with favor on the tennis court idea.

A year slid by. Mike vanished from the scene, departing for Chicago to reside with his uncle, the policeman, to complete his education in a good parochial school where he would be well protected from con-taminating influence of Protestants and heretics. Other things remained unaltered. Nelly was in high school, in her junior year. She sang at the commencement exercises, and Mitchell J. Ballou reported her per-formance in the Wyattville *Gazette*. He said: "Pretty, graceful Nelly Braden rendered her selections in a voice that holds great promise. We are mighty proud of Nelly. We venture to predict that, with proper training, she will one day grace the concert platform in the great cities of this country." Nelly was in raptures when Madge read it aloud—

"A concert singer!" she exclaimed. "Yes, I guess that's what I'll be. It's more dignified than opera—don't you think so, Madge?"

"Why yes, perhaps—" Madge sighed and smiled, picking up some sewing. She was busy all day long with the cooking and the house, and Mr. Daniel Price had not been back.

Eileen did not come home that summer, not even for a day. Instead she went to Europe—with her mother, and Aunt Daphne and the boys—a spectacular event at the turning of the century: except for the few born on the other side, almost no one in Wyattville had ever crossed the ocean.

"Oh dear—" Nelly groaned, when the fact was advertised in the *Gazette*, "—if only I could have a chance like that!"

"Shucks!" Sam was reading and he looked up from his book. "Just a lot of old churches and museums and things!"

"I don't care," Nelly said. "It isn't fair. She can do what she wants, and she hasn't any voice—or anything to train."

"Oh, well, I'd sooner go to California—" He went on reading, but he was consumed with envy: Eileen and Neill gallivanting about Europe! Yes, they were sure lucky.

Some post cards came—picture post cards mailed in Paris, in Lucerne and Venice, depicting local monuments and fashionable hotels, with a few words scrawled in schoolgirl French in the space where you could write, but no address to reply to.

The summer days droned by. His salary had been raised, and raised again—the last time to eight dollars. He was giving five to Madge and keeping three; and he had saved almost thirty dollars which were in Old Henry's bank, drawing interest at the rate of four per cent. But still he had misgivings: at this rate of progress, phenomenal though it was, it would take several lifetimes to get rich. He worked as hard as ever, was as punctual and polite, as diligent and careful; but perhaps Clem detected something in his eyes. Anyway one Saturday when they were closing up, he began to talk about it.

"Sam," he said, "you're a capable young fellow and I'd sure hate to lose you, but I know you won't go on here all your life."

Sam was startled—not knowing what was coming. He went on sweeping out.

"I'm paying you eight dollars," Clem continued. "In another year or so you might get ten, but that's pretty near the top. Miss Murgatroyd and Stahl are only getting twelve, and they been here for years. I couldn't pay you what I'm paying them—not for quite a while. It wouldn't seem quite fair."

"No sir—" Sam agreed.

"And twelve—well, that's the top."

"Yes sir—" He was taking up the sweepings in a dustpan.

"I've known you all your life, Sam, and I know you pretty well; you're smart and you're ambitious. There isn't any future in what you're doing now, and I think it's only right to tell you so, though—" He leaned against the counter watching Sam. "—though I guess you're smart enough to have got that figured out?"

"Yes sir," Sam admitted, sweeping up the last of it. "But, Clem—" He straightened with the dustpan in his hand. "—what shall I do?"

"Blamed if I know," Clem said. "In a little town like this there isn't much of anything." He scratched his head. "There's the banking business, though Old Henry doesn't pay as much as I do. Still, you might pick up from him some tricks of making money. Or—well, did you ever think you might want to study law?—something like that?"

"No, I never thought of that."

"Well, I tell you what you do—" Clem was getting out the keys to lock the door. "—you take a week's vacation—with pay, you understand —and kind of look things over, see what you can find. If you want to stay with me—well, you know I'm glad to have you. But if you can locate something you think is any better, I'll be just as glad as you are."

"Gee, thanks, Clem."

"That's all right, Sam."

He proceeded cautiously, not rushing around like a chicken with its head off—and caution was a quality which would stand him in good stead. He took a day or two to think things over, going off to Beaton's woods with a sandwich in his pocket, sitting on the bluff, looking out across the river to the shore of Illinois—to Chicago and New York, to the capitals of Europe—to the treasures of Cathay—

And he talked with Madge and Nelly, without practical result. Madge seemed to feel he ought to stay with Clem, but Nelly urged him on. She advised him to learn the banking business and then start one of his own.

"Everybody hates Old Henry," she affirmed, "and they'll bring their money to you. And when you get things going you can move your bank away—move it anywhere you like." She tore on with the idea and even mentioned something about a private yacht and a house at Lake Geneva—

"Aw shucks!" he said and changed the subject. He did not discuss the matter with his father.

But on Wednesday he put on the yellow suit and orange shoes, slicked back his hair the best he could, and paid a visit to the Wyatt bank. Young Henry, with an eyeshade on his forehead and black sleeve protectors from his elbows to his wrists, nodded coldly at him, looking through a wicket in the glass partition. There was only one wicket and Young Henry was the teller; he was also the cashier, bookkeeper, and vice-president. The other employees were two sad-faced looking men of middle age: Wallie Coot and Arthur Bridgeman. They were standing at a desk, in eyeshades and sleeve protectors exactly like Young Henry's, adding figures in the books.

"Well?" Young Henry asked.

"I'd like to see about a job—" He had rehearsed the matter.

"A job?" Young Henry looked surprised and mildly shocked. "What kind of job?"

"A job here in the bank." He kept looking at the vault which contained his thirty dollars.

"Oh—" Young Henry turned the matter in his mind. "You'll have to see my father about that." It was said in Wyattville that Young Henry wouldn't dare to obey the calls of nature—only they put it bluntly—unless he asked his father.

"Well, could I see him now?"

"Why yes, I guess so—" He opened the gate in the partition and ushered Sam into a dingy little room in the corner of the bank. Old Henry was sitting at his desk—a wizened little man with a white beard like a goat's, and his threadbare old blue coat a mass of spots. He would not submit to have it cleaned.

"Well? What?" He looked up impatiently. Sam's heart sank to his shoes and his hands began to sweat.

"It's the Braden boy," Young Henry said. "He's looking for a job."

"What for?" Old Henry barked, glaring angrily at Sam. It was a simple question but difficult to answer. "What for? Speak up!"

"I—I'd like to learn the business—"

"Oh, you'd like to learn the business!" Old Henry scowled or grinned; it was difficult to say. "Well, what for?"

"I'd like to be a banker—"

"Oh, you'd like to be a banker!—Well, why, I want to know?"

"I—I want to make some money—"

"Oh, you want to make some money!—Well, how much?"

"All I can get—"

"How much?"

"A lot," Sam blurted desperately. "A million dollars maybe."

"A million, eh?" Old Henry shook his head. "We haven't any jobs."

"I don't mind starting cheap—"

"We haven't any jobs." He picked up his pen and began to scratch again in the ledger on the desk. "I don't employ young fellows that want to make a million. I can't afford such luxury." He made a cackling sound

« 113 »

that might have been a laugh, and motioned with his hand as if brushing them away.

What were the proper answers to the questions that Old Henry had propounded and clung to like a leech?—"What for?" "How much?" He wondered about that, out in the street, aware that whatever they might be, he had not replied correctly.—"Because I need the work." "I have to make a living." "I'd like to learn to keep a set of books, and maybe sometime get as much as Wallie Coot." Yes, answers such as these might have landed him a job. Instinctively he felt what in time he came to know: that rich men didn't want ambitious men around them—as witness in himself his choice of Mike—that the making of money was a solitary business whose secrets, if they must be shared at all, had best be shared with unambitious men—loyal, mediocre men, content with crumbs.

And in the years to come he wondered more than once what his life would have been like had he made a proper answer?—had he been engaged to work for Old Henry in the bank? And he shuddered at the memory of the dingy, shabby place, and the grubby little men with eyeshades on their foreheads and alpaca sleeve protectors—adding up the ledgers, endless empty columns whose fruits, if fruits there were, they were certain not to taste. But he would not have stayed there, drifting into middle age—and yet, suppose he had—

The following day he called upon Judge Nicolls.

The Judge was very old—older than Old Henry, getting close to eighty, and not small or shriveled up, but big and round, with white hair like a mane that came almost to his shoulders, and a large red bulbous nose with blue veins sticking out. He was sitting in his office over Mr. Bascom's undertaking shop—an office lined with faded leather law books, smelling of hot leather in the sun which streamed in the open window through which he was gazing at Clem Wyatt's store across the street. He was sitting in his shirt with the sleeves rolled to his elbows, fanning himself with a big palmetto fan. His long black coat hung on the wall beside the stovepipe hat which he did not often wear now except to a funeral or something of the sort.

"Howdy, Sam," he said with a twinkle in his eye. "Have you come to start a lawsuit?"

"No sir—" Sam smiled, waiting near the door. He had on the yellow suit and orange shoes.

"Well, that indicates to me you're a pretty smart young fellow—" He reached out to swat a fly with the palmetto fan. "But you're all dressed up for something, like a suppliant for justice. Come in and have a chair."

"Yes sir—" Sam sat down. "I've been thinking that perhaps I'd like to study law—"

"To study law," the Judge repeated solemnly. "What put that in your head?"

"I've been thinking I'd like to be a lawyer—"

"Yes?—Why, Sam?"

"Well—I—" He was going to be cautious about this.

"Do you feel a burning passion for the lady with the bandage on her eyes, and the sword and scales of justice?"

"Why—"

"Now let's be honest, Sam."

"I never thought of it like that—"

"How have you thought of it?"

"I—I—"

"Why do you want to be a lawyer?"

"I have to make my living—"

"Is that all you want to make?"

"Well—" He was silent, not knowing what to say.

"Look, Sam!" The judge was pointing at the shelves of yellow books. "Books about the law, the law itself—hundreds of 'em, dull and dry as dust. You'll have to read 'em—read 'em all your life: red tape mostly, tying people up so justice can't be done. You'll get pretty sick of that, watching the innocent get punished and the guilty get away. And you'll never make much money—not if you're a lawyer."

"But—" Sam wet his lips. "—some lawyers get rich, don't they?"

"No sir, they don't." The old man struck the desk with the palmetto fan. "Smart businessmen get rich, and a few of them are lawyers—or so they call themselves: corporation lawyers who can show their wealthy clients how to cheat the law. But real lawyers don't get rich." He paused and fanned himself. "Why do you want to be a lawyer, Sam?"

"Well—" Sam said, drawing in his breath, "—perhaps I don't."

"Now we're getting somewhere—" The Judge was smiling at him, leaning back in his big chair. "What do you really want?"

"I want to make some money," Sam confessed.

"How much?"

"A lot. A million dollars."

"A million dollars, eh?" But the Judge didn't bark at him the way Old Henry had. "I see. You want to be a millionaire?"

"Yes sir—if I can."

"Why?"

"Why?" Sam stared.

"No matter, Sam. Don't try to answer that." He was smiling—kind of sadly: "It doesn't matter why. Anyway you couldn't tell me." He paused and sighed. "It's the spirit of the age—the spirit of America. I'm getting so old that I forget." And then he went on briskly. "All right, I understand: you want to make your fortune, and what you want to know is how to get a start?"

"Yes sir, I guess that's it."

"Like the boys in Babylon?—in Greece and Rome?"

Sam was discreetly silent.

"Well, first, don't waste your time, for time, they say, is money."

"Yes sir, I know—"

"*Don't* study law."

"No sir—" Sam nodded with a feeling of relief.

"And second—hum—" The old man seemed to drift away, to be dozing in his chair; then suddenly he roused and turned his shaggy head. "Telegraphy," he said.

"Telegraphy?" Sam stammered.

"Yes, telegraphy. Why not?"

"But could anyone get rich—just doing that?"

"Railroads!" the Judge exclaimed, and slowly winked his eye. "Railroads everywhere—snaking through the grass, climbing over mountains. Learn the railroad business, Sam. Learn to build 'em, buy 'em, sell 'em. But first you learn telegraphy. Railroads need telegraphers—hundreds of 'em, Sam."

"Yes sir—"

"Wires strung around like spiderwebs! People talking through the air, a thousand miles apart, in the twinkling of an eye!—Anything can happen—" He seemed to drift away again, staring through the open window at the lazy summer street.

"Well, thanks, Judge—thanks a lot—" Sam was edging toward the door; his hand was on the knob.

"Oh, Sam—" The old man did not turn his head.

"Yes sir?"

"Your mother used to mend my shirts for me—sew buttons on and such. I knew her from the day she came to Wyattville—the very night she got here on the 'Mary Queen,' down at the Wyatt House, with your father and the children, Madge and Tom. You weren't born then."

"No sir," Sam said.

"Your mother didn't have an easy life—" He kept on looking through the window. "—but I never heard her whimper or complain. She was proud and she was plucky."

"Yes sir—" Sam bit his lip; the tears were welling in his eyes.

"You stop and think, all your way through life, when you're in doubt—what your mother would have said."

"Yes sir, I'll try."

"All right." The old man waved his fan but he didn't turn his head. "Now go and learn telegraphy as quickly as you can, and when you get it learned—come back and see me, Sam."

"Yes sir, I sure will."

"The railroad's coming here, to Wyattville. They're going to build a depot, and they'll need a bright young fellow to sell the railroad tickets and run the telegraph."

"Yes sir, I know—" His heart was thumping.

"I'm their lawyer, Sam, and—maybe I could fix it for you to get the job."

"Gee, thanks, Judge—"

"But learn telegraphy."

"Yes sir, you bet I will." He went clattering down the stairs in a fever of excitement.

He didn't ask: "How am I to learn?" or "Who will teach me?"—didn't hesitate or question: "Would they pay me as much as I'm getting from Clem Wyatt?"—"Yes sir, you bet I will," was what he said.

A decision had been made. He would go on making them, not thoughtlessly nor hastily, but quickly when the need was; and he would unmake them, too, when their purpose had been served. He was never one to follow a false scent, once its falseness had been recognized, nor to fight for a lost cause, once the odds had been dispassionately computed. He was not intrigued by sinking ships; he never threw good money after bad. He had qualities of generalship: initiative, mobility; he could always change his plan to conform to the actions of the enemy; he could decide and act. He was a realist, and yet he was not completely that—

There were times when he looked back, as who does not, to the crossroads that checkered his career. Suppose, for example, that Judge Nicolls hadn't been a wise old man, or hadn't cared enough to cross-examine him?—that he had settled down to study law in that sun-drenched little room with the smell of leather books?—with farmers coming in with petty lawsuits—suits against the railroad which had killed a cow or pig, disputes among themselves over boundaries and fences—leases, contracts, and bad debts—the dreary, tedious trivia of rural legal practice.— It was of course unthinkable that this could have been his life—any more than going on working for the railroad, or for the wholesale paper house which followed that experience, for anyone in fact except himself, or for anything at all except for money. He would have stayed a while, reading those leather books, and then he would have known that he was wasting time; and one day he would have quit and gone on to something else—

He learned telegraphy.

He bought an instrument and big glass jars for batteries. Clem sent and got them from Chicago at a discount. He went on working at the store, but at night he learned telegraphy. He taught Nelly how to send so that he could learn to take. He would sit with his eyes shut, reading out the letters, and finally the words, which she painfully and inaccurately clicked.

"Oh dear!" she would protest at last. "It makes my fingers ache, and I'm sick and tired of it."

"Aw shucks!" And he would demand or plead, "Just a few minutes more."

"But you'll never get rich doing this—"

"I'm not aiming to do it all my life."

"Well then, what good is it?"

"You'll see—" he would grin, "—when I get to be the president of a railroad."

"Yes, well when?"

"Come on, Nelly, please—just five minutes more."

"I won't. It isn't any fun."

"If you want to go to Paris—"

"Oh well—" She would make a little face and go on tapping at the key. It had come to be a formula.

But he learned telegraphy—learned it in five months—to send and take Morse code with decent speed and accuracy. Early in November he went back to see Judge Nicolls. His birthday had just passed; he was seventeen years old.

He got the job.

The pay was sixty dollars—almost fifteen a week; not many men in Wyattville were making more than that. The hours were from seven in the morning until nine o'clock at night, with an hour off for dinner and another one for supper when he simply closed up shop and locked the door. On Sunday he was free and the depot was not opened.

The work was easy. There was nothing much to do but to keep the place swept out and sell occasional tickets or check a drummer's trunk. Commercial telegrams were rare events in Wyattville in those days. There were records and reports, bills of lading to be made; but no grave responsibility rested on his shoulders. The line which began at Muscatine, ended at Wyattville; it was twelve miles in length, with a single train that shuttled back and forth—thus reducing to a minimum the danger of collision. The train, which was jocularly called the Plug, arrived at ten-fifteen if it was on time which seldom happened, and returned to Muscatine at four o'clock. It was a "combination" with a coach and several freight cars, carrying passengers and livestock, milk and freight. In between were two small stations at which it stopped and lingered.

The crew of the Plug lived in Muscatine. The engineer was Mr. Rooney. He was quite old and religious. He seldom left the depot while the train was anchored there, but would putter with his engine, climbing all around it with an enormous oilcan; or if it was stormy, he would sometimes come inside and talk to Sam. He had spent his life with railroads—very pleasantly, it seemed, but with nothing much to show for it. Mr. Bullock, the conductor, was austere and elderly. He had friends in Wyattville with whom he passed the time. Mr. Jones, the fireman, was a grouchy, silent man. He stayed mostly in the engine, reading the *Police Gazette* or dozing in the cab. The brakeman's name was Nick. He was young and less substantial, and a frequenter of poolrooms in his leisure. He had nothing much to do—no switching cars around, since the train departed backwards with the engine on the rear.

At the far end of the wire which kept clicking in Sam's ear, twelve miles away in Muscatine, was a young man named O'Gara with whom he was at once on friendly terms. This O'Gara, one might judge, was a gay and blithesome spirit, cracking jokes along the wire, even telling smutty stories, and recounting his adventures with young ladies of the town and lurid anecdotes of blind pigs and poker games. He was generous, too, with questions of more serious import, answering patiently at length any query he received, and repeating endlessly if Sam was still in doubt.

It began the very morning that he started. Mr. Butts, the division superintendent who resided in Rock Island, had come over on the Plug to instruct him in his duties, and had left him for a moment to speak to

Mr. Bullock who was standing on the platform. Sam was in the cubby-hole in the center of the depot, checking bills of lading, when the silent wire spoke for the first time—

"Hello, sucker. What's your name?"

"Braden," Sam spelled out, startled but not sure that this method of address was unofficial.

"Mine's O'Gara."

"O'Gara," Sam repeated, adding dutifully, "OK."

"Is old Frizzletop around?"

Sam was stumped. It was explained that Frizzletop was Mr. Butts whose naked dome had been reclaimed with a curly black toupee.

"On the platform," Sam replied in some alarm.

"So long. I'll see you later."

"OK." The key was silent, and he went back to his bills.

But it wasn't as simple as it has been presented. O'Gara had a quick and flighty fancy to which the telegraph was not adapted. In defense he had evolved an abbreviated style better suited to his temperamental nature, and which, incidentally, greatly puzzled or defeated casual listeners. Even Mr. Butts whose ear was pretty keen, had been known to listen blandly to a painful description of himself. For example, in the morning, some minutes after nine, something of this sort was likely to come forth:

"plg plgd 9 3 ry brdg admrl bul com shd ar wyvil abt 2 wks" which reduced to language would have read something like this: "Train 28 departed 9.03 with Rooney on the bridge and Admiral Bullock in command. Should arrive at Wyattville in about two weeks." This latter prediction was not of course official.

"OK," Sam would reply.

Or something of this kind:

"o b wht hd ths am bg pty lst nite drk qt crn" which translated: "Oh boy, what a head I've got this morning! Was out last night on a big party and drank a quart of liquor."

It took some time and effort to master this technique, but his tutor was patient and indulgent. Whenever he was free he would wire-chat away in his breezy, friendly fashion; and when he wasn't chatting he would leave the key cut open so that everything that he received would come on through to Sam. It was splendid training for him; with the office window open, even on the platform, delivering freight or baggage, he'd be reading from the wire.

O'Gara was frank about himself: he was twenty-five years old and had come from Omaha where his father was a house painter. He'd been working for the railroad for five years, and as far as he could see it was a rotten business—no future in the thing and too much red tape about it. Like being in the Army you never got a boost until somebody died, and the guys that held the good jobs would live to be a hundred; they were too damn tight to die. He had started as a freight clerk and then learned telegraphy, but now he wondered why. The pay wasn't bad— he was getting seventy-five. "How much they paying you?" he asked abruptly.

"Sixty," Sam replied.

"Dirty robbers!" tapped O'Gara. He said the only chance was to be a train dispatcher at a hundred and a quarter or maybe even more, but then where in hell were you?—sitting at a desk for the balance of your life, switching trains around, and if there was a wreck you'd lose your job. Anyway he knew he'd never make the grade—he liked to take a drink and have a little fun, and it wasn't any secret. He was poison to old Frizzletop who was waiting for a chance to can him out entirely. "And a good thing, too," he said. "Say, what about yourself?"

Sam told him—something. But he lied about his age: he said he was nineteen. He didn't want O'Gara to think he was a kid.

Their acquaintance ripened rapidly. Early in December his unseen friend was urging him to come to Muscatine—

"Come over and we'll make a night of it."

"Can't now."

"Hop the Plug."

"Got to stick around till nine."

"Close up the dump. Nobody'll know you're gone."

"I can't."

"Oh nuts!" The key snapped shut.

But a week or two later he reverted to the subject:

"Party framed for Sunday—swell girl picked for you—come over."

"How?"

"Hire rig."

"Can't afford it." This wasn't true; he was keeping thirty-five out of his sixty. And he would have liked to go, but he didn't want to risk it— risk a lot of things. He had been in Muscatine—once long ago with the Baxters to a circus—and though it was no more than a modest country town, he had been much impressed by the shops and busy streets. In fact he was afraid—afraid he wouldn't look or act as city people did. And, too, he had formed a mental picture of O'Gara: a sporty looking fellow with a derby hat cocked over his eye and a big cigar gripped in his teeth. And how would he appear in such company as that? He was only seventeen. He had smoked but one cigar which had made him deathly sick; and though he occasionally drank a glass of beer, he had not been really drunk and had only tasted whisky—

"I'll loan you the price," the wire clicked.

"No thanks."

"Swell girl picked for you—real juicy peach."

"I'd like to." Even this was but half true. There was only one girl he really cared about. The others might be fun but it wouldn't be quite fair—

"Come on. Don't be a sap."

"Sorry." He was sorry in a way; he would have liked to go—to wear a derby hat and swagger down the street, and lean against a bar and drink a glass of whisky—to meet this juicy peach and take her out—and see what happened—

"Well, by God!" The wire fairly snapped with irritation.

"Sorry, really can't." And there was another reason—perhaps the most decisive: suppose that Mr. Butts should have knowledge of the fact that he and O'Gara were running round together—O'Gara who by his own admission, was already in disgrace and slated to be canned. It wasn't any use to take a chance like that—

"Are you man or mouse?"

"Some other time," he hedged, but he felt that it was settled.

"Oh, go to hell!" the wire cracked and stopped.

But O'Gara was not one to cherish injury, and a few days later he was on another tack:

"What kind of girls you got in Wyattville?"

"All kinds."

"Pretty?"

"You bet."

"Liberal minded?"

"Maybe."

"Guess I'll drop over there some day."

"Why don't you?"

"I'll step off the Plug some morning. I'll wear a red carnation so you'll know me."

"OK," Sam answered quickly, but he hoped it wouldn't happen—hoped it would and hoped it wouldn't.

"I'll be seeing you some day."

But O'Gara never came.

Jim Braden changed his schedule to fit the changing times and included the depot on his beat. It was rather out of things—on the edge of the town west of the Square, not far distant from the school—but a lunchroom and some stores grew up around it. Jim would be there on the platform when the train came in, and usually turned up again at four—sitting on a baggage truck, whittling a stick, or chatting with old Hogan on the box of Birney's hack, or if it was cold, he would come inside the waiting room and loaf around the stove. He seldom spoke to Sam.

Sometimes Mitch dropped in going home from school, and would lean on the counter looking through the wicket—

"How's the railroad business, Sam?"

"Getting better every day."

"What's that thing saying now?" pointing to the telegraph.

"Right now?—Oh, nothing much."

"You're a liar. I can read it."

"All right. Then what?"

"It says—" Mitch cocked his ear. " 'Turn again, Whittington, Lord Mayor of London.' " And he would laugh and maybe kid a while, and wander off. "You won't get rich," he would call back, "not listening to that stuff."

"Oh yeh?" Sam would shout after him. But he wondered about it all the same.

Sometimes Nelly came. At first she was impressed, but then her interest lagged. She didn't see, she said, that the depot or the railroad were combining to assist her to embark on a career, and Paris and New York seemed as far away as ever. She lamented the delay.

"Shucks!" Sam would exclaim. "Can't you give a guy a chance?"

She knew about O'Gara and would get around to that, urging Sam to go and take her with him. "Tell him that we're coming—coming over there tonight. No, wait, don't tell him, Sam. We'll just get off the train and take him by surprise."

"What for?"

"For fun." She clapped her hands. "We'll have supper in a restaurant, and maybe there'll be something at the Opera House—a concert or a play." She had been in Muscatine, with Jane Wyatt several times, and had visited a girl there. "Maybe I'd meet someone connected with the theater—a manager or actor, and he would hear me sing, and then— Let's go, Sam, please—"

"You're crazy, Nelly."

"You never want to do anything that's fun."

"Aw, shucks!"

"You don't—not just because it's fun.—Sam, please—"

He shook his head.

"All right—" And she would threaten, "I'll go alone sometime. I'll get on the train and go over by myself. I'll tell your friend, O'Gara, that I've come to have a party and I want to see the sights."

"Go on, get out, I'm busy."

"Oh well—" And she would toss her head and slam the depot door when she went out. But she wasn't really angry, and not really serious. She was restless, that was all; she wanted to do something—something gay and fabulous, and there wasn't anything. Boys liked her, but there wasn't anyone she cared about. Once she had imagined that she was in love with Neill, but actually she wasn't. He had been a kind of symbol for someone gay and dashing—for something that was fun.

Drummers, waiting for the train, sometimes chatted with him. They were mostly stodgy men of middle age, red nosed and bibulous, who sold their merchandise over anecdotal bottles. But the age of *friendly* salesmanship was waning. *Efficiency* had reared its ugly head; the industrial machine had crept out upon the road. There were still a few who traveled in black coats and stovepipe hats, but most of them wore shabby suits and fancy checkered vests, with Elk pins on their coat lapels or dangling from their watch chains.

There was one, a youngish, enterprising sort of fellow, who seemed to take an interest in Sam. His name was Mr. Brush and he traveled for a general paper jobber located in Chicago. He said one time, leaning on the counter, waiting for the Plug to get up steam:

"There's good money to be made selling on the road—if you've got the stuff and price, and no monkey business, see?"

Sam nodded.

"No hanging over bars telling smutty stories; no going home to dinner with your customers and playing with the children; no jumping home on Sunday half across the state. But tending to your business—writing orders, see?"

Sam nodded.

"No glad-hand stuff; that's finished. And the customers, themselves, are getting wise to it. 'Cut out the social stuff,' I've heard 'em say, 'and let's get down to business: what's the price and what's the terms?'"

Sam nodded.

"These old buzzards with their Elk pins and their Masonic badges, they're on the scrap heap now and they don't know it. This country's on the march and it's got no time for play. Efficiency—you got me?"

Sam nodded.

"You're too bright a looking kid to waste your life in this dump." He shoved a business card beneath the wicket. "If you ever take a notion you might want to make a change—well, let me know."

"Gee, thank you, Mr. Brush—"

"All aboard for Muscatine," Mr. Bullock interrupted from the door.

But Sam was thinking hard when the Plug had chugged away: good money to be made selling on the road—no more monkey business—efficiency's the word—this country's on the march and it's got no time for play.—These were things to think about. He put the card away. "Ned G. Brush," it said. "Acme Paper Company—Home Insurance Bldg.—Chicago—Illinois."

A few days before Christmas a commercial wire came—for Mrs. Henry Wyatt.

"Look out!" O'Gara warned, "This one's (cntgs) contagious." And started on the message. "Eileen—" he clicked and stopped, called away to something else.

Sam's heart stood still. He called back wildly.

O'Gara finally answered with a note of irritation, "hld yr hrses—r u crzy" and he relayed the message:

Eileen has mild case of German measles and is quarantined at school. No occasion for concern. Will see that she is comfortable and has happy Christmas. Love to all from all.

Daphne

German measles—that was all! He breathed again.

"Do u knw ths doll," O'Gara added.

He closed the key—So Eileen would not be home! Well, that was that. He had hoped she would come home on the train; and she would be surprised to find him on the platform—not in a grubby apron, weighing sugar, but in charge of things—representing the great Rock Island Railroad—getting on, in fact.—He sighed.—Well, it would be next summer— But he was wrong: it would not be next summer—or the next; it would be a long, long time.

He delivered the message on his way to dinner. Mrs. Henry, herself, came to the door—

"Oh dear!" she gasped when she saw the yellow envelope.

« 125 »

"It's nothing," Sam assured her. "Just measles that she's got."

"Oh dear—" She read the message, and then she stared at him. "But, Sam, how did you know?"

He grinned. "I have to read 'em before I write 'em down."

"Why yes, of course—" She smiled a little vaguely. Telegrams were not too common even then, in Wyattville.

He wrote a letter to Eileen, telling how he'd known about her measles sooner than her mother, about what he was doing and how he was getting on—warmly sympathetic and carefully composed. And he got a scrawly, hasty note in answer: it was certainly amusing that he'd got the telegram—nobody could keep secrets from him now—she wasn't really sick and it was rather fun—that sort of thing. He did not write again. It was better just remembering—

The day before Christmas Tom came home.

Sam was standing on the platform when he swung down from the car—the only passenger. Jim was there, leaning with his back against the depot wall, whittling a stick. It was a dreary, frosty morning, thick with mist, and the steam from the engine blowing white along the train— At first he wasn't sure, and he glanced back at his father who had stopped whittling now and was looking toward the coach—at the man who had got off and was slowly coming nearer, dragging his feet as if he had been sick, and not carrying a valise or anything at all, and without an overcoat—

"Hello—" Tom said with a kind of sickly grin. His face was thin and white, and his clothes were almost ragged.

"Hello—" Sam answered, and not knowing what to do, called back to his father. "Pa, it's Tom."

Jim waited, watching them.

"Hello—" Tom said again.

"Hello—" There was no change in Jim's face; he was just waiting.

"I been sick, Pa—"

"Yeh?" Jim closed his knife and put it in his pocket.

"I'm down to my last cent—"

"Yeh?"

"Would you mind if I came home?—just till I get my strength back."

"No, I don't mind."

"Thanks, Pa."

"All right," Jim said without any trace of feeling. But Sam's eyes were moist with tears, looking at them and remembering—

They walked away together down the street.

Tom's health recovered quickly. For a week he loafed around the house, having breakfast in his bed at nine or ten o'clock. His contrition was skin deep, and he was rough and boastful—bragging of the winners he had trained and of the easy money that had sifted through his pockets. He had been around a bit and seen the country, and he spoke of Wyattville as a "stinking little burg." The girls were silent in his presence; the household was upset; everybody was uncomfortable.

He treated Sam with some respect and got ten dollars from him—to buy some clothes, he said. But his clothes remained unchanged; the money went for whisky, and he came home late at night, stumbling on the stairs. He had resumed relations with his poolroom friends and the money didn't last long.

In time he got around to make another touch. He said there was a job waiting for him in Chicago, as soon as he was strong enough to take it—with a stable that was wintering at the Hawthorne track. There would be good money in it; he would send Sam's ten to him and the price of the bike which he still owed—

Sam nodded; he was reading. It was in the evening and there was no one in the room at the moment but themselves.

"Say, Sam—"

"What?"

"Could you let me have another ten spot?"

"What for?"

"Well, I'm feeling pretty good and I think it's time I was getting back to work. I'm figuring to pull out most any day now, and I'll need a little cash to get me back to Chi."

Sam didn't answer; he was thinking.

"A ten spot ought to do it."

"No," Sam said.

"I can't go back to Chi without a cent."

"No." Sam shook his head.

"Well, make it five. Maybe I could manage."

"No."

"You don't want me camping here forever."

Sam was silent.

"You won't lose your money. Say, I'll pay you interest on it."

"No." He kept on looking at the page that he was reading. "But I'll tell you what I'll do—"

"Yeh? What?"

"I'll buy your railroad ticket to Chicago."

"You're pretty smart," Tom said.

But in a week or two he closed the deal and left. Jim was on the platform when the train pulled out.

The days and weeks and months slid by. Sam was diligent and punctual, polite and competent; the Rock Island Railroad's interests in the town of Wyattville were scrupulously cared for. Mr. Butts came rarely and when he did, would glance around the depot and nod approvingly. The Plug chugged back and forth with Rooney on the bridge and Bullock in command; and O'Gara wire-chatted contemporary comment on railroad life in general and his personal affairs, growing steadily more caustic as the time passed. He was bloody sick of Muscatine, he said—of camping in the sticks in one-horse towns; it was very dull and boring; the peaches he had nourished had developed into lemons, and left him with no solace but the bottle; old Frizzletop was dogging him and watching like a hawk, waiting for a chance to set the skids. He kept hinting ominously that the end was not far off—

But the months fled away. It was one day in June when the wire, announcing the departure of the Plug without the customary humorous comment, added briefly and tersely:

"Am canned."

"Repeat," demanded Sam, startled and confused.

"Have got the skids. Am fired."

"When?"

"Right now"

"What for?"

"Slight misunderstanding," chirped O'Gara, and explained: he had garbled a message concerning disposition of a private car containing the vice-president in charge of operations, and the car had stood all night on a siding near Rock Island. It was possible, he added, he had been a little drunk as he couldn't remember much about it.

"Are you kidding?" Sam was horrified.

But the wire hurried on, ignoring this: there had been hell to pay; old Frizzletop, himself, had almost lost his job. He had come in pale and trembling and given him the gate—to take effect at once, this very day; and then had jumped the Plug as it was pulling out. "Maybe break for you," O'Gara clicked.

"What will you do?" Sam queried, but his heart was beating fast: Mr. Butts was on the way to Wyattville—

"Hopping 21 for Chi this afternoon."

"Awfully sorry."

"What the hell!" There was a pause. "Be seeing you sometime. So long, old top." The wire stopped.

Sam was waiting on the platform when the Plug pulled in. His hair was neatly combed; his shoes were shined; but his hands were moist with sweat. Mr. Butts swung down from the engine cab where he had been riding, and motioned him to come into the office. He did look kind of pale and shaken up—

"Sam," he said abruptly, "how soon could you get ready to go to Muscatine?"

"To Muscatine, sir?" He went through the motion of reflecting; his heart was stepping up. "When the Plug goes back this afternoon."

"No, no," Mr. Butts frowned irritably. "I mean, to stay there—to fill O'Gara's job."

"Oh—" Sam nodded, remembering to look decently surprised. "Well, I could go this afternoon."

"To take the job and stay there," Mr. Butts insisted.

"Yes sir, I understand."

"All right." The superintendent smiled for the first time that day. "Go on home and pack your things. You've got the job."

VI

LIFE PROCEEDS AT AN UNEVEN PACE, IN JERKS AND SPURTS, LIKE GROWING plants and children. It rushes headlong for a while and then it seems to stop. It is not unlike a river, tearing through a narrow channel over shoals and treacherous rocks, and then abruptly spreading out into a placid stream, ripples slowly on its way—or, trapped in an eddy near the shore, may actually flow backwards for a time.

It is good that there are eddies—periods in which there is nothing to remember, when the picture is blurred by the softness of the colors, when the sunshine is not bright and the shadows are not black—when nothing happens. But of course something is happening all the same, but so gently and persuasively that one is unaware of it. Life does not really stop, though now and again it rests upon its oars—preparing perhaps for fresh acceleration.

However one explains it, Sam retained in later years scarcely any memory of his life in Muscatine, except for those events which came close upon the end of it and were, in fact, not part of it at all. The town became confused with all the other towns in and out of which he subsequently hurried, selling paper on the road. And the people that he met, with two or three exceptions, had a nebulous identity; he would get them mixed with others that came later, and remember them as being somewhere else—in Peoria or Moline or Davenport. He had come into an eddy and drifted to a pause, circling round and round; and unconsciously he must have been aware of it—that progress was arrested, that he wasn't getting on. Perhaps his faulty memory was a recognition of it —an intuitive rejection of people and events unworthy of retention.

But consciously he could not have suspected such a thing. He had been promoted to a better job—or so, on the face of it, it seemed; his pay had been advanced; he had moved from a small town to a relatively big one. The illusion of success was a convincing one. Yet he was in an eddy, and one that could be fatal if he stayed in it too long, or if he failed to understand its purpose—as a breathing spell to think and look around, to carefully weigh the values and come to a conclusion—to change his course or hold it, but not hurriedly or rashly—

That first night in Muscatine he would remember—the first night in his life he had spent away from home. Mr. Butts had seen to that, had gotten him a room in a hotel and paid for it, himself, saying that tomorrow he could take an hour off and find a place to live, and then had left him there in what seemed to him luxurious magnificence, though in truth it was a cheap and shabby place. And he had gone to bed, afraid to venture forth into the street, afraid to go downstairs—to cross the empty lobby with the clerk behind the desk, afraid of making some mistake. He had been so excited and elated—and then suddenly so homesick and so wretched—

He would not forget that night—not the pattern of the paper on the wall, nor the washbowl on the stand, nor the gaslight he extinguished and then went back to sniff, in terror lest he had not turned it off, nor the poolroom which his open window faced—the clicking of the balls and drunken voices, and the stifling muggy heat rising wetly from the river—

But he did not remember the second night at all—not the name of the woman who rented him a room and agreed to do his laundry at no additional cost, nor much about the room except the price and the fact that it opened on the kitchen and was warm, the deciding factor in his choice. He remembered what it cost to live in Muscatine and was likely to mention it when speaking of the past: about ten a week if he was very careful. But if he stepped outside the groove, like going to the theater—there was a third-rate stock company in town, playing in the Opera House; he would have good reason to remember that—well, even though a ticket cost only fifty cents, it would upset his budget. But he did go to the theater now and then—"Sappho," "Trilby," "A Texas Steer"—they did a different play each week—tragedy and comedy, incredibly performed, but new to him and wonderful.

Every month he sent Madge fifteen dollars—a sum they had discussed and determined to be fair, and every month there would be something left to deposit in Old Henry Wyatt's bank—until toward the end when Nelly got to coming and staying over Sunday, and then some months he didn't save a cent.

He ate in a lunchroom opposite the depot where the train crews took their meals. There was a girl who worked there as a waitress—a girl called Jo, for Josephine perhaps. She was about his age, but she thought that he was older than he was—almost everybody thought so, including Mr. Butts. He had reason to remember her, but he never could recall her face—what she had looked like, beyond that she was small and dark and pretty.

But the people at the depot left no imprint on his mind, possibly because they were jealous and unfriendly, envious of his youth and his pull with Mr. Butts. Still, they had not liked O'Gara who had always spoken of them with humorous contempt. There was a station agent and a freight clerk, and a night operator who came on at six o'clock and who really hated Sam because he thought he should have had the job—a lazy, shiftless fellow. None of them were young; they were sour, disappointed little men—drifting in an eddy whence there would be no escape until they died. And it may be that unconsciously he sensed that and forgot them, as one who has no time to take note of futile things.

The work was not hard but it soon became monotonous, lacking the variety of Wyattville where whatever was to do, he had had to do, himself. Here in Muscatine he sat all day in the stuffy cubbyhole in the center of the depot, with an eyeshade on his forehead, facing the window which looked out across the platform—listening to the wire, sending and receiving, writing endless messages, official and commercial, on sheets of yellow paper. To be sure there were periods of leisure, like the ones in which O'Gara had found time to wire-chat, but he had no one to chat with and was not the chatting sort.

Trains came and went, but they were only numbers; they had no personalities—not like the Plug whose wheezy chug and flattened wheels were friendly and familiar. Mr. Rooney hurried home when he got down from his engine, and the drummers did not linger in the depot. Folks from Wyattville would sometimes pause to greet him and exchange a word or two; and about once a month Mr. Brush would come along and call to him through the wicket: "How they coming, son?" or something of that kind. And he would answer cheerfully, "Just fine—"

"Still like the railroad business?"

"You bet." He was sure that he did, but he wasn't very happy, though he couldn't have said why—not then, not yet.

"Well, when you get a bellyful—remember what I told you."

"Yes sir, I sure will."

The first few weeks he kept watching for Eileen—every train arriving from the East. She'd be coming home from school any moment now, he thought. But one day a message came from Wyattville, addressed to Neill Wyatt in Chicago:

Are you coming for a visit as you promised? Love. Eileen.

So that was it! She must have gone home on the boat—as, indeed, she had; she always took the "Mary Queen," as long as it kept running. A lot of folks in Wyattville did that: habit, or sentiment perhaps. He clicked the message on, pressing hard upon the key. Old Neill Wyatt —always butting into things!—Late in the afternoon an answer came:

Awfully sorry. Must go Boston for college entrance exams.
Love. Neill.

And that was that. Old Neill wasn't coming for a visit after all, but was going to Boston with all the other dudes, to gallivant around and waste his time. Likely enough he had never meant to come—just stalling her along. She'd get sick of that sometime—of being such a sucker. He even felt a little sorry for her.

He thought he would invite her to come over—to the theater, but she'd have to stay all night in a hotel and he didn't know just how to manage that, and it would be expensive. And then he thought he'd rent a rig and drive over there some Sunday, and take her for a drive—maybe out to Beaton's woods. He inquired at a livery stable and the best price he could get was two dollars and a half, and he kept postponing it until it was too late.

Mitch turned up one day on some business for his father, and stood outside the window, tapping on the glass—pretended dots and dashes. Sam pushed the window up.

"Hello—" he said.

"I was telegraphing to you. Did you get it?"

"Don't make me laugh."

"Shall I tell you what it said?"

"Yeh, go ahead—" But he looked around to see there was no one within earshot.

"It said—" Mitch grinned maliciously. "—Sam Braden's getting on—like a monkey in the zoo. Next time they promote him they'll put bars outside his cage."

"You go to hell!" Sam said good-naturedly, and added quickly, "You're not going back till morning, are you, Mitch?"

"Not unless I walk."

"Well say—" His voice was eager. "—you can spend the night with me. I'll be off at six o'clock. We can have supper, Mitch, and take in the theater, eh?"

"Can I do it for a dollar?"

"Yep, you bet."

"All right. I got to see a creditor, but I'll be back at six."

Sam had a beer or two and Mitch had several, in the blind pig next the lunchroom, before they went to supper. Mitch was a little drunk; he kept singing the song about "working on the railroad" with words which he made up and which were not complimentary to that kind of occupation. In the lunchroom he took out his eye and made the waitress laugh, and even some trainmen who were eating at the counter. He was really very funny, but Sam was almost sorry he'd got into it. The girl named Jo—he had hardly spoken to her except to give his order, and just to say good morning and good night—she was leaning on the counter, kidding back and forth with Mitch, as if she had known him all her life.

"Say, cutie," Mitch was saying, "what time do you get loose?"

"What's that to you?"

"Well, I'm going to a show and I'll let you keep my eye till I get back."

"Oh yeh?" she giggled, leaning closer. The edge of the counter pulled her dress down tight across her breasts—small, round breasts with the outline of the nipples in the cloth. "If you leave your eye around I'm going to pickle it."

"It's pickled now," Mitch said.

She threw her head way back and laughed. "Say, you're a funny guy."

"What time do you get loose?"

"Suppose I didn't tell you?"

"I can wait until you do."

A lot of stuff like that while Sam kept eating with his eyes upon his plate, wondering what he'd do if Mr. Butts walked in. But finally she told him she was through at eight o'clock.

"Let's take a walk," Mitch said.

"Where to?"

"Out in the woods."

"Say, what do you think I am?" But she was laughing.

It was really pretty raw—saying things like that to a girl you had never seen before.

"Well—" Mitch considered, "I'll tell you what we'll do: we'll take old Sam along."

"Shucks—" Sam mumbled in his plate.

"What for?" she asked.

"I'll tell you," Mitch explained, "it won't be any fun, but it's sure to be safe."

"How come?" She was laughing, watching Sam.

"Sam's got no time for fooling. He's a business fellow, see?"

"I've seen plenty of those guys—" She winked her eye. "—and I wouldn't call 'em safe."

"Well, you and Sam go walking, and find out for yourself."

"Aw, cut it out," he muttered, beginning to be angry.

And then she said, half serious, but laughing, "Go on, quit picking on him."

"Quit picking on him?—Why?"

"Because I like him, see?"

He looked up with a start and met her eye, and then she looked away and back at Mitch.

"I see—" said Mitch, affecting to be crushed. "The silent, steady man gets the gravy every time. You mean, you don't like me?"

"Sure, I do," she said. "You're funny—you're a scream."

"A funny guy!" He groaned. "That's all I get." He reached and grabbed her wrist. "You take a walk with me and I'll make you change your mind."

"Let go!" She jerked away. "You're pretty fresh." She wasn't laughing now, and she was watching Sam from the corner of her eye.

"All right—" Mitch grinned. "Some do; some don't. And you can't be hung for trying."

They took her to the theater—or anyway Mitch did, though Sam paid for her ticket; and then they took her home.

That was the beginning. You couldn't go back to "veal stew and apple pie, please," to "good morning" and "good night"—not after that. And he was really glad that Mitch had cracked the ice—

He said next day, making conversation lamely, "Old Mitch is quite a fellow—"

"Sure, he's all right." She shrugged, leaning on the counter, her dress pulling tight across her breasts. "But you never get nowhere with them guys. They ain't—" She hesitated for the word. "—they ain't reliable."

"Yeh—" Sam nodded.

"I mean they're always kidding—or, if they ain't, you never know."

"I guess that's right," he said. He kept watching as she moved behind the counter, kind of switching with her hips. Her ankles made him think of Cassie—

He came in late that evening and contrived to finish supper a few moments before eight.

"Do you mind if I walk home with you?" he asked.

"Okay by me," she answered carelessly.

They strolled along the darkening empty street in the hot summer night. He took her arm. Her hip kept brushing his, and presently he ventured to slip his arm around her, but she slid away and put it back through hers. He let it go at that; he thought she meant it. She didn't act like Cassie—teasing him along. They strolled on slowly, conversing in strained, half-finished sentences—not kidding, very serious: the wrong approach entirely to what was in his mind. She told him of herself: she was the daughter of a section foreman; her mother was dead and her father had remarried; her home life wasn't happy—she wished she could get out of it—

"I'm sick of being poor," she said.

"Yeh, I know," he nodded earnestly.

"I wouldn't want a lot," she added quickly. "I'm not such a sucker to think I could be rich. But just something of my own—"

"Yeh, sure," he agreed.

He left her at the door of the shabby little house, unpainted and run-down. He didn't try to kiss her.

But after that, every other night or so, he would wait till eight o'clock —sitting at the far end of the counter, reading the paper or some book he was carrying in his pocket. And they'd go out together—or, if there was someone from the depot in the lunchroom, he'd go out first and hang around the corner till she came.

There was nothing much to do. Usually they simply walked around. Two or three times he took her to the theater, but she didn't ask or urge it. He had told her that he had to be careful of his money, that he had to send some home, and to save a little, too, for he meant to get along— to get somewhere in the world—

"Sure, that's okay," she said. "That's only being smart." She clung closer to his arm, laughing softly in the dark. "We can have fun—for nothing." She never asked for anything, not even for a soda or a bag of candy.

A few times on rainy evenings they dropped in at a church—at some prayer meeting or something. It was a place to sit under cover of a roof, and they sat close together, holding hands. He kept saying that they'd get a rig some Sunday and drive out in the country—he was thinking about Cassie, and snugly hidden shelters, and the rows between the corn; but he never quite got to the point. And she always said she didn't care. She was content to stroll—or just to sit.

Sometimes they strolled through a vacant piece of ground known as the Park, with sycamores and unkept yellow grass, and a few murky light bulbs obscured by swarms of gnats—dark, and deserted save for occasional couples like themselves. They would sit on a bench making imitation love, holding hands and kissing—and going somewhat further as the summer waned, but never to the end he sought. She was compliant to a point, but then she would abruptly disengage his hands and slide away, good-humoredly but firmly. They never argued or discussed it.

But one night—it was toward the end of summer, hot and sticky, with the moon swimming in and out behind a gathering storm—she slapped his hands aside and jerked away with unconcealed exasperation, and she said a little wearily:

"You're all alike, I guess."

He didn't answer, still breathless from his effort and aching with frustration—his shirt soaked through with sweat.

"You only want one thing out of a girl. You ain't satisfied to have a little fun."

He leaned back, staring at the moon.

"Well, if that's what you want, you're wasting time."

And still he didn't answer.

"Come on." She got up, shaking out her rumpled skirt, holding out her hand in a placative gesture. "Come on, Sam, let's go home—"

They walked in silence. Once she took his hand, but there was no response and after a moment she released it. She was crying when they reached the house—but softly to herself. He would not have known it except for the teardrops in her eyes which the moonlight fleetingly revealed.

"I'm sorry, dear," she said.

"Aw, that's all right," he mumbled. He had suddenly gone cold and deadly tired.

"It wouldn't get us nowhere. You'd get sick of it—and me, in a little while."

He nodded, hardly listening—wondering what he could have seen in her—why he was there—

"I'm too fond of you, I guess—" She sighed and shivered. The storm was coming and a cool, clean wind swept through the street.

"It's going to rain," he said.

But she clung to his arm with her eyes upon his face. "Are you mad at me, Sam?"

"No, I'm not mad."

"Well—" But still she held his arm which was quivering with impatience. "Will you be around tomorrow?"

"Yeh, I guess so." Lightning cut the sky and thunder rumbled. "I better beat it home," he said.

"Sam!—Ain't you going to kiss me?"

He kissed her on the cheek. "So long—" he called, almost running down the street.

And it was over.

He went out with her again, but it was over. Now and then he waited for her, as he had, but more often he left early, inventing casual pretexts —matters at the depot, and some nights he ate his supper in another lunchroom. She did not reproach him or ask him where he'd been; if he came and waited for her, she was glad. And he came and waited for her because he was alone—because habits are difficult to break. They strolled about the streets, arms linked or holding hands, but they never went out to the Park again—

Their relationship had changed, was awkward and constrained—no longer anything. He had wanted something which had been denied; and she had been asked for something which she wouldn't give.—Why? —She had very likely given it before—would have given it again to someone else—to Mitch Ballou perhaps, to a fellow like O'Gara. The answer is not far to seek. She was in love with him. He was not in love with her. When two people reach a situation of this kind, there is no answer—no middle ground on which it is possible to meet.

The fact that, in later years, he could not recall her face—what she had looked like, testifies perhaps how completely it was finished, and rejected as unworthy of retention.

At all events he came and waited for her less frequently, then rarely. And when Nelly started coming in October—coming over on the Plug on Saturday and going back on Monday—after that he only saw her once or twice.

All summer long Nelly had been threatening to come to Muscatine. She had graduated from the high school, and had been writing to him ever since, saying she was bored with Wyattville, wasting her life, doing nothing with her voice, and soon she'd be too old (she was nineteen). She wanted to come and live with him, suggesting she'd keep house— do the cooking and the laundry, everything in fact. An arrangement of this kind would be a great economy and better for his health: he would have no board to pay and no greasy lunchroom food, and a cozy home to live in. She said that in a place like Muscatine she could certainly find someone to begin her vocal training, for the present anyway—a sort of preparation for Paris or New York. Her tuition would cost nothing; she could find some work to do to pay for that. She wanted to come and talk it over—"or you come home," she wrote. "You could come any Sunday, just drive over in a rig."

It was one of the reasons he had not gone home—had kept postponing it. He had no notion what to do with Nelly, and well-grounded apprehension of her economic reasoning. It was bound to be expensive; and, too, what would she do in Muscatine? As for keeping house and cook- ing—he shuddered at the thought. There was, finally, the girl with whom he was going out—not a girl he'd want to introduce to Nelly. She was all right, of course, he told himself; but the nature of his interest— well, it simply wouldn't do. He would have to break it off if Nelly came, and he didn't want to break it off—not then. He kept writing her to wait, evading things, promising to come and then finding an excuse.

"You are acting like a pig," she wrote him in September. "But I'm coming anyway. I'll come over on the Plug and take you by surprise.— Your loving sister—Nelly."

He let this slide. He didn't think she'd do it, but she did.

One Saturday, early in October, when the Plug came in at five o'clock, he looked up in response to a tapping on the glass, and there she was—very pretty and excited, dressed in her Sunday best. He pushed the window up and kissed her—

"You needn't look so cross," she said. "I didn't come to stay."

"Well, shucks—" He tried to smile.

"I came to talk things over. I'm going back on Monday."

"Yeh, well—" He felt relieved. "I'll be through at six o'clock."

She waited for him in the empty waiting room, flushed and happy and excited, with a battered old valise she had borrowed from Jane Wyatt.

He got a room for her in the house in which he lived, explaining their relationship with elaborate casualness, and then they went to supper in a lunchroom—a Greek place where he had been going lately. The food was cheap and bad, but Nelly was in raptures about everything —conclusive evidence, if evidence be needed, of the truth of relativity.

"I love it here," she said, finishing a fragment of soggy apple pie. "I think it's simply wonderful."

"Yeh, sure—" he agreed, but he was pretty sick of it—of the town and of the food, of a kind of lonely emptiness—really of his job, of the eddy he was in, though he hadn't reached the point of knowing that. And he thought: it was pleasant sitting here with Nelly, listening to her gay and eager voice, watching shifting fancies sparkle in her eyes, forgetting for a moment life was real—

He asked about Eileen. Nelly shrugged an answer: Eileen had come and gone; she had seen her once or twice—nothing to remember. Yes, she had asked about him—like everybody else. Old Henry had been ill; he had had a minor stroke, but was up and out again. Elliott had been there, but not Daphne or the boys. Jim was just the same and Madge was well; they had had no word from Tom. She finished Wyattville in one long breath; there were more important matters—

She had come to Muscatine to talk things over—to settle what to do about herself. She couldn't just go on the way poor Madge had done, giving up her life for nothing; and she wouldn't be a schoolteacher—no, not for anything. She had a voice, and dramatic talent, too—everybody said so; and it would be a crime to let it go to waste—

He nodded, balancing a spoon across his coffee cup.

She hurried on: she had put off a decision as long as she could stand it—even coming on the Plug, she had not made up her mind. But now that she was here she felt sure of herself—was certain she was right. She was not going back to Wyattville—

He moved uncomfortably.

"I mean," she added hastily, "not to settle down and stay—the way it has been, Sam." And she went on to explain that, coming on the train, she had had an inspiration—such a simple solution to the problem that she couldn't understand why she had never thought of it before, and about which there could not be any question of expense—

"Yeh, what?" he asked suspiciously.

"Just this," she said. "I can find someone to teach me, who could give me one lesson every week—on Sunday, don't you see?"

"On Sunday? Why?"

"Well, then I'd come on Saturday and go home Monday morning."

"Oh—"

"It wouldn't cost a thing except the railroad fare, and the lesson and my room and what I'd eat. And I'd have all week to practice."

"I see—" He nodded doubtfully, adding figures in his mind.

"Sam!"

"What?"

"You could help me that much, couldn't you?"

"Well, maybe, Nelly—"

"I can look for a teacher. I can look all day tomorrow."

"Yeh, but where?"

"I know a girl that lives here. I could ask her about it."

"Well, we'll see—" he said, and changed the subject. "Say, how would you like to take in a theater, eh?"

"A theater—" She caught her breath. "You mean, go to a play?"

"At the Opera House—" he nodded.

"But—won't it cost a lot?"

"I guess I could stand it—for a kind of celebration."

"Oh, Sam—" was all that she could say, almost in tears.

The play was "Camille." The leading man whose horselike face adorned a poster in the lobby, bore the romantic name of Wilfred Ashby. He was not young and beginning to be bald; such hair as he retained was dyed jet black and hung down in the back across his collar. He played Armand; he played the leading man in every play—from "Hamlet" to "The Count of Monte Cristo," and played them all in the highest tradition of bad acting. Sam had seen him many times and had begun to doubt his mugging and his ranting. He had asked Mitch what

« 140 »

he thought and Mitch had held his nose, but Mitch was being funny. As a matter of fact Wilfred Ashby was a ham of the first magnitude.

His wife was in the company—a faded blonde, billed on the program as Miss Margaret Liscomb. She appeared in minor roles—maids and things like that. And they had a child, an anemic looking boy of five or six, named for his father but called Willie, and occasionally presented to the public when a child was indicated in the script. Otherwise he could usually be found in the Ashby dressing room, next to that of Miss Cynthia Cavendish, the leading lady, playing on the floor or curled up in a corner fast asleep. Miss Cavendish, in her own way, was as bad as Wilfred Ashby, but she lacked the vocal strength to be as noisy. There was no love lost between them; every love scene that they played was a battle to the death.

The curtain rose—

Nelly clutched his arm. She had never seen a play before—just barnstorming troupes that paused in Wyattville, presenting "The Two Orphans" or "Uncle Tom's Cabin" in the Masonic Hall where you sat on folding chairs and had to lean to see around the big stoves on the floor—nothing resembling this: an opera house with scenery and real actors.

She hardly spoke. They sat through the intermissions, munching chocolates from a paper bag. He mentioned the other plays he'd seen —he had been going almost every week—

"Just think of that—" she breathed, "—being able to do that."

He went on talking, acting like a host, explaining that Miss Liscomb was really Mrs. Ashby and about their little boy, and he ventured to express a fleeting doubt of Wilfred's acting. "Don't you think," he suggested, "that he hits it pretty hard?"

"What?" she asked, as if she had been dreaming.

"I mean," Sam said, "he keeps worrying at the thing—like a dog that's got a bone."

"Oh, Sam! How can you say a thing like that?"

"I only meant—"

"Please don't—" She pinched his hand. "I think he's simply wonderful."

"Well, maybe—" he conceded. "But if I had to choose between them, I'd sooner take Miss Cavendish."

"Sam, don't!" She drew away. "I wouldn't say that even in a joke. Why, just look at the way he holds you in his hand!"

"Yeh—" Sam admitted, "that's what I thought at first. But—"

"Hush!" She clutched his arm. "It's starting—"

The curtain rose and fell, and rose and fell—

"Oh dear," she sighed, "it's over." Her handkerchief was soaked with tears.

Camille was dead—dead in her lover's arms. But behind the curtain she was very much alive, confronting him with passionate fury—

"You clumsy brute," she hissed. "You poked me in the stomach with your elbow."

"Mr. Ginsberg!" Wilfred Ashby recoiled a step, calling to a dirty looking man who was crossing through the set. "Mr. Ginsberg, if you please—" He spoke with elaborate restraint. He was a little drunk.

"What's the matter, Mr. Ashby?" the dirty man asked wearily.

But Miss Cavendish resumed in a high-pitched, shaky voice: "He poked me in the stomach. It's the second time this week. He wants to hog the scene so he knocks the breath out of me—"

"Now, now, Miss Cavendish—" the dirty man said soothingly.

"Mr. Ginsberg—" Wilfred Ashby crossed his arms. "—I have played with Modjeska, with Olga Nethersole, with Ada Rehan. I have never in my life been subjected to such insult. There is nothing in my contract to oblige me to submit—"

"Now, now, Mr. Ashby—"

Miss Cavendish took the stage again. "I'm accustomed," she said, "to appear with gentlemen."

"You hear that, Mr. Ginsberg?" demanded Wilfred Ashby.

"Now, Mr. Ashby, Miss Cavendish don't mean—"

"Yes, I do," she stormed. "And the next time it happens I shall cancel this engagement. I shall return to Broadway."

"To where?" inquired Wilfred, as if he thought he must have misunderstood her words.

"To Broadway," shrieked Miss Cavendish.

Wilfred shrugged and spread his hands in a gesture of indulgence, and he looked up at the fly loft, murmuring sadly to himself. "What could she do on Broadway?"

"You dirty cad!" Miss Cavendish replied, and fled weeping to her dressing room where she found her colored maid and sent her out posthaste with a pitcher for some beer.

"I guess she's tired—" Mr. Ginsberg ventured.

"Tired, Mr. Ginsberg?" Wilfred smiled with lofty condescension. "I would say she was exhausted—I would say, completely spent—as limp as a rag, without a spark of life. She was born that way in fact. Why, I have to carry her through every scene."

"Yeh—" Mr. Ginsberg nodded wearily. "But you better try not to poke her in the stomach." And he hurried away into the wings.

It was just then, to be exact, that Nelly spoke. They had been walking slowly and in silence. It was a fine, crisp, moonlit night—

"Sam—"

"What?"

"Perhaps I'll be an actress after all—"

"An actress?" He was startled, though being an actress no longer seemed immoral—or at least not as immoral as it had in Wyattville. "But I thought you wanted to train your voice and sing—"

"Well, of course I do," she said. "But you have to be an actress if you want to sing in opera."

"Oh yeh—" he nodded, yawning.

"It's just a question which comes first. If I learn to act, I'll be that far ahead. Then I could act in plays until my voice was trained."

"Well, I don't know," he said, not quite sure what he might be getting into.

"But don't you see—" Her nimble fancy was accelerating. "—I'll be getting paid for that, for acting on the stage—earning money for myself. How much do they get paid?"

He shook his head.

"An actress like Miss Cavendish?"

"I don't know, Nelly."

"Well, anyway, I'd get as much as she does. And I'd only act in the theater in New York, so that all the time I'd be working on my voice. You won't need to help me, Sam. I'll have money enough to pay everything myself."

"Uh-huh—" He nodded, beginning to be sleepy.

"Perhaps I could help you. I'll be meeting lots of people—influential ones. You could give up this stupid railroad business and come on to New York. We'd rent a little flat—"

"Say, wait a minute, Nelly." He shook himself awake. "Somebody's got to teach you how to act."

"Well, yes—" she admitted with a sigh. "But it can't be very hard if a person has the talent." She was silent for a moment. "Sam!"

"What?"

"No, never mind." She shook her head, smiling to herself. "I was just thinking about something—"

« 143 »

They had late breakfast in the lunchroom, a habit he had formed to reduce the Sunday meals. They had baked apples, and hot cakes and sausage. Nelly was as gay as ever but she didn't eat much breakfast. She said she wasn't hungry. After breakfast he suggested they might stroll around a while and drop in at a church. But she said she must go and see her friend—the girl she knew, and inquire about teachers, and maybe call on some. It would probably take most of the day—

"All right," he agreed, secretly relieved. He'd been wondering what to do to entertain her. He said she needn't hurry, he'd be waiting at home when she got back. She left him in the lunchroom, waving gaily from the door—

"I'll have something to report—"

"Good luck," he called, but he really wasn't thinking much about it.

It was almost suppertime when she burst into his room where he was sitting, reading. She was flushed and so excited she could hardly speak—

"Sam!"

"What?" He looked up from his book.

"Oh, Sam—"

"Say, what's the matter with you?"

"The most wonderful thing—"

"Wonderful?—Well, what?"

"Guess where I've been."

"Shucks, I don't know."

"Who I've been talking to."

"Well, who?" He was accustomed to her wild enthusiasms which usually turned out not to amount to much.

"No, guess!" she urged. "Just sitting talking to, the way I would to you—or anyone."

"Admiral Dewey," he suggested.

"Please don't make fun. It's serious—the most serious thing that ever happened to me."

"All right," he said. "Then who?"

"Wilfred Ashby, Sam."

"What?" He got up from his chair.

"Yes, Wilfred Ashby—in the Opera House."

"You're joking."

"No, I'm not."

"Have you gone crazy, Nelly?" He stared incredulously.

"Wait! You don't understand. He's going to teach me, Sam."

"Teach you?—Teach you what?"

"Teach me to be an actress."

"Well, shucks—"

"I thought of it last night when we were coming home. It just popped into my mind, but I didn't dare to dream—"

"You mean you went to see him—in the theater?"

"Right in his dressing room."

"Nelly!"

"Oh, you needn't look so shocked. I didn't go alone, and anyway his wife and little boy were there. And what difference would it make—with a perfect gentleman like Mr. Ashby?"

"Go on," he said.

She explained in eager, breathless words: she had taken Rita with her—Rita was her friend. They had gone to the matinee, sitting in the gallery; it was pretty far away but it didn't matter much because she had already seen the play. And then they had gone to a back door in the alley, to which they had been directed, walking twice around the block before they mustered courage—

Sam groaned and shook his head.

They had knocked but no one answered and so they had walked in—right onto the stage, with scenery and everything just the way it had been when Camille had passed away, but very dimly lighted—almost dark. Rita had been frightened and had wanted to run back, but a dirty-looking man had suddenly appeared and asked them what they wanted. And when they told him, he had showed them where to go—down a dingy, narrow hall with several doors, to Mr. Ashby's dressing room. And they had knocked again, shaking in their shoes, and Mr. Ashby's voice had told them to come in. But Rita had lost her nerve and run back to the alley, and she had gone in alone—

"Oh, Sam," she breathed, "he's wonderful." He was sitting in his costume at a shelf before a mirror, rubbing something on his face, but had gotten up to greet her—just as friendly as could be but so courtly in his manner—like Armand in the play. He had introduced his wife who was doing up her hair and had not had much to say—a sour-looking woman, not young and even plainer than she seemed upon the stage—not at all the kind of person you would think he would have fancied. The little boy was playing with some bottles on the floor, building them like blocks—

"Yeh," Sam said, "go on."

"Well, everything is settled."

"Settled?—How?"

"I mean—" She plunged into it again: she had told him her ambition —why she had dared to come and intrude upon his kindness; and at first he had laughed lightly, but not making fun of her. He explained he didn't teach—really couldn't spare the time, unless, as rarely happened, he was conscious of a talent which demanded cultivation, which could not be ignored. Then he asked her to go on—just to keep on talking to him, about anything at all. And all the time she could see that he was watching her—watching in the mirror from the corner of his eye— making up his mind— She paused dramatically.

"Go on," Sam prompted.

"I met the test," she cried with a gesture that Wilfred might have envied. "He's taken me to be his pupil." It had worked out perfectly: Mr. Ashby was busy with rehearsals every day—every day but Sunday. He would give her lesson before the matinee—in the theater, on the stage. They would have it to themselves, there would be no one around. And he would give her parts which she could learn at home. And on Saturday nights she could come and see the play, and again two times on Sunday, both matinee and evening, to study his performance and see actually effected the precepts he would teach. And this would cost her nothing—she would be there as his guest, with her brother or anyone she chose as a companion. He would see that seats were waiting in her name. If there was any question she must ask for Mr. Ginsberg to whom he would give instructions—

"Say, wait a minute," Sam contrived to interrupt. "What about the lessons?"

"The lessons?"

"What'll they cost?"

"Oh!—Well, we didn't settle that."

"You mean—you didn't ask him?"

"Of course I did," she said. But Mr. Ashby had jokingly replied that he could not discuss business with so charming a young lady, and had quickly changed the subject. He was picking out a part for her to study and wanted her to call again tonight after the play when he would give it to her. He had suggested she might bring her brother with her—

"Well, shucks—" Sam was wary but impressed.

At supper in the lunchroom he kept looking at Nelly and seeing someone else—an actress like Miss Cavendish, acting on the stage. And Nelly, herself, was abetting this illusion—holding out her little finger when she used the salt and pepper, and talking to the waitress in a voice he hardly knew—like an actress in a play—

And he was still impressed, sitting in the theater in seats which had cost nothing, watching the unfoldment of Camille's disastrous life—not so exciting now that you knew what would take place but intriguing all the same, watching Wilfred Ashby rant about and tear his hair, with the knowledge that your sister, sitting here beside you, had been walking on that stage a little while ago, conversing with that man. The whole thing was amazing and incredible—

And going through the alley, through the back door to the stage, across whose dark and littered breadth Nelly led him by the hand, and down the dingy hall—well, it was like a dream. His heart was thumping and his hands had started sweating when Wilfred Ashby's booming voice bade them cheerfully to come in—

He did not like Wilfred Ashby at the start, but still he was impressed; his instinctive mistrust was neutralized. And Wilfred was most gracious. He introduced his wife who was sitting at a shelf across the way, removing the makeup from her face which was plain and tired-looking. She had been polite enough, but then she had gone on with what she had to do, not taking any part in what was said. The child was asleep on a sofa in the corner. Some empty beer bottles with which it had been playing, were scattered on the floor. The room was small and crowded with two big costume trunks, and messy and disordered. But still it was impressive, no matter how cheap and fraudulent and tawdry—because it was the theater. To one who loves the theater the illusion of the play pervades the empty auditorium, still exists upon a dark and naked stage, is everywhere within its walls— a mysterious affair involved with the emotions. Even the smell of it is potent and like no other smell—that odor, indescribable and not easily classified, of paint and yet not paint, of canvas yet not canvas, nor of painted canvas either, which comes drifting from beneath the rising curtain—

Wilfred Ashby talked into the mirror. It was indeed a pleasure to make the acquaintance of Miss Nelly Braden's brother. The young lady had great talent; there was no doubt of that. With proper tutelage she should go very far—yes, very far— He smiled convincingly.

In the mirror on the other side Sam caught an expression on Miss Liscomb's face—an expression of annoyance, of something more than that. She stood up, almost roughly pushing back her chair, and went to change her dress behind a screen, and then she woke the child who cried out fretfully, rubbing his sleepy eyes against the light. She would go on, she said, to the hotel and get Willie into bed. She said good night to both of them, pleasantly but shortly. Sam felt that she was irritated with her husband, with something he had said, and disdainful of him, too. But still he was impressed—

Wilfred went on talking through the mirror, removing specks of makeup, rubbing with his thumbs at wrinkles in his chin. He had glanced through some scripts and had selected one—the role of Trilby which would serve to give notion of her range—whether her forte would be comedy or drama; he rather thought the latter. It would simplify the lessons since he knew the play by heart, having played Svengali more than a hundred times—

Sam ventured to remark he had seen him in the part.

"Indeed? May I inquire where?"

"Right here in Muscatine."

"Ah well—" The Ashby shoulders shrugged. "I wish you might have seen me with adequate support."

"I enjoyed it very much," Sam hastened to assure him.

Wilfred smiled and changed the subject. He said he could not promise how long he would remain in Muscatine. There were some discordant factors in the company— He shrugged again. He had taken the engagement to oblige a manager to whom he felt under obligation, intending to remain for a few weeks until the company should be established. But the matter had dragged on and the manager kept urging him to stay a little longer. He was not accustomed to playing in the summer, or indeed to playing stock at any time— He shrugged again. Still, much might be accomplished with a pupil of such talent in a narrow space of time. It was possible, he thought, that almost before they knew it, Miss Nelly might be ready to essay a minor role on the commercial stage—providing, of course, that nothing interfered with the program of instruction which he had in mind. But he must inform them—it was only fair to do so— that there were urgent calls coming to him from New York—almost daily telegrams—

Sam nodded. He could not recall any telegram of this kind passing through his hands, nor indeed any message addressed to Mr. Ashby.

"Oh, Mr. Ashby," Nelly groaned, "I hope you won't go for a long time."

"I begin to hope so, too, my dear young lady." Wilfred smiled into the mirror. "For now I foresee a purpose in my presence, and a duty I shall cherish." He handed her the script, a dog-eared volume. "The role of Trilby, Nelly. I shall count on you to have the first act letter-perfect a week from today—at noon exactly. You will find me waiting for you on the stage. And then we will see what we will see—" He rose as if to terminate the interview.

"Yes, but—" Sam stood up, fumbling with his hat.

"But what, sir?"

"I mean—about the price?"

"The price?" Wilfred looked blank.

"We didn't settle that."

"The price! Oh yes, of course! My honorarium—" Wilfred laughed softly. "Dear me, I had forgotten it entirely. Well now, let's see—" He appeared to be reflecting, communing with himself. "I have been offered as much as fifty dollars for one lesson. But," he added quickly, noting the expression on Sam's face, "by a person whom I would not instruct at any price." He smiled disarmingly. "How much?—How much?—I'm so stupid about business.—What would you suggest?"

"I—I wouldn't know," Sam stammered.

"No—well—" There was a shifty look in Wilfred's eyes. "Shall we say ten dollars then?"

"Ten dollars?—for each lesson?"

Wilfred nodded carelessly.

"Well, shucks—" Sam shook his head. "I'm sorry, Mr. Ashby, but we'll have to give it up."

"Oh Sam—" moaned Nelly.

"Come, come," said Wilfred with a very jovial air but a hint of disappointment in his face, "I won't hear to such a thing. I was offering a suggestion. Let's be frank with one another: how much can you afford to pay?"

"I could pay—" Sam gulped—he had long since set a figure as the limit he would go, and had hoped it might be less. "—well, I could pay two dollars."

"Two dollars, did you say?"

"Yeh, two dollars," Sam repeated, feeling terribly embarrassed.

"Then two dollars it shall be," boomed Wilfred Ashby, albeit he did not look very happy. "Miss Braden's career will not be sacrificed on a mercenary altar." He strode to the door and put his hand upon the knob. "And now, my young friends, I must ask to be excused—"

"Oh, Mr. Ashby," Nelly breathed, "how can I ever thank you or repay your generosity?"

"A privilege, dear young lady," Wilfred murmured, and held her hand a moment before he bowed them out.

As they stepped into the hall a woman hurried by, swishing her skirt aside with a disdainful air and avoiding looking at them.

Nelly nudged his arm. "Miss Cavendish," she whispered.

"Oh—" Sam said, impressed.

"Mr. Ashby says she's very difficult."

"Yeh?" He watched her disappear around a corner. "Well, she does look kind of touchy."

The dirty-looking man was doing something on the stage, tinkering with a light stuck on an iron pipe. He glanced at them and glanced away.

"Mr. Ginsberg," Nelly whispered. "He's the business manager."

"Oh—" Sam said.

"I better let him know." She stopped and spoke—triumphantly; her head was in the clouds. "I'll be coming every week," she said.

"That right?" He went on tinkering with the light.

"Mr. Ashby is going to give me lessons—"

"Lessons, eh?" He didn't laugh exactly. He looked at her and then he looked at Sam, a funny kind of look—as if he were sorry for them.

"My brother—" she explained.

"Oh, your brother!" he said in a funny kind of way.

"Well, good night, Mr. Ginsberg."

"Good night," he answered.

They walked in silence. Sam was thinking of Miss Liscomb, the expression on her face he had noticed in the mirror—an expression of annoyance, of something more than that, of injury perhaps and contemptuous irritation; thinking of Miss Cavendish swishing through the hall with her chin stuck up and face averted; of the dirty-looking man and of something in his voice; of Wilfred Ashby whom he didn't really like— But still he was impressed.

"Sam, dear—" Nelly squeezed his arm, standing at the door. "—you've been so good to me. It's all so wonderful."

"Aw, shucks—" he mumbled, fumbling with the key.

"You'll be proud of me some day. You won't regret it, Sam."

"Yeh, sure," he agreed. But he wasn't sure of it.

The weeks slid by. Nelly came and went. He didn't see much of her: Saturdays at supper and afterwards the theater, but it got to be a bore to go again on Sunday, and so she went alone. He let her take his door key. Sometimes he didn't see her after Sunday breakfast until the Plug pulled out on Monday morning. She would get to the depot just in time to wave good-by. The woman of the house complained to him one day that his sister had come in very late the night before—at two o'clock, she said, looking pretty grim; she had no use for theaters or for actors. He smoothed it out, but he mentioned it to Nelly. She shrugged impatiently; she said Wilfred often kept her after the performance to go over certain things—she called him Wilfred now.

"Well, you shouldn't be out so late," he grumbled.

"Why not?"

"It doesn't look good, Nelly."

"Nonsense!" she snapped. "I don't care how it looks to stupid, poky people. Nobody in the theater ever thinks about such things."

She was irritable with him several times, and she did a lot of acting —in the lunchroom, anywhere. Sometimes he was embarrassed. And things were always happening to upset her. One day Miss Cavendish was rude. She had met her in the alley and had started to speak, but Miss Cavendish had turned her head and looked the other way. She was hurt and furious.

"Perhaps she didn't see you," Sam suggested.

"Oh yes, she did!"

"Then why—"

"Because she doesn't like me, because she's mean and hateful—" She went on to tear Miss Cavendish to shreds: the woman couldn't act and she was not a lady. She didn't see how Wilfred could put up with her.

Another day she was in tears. Miss Liscomb had done something; he could not discover what—

"She's mean because she's jealous," Nelly stormed.

"Jealous?" Sam was startled. "Jealous—why?"

"Of me, of course."

"Of you, Nelly?"

"Oh, I don't mean what you think," she cried confusedly. "She's jealous of my talent—because I'm a better actress—and because I'm young and pretty."

"Well, shucks—" he said.

He did not know what to make out of these tantrums. It was hardly ever pleasant being with her any more. She was always picking up something he said and being hurt or angry. And she was rude to other people, too—like the waitress in the lunchroom, rapping on the table and complaining of the service. And if he breathed a word of criticism, as likely as not she would burst into tears—

"Oh, Sam," she sobbed one day, "I'm so unhappy."

"Unhappy?—Why?"

"Because—because—" She shook her head.

"You're getting what you wanted—"

She didn't answer.

"Maybe you're working too hard," he suggested. "Maybe you ought to quit—"

"Quit?" She looked up quickly. "You mean—to stop my lessons?"

"Just for a while—"

"Don't be absurd!" Her eyes were angry, and a little frightened.

"But, Nelly—"

"No, don't. Don't say another word. I wouldn't stop my lessons for anything on earth." And she flung out of the room.

He did not know what to do. He thought of consulting Wilfred Ashby, and suggested one day going with her to a lesson, but she wouldn't hear to it. She said Wilfred wouldn't like it—no one was permitted to be present at a lesson, not even Mr. Ginsberg. Maybe later on, when she was more advanced—

"I wouldn't bother you," he said.

"No." She stamped her foot. "You can't, you can't."

"All right—" He let it go.

In November Madge wrote to him: she was worried about Nelly who seemed nervous and depressed—not a bit like her sunny, happy self. She was cross and irritable and uncommunicative. All week she stayed around the house, studying different parts and practicing her acting, never going anywhere in Wyattville, though she was often asked, and turning up her nose at the boys and girls she knew, as if she thought she was too good for them. When Madge spoke to her about it, she flared up in a rage. She wouldn't lift her hand about the housework. Almost every day a letter came from Mr. Ashby, and if she didn't get one she was more upset than ever. Madge assumed that these letters had to do with Nelly's lessons, but lately she had wondered. Nelly had no appetite and was looking pale and thin. Did he think that everything was going as it should? Did he feel that Mr. Ashby was completely trustworthy?

He put off answering. He did not know what to say.

The end came with electrifying suddenness.

Late one Sunday night Nelly burst into his room in a condition verging on hysteria. She was laughing and crying all at once, strung up to such a pitch that it was hard to follow what she said. And he had been asleep and was only half awake.

It appeared there had been a dreadful row between Miss Cavendish and Mr. Ashby. It had happened on the stage after the performance.

Nelly had been present at the moment, crossing through the set to go to Wilfred's dressing room. The woman had accused him of doing something to her and had called him awful names, vulgar and insulting; and then had snatched a vase from a table on the stage and shattered it to fragments on Mr. Ashby's head which had been cut and bleeding. Mr. Ginsberg had rushed up but had not been in time. Wilfred had fallen back into a chair and she had run to him to see what she could do, but Miss Liscomb had screamed at her and given her a shove which almost knocked her down—

Dear Wilfred! Whatever he had done had of course been meant in kindness and Miss Cavendish had acted like a vicious, jealous snake. He had leaned back in his chair with a towel wrapped round his head to staunch the blood which was trickling down his face. And he had said with simple, gentle dignity: "This is the end—the end—"

"Oh Sam!" She clasped her hands. "The end—you understand?" She had tried to speak to him but Miss Liscomb had snarled at her and shoved at her again. And even Mr. Ginsberg had spoken to her roughly: he had told her to get out—to go on home.

"What can I do?" she wailed. "What can I do to help him?"

"I expect," Sam ventured mildly, "he can take care of himself."

"Oh, you don't understand," she moaned distractedly. "You don't; you never could."

"Well, maybe not—" he said. He was not much concerned. There had been too many excursions and alarms.

She stopped crying after while.

"You've been awfully kind," she said. "I'll never forget it—not ever in my life."

"Aw, that's all right—" he mumbled.

"You're my brother and I love you—" She leaned down and kissed his forehead. "I'll always love you, Sam—no matter what—"

"Yeh, well—" He moved uncomfortably; it didn't seem quite proper, and he pulled the blanket tight around his neck. "You better go to bed, Nelly—"

"Yes—" she nodded and went slowly to the door—as if there was something else she hadn't said. "Good night, Sam dear—"

"Good night," he answered, and dropped off to sleep reflecting that the end of Mr. Ashby would be a great relief.

That was Sunday.

Monday morning she did not come hurrying down the platform, waving to him through the window. The Plug pulled out without her—

at least he didn't see her, though she might have hopped aboard at the last moment. He was not concerned about it. Several times she had almost missed the train. It was likely, he thought, that she had overslept after the excitement of last night, and it wouldn't do her any harm to have a good long rest and wait over until Tuesday. Later in the day she would probably drop in and be apologetic and contrite. He did not think much about it; he was busy with his work and presently the matter slipped out of his mind.

And then—

It was after three o'clock when he glanced up from a message he was writing in response to a tapping on the glass—

He had seen the girl, called Jo, only once or twice since Nelly had been coming. He had stopped eating there. One day a month ago Mr. Butts had been in town and had taken him to lunch in the place across the street. Her face had lighted up when he came in but she didn't say a word, seeing him with Mr. Butts—just nodding and smiling as she would to anyone, waiting for his order. But while he was eating he could see that she was watching him, going up and down the counter—watching all the time. It made him feel uncomfortable.

Finally Mr. Butts excused himself to go and speak to someone, and then she came and leaned across the counter—

"Why don't you never come in no more, Sam?"

"Well, I been pretty busy."

"Yeh?" She filled his coffee cup. "You got to eat some place."

"I been eating up the street."

"I know," she said a little wistfully, adding with a smile, "I don't get paid for driving trade away."

"Aw shucks—" he grinned, explaining lamely, "My sister's been here with me."

"Yeh—" she nodded. "I seen you on the street a couple of times. I thought at first—" She leaned a little closer. "—maybe you had another girl."

He laughed, looking back over his shoulder to see that Mr. Butts was not returning or observing.

"But a fellow at the depot said it was your sister."

"That's right," he said.

"Why don't you bring her in here sometime, Sam?"

"Sure," he agreed, "I been meaning to do that."

And then Mr. Butts came back, and she wiped away the crumbs and went on along the counter.

That was a month ago, and he had not gone back there, nor seen the girl again until, looking up now from the message he was writing, he saw her on the platform, in her gingham dress and apron, though it was cold and snowing, tapping on the glass—

He was startled and annoyed. She had never done a thing like that before, not even when they were going out together. It was pretty raw and nervy—coming over to the depot. He glanced around: there was no one in the office at the moment. He motioned her to wait until he finished with the message he was taking from the wire, and then he went over and pushed the window up.

"I hate to bother you," she said. She was shivering with the cold and her face looked very serious. "I know you're busy, Sam, but I thought I ought to tell you—"

"Yeh? What?"

"Could you come out on the platform for a minute?"

"I can't leave the key," he said with a vague sense of alarm.

"Well, I'll have to tell you here."

"All right. Go on."

"Maybe I'm butting in, but I thought you ought to know—" She hesitated, shivering. "Gee, it's sure cold. I should've wore my coat, but I run across the street as soon as they went out—"

"Who?"

"Your sister and—"

"Nelly?" He caught his breath; he felt it coming now.

"Yes, that's what he called her—the fellow she was with."

"What fellow?"

"That actor from the theater."

"Wilfred Ashby?"

"Yes, that's the one."

"Well, what—"

"They came in for some lunch a while ago. They were sitting in a booth. I knew it was your sister and I couldn't help hearing something that she said, and then—well, I listened to them, Sam. And I thought you ought to know—"

"Yeh? What?" His heart was thumping. "Go on and tell me—what?"

"They were planning something, Sam—to run away together."

"To run away," he echoed.

"That's what they said. And I know he's got a wife—"

"Sure. Yeh, of course." He felt confused and sick. "But run?—run where?—and how?"

« 155 »

"Right now—this afternoon."

"But where?"

"To Chicago first and then New York—" She hadn't heard it all, just snatches of their talk. They meant to get a rig and drive to another town where they could catch a train—not coming to the depot here in Muscatine where they might be recognized—

"What town?"

She shook her head; she hadn't heard the name.

"Yeh, well—" His head was whirling. There were half a dozen towns to suit their purpose. The wire at his back was calling him. He half pushed down the window and then he shoved it up. "Thanks, Jo," he said.

"Oh, that's all right. I thought you ought to know—"

"Yeh, sure."

"If there's anything that I could do—"

"Well, I don't know. I got to think about it." The wire kept on calling. "You better run along. You'll catch cold standing there."

"Yeh, I guess I better, Sam." She backed away, clinging to him with her eyes, and then she turned and ran.

He pushed the window shut and went back to his table and began to write mechanically, not thinking of the words that he put down.—His little sister, Nelly, whom his mother, on her deathbed, had confided to his care. A lump rose in his throat. He should have seen it coming; it was plain enough, what had been going on. And he hadn't been completely blind about it—just unwilling to believe that such a thing could happen. If only he had answered Madge's letter! If only he'd done something!

And now what?—Perhaps they hadn't gone yet. Perhaps she was at home packing up her things. But he couldn't leave the office; there was no one to relieve him. And if he could, what then? The way she had been acting, she wouldn't listen to him. Likely enough she would fly into a tantrum, and if he tried to stop her there might be a public scandal. And they'd know in Wyattville, and Eileen would hear about it. No, that wasn't any use. Anyway he couldn't go, not till six o'clock. He was chained here to the wire like a prisoner in a jail—like a monkey in a cage, as Mitch had said. And suddenly he hated the thing that he was doing—the long, dull, tedious hours, the wire and the railroad, the implacable machine in which he had been caught—

His thoughts went racing on. Did Miss Liscomb know about it? He remembered again the expression on her face he had noted in the mirror.

Perhaps she had expected something of this sort. If he went to the hotel and told her what he'd learned—well then, what could she do? Could she prevent her husband from taking such a step? He didn't think she could. And there might be a scene, and publicity and scandal—

And probably they had already gone—were driving through the country at this moment to some small neighboring town. Yes, but what town? He spread a railroad folder on the table, circling with his pencil the ones that seemed most likely, and checking the departures of trains bound for Chicago. They were at his finger tips; he could query them by wire, but what was he to ask? "Have you seen a man and girl—" and then he must describe them—"buying tickets for Chicago?" And if they had, what then?—No, no, that wouldn't do; and they wouldn't be there yet, wherever they were going. He phrased the thing again: "Notify immediately when man and girl—" followed by descriptions "—buy tickets for Chicago." But there was no good of that, for it would then be too late. There was no use knowing where they were unless you had authority to stop them—

But he went on struggling with it. The livery stable where they got the rig—well, they would know of course. But there were several liveries in the town; you'd have to make the rounds and question them. "Did Mr. Wilfred Ashby rent a rig this afternoon?"—And would they tell? Likely as not they had been paid to keep their mouths shut and would lie about the thing. No, it wanted an authority which he did not possess—

The wire woke and cut across his thoughts. Wyattville was calling. "Plug—" it began.

He glanced up at the clock: the Plug was pulling out. He caught his breath and jerked around, reaching for the key.

"Hold Plug," he said.

The wire was silent. He waited with his eyes upon the clock—one minute after four. There was just a chance, he thought. An interminable minute ticked away, and then—

"OK," said Wyattville, "I got her stopped but I had to wave to Rooney down the track."

He leaned back in his chair and wiped his hands upon his knees.

"What's up?" the boy at Wyattville was asking.

He pressed the key again. "Is my father on the platform?"

"Wait till I look."

Again he waited, drawing little squares on a scrap of yellow paper and lacing them with bars.

"I got him."

"Ask him come to Muscatine on Plug."

"He wants to know what for."

"Tell him important."

"All right he says." A pause. "What about the train?"

"Let her go," he tapped and added, "Thanks."

The snow had turned to rain and it was almost dark when, watching through the window, he saw his father's figure coming down the platform—a tall, gaunt figure with signs of age upon it, but a figure of authority. He pushed the window up and called to him.

"Hello—" Jim said. His hands were in the pockets of his shabby overcoat. He didn't take them out.

Sam told him what had happened in as few words as he could. There was no time to waste. He had made a list of liveries and he held it out to Jim. "We've got to find out where they went," he said. "The first one's just a block or two away."

"Yeh, I know," Jim nodded. There was nothing in his face, and had not been, beyond a little tightening of the lips. His coat rolled back when he pocketed the list, disclosing for a moment the nickel-plated star.

"I guess they'll tell you, Pa."

"I guess they will."

"You better hurry now."

"All right." He turned and strode away.

He was back in a few minutes. The first one on the list had yielded information. They had rented a surrey with a driver and a team, and had left at five o'clock for Miller Junction—

"Miller, eh?" Sam said. "I thought it might be that." He had some railroad folders and he opened one and scanned it.

"It's about six miles," Jim said.

"On the Burlington," Sam nodded. "There's a train for Chicago leaving there at 7.05." He glanced at the clock—5.40 now. "Can you make it in a rig?"

"I might," Jim said, "if I didn't have no trouble." He considered for a moment. "I could telegraph 'em over there to hold her."

"No." Sam shook his head. "You can't do that. It might get in the papers. We've got to keep it quiet."

"Well, I don't know—" His eyes were grim and stubborn.

"You can't use force or anything like that. You've got to make her see what a crazy thing she's doing—or maybe she won't come."

"She'll come all right," Jim said. "There won't be nothing else for her to do." He looked down at his hands—big, bony hands they were—with the flicker of a smile. "That fellow that she's with won't be traveling for a while."

"Yeh, well—" His heart was sinking. It was no use to argue; they were too far apart. And the wire was calling him and time was running on. "You better hurry, Pa." And then he called him back. "You got some money?"

"No, I haven't, Sam."

"Well, here's ten dollars." He put the bill into Jim's hand. "Send me a telegram. I'll be around here waiting."

"All right, I will."

He pushed the window shut and went back to the table, writing down the words that came clicking from the wire, heedless of their import. —Suddenly he had no hope about it. He was half sorry he had stopped the Plug, that his father had been there on the platform, that he had done anything or known about it; for what was there to do that wouldn't make things worse? Authority was not the answer. It hadn't worked with Tom; it wouldn't work with Nelly. Maybe force had been effective when his father was a boy, but the world had changed since then. You couldn't knock things down and make them right. If his mother were alive she would know what to do. But if she had been alive the thing would not have happened. She would have seen it coming before it was too late—

He finished with the message he was taking and wired one to Wyatt-ville, to Madge. "Pa here on business. Nelly staying over. Everything OK." There was no use worrying her about it yet. He almost wished that Jim would be too late to catch them. He got through to Miller Junction and asked about the train. It was on time.—Jim would be started now, driving through the darkness and the rain with a strong and sure hand. It would be nip and tuck. But he knew deep in his heart that his father would come back empty-handed—as he had come back that time when he went to get the bicycle, as he had come back from everything.—Poor little Nelly—

The surly night man came in to relieve him, and he got his hat and coat and hurried home, almost running through the street. He thought she might have left a message for him, and she had—a note pinned to his pillow:

Dear Sam, [it said] we love each other. That's really all there is to say about it. We're going away together so we can be happy. I know it will be an awful shock to you and Madge but there's nothing else to do, and it isn't wrong or sinful. Wilfred will arrange for a divorce as quickly as he can and then we will be married. We are going to New York, and I shall train my voice and also act, but only in the company with him. I'm crying so I can't write any more. I'll send you our address.

My dearest love
Nelly

It was terrible enough, but he was spared the fullness of its measure. He did not know that Wilfred was of less than no importance, that here in Muscatine he had been at the zenith of his professional life, that he had no money and no character, that he had done this sort of thing before, that he was in fact a rascal.

He thought, sitting wearily on the bed in his dingy little room: perhaps it would all be for the best; perhaps no one would ever know about it. They would say, when people asked, that Nelly had gone East to train her voice, that she was studying music in New York. And then when they were married everything would be all right. He tried to think that this would be the case.

He thought he would go out and get his supper. It would help to kill the time until he could expect a message from his father. The woman of the house came out into the hall, as if she had been watching for him. She was curious and snippy. She remarked that his sister had missed the train that morning.

"That's right," he said.

"I guess she overslept, coming in so late at night."

"Uh-huh," he nodded.

"Will she be back tonight?"

"Why yes—" he mumbled, fumbling with the door latch.

"She packed her things and took 'em when she went."

"Oh, did she?" He was outside on the step.

"I'd like to know what to do about her room."

"I'll pay for it," he said and hurried on.

He went into a lunchroom, not the one he had been going to with Nelly. There was an evening paper on the counter and, glancing through it, he came on an announcement: there would be no performance at the Opera House tonight. Mr. Wilfred Ashby had been taken ill. That was all it said about it. He ate his supper with his eyes upon the clock. At a quarter after seven he went back to the depot. The night man was sitting at the table, sending. He did not look up when Sam came in.

"Did you get a message for me?" Sam inquired stiffly. They were on barely more than speaking terms.

The fellow shoved a yellow paper at him. "Missed train," it said. A wave of relief flooded through his tired body. Thank God for that. He had had a vision of his father pounding Wilfred Ashby with his fists, flinging him across the depot platform while Nelly stood by screaming and the people of the town came running to the scene, and stories in the papers—scandal and disgrace—

He turned back to the door; his hand was on the knob when he became aware of the words the operator was clicking on the key. He had been hearing them ever since he had come in—just words he had not bothered to interpret. But suddenly they registered and he was listening to them with riveted attention—

"—Margaret Liscomb, actress wife of Ashby, found unconscious in hotel suite late this afternoon. Hotel employees, alarmed by crying of couple's child, aged five, locked in room with mother, summoned L. M. Ginsberg, manager of company and guest in same hotel, who called in the police—"

He went back toward the table.

"—Woman, suffering from poison thought self-administered, removed to hospital where doctors say recovery probable—"

He found his voice. "What's that? What are you sending?"

The fellow looked up at him with a half-embarrassed air. "AP dispatch," he said and pressed the key again.

Sam sat down in a chair across the table from him. His legs were trembling.—AP dispatch—Associated Press, spreading out across the country like the ripples in a pond—to Wyattville—Chicago—

The man was speaking to him through the clicking of the key. "The police were in a while ago," he said. "They were looking for you, but I told 'em you'd gone home."

He nodded dully. They'd be looking for him there, talking to the woman, asking questions about Nelly. She'd be pleased enough to tell the little that she knew—

The fellow was saying something else, not looking up this time. "Too bad your sister got into this mess."

He didn't answer. He wasn't listening to the wire now. He was thinking of the papers pouring from the presses to be read at breakfast tables in the morning. Mr. Butts would read about it in Rock Island, and the Wyatts in Chicago, and Neill Wyatt at his college, or wherever he might be, and Eileen would read it, too.—His sister, Nelly Braden—

He was thinking that his father could sleep in Nelly's room which he had said he'd pay for—that he had better wait at the depot till Jim came since he might not remember the address where he lived—that he couldn't have needed to use much of the ten dollars. He did not want to go back to the house. The police might still be there, and the woman would be waiting, listening for his step, ready to pounce out, exultant of the fact that she had known how such goings on must end—

He was thinking of the faces he must meet tomorrow, people at the depot, in the lunchroom, on the street—thinking that he hated Muscatine, and the wire and the railroad, and his job which was really nothing more than a cog in a machine, and a very little cog buried in immensity—a cog that would keep turning until it was worn out, and would then be cast aside and a new one fitted in. O'Gara had been right. Even Mr. Butts who had seemed like God to him, shrank to a puny figure—a futile little man beneath a comic wig. It was all a waste of time—not getting anywhere. And suddenly he knew that it was finished.

It was still raining, beating on the dirty windowpanes like fingers lightly tapping on the glass—calling him to come, to get it over with. He took out his leather wallet, and out of it a card. NED G. BRUSH, it said. ACME PAPER COMPANY—HOME INSURANCE BLDG.—CHICAGO—ILLINOIS. At the top was printed, *"If it's paper, come to us."*

He reached across the table for a sheet of yellow paper and dipped a pen into the ink—

"Dear Mr. Brush," he wrote, "I guess I'm finished with the railroad business—"

The first year of a new century was drawing to a close. Some important things had happened. In May a group of daring speculators caused a panic in the stock market. Northern Pacific, cornered, shot to a thousand dollars. A lot of people lost their shirts. Old Henry wasn't hurt; he didn't gamble, except on sure things. And Elliott was rumored to have made a million dollars. In September the President of the United States, William McKinley, was assassinated by an anarchist whose name nobody could pronounce, a foreigner of course. Many people thought that William Randolph Hearst had been more or less responsible, stirring up the working people with yellow editorials and blistering cartoons, trying to persuade them that the President took his orders from Wall Street and the trusts, and inciting ignorant men to violent deeds. Theodore Roosevelt had succeeded to the office, and conservative elements were rather doubtful of him. He talked pretty noisily and had mentioned a "big stick." Presidents had not talked that way before. But the country was all right, marching straight ahead, getting bigger and richer every time the clock ticked. There were some other things that didn't seem important at the time. An Italian, named Marconi, telegraphed the letter S across the ocean, without wires, through the air. Few people understood how it had been done or foresaw any purpose in the thing. But "horseless carriages" were attracting some attention— "automobile" was the name given to them by the French. They were clumsy looking things and always breaking down. It was generally believed they would not amount to much, and a good many people were afraid to ride in them. One had passed through Wyattville, going down the river road toward Beaton's woods, but had not gone very far. Dave Birney had been summoned with a team to tow it back. In some vaudeville theaters, at the end of the performance, they were showing on a screen photographs which seemed to move, an invention of the French called the "cinematograph"—regiments of soldiers, galloping hussars, and things like that. They were pretty hard to look at, blurred and much too fast; and they flickered in a way that hurt your eyes. All in all it had been quite a year.

VII

CHICAGO, PROUD CITY WHOSE MOTTO IS "I WILL."
    Sam loved it from the start, in common with countless other boys who came flocking from the farms and country towns throughout the Middle West. And it opened wide its arms and took them in. It was made for them and they for it—like Mecca of the Moslems, a holy city and their own, the heart of their America, the fulfillment of a promise.

Only Mitch was cynical about it. One night, sitting at a table in some bar, they had an argument which Sam afterwards remembered. Mitch was working for the *Tribune*, a police reporter then. Sometimes when he was drunk he would take out his glass eye and lay it on the bar, and announce to anyone who happened to be listening: "I'm the best police reporter in Chicago, and the best goddamn one-eyed one in the world."

He was a funny fellow. He had worked his way through Chicago University, coming down at night and setting type for the morning papers. Every night he would come down to the Loop and make the rounds, and if they were short of help he would get on, and would pick up several dollars.

This night he said abruptly, apropos of nothing:

"What do you like about Chicago?"

"Like about it?" Sam reflected. "Well, it's beautiful for one thing."

"Beautiful!" Mitch snorted. "It's uglier than hell."

"How can you say that? Look at the parks, the boulevards, the lake front—"

Mitch curled his lip. "Like a fringe of lace," he said, "on a pair of dirty drawers."

Sam laughed indulgently.

"It's dirty and it's ugly."

"That depends on where you sit."

"I'm sitting in Chicago." He paused to take a drink. "What do you like about it?"

"Everything," Sam said. "The smell of it, the sound of it, the people in the street—"

"Which street?" Mitch asked. "You mean the Lake Shore Drive where Stanley Adams lives?"

Sam didn't answer.

Mitch went on talking, painting pictures of the city that he knew, the hinterland behind the Gold Coast: the open red-light district, spreading like a fan from the south edge of the Loop, and the dives that flourished in it and around it; negroes swarming through abandoned mansions of the rich who were always on the move, flying from the Jews who kept close upon their heels no matter where they went; the stockyards and the hunkies in their clapboard tenements (a million of them came to America that year), and the reek of the slaughterhouse descending on the city when the wind was right for it; West Side hoodlum gangs, the beginning of the gangster; rotten politics; poverty and viciousness nicely screened from view by boulevards and parks; maggots in a cheese with a ribbon tied around it. He came back to his question at the end:

"What do you really like about it, Sam?"

"It's been good to me," Sam said.

"Good? How?"

"It's given me a chance to get along."

"Yeh?" Mitch rolled the liquor in his glass. "Get where?"

"Oh well—" Sam shrugged impatiently, beginning to be angry.

"That's it," Mitch nodded, grinning. "That's the trouble with you both—you and Chicago."

"What?"

"You haven't any answer.—'I Will,' but I will *what?*" He put down his empty glass. "It all adds up to nothing."

Sam paid the check.

He got on a car on Randolph Street, standing on the platform to finish his cigar. It was a warm spring night. The lights were bright on Randolph—marquees of theaters, the Garrick, the Colonial, Powers; Henrici's restaurant, and the Sherman House; people on the street; strolling up and down; automobiles threading through the traffic; an air of gaiety. Chicago was all right.—"I Will," but I will *what?*—He was still irritated. Old Mitch was always saying things like that, figuring out some way to make you feel uncomfortable, showing off his college education which had not done much for him—maybe twenty-five a week, and he was always broke. People with no money could afford to talk like that, to pretend that money didn't count, but of course it was a gesture, a resentment of success. Still, he wished Mitch hadn't said it. And on a day like this—the day that he was leaving Acme Paper, going into business for himself, taking another chance, but not hurriedly or rashly—

He glanced down Dearborn Street, dark and deserted. The *Tribune* was down there, and Stanley Adams' bank. He had six thousand dollars on deposit in that bank. He had never asked for credit, not a cent, but he would need it now, and he would get it, too. They thought pretty well of him; they knew that he was steady. One of the vice-presidents had given him a hint, had practically said to go ahead.—Six thousand dollars saved out of his salary. That wasn't bad, considering the fifty he sent each month to Madge, and helping Nelly out, and the time that Tom was sick and on his hands. Chicago was all right and so was he. Of course there were people who didn't get along, but the blame was on themselves. They were lazy, ineffectual, good-for-nothing—

Clark Street.—Hub Baxter was with a firm of lawyers on that street and doing very well. He had been in Hub's office half that day, drawing up the partnership with Jules. The old man had been as fussy as a setting hen, reading the agreement twenty times and disputing every comma. The French were like that, annoyingly suspicious, penny-wise. But finally they had got it signed and sealed. A partnership. You had to get along like man and wife, had to agree. It wouldn't have helped to incorporate the thing, for Jules would not have parted with a fraction more than half. Well, they would see. If Jules would be content to run the factory and keep his nose out of the business end—

The City Hall.—Mike Hogan was working in the tax assessor's office. You could find him in the daytime leaning on the counter, black hair slicked on his forehead, whispering confidentially from the corner of his mouth, intimating he could "fix it" for a friend. His uncle, the policeman, now a captain, had gotten him the job. Mike had married recently an Irish Catholic girl, the daughter of a bailiff, and they lived in a flat in Ravenswood. He rarely saw Mike any more. Once he had gone out for Sunday dinner, but had dodged a second invitation; it had been pretty dull.—The boys from Wyattville. There had been five of them. But Grover had gone home to practice medicine, and had married Susie Baxter.

La Salle Street.—The Elliott Wyatt office was down there, with its board room, leather chairs, mahogany and brass, and eager speculators. He dropped in now and then to see how things were going and occasionally would catch a glimpse of Wayne. But old Neill wasn't there. You wouldn't catch him sitting at a desk. It was hard to tell where he was—jumping around from one place to another, squandering money that his father gave him, running automobile races, playing tennis in England or Long Island, or in Switzerland climbing mountains, or mixed up with some actress in New York. Now and then when he went home he heard stories about Neill which always sifted back to Wyattville. People said that he was like his father, and they said it with a smile, seeming rather pleased and proud. It was funny, the credit that you got for things like that—

The car turned north and dove into the tunnel.

They said that Eileen Wyatt was still in love with Neill, waiting patiently for him to settle down. Perhaps she was—if she had ever been. He had never quite admitted that. But the years were slipping by and the rolling stone showed no signs of slowing up. She must be pretty sick of it by now. He hadn't seen Eileen since the summer she came home with Becky Adams, the time she gave the party on Old Henry's croquet ground, and they were youngsters then. Long time ago. Old Henry had passed on, and Judge Nicolls, and King Cole. But the town had not changed much. Clem Wyatt had retired and not a day too soon. The "five-and-ten" had all the business now. There was a new hotel halfway up Main Street. People wondered how the Wyatt House hung on. The "Mary Queen" had quit some time ago, and the levee was deserted. Madge wasn't getting any younger; she had an expression in her eyes—

a kind of resignation. Mr. Daniel Price had not come back. The house in Shanty Town, he wished they could move out of it. Of course the rent was free, partial compensation for his father's job as Marshal, and it would be silly, paying rent for something else. But he didn't like the idea of the family living there, on the wrong side of the tracks. It made him feel uncomfortable. Madge never mentioned it but he knew how she must feel when her friends came there to call. Recently he had thought a lot about it, of something he might do a little later on, if things went right: the Elliott Wyatt house on the north side of the Square, empty all these years—perhaps it could be bought at a bargain-counter price. It would be a proper place for his father and his sister.— Some day he would drop in at the bank and sound Young Henry out—

The car emerged from the damp and musty tunnel.

Eileen.—He had not seen her since that summer. She had never been at home when he was there. But he had not been there often—two or three times a year to spend a Sunday. He might have seen her when he first came to Chicago, at that school out in Lake Forest, but then he was embarrassed about Nelly and avoiding everybody. And then she had gone to college in the East, and then she was in Europe studying something—or maybe only chasing after Neill, and then in California with her mother, and then— He didn't know. She must have been in Chicago many times, but he hadn't known about it. It was hard to say offhand how he felt about Eileen—not the way he had when they were kids, but sometimes even now on lonely Sundays— He really hadn't thought about her much in recent years—like a fellow on a ladder, feeling for the rungs, with his feet firm on the last one and his eyes fixed on the next one. No time for idle dreaming—

Illinois Street.—That's where he began, almost ten years ago, in the Acme Paper warehouse.

And he saw himself again, standing in the lobby of the Home Insurance Building on a cold and blustery January evening, feeling frightened and bewildered. He had come straight from the station, carrying his suitcase, a cheap one made of cardboard. He had never seen a building more than five stories high, never ridden in an elevator. The Acme Paper office was an imposing room filled with desks and clicking typewriters. Mr. Meyer had been brisk and to the point. Mr. Brush had recommended his employment and no further reference would be needed. The first thing on the program was for him to learn the stock, a sort of an apprenticeship before he could expect to sell paper on the road.

"Yes sir," he said. Mr. Brush had written him that this would be the case.

Mr. Meyer hurried on. He would start in the warehouse and be there for several months, depending on how fast he got along. The hours in the warehouse were from seven to five-thirty, and the pay would be eight dollars.

"Yes sir," he said. He had guessed that it would not be much. But it had taken guts—like beginning life all over when you didn't have to do it. And Mr. Butts had offered him a raise, had pleaded with him to remain, hinting at a train dispatcher's salary in a little while. But he had not wavered even then.

Mr. Meyer was writing directions on a card, explaining that the warehouse was on Illinois Street, just across the river. "I will notify the shipping clerk," he said, "to expect you in the morning. Good evening Mr. Braden."

He had gone down in a crowded elevator; offices were closing and people going home, streaming from the building onto Adams or La Salle Street. He couldn't think which way he had come in and he had no notion where to go. He was standing in the lobby with his back to the cigar stand in an eddy of the traffic, clinging to his suitcase, debating what to do, when he heard the voice behind him—a pleasant, friendly voice with quite a German accent—

"Can I help you?"

He turned and saw a smiling, round-faced man behind the counter— a man with a mustache and thick-lensed spectacles, but not waiting on the customers; a clerk was doing that. His name was Otto Kranz and he owned half a dozen of these stands in different office buildings in the Loop. Mr. Kranz was speaking to him, had been watching him perhaps, sensing his bewilderment.—What had he looked like then?—A comic figure really, with a derby hat perched on his head, the first one he had owned, and the worn-out, old ulster that came almost to his ankles. But the freckles had nearly disappeared, and the cowlick was yielding to inexorable brushing. And the suitcase made of cardboard, and the mittens on his hands—

"Can I help you?"

"Why, yes sir—" He had liked Mr. Kranz from the moment that he saw him. There was something warm and comfortable and safe—the way you'd like to feel about your father. "Could you tell me where to go to get a room?"

"A room?—in a hotel?"

"Well, not expensive." He explained that he had just arrived, his first trip to Chicago, and the Acme Paper job—

"Oh yes, I know them well—Mr. Lubin, Mr. Schultz, and Mr. Meyer. A splendid firm. Then you are looking for a permanent place to live?"

He nodded earnestly.

"I see—" Mr. Kranz had reflected, taking time to look him over, and then he had said with a twinkle in his eye, "It is difficult to settle such a matter in a moment. But perhaps you will come home with me and be my guest tonight? We have an extra room and tomorrow we will see. Possibly my wife will have something to suggest."

"Oh, thank you very much—"

And so he had gone home with Otto Kranz, wedged into a Clark Street cable car, hanging to a strap, around the Loop and through the tunnel, on and on—to the comfortable house in Deming Court, with its reddish sandstone front, and stoop and steps down which, on summer nights, Otto Kranz would spread a carpet, and the family would sit out beneath the stars. The family then were four: Papa Kranz and Mama Kranz and little Emilie, and the old grandmother who did not speak any English and had passed away a year or so ago. It was pleasant sitting out there in the evening—the quiet street, the yellow gas lamps not too bright, and people strolling by, going to and from the park which was just a block away, and neighbors coming over to sit and chat a while, and children playing on the sidewalk. Little Emilie would come and cuddle in his lap when it got along toward bedtime. She always hoped that he could put it off, getting started with a story Mama Kranz would let him finish. She called him Uncle Sam; she still did that. She was quite grown up now—very lovely looking, with auburn colored hair and soft brown eyes.—Yes, those had been pleasant evenings—

But that night he had gone home with Otto Kranz— Funny how it happened, all of it. The dinner was delicious, good German cooking and such coffee. They kept a hired girl but Mama Kranz looked after things herself. And the bed in which he slept, so immaculate and comfortable —the same he slept in now, in the same room at the back on the second floor, next to Emilie's. Papa Kranz had done the talking after dinner but no mention had been made about where he was to live, and then he was so sleepy he forgot it. He was up at half-past five, and tiptoed down the stairs, and took a Clark Street car, and found an open lunch-room down near Illinois Street, and was at the warehouse door a quarter before seven. And then the day was gone and there was no place to go except back to Deming Court. And the next day and the next—

They didn't need a lodger, hadn't dreamed of such a thing. Papa Kranz used to laugh about it afterwards:

"I bring him home for dinner and he stays here all his life."

North Clark Street.—Honky-tonks, penny arcades, nickel picture shows, streetwalkers lurking in the shadows. Pretty shabby and run-down. But it never had been much, not when he first saw it. Saloons and cheap hotels where you could take a girl, and workmen's lodging houses. There was the Greek place where he'd eaten his first breakfast —almost ten years ago. And there was a saloon where he used to get his lunch—off the free lunch counter. A nickel for a beer was all it cost. You could do it in those days if you wore a decent suit and didn't look as if you might be hungry. The Star and Garter Burlesque with lurid colored posters of half-naked chorus girls. He never passed that place without stirring up a memory—

He hadn't recognized her at the start. The makeup on her face was like a mask, and the way her hair was done, in a way she'd never done it, and the color of it, too, for it was dyed. But he had kept looking at her more than halfway through the show, not suspecting in the least, but attracted for some reason that he didn't understand. She was on the right-hand side, third from the end, when he first noticed her, and then he'd pick her out in some other spot, running with his eye until he found her. When they pranced along the runway he could have reached and touched her.

It was in Omaha, five or six years ago, but the memory was still vivid. He had walked out in the lobby during the intermission, to smoke a cigarette with the fellow he was with, a customer with sporty inclinations. He had written his order and taken him to dinner, and the man had suggested going to the burlesque show, and so of course he went, though he would have preferred to go back to the hotel and go to bed.

They were standing in the lobby waiting for the buzzer when the fellow said to him, cracking jokes about the girls who were mostly big and beefy like the kind they have in burlesque, "Sam, you sure got an eye. You picked the only one I'd want to sleep with."

"Yeh?" He laughed uncomfortably. "She makes me think of some-one."

And suddenly his words put the idea in his head. She *did* make him think of someone; she reminded him of Nelly. His hands began to sweat and he felt sick at his stomach. The fellow he was with was looking at him.

"You all right, Sam?" he asked.

"Sure, I'm all right," he said. "Maybe something that I ate for dinner—"

"If you want to go back to the hotel—" The man kept looking at him.

"Hell, no." He laughed about it. And he wouldn't have gone back if he had been really ill. He could hardly wait to get back into his seat, to look at her again, for this time he would know. Not the makeup on her face, nor straw-bleached hair, nor legs in cotton tights would fool him now. But of course it wasn't Nelly—kicking up her heels, smirking at the men, making dates across the footlights, sleeping with them maybe— "Let's go back in," he said.

He read the program, the names of chorus girls lumped together at the bottom—silly, fancy names, but no Nellys and no Bradens. But she wouldn't use her name; that wasn't likely. And of course it wasn't Nelly. He had had a letter from her not so long ago—like all her other letters, optimistic and excited, always on the verge of something big. Things were looking up, she said. She had promise of a job which might really lead somewhere; she wouldn't say just what but would keep it to surprise him. Could he spare another loan of fifty dollars? She always put it that way.

And he had sent it to her.

He had very little notion of her life. She was always vague about things, even at the start. It was months before they knew that Wilfred had abandoned her within a day or two after they reached New York. She had written him for money but had not disclosed the truth. When they found out what had happened both he and Madge had written, urging her to come back home, but she never answered that. And it wouldn't have been easy to go back to Wyattville, not after all the stuff that had come out in the papers. He didn't blame her much for refusing to do that. Once he had suggested her coming to Chicago, but he hadn't urged it then or afterwards repeated it. He hadn't felt sure it would work.

The theater was her métier, so she said. She loved it, she adored it, and would never be content with any other life. And success was always just around the corner. She had had some minor parts which were "bound to lead to something," but none of them ever did. The plays had failed or never gotten on; she was very vague about it. And she had earned some money with her voice—"ten dollars in one evening," she had written jubilantly, but she didn't mention where. A manager had heard her and had sent for her to come and see him in his office. She was certain that this was the turning point. But when another letter came it would be something else—

The curtain rose.

It *was* Nelly. He knew her instantly. He couldn't understand why he hadn't known before, except that it was something rejected as impossible until he partly put it into words. But there she was, cavorting, ogling the bald heads in the front, giggling at the smutty jokes that the comedians cracked, flinging up her legs—slender, graceful legs, different from the others. There were little metal shields tied on her breasts—

"She's sure got your goat," the fellow said.

"Yeh—" He rubbed his hands dry on his knees. He couldn't look away.

They went and came, prancing up and down the runway which was level with his head, a few seats to the side, spreading the smell of makeup and cheap perfume. At the end, in the finale, they came out dressed like birds, with headdresses and girdles made of feathers, singing a song about getting in their nests and hatching out their eggs—a song with smutty implications. And they spread out on the runway. They had bags tied at their waists, filled with little cotton balls that looked like eggs, and they tossed these out among the audience. She was standing at the row in which he sat. A fellow close beside her pulled a feather from her girdle and stroked it on her leg, kidding in an undertone; and she was laughing at him, pretending that it tickled and kicking at his hand. And then she threw a cotton ball and her eyes went with it straight to his. She recognized him. He saw her catch her breath and cringe—

They went prancing back again and lined up across the stage. She didn't look in his direction. She missed a step in the routine, and the girl beside her glanced at her and made some laughing comment. The curtain fell.

Nelly, his own sister, the daughter of their mother, confided to his care with her last breath.—Well, what could he do about it? What could he have done at any time?—in Muscatine, in Omaha, or later?— He had gotten rid of the fellow he was with on the plea that he was tired and didn't feel too good. You had to be careful how you dodged things with a customer, but it had worked all right. And then he had gone back to the theater, dark and deserted now except for a pair of drunks arguing on the sidewalk about picking up some girls out of the show.

He found the stage door in the alley. Already they were coming out;

he could see their faces as the door swung to and fro.—There were the comedians who cracked the dirty jokes, sour looking men with puckered faces; and the boy who sang the songs in a navy uniform, very natty on the stage but pretty sloppy now; the chorus girls in groups of two or three, with their makeup half washed off, calling out to one another in hard, flat voices, "Hey, Judy, wait for me," or things like that—not girls that you would notice on the street. None of them were laughing or having any fun; they had left their smiling faces on the stage. They hurried past him—not to waiting gentlemen with boxes full of flowers, not to parties and cafés, champagne and lobster suppers, not to anything like that; but to all-night lunchrooms where coffee and sinkers cost a dime, and then to shabby rooms in cheap hotels—

Fewer of them came and then not any. Was it possible he could have missed her?—or perhaps she was waiting for him to come inside?—When he opened the door he was conscious of the smell, the odor of the theater—not canvas and not paint, nor painted canvas either, something that sunlight never reached. It made him feel a little sick. He paused in the narrow vestibule with its dingy yellow light bulb, and the call board on the wall with notices and things, and the rack with unclaimed letters—the shoddy, mucky entrance to a shoddy, mucky life. He could see the darkened stage which had been so gay and glittering, but it wasn't glittering now—the dirty backdrop with the paint cracked off, the floor cloth full of holes, the tangled maze of ropes and flats and lights.—He did not know what to do, and he had no slightest notion of what he meant to say; he was still shocked and confused, almost incredulous.—A surly looking man came across the stage and asked him what he wanted. He said embarrassedly, he was looking for someone—

"Yeh? Who?"

"A girl that's in the chorus." He had the program in his hand. "I don't know her name—not the name that's on the program."

"They've all gone home by now."

"No, I don't think she has. I've been waiting in the alley and I would have seen her pass."

"They've all gone home, I tell you."

"Well, I'd like to know for sure," he persisted. "You see—well, it's my sister."

"Your sister, eh?" The fellow changed his tone. "What's your name?"

"Braden. Sam Braden."

"She left a note for you." He took it from the rack and held it out.

"She scooted outa here before anybody else. I guess that's how you missed her."

"Yeh—" he said, but he was reading—a few scrawled lines on a mussy scrap of paper with spots of rouge or lipstick. "Sam dear," it said, "I know the way you'll feel and I just can't talk about it—anyway not now. But I'm really getting valuable experience and I know it will pay out in the end. I'll write you all about it. We're leaving in the morning and I have to be up early. Don't worry. I'm all right. Love. Nelly."

"Yeh—" he said again, and turned back to the man who was waiting by the door. "Could you tell me what hotel she's stopping at?"

"I wouldn't know."

"Is there anyone that would?"

"They've all gone home by now."

"Could you tell me her name—I mean the one she uses?"

"I never know their names."

"Oh—" The man was waiting for him, rattling a bunch of keys. "Well, thanks," he said and went out into the alley—

Division Street.—Down there three or four blocks, around the corner of the Drive, was the Stanley Adams house. On the rubberneck wagons the fellow with the megaphone would point it out and say: "Residence of Stanley Adams, financier and banker. This palatial home, built of Indiana limestone, contains twenty-seven rooms and fourteen baths, cost half a million dollars."—He remembered the first time he had heard it, that summer he was working in the warehouse and riding round on Sundays in rubbernecks and streetcars, finding out about the city. Sometimes he would take little Emilie along—she was five or six years old then, and she loved to go on trips with Uncle Sam. He had turned his head and watched until the house was hidden by the trees along the Drive, and he had told the child that he knew someone who lived there. Emilie was impressed—

"Why do they have so many bathrooms, Uncle Sam?—Do they have a lot of children?"

He laughed—just the father and the mother and the girl he knew, named Becky.

"Is she pretty?—Is she nice?"

"Oh, she's all right," he said. But he never thought of her without resentment. It was she who first put the bug in Nelly's head, that night of the party on Old Henry's croquet ground, passing out bouquets that didn't mean a thing, suggesting in her airy, casual way that she could sing in opera if she had a little training in Paris or New York—like suggesting to a blind man he could see if he had eyes. Rich people butting in when they ought to keep their mouths shut—pampered brats like Becky Adams and Neill Wyatt—

The Elliott Wyatt house was off the route of the rubbernecking wagons. But he had looked it up in the telephone directory and had strolled by one day. It was on Astor Street, a pretty snooty neighborhood, not a big, imposing place, but impressive all the same—with the brass grille at the door polished up like gold, and a kind of jaunty look, like Elliott, himself, but with a lot of dignity behind it—classy was the word.—He had half thought he might stop and say hello, but the windows were boarded up; they were away of course—maybe up at Lake Geneva, maybe Europe. He walked on around the corner to the Drive, feeling disappointed and relieved. The house was through the block from the Stanley Adams mansion, almost behind it. From the windows at the back Becky Adams and Neill Wyatt could have waved to one another, but it wasn't likely that they did. Being neighbors in Chicago didn't mean much. Still, that time he had run into them—

It was two or three years after he came—the second or third summer. He was traveling on the road then, tank towns in Illinois, and some weeks he would get home to spend a Sunday. He had taken Emilie to the zoo in Lincoln Park and they were walking back along the outer drive—

"Hi, Sam!"

He looked around. There was an automobile stopped against the curb and a fellow standing in it, beckoning to him, and a girl in a duster with a veil around her hat, sitting in the seat beside him. He had thought for an instant that it might be Eileen—

"Hi, Neill—" He crossed the parking, holding Emilie's hand. The automobile was a sporty looking one, with glossy yellow paint and big brass lamps and horn—the kind that Neill Wyatt would be driving. It had another seat and a door in the back to get into the tonneau, but it had no top or windshield. And Neill, himself, looked as sporty as the auto, with thick glass goggles pushed up on his forehead, waving a leather cap, and his brown hair brushed straight back—

"Old Sam," he grinned, and reached to grip his hand. "I was sure it was you. Say, you haven't changed a bit." And then he remembered and introduced the girl. "You remember Becky Adams?"

"Oh yes—" he said politely. She was being coy and giggling—just as pert and smart as ever.

"What a darling child," she cooed. "Don't tell me that she's yours, Sam." Kidding of course, trying to embarrass him.

He explained who Emilie was. The child was clinging tightly to his hand, fascinated by the auto—

"Will it go fast, Uncle Sam?"

"What?" Becky leaned across the door. "What did she call you?"

"Uncle Sam," he said. "That's her name for me."

"Uncle Sam?—Not really?" She was giggling again, as if it were a joke. "Did you hear that, Neill?—It's simply priceless."

He disliked her more than ever. He asked about Eileen, but it was Neill who answered; Becky didn't say a word. Apparently they weren't such close friends any more. Eileen, Neill said, was somewhere, traveling with her mother—

"But say," he changed the subject, "I hear you're getting on, doing mighty well."

"Oh, all right, I guess—"

"Traveling on the road and selling stuff?"

He nodded.

"That's swell, Sam." And he added almost wistfully, "You're way ahead of me."

Ahead! That had struck him funny—the idea of Neill Wyatt selling paper in tank towns in Illinois; getting up at five o'clock to catch a milk train; sleeping in hotels, in beds with bugs sometimes, where you had to break the ice in the pitcher in the morning before you washed yourself, or lie naked in the stifling, muggy heat of summer nights; eating greasy food off thick white plates, where the waitress didn't ask you what you wanted for dessert, but only if you were ready for your pie; waiting endless hours for the chance to show your wares; spreading out your samples by lamplight on the counters of messy little stores whose owners were determined not to buy. But there were many ways to get an order—if you never got impatient, never lost your temper. Toilet paper, tissue paper, butcher paper, stationery, wrapper, newsprint, catalogues and samples spread out on the counters—

Ahead! Yes, it was funny, thinking of Neill Wyatt doing anything like that. But he had merely smiled and said, perhaps a little grimly, "Well, I had a long head start." And a long head start he'd had.

And then the Becky girl had butted in. Perhaps she hadn't heard or had forgotten—

"Your darling sister with the lovely voice—what's she doing, Sam?"

But old Neill had interrupted—intentionally, he thought.

"How do you like her, Sam? (He meant the auto) Isn't she a beauty?" He pointed out the features: the big brass generator which produced acetylene to light the lamps, and the coil box on the dash—a new kind of ignition. The engine underneath the floor kept chugging while he talked. He explained the dials and buttons on the dash. This one was the speedometer which told how fast you went, though it was hard to read on account of the vibration. She was geared for speed, he said, could scoot along at thirty—do forty if you pushed her and she was in the mood. "S-s-say, Sam—" He was stammering with excitement. "—why don't you come along and take a ride?"

He hadn't wanted to. He felt uncomfortable—the way he'd always felt when Neill Wyatt was around, anxious to get away. And he didn't want to talk to Becky Adams, or to listen to her either; and he didn't think that she was pleased with the idea, though she was polite enough. But of course she'd sooner be alone with Neill. He mumbled some excuse about having to get home, but then he caught a glimpse of Emilie's face—the breathless longing in her eyes fixed so eagerly on his—

"C-c-come on, get in," Neill urged.

"Well—" And he had yielded, climbing into the back seat with his arm around the child who was in the seventh heaven of delight.

It was exciting, his first ride in an auto—racing along the Drive through the crowded Sunday traffic; and Neill Wyatt sitting up there, as unconcerned as could be, with the goggles on his eyes and his leather cap pulled down, dodging in and out and tooting the big horn—

"We're doing thirty, Sam," he called over his shoulder. "When I get a chance I'll let her out."

But thirty had been plenty fast enough. The horses that they passed seemed to be standing still; the monument of General Grant tore by. At this rate they'd be through the park in no time. The wind was like a hurricane. He hugged the child close to him, clinging to his hat—

"Now—" Neil shouted. There was a fairly open space ahead. "I'm going to let her out."

The engine speeded up; the auto was vibrating so that it blurred your eyes. The horn kept tooting, and the people in the rigs pulled in against the curb as quickly as they could, looking pretty mad, and some of the horses reared. A policeman shouted at them, but Neill did not slow down—

"Thirty-five," he called, "and she's still picking up." They were coming to the end of the Drive where the road curves to the left and down a little grade to the intersection of Diversey Boulevard—

"Yeh," he shouted back, "but you better slow her up now." And the Becky girl had turned and looked at him with a kind of taunting smile—

And then it happened—

A phaeton with a man and woman in it and the woman driving, coming down Diversey, not turning on the Drive as everybody did, but across the intersection toward the beach—

"Look out!" he yelled.

Neill slammed the brakes, the tires screaming on the asphalt. One of them exploded and the auto lurched and swayed, almost turning over, skidding through the intersection, missing the phaeton by a hair, and crashing broadside on into the curb. The wooden wheels collapsed, and the front end struck a lamp post which snapped off at the base and fell across the hood in a rain of broken glass—

For a moment there was silence, and then the Becky girl had turned around, blood streaming from her face—

"Is the little girl all right?"

He hadn't answered her, but had climbed out on the side because the door was jammed and wouldn't open, carrying the child who seemed to be unharmed. And people had come running, crowding round, but not offering any help. And Neill had gotten out with his right arm limp and dangling, but seeming unaware that he was hurt. And he had helped Becky out, and tried to persuade her to sit down on the curb. And she had laughed and said that that was nonsense. Her face was bleeding terribly, and Neill had tried to stanch it with his handkerchief, discovering then that he couldn't use his arm, and looking so incredulous about it. And he had tried to help and had seen the jagged cut from the corner of her eye almost to her chin—a wound that bared the bone. But she had kept insisting that she wasn't hurt at all—only a scratch, and wanting to be sure that the little girl was cared for and that someone got a doctor for Neill's arm—

Whatever she might be—pert and smart and giggling, she certainly had guts. It was funny—those people that you'd think would be so soft. You could wham them around but you couldn't make them yell or get them down. There was something that they had that kept them on their feet—

When the ambulance got there one of the interns looked at Neill and said, "You better sit down, mister."

Neill smiled and shook his head. His face was white and dripping sweat, but he did not sit down.

"I'm awfully sorry, Becky," he kept saying.

The police had got their names. He could hear people whispering in the crowd: "It's one of the Wyatt boys and Stanley Adams' daughter." But both of them acted as if no one was there, as if they didn't see the clustered faces, joking with the interns about the ambulance. Neill tried to take her arm to help her in, and paused at the step, holding out his hand—

"Excuse the left," he said. "I'm awfully glad you both came out all right. Let's get together, Sam, and we'll really have a ride." And he smiled and waved to Emilie, "So long—"

And Becky had leaned back through the door while the intern held some gauze against her face. "Sam, be a darling please and telephone my family, and be sure you explain that I'm not the least bit hurt—just a tiny little scratch that needs a stitch or two. And call me up some-time—"

The ambulance had clanged away. A policeman who had overheard her, shook his head and said, "She'll wear the scar of that cut to her grave."

He had walked up Diversey, holding Emilie's hand, till he came to the Rienzi where there was a telephone. Someone, the butler maybe, said that Mr. Adams was at home. He gave his name, explaining that he had a message from Miss Adams for her father. And then he waited, feeling pretty nervous at the bare idea of talking to a man like Stanley Adams, even on the telephone. The voice that answered was a grave and quiet one, not in the least excited by his information—

"St. Joseph's hospital, I believe you said?"

"St. Joseph's. Yes sir."

"Thank you very much. It was kind of you to call."

"Oh, that's all right—"

"Good-by."

And that was that. He would still feel nervous—a little anyway—talking to a man like Stanley Adams, but not the way he had felt seven years ago. A lot of water had gone down the stream since then. Today he was in business for himself—

North Avenue.—Something had happened on that street a week ago which he would not soon forget—an unpleasantly disturbing scene to which he had been witness. He had gone out with Jules on West North Avenue, bargain hunting for a lathe which was needed in the factory to turn down the pattern rollers, but the man had wanted more than he felt they ought to pay. They had come back to Clark Street where their paths diverged, Jules going south to Woodlawn where he lived, out near the university. But before they parted they had stopped to have a drink in a decent German place familiar to him, where sometimes going home he would drop off the car and then walk on through the park.

There was no one in the place except the moonfaced, pig-eyed bartender and the owner, Mr. Schneider, a big, sleepy-looking German who was sitting at a table in the back, going over his accounts. Jules ordered sherry and he had a highball, and they were standing there talking about the lathe which Jules felt they should have bought, when two men came through the swinging door—young fellows in high spirits. He could see them in the mirror as they came up to the bar, and then suddenly he saw that they were black—negroes far away from Cottage Grove, from the South Side section they belonged in. He had never seen a negro in that place before—not in any place he went. It made him feel uncomfortable, anxious to get away and yet curious to see what, if anything, would happen—

The bartender went back and spoke to Schneider and then returned and stood waiting for their order with his fat fists on the bar. In the mirror he could see the colored men who were laughing and kidding with each other, talking loudly but not noisily—young bucks, flashily dressed, having a good time, not thinking of whether they were wanted in the place. Maybe boys from out of town—

There was something familiar about the smaller one who was as black as ink, and, looking closely in the mirror, he recognized the boy as Peewee Cole.—Yes, it was Peewee, Cassie's little brother, a playmate of his childhood, in whose home he had been welcome.

His impulse was to turn and say hello—"Old Peewee, well, how are you?"—to invite them to have a drink with him, to ask about his mother and how he was getting on and what he was doing in Chicago. Perhaps if he had been alone he would have. He went on sipping the liquor in his glass with his back half turned away but still watching in the mirror, scarcely listening to what Jules was saying to him.

They ordered two Manhattans and the bartender mixed them, not making any comment or changing his expression but rattling the ice behind the bar and putting down the glasses so that they slopped a little. But the colored men, intent upon their banter, seemed not to notice anything unusual. They kept kidding with each other, drinking slowly, leaning with their elbows on the bar. And the bartender stood near them, waiting for them to get done. They finished up at last and ate the cherries, and Peewee, who was treating, put a quarter on the bar, the price of two Manhattans anywhere—

"Half a dollar," the bartender said gruffly.

"How much?" The boy looked startled.

"You heard me. Half a dollar."

"But—" And then he stopped. He dug another quarter from his pocket and laid it on the bar, knowing better than to argue with a white man. But he wasn't laughing now, nor the fellow that was with him; their lightheartedness was gone, all their gaiety and kidding vanished in a moment. They knew they were not wanted, and were suddenly self-conscious, furtive and ashamed, looking round to see if they were noticed, edging away.

The bartender didn't touch the coins, but before their backs were turned, he picked up the empty glasses and threw them with a crash on the floor behind the bar.

A pretty dirty trick!—He had winced and felt the sweat start in his hands.—The negroes had gone out, slinking through the swinging doors like dogs with their tails between their legs. And then the fellow took the coins and rang them on the cash register, and turned with a smug grin on his fat, German face—

"Them niggers won't come here again," he said.

Jules had been furious. He had said things to the bartender, calling him a pig, saying that he ought to be arrested, and refusing to finish the sherry in his glass, to refresh himself in such a place. Schneider had come hurrying from the table in the back, misinterpreting the matter, thinking they were angry at the negroes being served—

"Please, gentlemen," he pleaded. "I cannot refuse to serve them. That's the law."

"Bah!" And Jules had turned on him, mixing French and English as he did when he was angry. "It's not enough to rob them," he shouted at the end, "but then you must insult them."

The bartender had stared with his fat jowls hanging loose, and Schneider had finally turned his back and walked away, shrugging his shoulders and muttering to himself.

On the sidewalk he had tried to make Jules understand: Schneider couldn't help it, if he let the negroes in his customers would quit and he'd soon be out of business—

But Jules refused to listen. Ten years, he said, he had been here in this country but he did not understand it any better now than the day he had got off the boat. Such a thing could not take place in France. "Figure to yourself," he said, "two Germans and a Frenchman, and three Americans in the country that they own, and two of them are robbed and insulted by the Germans because their skins are dark. No, no!" He waved his hands. "You cannot explain such matters."

It did seem pretty raw, putting it like that.

"As for me," he had concluded, "I would sooner drink with black men than with Germans, but I don't insult and rob them because I do not like them." And he ran into the street to catch his car.

Of course Jules had been right—right but not practical, the way he was in business: a good designer, good production man but not realistic about things. And they were partners now—since five o'clock this afternoon. Funny how the thing had come around—

Jules had been his customer. He had started the account about two years ago, passing on the street and noticing the sign outside an upstairs loft: TRONCHET WALLPAPER COMPANY. (*Not Incorporated*) And he had called and sold the man a car of hanger stock, showing him how to save a little money, figuring 500 to the ream instead of 480, the way he had been buying; the stock would run a little lighter but nobody'd ever notice it. He had been afraid about the credit but Mr. Lubin had okayed it finally, and it had been promptly paid. And he had sold another and another, and bit by bit they got acquainted.

Jules wasn't young, probably near fifty. He had been a designer in a factory in France, and some outfit in the East had brought him over here to design and color wallpaper. And he had worked for them for several years, saving his money the way a Frenchman would; and then one day he'd had a row and quit. And he'd come out to Chicago and started up this plant, a very modest one—two eight-color print machines was all, and they were secondhand—in a long, narrow loft in a tumble-down old building on Canal Street. And there he had been for the past five years or so, making a decent living but not growing or expanding—not getting anywhere—

One day some months ago Mr. Lubin had sent for him.

"Sam," he said, "what about this fellow, Tronchet?"

"What's the trouble, Mr. Lubin?"

"He's into us about five thousand dollars, most of it past due."

"I didn't know he was that far behind."

"That's the way it stands. Where do we go from here?"

"Well—" He thought about it. "—if we quit selling him, he'll fold."

"If we quit, can we collect?"

"I'm afraid not, Mr. Lubin."

"What would you suggest?"

"I'm sure that he's honest. I'd like to have a talk with him and kind of look things over."

"All right. But you better make it snappy. I'm no hand to throw good money after bad."

He had found Jules in the boxed off cubbyhole in the corner of the loft, known as the office, poring over badly muddled books with his elderly stenographer; and the place packed full of wallpaper, stacked up to the ceiling in the office, in the aisles between the drying racks, even in the hall outside the door.

"My God, Jules," he remarked, wedging through a narrow passage between the piled-up bundles, "why don't you sell this stuff?"

"Sell it?" The Frenchman wiped his dripping face. It was sweltering in the loft from the steampipes underneath the drying racks. "I have no salesmen, Sam. And how can I go out and run the factory, too?"

"But the stuff'll push you out into the street. You've hardly got room now to turn around."

"I know, I know, but I won't shut down my plant."

"What's happened to your salesmen?"

"Ah, bah!" They were no-account, he said. He had had one that was fair but the fellow had quit to take a better job, and the others he had hired had turned out to be worthless, wasting money on expense and getting drunk, but not writing any orders. The last one he had fired just a day or two before—

"What're you going to do?"

"I don't know, Sam." He sat down at his littered desk, the picture of despair.

"Lubin's on his ear about the size of your account."

Jules groaned. He wasn't broke, he said. There was merchandise on hand to cover all he owed and more than that, but he had no cash to pay his bills—just enough to meet his pay rolls for another week or two.

"You can't go on like that, Jules."

"I'll get out of it some way." But it was plain enough that the man was up against it.

"Can I see the stuff you're making?" he suggested, thinking to himself it was probably no good or priced too high. He knew nothing about wallpaper and had never even looked at the goods that Jules turned out.

"Why, sure, Sam." The Frenchman got some books and spread them on the desk. "The best cheap line on the market," he insisted. "And the lowest prices, too. A wooden man could sell it. Look at that—" He turned the sheets. "—and that, and that—"

It looked all right—nice patterns, tastefully colored.

"How much for that?" he asked.

"Two dollars and ten cents a hundred rolls."

"My God, that's cheap enough."

"That's what I tell you, Sam. It's cheap, it's good."

He had gone on looking at the stuff with growing interest, with an idea germinating in his head—three slim books of samples, nothing fancy or expensive, bread-and-butter merchandise, the kind you'd find in every house in Wyattville—and a line you could carry underneath your arm.

"It looks all right," he said.

"It is all right. Say, Sam—" Jules looked up hopefully. "—maybe you could find a salesman?"

"I'll look around," he said.

He went back to Mr. Lubin and explained the situation, adding that he thought he could sell the stuff, himself, in odd times now and then, without interfering with his work for Acme Paper. He was conscious while he spoke of Mr. Lubin's eyes, shrewd and penetrating, and was careful not to make an issue of the matter. "It's the only way I know to get us out," he said.

"Okay, Sam, go ahead," Mr. Lubin smiled.

And the stuff had sold like hot cakes, as he had thought it would. In three months he had Jules Tronchet out of debt and there was room to walk around the loft, and he had learned a lot about wallpaper—enough to be certain there was money in the stuff—

And then one day he said to Jules, "Well, you're on your feet again, all square with Acme Paper."

"Thanks to you, Sam."

"Oh well," he laughed, "I saved a customer." He'd been getting a commission on his sales and had offered to turn it in to Acme but Mr. Lubin had smilingly refused. He had the sample books under his arm and he dropped them on the desk, aware that Jules was watching him. "There you are," he said, trying to sound careless.

"You need some fresh ones, Sam?" But the Frenchman suspected what was coming.

"No thanks." He laughed again. "I'm bowing out, resigning."

"Sam, no!" Jules clutched his arm.

"But I've got to, Jules," he said. "It was only temporary, till you got back on your feet. Acme isn't paying me to sell a line of wallpaper."

"I know—" Jules caught his breath. "But I can't get along without you."

"Sure you can. I'll find a salesman for you."

"He won't be any good."

"I'll look around until I find a good one."

"Sam, please—" Jules was trembling with anxiety and thrift.

"Well?"

"Sam, would you consider to come to work for me?"

He smiled and shook his head.

"How much?—Just tell me, Sam."

"I wouldn't take another salary job."

"Commission then?"

"Nor that."

"Well, what?"

"If I ever quit with Acme, I'll never go to work for anybody but myself."

"Oh—" The Frenchman wet his lips, sitting in the creaky chair behind his littered desk—a pudgy little man with a bristling mustache but already getting bald. His small slate-colored eyes were thrifty and suspicious, but worried, too, and eager. "Perhaps we could—" It was hard for him to say. "Perhaps we could make some arrangement, Sam?"

That's how it had started. But it had taken months to bring it to an end—months of pretending that he wasn't interested, endless fencing contests, in the office on Canal Street, in saloons, in restaurants, always winding up, "Oh, you'll get along all right," or something of that kind; but not looking for a salesman, though he had his eye on several that he thought would be okay under his direction; letting Jules do all the talking, not having much to say, but dropping in ideas to egg him on: painting pictures of a factory on the outskirts of Chicago where labor would be cheap and there'd be room to grow, and up-to-date machinery, and a sales force on the road, maybe twenty men or more, traveling through the land from coast to coast. The Frenchman's eyes would sparkle and he would begin to sputter and gesture with his hands. He spoke English well enough until he got excited, and then he'd get mixed up, using words that didn't fit, and sometimes talking French. One night in a bar—

"*Combien?*" he fairly shouted. "Say now, what do you want?"

And he had calculated that the moment had arrived, that it was now or never. "All right," he said, "I'll tell you: not a penny less than half."

Jules gulped. His face flushed red and there were beads of sweat on it. He had thought for a moment that perhaps the jig was up. And then—

"Très bien," he said with his shoulders drawn tight against his neck. "Très bien." He nodded slowly. "It is a bargain, Sam." And they had shaken hands across the table.

"I Will," but I will *what?*—A hell of a remark for anyone to make; it had no sense in it. But Mitch was always saying things like that.— His cigar had burned down to a butt and he threw it from the platform, watching the sparks spring from the pavement.—There was plenty to be done, to exercise your will on—to convert that loft of junk into a thriving factory, maybe into something big—oh, not measured in the scale of oil or steel, but big enough to satisfy an ordinary man, a boy from Wyattville.

There were possibilities, a future that the Frenchman hadn't dreamed of. No fancy, arty stuff for a handful of rich people. Bread-and-butter merchandise, the kind they'd use in every farmhouse in the country, the kind the other factories didn't want to make or sell—the suckers didn't know that there was money in it; and they'd all be plugging for you, saying to their customers, "Buy your cheap stuff from Sam Braden." He had found that out already. And if they did get wise to what they were passing up—well, he'd have a long head start; he'd be pretty hard to catch. Yes, there was money in it; not big money maybe, but plenty big enough. If Jules would go along and do what he was told, if he knew which side his bread was buttered on—

Deming Court.—He swung off the car and walked briskly down the street—a quiet, pleasant street of modest houses with reddish sandstone fronts and a few apartment buildings. A neighbor called out to him. He knew most of the families in the block—friendly, German people who had brought their way of living to the country. They were clustered in that section of the city and they had made it seem a little like their homeland, clinging to the customs that they loved: their food and ordered neatness, their close-knit family life, their clubs and *Turnvereins* and beer gardens where, in the summer, they gathered out of doors at tables under spreading trees, and ate good German food and drank good German beer. And for the winter there were indoor places with frescoes on the walls depicting German legends, and words in German script. And always there was music, orchestras and singing—music of the homeland. They had brought so many things when they came across the ocean: their German Christmas with the candlelighted tree, their birthday celebrations. They had not been here long enough to change or to forget. In almost every family there would be one quite old person who did not speak any English. The children who were born here didn't like that very much; it embarrassed them with their companions.

Chicago was all right.—He was thinking of the evenings he had spent at the Rienzi or the Bismarck Garden, with Papa Kranz and Mama Kranz and Emilie, and the old grandmother, too, until she got too feeble to go outdoors at night—drinking beer out of a stein and listening to the music, like a member of the family; of evenings when the carpet was rolled down the sandstone steps and they would sit till bedtime, chatting about things that were happening in the world, maybe strolling to the drugstore for a glass of ice-cream soda as a special treat for Emilie; of Sunday family picnics in the park, and the good things Mama Kranz would unpack from the basket. It was something to get back to after traveling on the road. He had really learned from them what a family could be like.

He went up the steps and let himself into the house. It was after ten o'clock but they had not gone to bed. They were waiting up perhaps for news of what had happened. Emilie was in the parlor, playing the piano. When she heard the door she stopped and looked out into the hall.

"It's Uncle Sam," she called.

Otto Kranz came out from the back parlor where he and Mama Kranz were playing dominoes.

"Well, Sam?" he asked.

"It's settled, Papa Kranz." He always called him that when he was with the family; he had started it in mimicry of Emilie. "I'm in business for myself."

"Ah, good!" beamed Papa Kranz, and Mama Kranz was nodding approval from the door, buxom and placid as she had always been but getting older now. "I bet you," he said, "Mr. Lubin was surprised?"

"I haven't told him yet."

"Ah, so?"

"Tomorrow's soon enough." He was like that: not burning any bridges until his feet were set upon the other side.

"Well, we must celebrate this great occasion, Sam. A bottle of good Rhine wine, one I have been saving. The best we have, eh, Mama?"

"Of course," she nodded.

And Papa Kranz went hurrying to fetch it from the cellar. Mama

Kranz sat down, hands folded in her lap. She said, half-humorously, that she felt a little sad, for some day now he would go away and leave them. And Emilie looked up startled—

"Why, Mama?" Her big brown eyes reflected her concern. He had been like a brother and she was devoted to him. She was still a little girl although she was sixteen. She shook her head impatiently and her auburn colored hair which hung down to her shoulders, shimmered warmly in the light of the piano lamp. "Why should he go away?"

"Nonsense!" He laughed. "I'll be here all the time instead of once a week."

"Well, maybe—" Mama Kranz seemed unconvinced. "But in business for yourself, you will want to settle down."

"I'm settled down," he said.

"You'll want your own home, Sam, and you will want—a wife."

"A wife!" He laughed again. "I'm going to wait till Emilie is old enough to marry me."

"Oh, Uncle Sam!" She was confused and blushing. "I bet you won't," she said. "And I'm almost old enough—" And then she changed the subject. "Oh yes, I meant to tell you—"

"Tell me what?"

"A friend of yours is going to be married."

"A friend of mine?"

"I read it in the paper. That girl in the auto, the time we had the wreck."

"Not Becky Adams?"

"Yes."

"To whom?"

"It's in the evening paper, and both their pictures, too." She brought the paper, open at the place.

"Neill Wyatt!" And he stared; his heart was thumping. Of all things that he hadn't thought would happen. And yet, why not? He had not seen Neill Wyatt since that day in Lincoln Park; he had seen Becky only once since then and that was long ago. What did he know about them? Why should he be surprised?—Perhaps deep down he had actually believed what everybody said: that Eileen would get Neill Wyatt if anybody did. But he never had admitted it.—He read the opening lines: "Mr. and Mrs. Stanley Adams announce the engagement of their daughter, Rebecca—" And pictures of them: a little one of Neill, smiling at you carelessly, shirt open at the neck, as if he might be playing tennis; and a big one of Becky, looking pert and rich and classy, but in profile so you couldn't see the left side of her face. "Well, well!" he said.

"Are you glad about it, Sam?" Mama Kranz inquired.

"Glad?" he shrugged. But he was glad, though he didn't yet quite know the reason why—as if a thing that he had willed and planned, had come to pass when he had abandoned hope that it ever would, when, indeed, he had almost forgotten it. "Oh, I don't care." he said, "one way or another."

"You act kind of funny though," Emilie was watching him.

"Do I?" He grinned.

"Maybe," she teased, but not entirely teasing, "you wanted her, yourself?"

"Maybe," he agreed, laughing overloudly to cover his elation which was mounting like the feeling from a highball.—No, he had not wanted Becky for himself, never in a moment of his life—not with all her money, all the money in the world.

"Anyway you wouldn't tell us—" Emilie was looking at the paper, studying the pictures. "Why yes, of course," she said. "Isn't he the man who owned the auto?—the one that caused the wreck?"

"That's right," he nodded.

"Ah so!" Mama Kranz sat straighter in her chair. "And the scar on her face—did it ever go away?"

"Well, I don't know," he said. "I've only seen her once; she had it then."

"Was it a bad scar, Sam?"

"Yes, bad." He drew a line across his face, from his eye down to his chin. "Like that," he said. He had seen it through the dotted veil she wore, that time he had met her on the street. He would not have recognized her through the veil but she had called his name. And he had seen the scar, trying not to look at it—a white, disfiguring welt across her face.

"Was she a pretty girl?—I mean, before it happened?"

"Cute looking," he admitted.

"Perhaps," said Emilie cheerfully. "perhaps he felt he had to."

"Had to? Had to what?"

"To marry her, I mean."

"Nonsense!" He laughed, but the idea was unstartling, as if it had already cross his mind.

Mama Kranz corrected her for expressing such a notion.

"But, Mama," she protested, "why else would they wait until they're both so old?"

"Am I so old?" he frowned, pretending to be hurt.

"Oh no, I didn't mean—" She was terribly confused, blushing prettily in the lamplight. "But if people love each other—well then, why should they wait?"

"Perhaps they didn't know it," Mama Kranz suggested. "Love comes quickly sometimes, sometimes very slowly."

"I would know it," Emilie said. "I would know it right away."

But he wasn't listening to them, and the thought that had been started, went galloping along. Could it be *that?*—the sporting thing to do, "cricket" as they called it? But it wasn't likely Neill would marry anyone unless he wanted to; nor likely that Becky had lacked suitors. A scar across her face wouldn't keep the boys away, nor a pair of wooden legs—not from Stanley Adams' daughter. And yet it could have been a means to gain her end, if she had had an end, waiting for Neill Wyatt, outwitting poor Eileen or any other rival, feeling confident perhaps that he would never marry anybody else while she remained unmarried. But it wouldn't be like Becky to play that sort of game. Still, what else was she to do? If she was in love with him, she couldn't marry someone to ease his conscience for him—

Papa Kranz returned with a bottle of good Rhine wine and the subject blew away in a gust of merriment as they drank to his success, clinking glasses all around. But his thought kept straying from them, from their kindness and good wishes, straying backward and then forward into nebulous elation.

He was glad to get away to the shelter of his room where, stretched out in his bed, he could think about it calmly. He had only seen her once, that one time on the street, four or five years ago. At Mama Kranz' suggestion he had sent some flowers to her after the accident, and had received a breezy note of thanks, adding in a postscript, "Why don't you call me up?" And then, after some time, he had had another note inviting him to come to a party at her house—"a supper dance, informal." But of course he hadn't gone. He wasn't mixing up with a lot of rah-rah boys and snooty, giggling girls from around the Lake Shore Drive, not if he could help it. If it was to do again—well, he might go, hoping for the chance to meet her father. It might come very handy, knowing Stanley Adams socially. He had written his regrets, making some excuse about being on the road.

And then one day, after a year or more, he had met her on the street —on Washington, by Field's. He hadn't noticed her until she called his name, and at first he wasn't sure who she was. He stopped and tipped his hat.

"Don't you know me, Uncle Sam?—Remember little Becky?" Pert as ever, kidding through her veil which had big black dots on it. You could hardly see her face but you couldn't miss the scar. "So you won't come to my house?" She had started out like that, and he had mumbled something. "You think you're too good for us, don't you, Sam?"

He had never in the least known how to talk to her.

"You're an awful snob," she said, "the worst I've ever met."

Calling him a snob—well, that was funny. He laughed and changed the subject, asking about Neill, not knowing what to say.

"Oh, Neill's all right," she answered petulantly. "He's eternally all right; that's the trouble with him. He's in Africa or somewhere." And she added with a shrug, "Must we talk about our friends?"

"Well, I just wondered—" He wished to God she hadn't seen him.

"Neill's all right," she said again, "even if he didn't go to work when he was twelve, or whatever age you started."

"Why sure, Neill's all right."

"But you don't think so."

"Of course I do."

"You're a liar, Sam. You hit him in the face once with a piece of lemon pie."

"Oh well—" he laughed.

"And you'd do it again if you ever got a chance. Neill wouldn't. He likes you—if he ever thinks about you.—Why?—I mean, why would you?"

"I wouldn't," he protested.

"Oh, come along," she said and took his arm. "I'm going into Field's to tea. I'm late. Why are you such a liar?"

You couldn't get sore because of how she said it: a kind of careless kidding, though she might mean some of it, but he was never sure which was which. He asked about Eileen, just to be saying something.

"Eileen!" She shrugged impatiently. "There you go again. Really, Uncle Sam, you should cultivate a light touch." She paused at the entrance to the store. "Who cares about Eileen? Oh yes, you do, of course. Well now, let's see—" She cocked her head mischievously. "I seem to see her sitting in the musty family mansion, looking at the family album."

"I thought you two were friends," he said uncomfortably.

"Did you? How naïve!" She studied him a moment quizzically. "Why don't you ask her, Sam?"

"Ask her?" he repeated.

"To marry you, or how she is, or something?"

He stood there grinning foolishly.

"She's not getting any younger and blondes don't last forever."

He tried to laugh it off.

"I've simply got to run now—" She turned away, calling back over her shoulder, "So nice to have a chat—"

And he had not seen or heard from her since then. What was she driving at?—those cracks about himself and Neill, and the catty way she talked about Eileen? At the time he had thought it was just her usual line: to embarrass a person and make a sucker out of him. But perhaps it had been something more than that. Maybe she had been in love with Neill for years, and maybe she had got him in payment for that scar.

Well, it didn't matter much; all that mattered was the fact. And elation swelled within him as the source of it grew plainer: Neill Wyatt was removed from his affairs; a shadow on his path had been finally dissipated—

He could like Neill Wyatt now—like him well enough.—It had been a long hard day and he was getting sleepy. He put out the bedside lamp and lay back upon his pillow, seeing in the dark a boy in sailor pants and a pretty little girl with leather leggings and a red cap cupped around her flaxen curls. Nostalgia crept out of his childhood and he remembered things long since forgotten: the time that she had kissed him in a game of post office—the only time he'd ever felt the softness of her lips, but *she* had sent for him; the time he'd walked with her along the levee when his bicycle was coming on the boat, picking a path for her around the mudholes, holding his elbow tight to conceal his torn shirt; the time he sat beside her at the party on Old Henry's croquet ground, and the colored paper lanterns and the songs that Nelly sang; the way her hair had looked in school with the sunlight shining on it; this thing and that. There wasn't much and for ten years had been nothing, but he made the most of it, adding warmth out of himself.

He tried to picture how she would look now—older of course, and her hair would be done another way, but her face would look the same, serious and calm without any worry lines, and the same expression on it, not indifferent but detached—enigmatic was the word. It would be hard to tell what she was thinking. She wouldn't seem to hurry but that wasn't indolence, and when she was sitting down she wouldn't lounge around or cross her legs. She would have a lot of poise and dignity. In an evening gown she would be stunning—going to the theater or into a café; people would look around and inquire who she was—or at her table at a dinner party, she would be a gracious hostess, sought after and admired. You'd be awfully proud of her. Her voice would be the same, soft and rather low—not wasting words, half saying things and leaving you to guess.

He fancied her head on the pillow at his side in a tangle of spun gold, cheek cupped in her hand and blue eyes smiling at him. He had always loved Eileen, had never seen another girl that he would want to marry. He had buried it away, forgotten it sometimes, but it hadn't ever changed.

"I Will," but I will *what?*—Old Mitch and his ideas! He smiled indulgently—

The first decade of the century had drawn to a close. Everything was going fine. William Howard Taft was President and substantial people felt he could be trusted. The country had been muckraked from one end to the other. Baker, Tarbell, Sinclair, Steffens, and that renegade, Tom Lawson, had turned it inside out, exposing everything that they could lay their hands on, from sausage to finance. Even Mitch Ballou had written a book about Chicago politics, but nobody would publish it. The game was up; it was too late. The public had lost interest in the subject; the country had survived the hysteria of reform. The train was rushing on a mile a minute and it wasn't going to stop while a lot of long-haired bums poked around the engine and pulled the wheels apart.—Droves of people went to Europe in the summer; the boats were packed. They did not pay much attention to anything they saw, loafing around with a patronizing air and their pockets full of money which they carelessly disbursed, making cracks about the natives and complaining about things. Mitch Ballou had gone one summer—on a cattle boat.—Chicago was all right, right on its toes. Labor was plentiful and cheap—fifteen cents an hour for a pick and shovel man, sixty hours in the week, or sometimes longer. But other things were cheap: a nickel for a beer, two cocktails for a quarter, a classy suit of clothes for eighteen dollars, and two fifty for a pair of Frazin's shoes. For thirty cents you could get a hearty meal, not in an A 1 restaurant, but plenty good enough; for a dollar you could eat almost anywhere in town. "Ten, twenty, thirty" was the price of vaudeville—best seats a little higher; "legit" attractions in the Loop rarely scaled above a dollar and a half. A haircut was a quarter and a shave was fifteen cents, even in the Palmer House where the barbershop was tiled with silver dollars. On a hundred a month a man could raise a family and do a decent job; a three thousand dollar salary was considered affluent.—Yes, Chicago was all right—if you didn't snoop around like Mitch Ballou. A group of worthy citizens had decided on a plan to make the city beautiful—"The Chicago Plan" they called it. They figured that there wasn't much to do about what was already done, but they had the lake to work on; they would put their beauty there. It was a clever notion: the urban excrement, like oriental night soil, would serve as a foundation for architects and artists—for a city which would rise from the bosom of the lake. Mitch was unimpressed. He remarked that, from the windows of the el, the town would look the same.—Everything was going fine in Wyattville, population now three thousand. They were making buttons in the warehouse on the levee. Young Henry had some stock which he had accepted in part payment for the property. He had bought a little house in Long Beach, California, and went out there in the winter with his wife. He was stepping out, folks said, since his father died. An interurban line was coming into town, and the Rock Island Railroad was trying hard to stop it, threatening, if it did, to pull up its track and quit. The Elliott Wyatt Company, so everybody said, was financing the interurban line.

VIII

Sam married Eileen Wyatt—but not hurriedly or rashly. They were married in Chicago in the spring of 1912. Quite likely Fate had tired, and Eileen too perhaps, of trying to avert it.

They lived together for five years, though not the last two years as man and wife, not after Neill and Becky separated—or, to be exact, not after Becky's suit for a divorce—a brief complaint which specified desertion—was filed in the Superior Court and published in the papers. But this could have been coincidence. At all events it did not at the time occur to Sam that the end of his marriage—the real end of it—might have been related to the ending of the other; and then it was impossible to say, nor a thing he would admit without contributory evidence, and the evidence was lacking.

It was he who had got through, or so he thought, and so it would appear to an observer—through with a relationship which from its inception, had been destined to this end. It was he who took the step, who said what had been said—cruel and brutal things, long gathering in his heart, goaded into utterance by a cankering frustration, by a voice that would not answer, by eyes that told him nothing, by a wall he could not scale or penetrate—things which could not be unsaid no matter how you tried; and he *had tried*. But the truth was in his words, and his efforts to unsay them were unconvincing lies. There was no chance after that night, and indeed had never been one, though he did not know that then. So, no matter how or when, there was no other end to it. But it had no connection with anybody else—

Hub Baxter put the notion in his mind, or brought it to the surface. It was in 1918, in the spring, the last year of the war. She was in France and she had written him, after many months of silence, asking his consent to a divorce which could be had in Paris with his co-operation—a brief and formal note, not adding anything to her request beyond that there would be no question of expense or alimony since she had ample means in her own right. "Dear Sam," it began, and ended at the page end with "Sincerely. . . ."

He had not been much surprised, not emotionally upset. The pang of her had long since passed away, spreading thin in time. He had not seen her for a year. He had dropped in to talk to Hub about it, in a mind to give consent and let her have her way, only making sure that it would be in order, with no loose ends about it. But Hub had hemmed and hawed as lawyers do—he knew of course that they were separated. He didn't like the idea of a French divorce, he said; some of the states looked askance at them, and complications might result; it was safer to proceed in the constituted channels. Let it wait till she came back, was his advice. There wasn't any hurry after all this time. And then he asked a question:

"How long is it, Sam?"

"About a year."

"I mean, since you separated?"

"Oh!" He thought a moment. "We didn't really separate until she went away. I gave up the apartment when she left."

"No." Hub shook his head. "I mean, since you've lived as man and wife?"

"Oh . . ." He winced and looked away. "Three years ago," he said. "The twenty-third of June, 1915."

"That's definite anyway." Hub smiled, drawing figures on a scratch pad. "Well, after waiting that long, it can wait a little longer." He was looking at the pad. "That was about the time the Neill Wyatts were divorced."

"Yes," Sam nodded. "It came out in the papers on that day, the twenty-third of June."

"Oh!" Hub kept on drawing. "Kind of a coincidence, things breaking up like that—Eileen and you and Neill."

"Coincidence?" Sam said. "What do you mean by that?"

"Why nothing, Sam." He laughed. "It just struck me as funny."

"Funny? Why?"

"Oh, I don't know . . ." He broke his pencil point.

"Well, look . . ." Sam got up from his chair; his hands were dripping wet. "My breakup with Eileen was *our* affair. It had nothing to do with anybody else. It happened at that time, but that's all there is to that."

"Sure, Sam, I know."

"Just to keep the record straight."

"Of course . . ." Hub shrugged and changed the subject. "You were asking my advice about a legal matter."

"That's all I want to know," Sam answered drily.

"Well . . ." Hub leaned back in his chair with his eyes upon the ceiling. He was doing very well for a young man—a junior partner in a big, aggressive firm whose practice was confined to corporation law. He had married a girl whom he had known in college, and already had two children. They lived in Hinsdale in a modest stucco house which Hub had bought on contract. "Well . . ." he repeated, as if he were considering a question of importance, ". . . I'd say to let it go till she gets back. The war won't last forever."

Sam made no reply. He was standing at the window, looking down Monroe Street.

"If you like," Hub suggested, "I'll write to her myself, advising her to wait."

"No," Sam said at last. "If she wants it, she can have it."

"All right." Hub laughed. "You're paying for advice, but you don't have to take it. That's what keeps us busy."

"But you can write her, Hub." Sam came back to the desk. "Tell her it's okay so far as I'm concerned. You can help her, I suppose?"

« 196 »

"Probably . . ." Hub nodded. "I'll get it off tomorrow. Leave her letter with the address."

Sam dropped it on the desk.

"Red Cross," Hub noted, "Base Hospital 19, Soissons—that's rather close behind the front," he said.

"Is it?" Sam shrugged, and added with a smile, "That's where she'd want to be."

Hub got up to go with him to the door—got up heavily; he had taken on a lot of weight, notwithstanding golf on Sunday at the Hinsdale Country Club. "How's business?" he inquired, to be saying something.

"Fine," Sam said, and smiled wryly to himself as the door was closed behind him.

It was very far from fine. The big, new factory out in Clearing, where labor *had been* cheap, was fighting for its life. It wasn't paid for, but that was not the problem; the Stanley Adams bank could worry about that. The problem was how to keep it running. The war was playing hell with it: prices were sky high, raw materials hard to get, some almost unobtainable; labor was scarce and beginning to be cocky. They ran an open shop, a twelve-hour shift at times, and not paying any more than the ordinary scale. But it looked as though the end of that was coming: organizers were around, holding meetings in the lunch hour; there had been a lot of grumbling and some talk about a strike—

He wedged into a crowded elevator. It was half-past five and people going home—a bad hour of the day for a man who lived alone in a room in a hotel. The stenographers and clerks pushed back to make room for him; the elevator man did not click the latch to hurry him. He was obviously a person of importance—a high-priced man, an executive perhaps. He was thirty-four years old; his body had filled out and the pinched look in his face had disappeared; the freckles were all gone and the cowlick reduced to a becoming riffle. His gray, conventional suit was custom made; his shoes were shined; his necktie was discreet and in good taste. Eileen had taught him how to dress, had taught him many things, not by criticism or suggestion, but by rare and casual comment of her eyes; and he had been quick to learn.

The sales end was all right, he told himself. He could take care of that, distribute every roll the factory made. Production was the problem, and that was up to Jules, and Jules was cracking up—acting like a Frenchman, crazy and hysterical. He didn't like the French, had no patience with them. He had hoped in the beginning that they would lose the war to the sturdy, honest Germans—men like Papa Kranz—

He crossed the lobby toward Monroe Street, passing a cigar stand which had once belonged to Otto, but there was another name above it now. And Papa Kranz was dead, but that was not the reason that the stand had changed its name, for the changing of the name had happened first. Papa Kranz had lost it; he had had a dozen of them when the war began, and he had lost them all, one after another. His customers had quit him because he was a German—some had even threatened to move out of the building unless his lease was canceled. They had acted like a lot of goddam fools. No doubt Papa Kranz had talked too much, anyway in the beginning; he was not a man to pussyfoot around. And he had paid for it: his business kept on shrinking and leases that expired could not be renewed. Papa Kranz had grieved about it—grieved himself to death—

He came out onto Monroe Street and his thoughts went back to Jules. The man was getting old and he had some heart disease. He acted like a nut: he would sit down at his desk and cry about things—tears trickling down his cheeks. The boys around the factory knew they had his goat and they wouldn't be afraid to put the screws on. He was always talking of the old days on Canal Street and wishing he was back there in that messy little loft. Very likely he'd be glad to sell out his half and quit—at a bargain-counter price. Yes, this would be the time to buy him out. But buy him out *with what?* He was stubborn as a mule; if he thought you wanted something he would quickly change his price. Elliott Wyatt would know how to make a deal, how to juggle things around without changing any money; but he'd want his pound of flesh—

The current of his thoughts was diverted to the Wyatts.—What was Hub intimating about Eileen and Neill?—Well, that was nonsense! Neill Wyatt wasn't even in Chicago at the time; no one knew where he was. He and Becky had been living in New York, if they could be said to live anywhere at all. And then he had gone over and joined the British Air Force, not even waiting until the divorce was granted. It had all been in the papers. And he'd been there ever since—almost three years. He had been wounded once, and a great fuss made about it. He was pretty old to be flying airplanes, but of course that's what he'd like—grandstand stunts and cricket—

There was nothing in that stuff. Neill had never given a tinker's dam about her, and, whatever she had felt, she had gotten over it when he married Becky Adams. She had hardly seen him since then, and never talked about him, never wrote or heard from him—not as far as he knew. Suppose she was in France? That didn't mean a thing. She had wanted to do something, like a lot of other women. And he had said she could—but she would have done it anyway; it was just a pleasant gesture, asking his consent. So what the hell! The whole thing had been over two years before that. If there had been a reason, would she have stuck around? It wasn't likely. Anyhow, it was he who ended it—who had said those things that couldn't be unsaid—

He walked along Monroe Street, aimlessly but briskly. There was no place to go—a bad hour of the day since Eileen went away, but it had never been a very good one. He wished he had an office in the Loop. If the business ever got back on its feet, that was one thing he'd do. It was too early for dinner. Should he stop and have a drink?—should he eat downtown?—and where?—And after that, then what? He could take in a show but he wasn't in the mood. He'd like someone to talk to—not to be alone. The hotel where he lived was out by Lincoln Park, an apartment hotel, sedate and gloomy. He had thought of going back to live with Mama Kranz, but you couldn't pick things up where you had put them down: and now that Papa Kranz was gone, it wouldn't be the same. And Emilie grown up—perhaps already married, though they would have let him know if that had happened. He had hardly seen them since the funeral. It might be they were having tough sledding by themselves. He ought to call them up or drop around sometime.—Sometime but not tonight—

He wished there was someone that he felt like telephoning, and he checked in his mind the few he knew outside of business hours. Their friends had been *her* friends, married couples like themselves, and not many of them either. In a way he had been disappointed about that; she was not a social person. After she went away he had avoided them: he didn't really care about them anyhow. They suspected of course that something had gone wrong; it was embarrassing for him and for them, too. "Where's Eileen?" they'd ask, and "What's she doing now?" And he couldn't answer them with any certainty. It was likely enough that they knew more than he did, and were fishing around to see what they could find. Anyway it was uncomfortable—

He wished he could sit down and talk to Mitch—or listen to him. But Mitch was overseas, a foreign correspondent, writing stuff about the war. He had been up to the front and had nearly gotten shot, according to his story—an exciting kind of job but no future to the thing. When the war came to an end he would be back where he started. Still, Mitch wouldn't care. He would have enlisted but for his sightless eye. He said he'd never missed it until then. He'd been writing pretty

« 199 »

well, with his name signed to his stuff, a good war correspondent—probably the best one-eyed one in the world—

He even wished that he could talk to Mike. But Mike was in the Army, had enlisted at the start, no doubt glad to get away from the tax assessor's office, and to interrupt the sequence of Mrs. Hogan's pregnancies—they already had five children. Being in a war would be a break for Mike. The boys from Wyattville—himself and Mitch and Hub—had given him a party at the College Inn the night he left for camp. They had been a little drunk and sentimental—

He turned north on Dearborn Street, resolving to walk home. It would serve to kill an hour.—Mike and Mitch and Hub, the old friends of his childhood. Grover had gone as a doctor to the war—as an officer of course. Hub was safe enough, with his family out in Hinsdale. But what about himself?—There wasn't any use to kid yourself about it: if the thing went on a while, he could be drafted. What was there to prevent it? He was in the age group, the next one that they'd call; he was physically okay, without children or dependents; he wouldn't have a wife much longer now; his business didn't matter to anyone but him. Sure they could get him—if the thing went on a while—

No, this was not the time to buy the Frenchman out, not even if you could at bargain-counter price—

"Sam!"

He stopped and stared, for there was Mitch Ballou coming through the swinging doors, out of the Tribune Building—old Mitch in mussy, unpressed clothes, a coat that didn't match his pants, a necktie like a piece of string, a weather-beaten hat stained black around the sweatband—

"My God," he said. "I thought you were in France."

"That's right." Mitch pumped his hand. "I just got in. I'm busting up with this gang—" He motioned toward the *Tribune*. "The bastards think it's *their* war; they cut my stuff to ribbons. I just resigned—or else they fired me; I'm not quite sure which."

"That's tough," Sam said.

"It's swell." Mitch laughed. "I got a better job, on a paper in New York. I'm going back tomorrow. They're sending me to Moscow."

"Moscow?" Sam said blankly. "I guess you won't like that."

"It's the one place on the globe I want to go."

"You do? But why?"

"My God!" Mitch stared at him. "Don't you read the papers? There's something going on in Russia, Sam,—something different, something new. Maybe it's a racket, like all the rest of them. But I want to see, myself. I want to have a look."

"Well, yes—" Sam nodded vaguely. "But starvation and disease and those crazy Bolsheviki—"

"Sure," Mitch agreed and changed the subject. "How's everything with you?"

"Fine," he said and smiled, "Well, pretty good."

"Still grinding out the stuff to beautify the home?"

"You bet."

"Well, don't get smothered with it."

"No—" He shook his head. "The way it's going now, that isn't likely."

"Swell," Mitch grinned. "It's lucky that we met. I was going to call you up, but I'm running on a schedule—"

"Well, say—" His voice was eager. "—can't we have dinner, Mitch, and spend the evening?"

"I'd like to, Sam, but I've got to see a gal I used to play around with."

"Oh yeh—" His heart sank.

"But look—" Mitch grabbed his arm. "—we can dash across the street and have a quick one."

They scuttled through the traffic across Dearborn to the bar where the *Tribune* gang held out—a crowded, noisy place. Half a dozen fellows hailed Mitch, slapping him on the back, wanting to buy a drink—careless, seedy looking fellows like himself. They elbowed to the bar and had two scotch and sodas pretty fast. Mitch kept talking like a whirlwind, interrupting now and then to greet an old acquaintance—he was popular, it seemed—and picking up his story at the point where he left off: the Germans would be whipped, the skids were under them, the French had done the trick of holding them in check until we could make a start; when the might of America really hit the line, it would crumple like an empty paper bag—

"Yes? When?" Sam asked.

"Before the year is out."

"You really think so, Mitch?"

"I'm betting money on it." He put down his empty glass. "Say, Sam, I've got to run."

"One more?"

Mitch shook his head.

"A quick one, eh?"

"I can't." He stepped back from the bar. "Oh yes, by God, I almost forgot to tell you—"

"What?"

"I saw Eileen in Paris."

"You did?" His heart stepped up.

"About two weeks ago—just before I sailed."

"How was she?" He kept looking at his glass, moving his hand to stir the ice around.

"Swell," Mitch said. "And stunning, too, in her Red Cross cape and cap. She was on a holiday, from some hospital somewhere."

"Soissons?"

"Yes, that's the place."

"Is she—all right?" He was going to say *happy*, but changed the word half spoken.

"I'd say," Mitch answered drily, "that she was in the pink."

"Oh—" He nodded slowly. "Where did you run into her?"

"In a restaurant," Mitch said, "a ritzy place, not the kind I go to unless somebody takes me, but I was with a fellow from the Embassy. When we were coming out somebody called my name, and I looked around and there was Neill—"

"Yeh?" Sam said, watching his fingers turning white against the tumbler.

"Old Neill Wyatt," Mitch went on, "natty as hell in his Air Corps uniform with a row of colored ribbons spread across his chest. He was waving me to come, and then I saw Eileen sitting at the table—"

"Yeh—" Sam said again.

"Just the two of them," Mitch said. "A platter full of oysters worth about a franc apiece, champagne in a cooler. Neill wanted me to stop and have a drink, but the fellow I was with was waiting for me."

"Yeh—" Sam nodded, counting out some money on the bar. "Did she say—anything?"

"No," Mitch said, "I don't remember that she did." He shrugged. "Well, hell, you know Eileen."

"Yeh—" He pocketed his change. "When did you say it was?"

"About two weeks ago, just before I left. Say, Sam, I've got to run. Thanks for the drinks."

"Okay," he said. "So long—"

Mitch knew about them, knew that they had parted long ago. He had confided it to Mitch not long after it happened, but not saying much about it. And Mitch had been as brief. "A lucky break," he said, "for both of you." He had not pursued the subject; there were things you couldn't talk about to anyone on earth. And Mitch wouldn't understand:

he wasn't lonely. Women dropped into his lap and he played with them a while and then slid out from under. They expected him to do that and didn't seem to care. And he would find another and enjoy her just as much—

He walked along the crowded pavement, his hands clenched so tightly that the nails dug in his palms. It was July and the sun still slanting hotly in the canyon of the street. The highballs made him hotter; sweat trickled through his hair where his straw hat pressed his temples. He bought an evening paper at the corner, glancing at the headlines: "Huns Retreat Across the Marne," but the words made no impression on his thought—

Just the two of them—a cozy little party—ritzy and expensive— oysters on a platter, champagne in a cooler—a natty uniform with ribbons on his chest. God damn him anyway!—Not *them* but *him*—, he thought.—Pretty soft to be in Paris with a pocket full of money that someone else had made, acting like a hero, swaggering in the night spots with another fellow's wife. But he knew this was a lie: Neill Wyatt wouldn't swagger, wouldn't care enough about it, would be a lot too busy doing what he pleased. And he wouldn't be a hero, or act like one at least. And Eileen was his cousin; they had grown up together. What would be more natural than to take her out to dinner? If it was on the sly, would he call across the room to Mitch Ballou?—God damn him anyway!

The two of them—out having fun. And he was going home to a room in a hotel. But it hadn't been a *home*, in the apartment. All the furniture and stuff, and the dining table set with sparkling glass and silver, and the maid in cap and apron, and fresh flowers in the vases—oh, Eileen knew how to do things, and she did them to the end, to the day she went away. She had spent her money, too, buying things for the apartment, though he hadn't liked the idea. Old Henry had left her a hundred thousand dollars—the income from a trust, and she had been generous with it: the oriental rugs, the Steinway grand piano, the cuff links that he wore, a stickpin for his tie, his evening studs—

But it hadn't been a *home*, not even at the start—not the living room, nor dining room, nor the one he called his den, which was snugly lined with books—not their pleasant bedroom which looked out across the lake, with its twin beds side by side in their silken counterpanes, and the night stand set between them—just a yard apart they were; you could reach across to her. And then one day you couldn't. But it never had been easy, not the way it should be. How many, many times he had wakened in the night, listening for her breathing, to be certain she was there, and then certain that she wasn't—and turning on the light, and getting up to find her. It might be two or three or four o'clock. And she would be sitting somewhere in the dark, but she would hear him coming and quickly turn a light on. She would say that it was nothing, she had been awake and restless—just sitting there and smiling, never adding anything, any reason or complaint. But sometimes her eyes were rimmed, as if she had been crying. There had been a factor which he would not look at closely, an element of timing in these matters. He had refused to take it seriously, and he did not wish to think about it now. Perhaps all wives did things like that—

Would it have been different if she had had a child? But she hadn't wanted children, though she never put it that way, never really put it any way—evading with her eyes, if he hinted at the subject. Perhaps she was afraid? But no, that wasn't likely; she seemed to have no nerves; he had never seen her frightened. Maybe there was something lacking from her nature, that she simply didn't have, was incapable of giving, or of wanting to receive? Could it be that she was cold, as Nelly always said—a frigid woman?—He shook his head, as if to shake it clear. He had been all over this so many times—

Regardless of the reason, it hadn't been a *home*. There had been something wrong from the beginning. But whatever it might be, it did not concern Neill Wyatt—

He had never had a home, not since his mother died.—He welcomed the intrusion of this thought, a diversion of his bitterness onto safer ground.—No, he'd never had a home, not since he had been old enough to understand his father—to be ashamed of him, of the nickel-plated star, of Shanty Town, of poverty. He could put his finger on the day when it began—sitting on the ground beside his broken sled, with Madge standing in the doorway—"Because we're poor," she said. Not even his mother could compensate for that. And he had determined then, little fellow that he was, that he would not be poor when he grew to be a man, not a father like his father, who hadn't cared enough to see that they were fed, that they had a decent break to face the world. And he had never faltered in pursuit of that resolve—

His brother and his sisters hadn't fared so well—hadn't had the guts. The handicap had been too much for them. Tom was no-account and he had despaired of Nelly; she would never make the grade, was slipping down the hill toward things he didn't like to think about. She had married an actor—a no-good, shiftless fellow, and then had been divorced. She seldom wrote, except to ask for money; and while she still pretended that golden opportunity was just around the corner, between the lines he read a bitter disillusion—the echo of defeat. He did not know how she lived, tried not to speculate. A recent letter was almost incoherent. She said she had been sick and asked for "fifty bucks"— "till I get back on my feet." It was written with a pencil, barely legible, confused—as if she had been drinking—

He thrust that thought aside. She had been sick of course— And poor old Madge had missed the boat, missed everything she wanted—a husband and a family. Mr. Daniel Price had not come back. She had sacrificed herself as somebody always did. But at least he'd got her out of Shanty Town, decently installed in a comfortable home on the north side of the Square—the Elliott Wyatt house he had bought four years ago and given, in joint ownership, to Madge and to his father. She had that coming to her. It had cost eight thousand dollars which was half what it was worth. He had been prepared to go a little higher, but Elliott had nodded his acceptance of the offer, not bothering to bargain on a deal of such proportions. He had afterwards regretted that he hadn't offered six, but anyway they had it. It was a pretty place with a well-kept patch of lawn and a garden at the side and big shade trees all around it. And that old man, his father, living on and on without a care on earth, sitting on the porch in a cushioned wicker chair, with the nickel-plated star pinned to his suspenders—

But it wasn't any use trying to divert it, to pretend your sense of injury had another source, to blame it on the past, feeling sorry for your childhood. That was all well enough, but it was not the question—not the one that had been hammering in his head from the moment Mitch had told him—

Was that the reason she wanted a divorce?—the reason she had gone to France, by plan or in the hope?—Now that it was phrased you could look it in the face. And it was nonsense. There was not a shred of pretext to imagine such a thing; and even if there were, what was it to him? Why should he care about it? He had been the one to end it—

She had married him out of her choice, because she loved him— anyway as much as she could love anyone.—He dodged away from this: "love" was a word that he found hard to use in connection with Eileen; it seemed inappropriate, presumptuous in himself.—She had liked him well enough to marry him. There could be no other reason. She did not need a provider; and it wasn't loneliness—she was not the lonely kind; nor because he was the only one that asked her. She was beautiful to look at, socially well connected, cultured, educated; and she had a tidy income of her own. A lot of men must have been attracted to her; still, he didn't know of one. She had never suggested that there had been others—old sweethearts in the background, in Wyattville or elsewhere. But she wasn't one to talk about herself—

However that might be, she had married *him*. And it wasn't on a rebound, out of pique or disappointment. She'd had time enough to get all over that—if there had been anything that she needed to get over; and that was idle gossip in a sleepy country town. It had been two years before he asked her, getting closer friends as time went on, seeing her more often, first in Wyattville—she was home all that first summer and he managed to run down for several week ends; calling at the house, renewing, getting started, casual to begin with, having family Sunday dinner, taking her to drive—to Beaton's woods one day; telling her about his business, Jules Tronchet and the factory, and the things he saw ahead. And she had listened to him, appearing interested, never saying very much, but he was used to that—

That winter she had gone to California with her family, and they had corresponded—not romantically at all; he hadn't pushed things. Although she didn't say so, he gathered from her letters that Long Beach was pretty dull; but it would be dull in heaven with Young Henry and his wife—stupid, small-town people, beginning to get old. And, too, she had been so much with Elliott and Daphne that being with her parents must be an awful bore, though she never suggested such a thing. She seemed devoted to them, as indeed they were to her, but she didn't spend much time in their society. Mrs. Henry's gabbling would get anybody down; and Young Henry, glum and silent, walking stiffly with arthritis. No, it wouldn't be exciting—

It was the second winter that things came to a head, when she was in Chicago, going to an art class, studying drawing and design, living by herself in a boarding house on Rush Street, but a fashionable one, more like a small hotel. The Wyatt house was closed. Elliott and Daphne were in New York that winter; and Neill and Becky were hardly ever there. Only Wayne was on the job, and he was married now to a Gold Coast debutante, and lived in Highland Park. They had gone there once to dinner—a pretty fancy place, with a butler and a maid. Wayne was all right. He looked like Neill: lithe and trim and careless, but resemblance ended here. He was a steady fellow—no grandstand stuff about him. Strangely enough he didn't seem to mind that Neill had all the gravy: he actually seemed proud of the things his brother did, like sailing boats in races and winning tennis matches. They were a funny family—

He saw her often, once or twice a week, taking her to dinner—expensive, ritzy places, like the Blackstone and the Congress; to the theater and the opera. And she had seemed to like it—playing round with him; he never called her up to be told that she was busy. "Why yes," she'd say, "I think that would be nice." They had had fun together, more fun than they would have again; they were closer to each other then. He had not made love to her—hadn't wanted to until it should be settled. And he had known that the day was drawing near, that a great dream of his life was approaching its reality. But he didn't mean to ask her till the moment was at hand, feeling certain he would know when it was time to speak—

The end of March it was—an evening with the hint of spring. He had suggested showing her the factory—still on Canal Street then, but already it had grown to occupy the building, with three floors of print machines and three more for storage space and a decent looking office with stenographers and clerks—a modest enterprise but not one to be ashamed of; they made a hundred thousand net that year. He had ventured the suggestion while they were having dinner, that it might interest her, particularly since she was learning to design. But he wanted her to see it for reasons of his own—to see what he was doing, what he had made from nothing. They were running day and night, two twelve hour shifts; and he often went back to the factory in the evening, strolling through the place, watching to see that the men were on their toes—or sitting in the office, silent and deserted, figuring, making plans—

"Why yes," she said, "I think that would be nice." And they had driven over in a cab.

She had never looked more beautiful: her plain black dinner gown, her hair like woven platinum in the white glare of the arcs, standing in the muck of color mills and barrels, watching the printed paper spin from the clattering presses, to be caught by cunning sticks and draped in long festoons above the drying racks. She was really interested; he had never seen her face so animated—so beautiful, in fact. She didn't mind the racket, the dirty, slippery floor, the smell of glue and color, the humid, stifling heat; she wanted to see everything and have it all explained. And she had talked with Jules, shouting through the clamor. The Frenchman had been flattered, jabbering French at her, waving his hands around, eager to explain the presses and the colors and the technique of designing for the wooden pattern rollers—

Afterwards they had gone into the office—just the two of them; and he had lit the light which hung above his desk, and placed a chair for her across the desk from his. He had said she must cool off before going out of doors, and he had put her wrap across her shoulders—

"I wish—" she said, rather to herself, "I wish I were a man."

"Do you?" He laughed and sat down in his chair. "Well, why?"

"Because—" She hesitated, seeming to look beyond him. "Because I'd like to do the things that men can do."

"Grubbing in a factory, for example?"

"I shouldn't mind that."

"I think—" he spoke quite slowly, thinking of his words, "that the finest work of all is to be a reason for it, to be an inspiration to a man."

"Do you?" she said, looking at him quickly, with a pucker in her forehead—searchingly, he thought.

And suddenly he felt that the moment was at hand. He had leaned across the desk and put his hands on hers, the palms spread on her knuckles. And he had asked her then in just so many words: "Will you marry me, Eileen?" And she had answered yes—

But it wasn't quite like that. . . .

"You've always been so right—" was what she said, looking at him steadily, but her eyes were enigmatic. And he had looked away, embarrassed and confused, not knowing what she meant or paying heed to it, or afterwards remembering it—perhaps not really hearing through the throb of the machiney.

What did she mean exactly?—"You've always been so right—" with a question mark behind it, the shadow of a doubt debated with herself. She must have been prepared for the proposal, must have thought what she would answer when it came, for she was not a fool and the depth of his devotion could not have been mistaken. Likely enough she had come to no conclusion, hoping that events might serve to clarify her mind, answering to herself sometimes "yes" and sometimes "no," and more frequently the latter.

Thus the statement, or the question: "You've always been so right—" was an appeal to him from the depth of her uncertainty. It was as if she said, "I admire you, respect you, but I do not love you as I think a woman should love the man she marries; still, perhaps that may resolve in the new relationship—one with which I have as yet had no experience If I answered by myself, the answer would be 'no,' but I cannot leave you out at the risk to cheat us both. I am disposed to trust you, to rely upon your insight, to believe you will succeed with *us* as you have done with yourself, to make things work in the face of every obstacle."

And, too, she might have added, for the moment he had chosen was in truth the proper one: "In the wealth of your activity I shall have a living part, a vicarious achievement, but an end to aimless drifting, to emptiness of purpose, to waiting—and for what?"

In substance it may be that this was what she meant.

But that was what she said: "You've always been so right—" And then there was a pause, so that he asked again, thinking perhaps she hadn't understood: "Will you marry me, Eileen?"

And this time she said, "Yes," looking straight into his eyes, with that strangely searching look, as if she looked for something that was very far away. . . .

"My dear—" he said, and went around the desk, still holding to her hands, and drew her to her feet, and put his arms around her, feeling for a moment the pressure of her hands against his shoulders, holding back from his embrace, then yielding to it; and conscious, too, of being awkward, that the contours of their bodies did not seem to fit together, that he trod upon her slipper. He kissed her on the lips, but he could not see her eyes.

"Eileen, Eileen—" It was the greatest moment of his life.

They were married two weeks later, in a private dining room in the Blackstone Hotel, at high noon, or thereabout, so that they could catch the Century. He had not known where to go for a honeymoon, and Eileen seemed not to care, so he settled on New York—there were some business matters that he could attend to. "Why yes," she said, "I think that would be nice."

The wedding party was a motley one: her parents, and the clergyman they brought from Wyattville—not the Reverend Huntziger, who had long since been gathered to his fathers; Wayne and Cecily Wyatt, like a pair of fashion plates; Mitch Ballou, with frayed-out cuffs, muddy shoes, and uncombed hair; and Papa Kranz and Mama Kranz and Emilie, none of whom had seen Eileen until that day. He had meant to take her out there but—well, he never had. Papa Kranz was in high spirits, cracking jokes with everyone, but Mama Kranz looked sad, and Emilie was shy—she was eighteen that year. She had made a bouquet of lilies of the valley, as a bridal gift; and Eileen carried it, putting aside the one he had ordered from the florist.

"You darling child," she said. And when she pinned it on she took the other one, which was of orchids, and presented it to Emilie, saying that she wished it might bring her happiness and a husband of her own in proper time. And so it was that Emilie, blushing and confused, had held the bride's bouquet—

He had wanted Madge to come—some member of his family, but his father was ailing and she felt she shouldn't leave him. Just as well perhaps she didn't; the wedding was not gay. But he did not on the whole remember much about it except the way she looked—so trim and chic in her tailored traveling suit, and the lilies of the valley, and the sunlight on her hair—and her hand when he slipped the platinum band upon her finger, that it was cold as ice—

But that wouldn't be unusual when a girl was getting married. He, himself, was pretty nervous. And they'd had a strenuous time in those two weeks. They'd rented an apartment and bought the stuff to furnish it; it was being decorated, would be ready to walk into in ten days when they got back. They had even got a maid already hired. And Eileen had done most of it, shopping all day long for herself and for the house, and then having him go with her to see if he approved of the things she had picked out. It had all been pretty hectic, but through no fault of his. She had named the day herself. He hadn't dreamed that it would be so soon, had thought it might be months. "Why, any time," she said. "Tomorrow if you like."

Even the wedding had been hurried: he had kept an anxious eye upon his wrist watch while the minister was praying. And then there was a luncheon, or breakfast, as they called it, at which Mitch Ballou and Papa Kranz had saved the day, cracking jokes with everybody and proposing humorous toasts while the waiters ran about filling glasses with champagne. But in the midst of that they had left to catch the Century. It was then that Wayne had mentioned that his father and mother were somewhere on the ocean, coming home from England; he had had a cable from them. He named the ship and said that it would be amusing to meet them at the dock.

Old Mitch had grinned sarcastically, a little tight by now, and whispered in his ear, "You're a Wyatt now, my boy—one of the clan."

He had laughed good-naturedly, half pleased and half annoyed—concerned a little, too, at the thought of meeting them in this new relationship, as a member of the family, almost wishing he had chosen some other place to go. But he might have spared himself anxiety on this score: it would be a tragic meeting, but nothing he foresaw—yet it may have had a bearing on everything that followed—

But the truth was that the thing had started badly. It was hard to say just how; in a lot of little ways, as for example: he had never traveled in a drawing room before, but *she* had; when the Pullman car conductor stuck his head in at the door and greeted her by name—

"Mrs. Braden," she corrected.

And he had got it wrong, thinking she said Brady, and she had had to spell it. He lingered at the door, referring to the time when she used to travel with him going back and forth to college, and inquiring about Neill and her uncle and her aunt. The steward in the dining car remembered her at once, had something special for her—and how was all the family?—Little things like these, but important all the same: honeymooning in *reverse*—

They sat there after dinner, side by side, while the twilight faded out, and on into the darkness; and he had done the talking, as indeed he always did—the plays they'd see, the restaurants where they'd dine, this thing and that. He had written to the Holland House for a parlor-bedroom suite, asking for twin beds which were not common then, remembering she had chosen them for their room in the apartment, and he had approved her choice though the idea had been startling. He meant to do things right regardless of the cost; he had even ordered flowers. He mentioned the hotel, a fashionable one where he had never stayed, but *she* had. The porter came to make the berths—

They waited in the Observation car. He picked up a magazine, thumbing through the pages, holding it for her to see, not seeing it himself. When they went back he left her at the door, suggesting he would smoke a cigarette. He meant to be considerate. He had watched the minute hand creep round the dial—five minutes, ten, fifteen, in a tumult of emotion: excited and elated, frightened and confused—as any man might feel on that first night—

At length he knocked upon the door, then opened it a crack. "May I come in, Eileen?"

She answered from the darkness of the lower berth. But he could see —her hair undone and spreading on the pillow, the lace that trimmed the satin of her gown, her arm, her hand, the finger with the shiny platinum band—all that he had dreamed come true at last. He had wanted to kneel down and crush her in his arms, to melt into her body, to fuse himself with her—

"You're beautiful," he said.

"Sam, please—" She motioned him to come and sit beside her, and he had come and sat there on the bed, reaching for her hands, bending down to kiss her. But she had held him back with her hands against his breast, not pushing him away. "Please, wait—" she said. And he had waited. "There's something that I want to tell you, Sam—"

"Yes, dear?"

"You're such a good man, Sam—" She took his hands and held them, their fingers interlocked. "—good and kind and generous, with a very sensitive heart." Her fingers tightened. "I wouldn't want to hurt that."

"You never will," he said. He was very deeply touched; no one had ever said such things to him before.

"I wanted you to know—" she said, still holding to his hands, almost clinging to them. "I wanted you to know the way I felt about you. I trust you, Sam—trust you to understand. I want to be your wife, a good and loyal wife, to go with you hand in hand wherever you go. If only you will be a little patient with me?"

Perhaps the longest speech he had ever heard her make—

"Don't you worry about that." He laughed to reassure her, but his voice was close to tears—emotionally unstrung. It had all been pretty hectic: not knowing what was coming or what was expected of you, in the masculine position of having to decide. And of course in her case too: not knowing what he'd want, or take without the asking, and with no experience of it—things they had not discussed, not even mentioned. "Don't you worry," he repeated and felt her hands relax and the tension melt away. He spread the covers smooth and carefully tucked them in around her shoulders; and then he knelt beside her with his face quite close to hers. "I understand," he said. "And I'd like to be to you all that you think I am."

She thanked him with her eyes.

"Good night, my dear," he said and kissed her lips.

"Thank you, Sam," she whispered. "Thank you for everything—"

Strange wedding night perhaps. But was it any stranger than the other fellow's, about which you knew nothing? What should a wedding night be like—when two people meet in bed for the first time. You wouldn't like it if your wife took it in her stride, if she knew too much about it. And if that night had been strange, then what was to be said about the one that followed—

The day had dragged away—an interminable day of paralyzing strangeness, when the clock hands seemed to stop, when you went down to the office half a dozen times to ask about the trunk, to the newsstand for a magazine or paper, running out of conversation, not knowing what to do—reasonable enough for a man who was accustomed to a desk of piled-up work. They had got unpacked at last, clothes hung in the closets, toilet articles set out—embarrassing procedure. The rooms were pleasant ones, and there were flowers: daffodils and tulips, and a big vase of white lilac about which she exclaimed and which made him think of home—the old house in Shanty Town. They had lunched and gone to stroll along Fifth Avenue—

He had visited New York on hasty business trips, but he did not know the city—not the way *she* did. Like most Midwesterners he was a bit afraid of it, inclined to feel provincial, conscious of his dress as being not quite right, over-tipping waiters in an effort to convince them, complaining of the service, comparing everything with something in Chicago which was "just as good, or better"—mechanisms of defense against a rooted sense of inferiority. At the desk when they arrived, he had more than half expected that the clerk would greet Eileen as an old friend. And later at the newsstand, buying theater tickets, when it seemed he might not get the ones he wanted, he was tempted to explain: "For Elliott Wyatt's niece." He felt convinced that this would turn the trick—

They had dined in the hotel—an old-fashioned dining room, quiet and subdued, very elegant no doubt, but certainly not gay; and there were not many guests, most of them elderly; but Eileen had seemed to like it. It was restful in a way: people talked in lowered voices, and the tinkle of an ice cube could be heard across the room. The food was good —no better than the Palmer House but served with much more style, if you cared about such things. He wore his dinner coat, the first one he had owned; his pointed bat-wing collar kept scraping on his neck. Eileen was in an evening gown, black velvet, plain and rich, with just a sprig of lilac pinned against it—she never cared for jewelry. In the shaded candlelight her hair was like red gold. They talked about the wedding: how funny Mitch had looked, what Papa Kranz had said. It went off very well, beginning to feel comfortable. He left a dollar for the waiter—twice what he would have left at the Congress or the Blackstone, but he was in New York and on his honeymoon; and if you wanted service in a snooty town like this, you had to spend your money—

They took a taxi to the theater, threading through Times Square which was like Randolph Street, only brighter and more crowded, but really pretty thrilling. Their seats were excellent for a musical revue; the comedians were amusing and the chorus girls were pretty. He had one anxious moment when the curtain first went up, seeing someone on the stage that reminded him of Nelly; but this had happened many times before. Anyway he knew, if he stopped to think about it, that Nelly had long since outlived that sort of thing—she was thirty now.

He meant to look her up while he was here and find out for himself what she was doing—

Afterwards they went to Jack's, where he had been one time with some wallpaper acquaintances, but *she* had never been there. He felt that at last he had a chance to show her something; but the place seemed rough and noisy, not as he remembered it, and he was a little sorry that he had suggested it. But Eileen had seemed to like it: the Broadway atmosphere, sporting characters and people of the theater. She kept glancing round the room, calling his attention: "Look, Sam, over there; I thinks that's so-and-so." And he would smile and nod, but the faces that he saw were unfamiliar. They had a bite to eat and he had ordered wine, debating with the waiter like a connoisseur, but this was just a bluff—

He felt that things were coming on—the problem of last night dissolving in the light of a growing easiness in their relationship, of strangeness yielding to quickened habitude, for last night already seemed a thousand years away. They had sat together many times as they were sitting now—as they would go on through life, just the two of them; and this was solid ground to which they were accustomed. And then there was the wine which he was counting on; he kept filling up her glass, thinking well ahead of the moment they were in: You couldn't just go on *not making love*, for that habit could be formed like any other, and delay would but expand the dimensions of the obstacle. No, someone had to act, had to take the thing in hand before it was too late. And that was up to him—gently, yes, of course, but firmly all the same—

It was after two o'clock when they left the restaurant. In the taxi he put his arm around her and drew her, unresisting, close to him, her head upon his shoulder; and he held her hand and pressed it to his lips. He was passionately in love—

"Are you happy, Eileen?"

She nodded on his shoulder, her hair against his cheek, the fragrance of it almost more than he could bear—

He had let her go upstairs alone. A telegram which he must send, he said; but there was no telegram. He had gone into the bar which was on the point of closing, and had had a shot of bourbon, lingering over it, watching again the minute hand go round—five minutes, ten, fifteen. And then he had gone up, aflame with his desire, but certain in his mind—

"Are you in bed already?" he called cheerfully from the parlor.

"Long ago," she answered sleepily.

He glanced in at the door. The bedside lamp was lighted; she was lying with her head pillowed on her arm. "Have you had a happy day?"

"Yes, happy, Sam," she said.

"I'll be there in a jiffy."

She didn't answer that.

He had hurried with his toilet, undressing in the parlor where there was a closet for his things and a door into the bath—his silk pajamas, bought for the occasion, his slippers and his robe, his hair smoothed down, switching off the parlor light, coming on into the bedroom, humming something to himself from the show that they had seen, trying so hard to be casual—as if he were describing an habitual formula; but his hands were dripping wet and his heart was like a hammer—

She had turned her head so that she could see the door, and her eyes went with him as he moved about the room, fixing the shade, the window. Wide eyes they were, not sleepy in the least; and there was that look in them which he could not analyze and never had, but which in three years time would drive him almost mad, drive him into something like brutality—

His bed had been turned down. He threw his robe upon it, set his slippers side by side beneath the edge, snapped off the shaded light—

"Good night—" she said, with an interval between the words, as if they weren't the words she meant to say.

"Eileen, my darling—"

"Oh, Sam—" she said, and that was all. And she had lain still, not pulling back from him, not struggling with his hands, passive, non-resistant. He had kept on talking to her—love names and love words, broken passionate phrases, urging her toward him, to rouse her to response, but gently, very gently—until at length the matter had passed beyond control and there was no turning back—

It had not been a success, even measured with his second-rate experiences—a stenographer or two, and semi-, or professional, prostitute. In terms of Cassie Cole— But this was not a memory that he wanted to recall, and yet all through the years it would present itself, would stand there for comparison despite his every effort to suppress it. It had not been a success, that was enough to say—like ravishing a woman who had been drugged unconscious, or as you might imagine such a thing would be, like taking something from her with nothing to give back—not anything she wanted, or that made it worth the doing, that divided it from obscene ugliness—

But was this a rare experience?—or the common course of marriage?

And how was one to tell? Perhaps it often started out this way—as *he* had started. And he saw himself again, a frightened little boy, standing in the warehouse among the tumbled barrels, with the thunder and the lightning and the beating of the rain—and his agony of soul, shame and remorse—

He had wakened in the night with the pain of that remembrance, melancholy and depressed, seeing some strange parallel between himself, the child, and the girl whom he had married—trudging through the mud along the levee in his ragged, torn shirt, with the fish pole on his shoulder; sorry—oh, so sorry. He felt he couldn't stand it not to tell her so—to put his arms around her and ask her to forgive him, to assure her that he understood, that it would be all right. He wanted to reach out and touch her hand, but not to wake her. But perhaps she was awake, thinking in the dark. He listened for her breathing, and then suddenly he knew she was not there. Panic gripped his heart. He lit the bedside lamp; her bed was empty. He sprang up, running to the door, groping for the light switch—

"Eileen!"

And then she answered, and a wave of such relief went flooding through him. What had he been afraid of? He could never answer that —not in rational words. That she was gone?—gone *where*? It was ridiculous; and yet it would always be like that—that panic feeling clutching at his heart—

She was sitting by the window, a dressing gown around her. There was a clock on the marble mantlepiece it was near morning—

"What are you doing, dear?"

"Nothing," she said.

"But why, Eileen?"

"I wasn't sleepy."

"Oh—" He pulled a chair close and sat down. "Is it something to do with me?"

She shook her head.

"I'm sorry if it is."

No answer.

"I don't know what to say—"

"It isn't anything."

"But I think it must be, dear?"

No answer.

There was no use going over that: the endless questions and the empty answers which never gave a foothold to go on. You couldn't pour your heart out into eyes that were not there—not resentful or reproachful, but inscrutably remote. And it hadn't to do with what he had thought then—or, if it had, what of it? It was a part of her which had intrigued him greatly, even as a child: the enigma of her eyes; but you couldn't live with it. You simply never *knew*—

Perhaps it would have yielded if they had been let alone to survive their honeymoon, if tragedy had not come knocking at the door—not bringing them together, as indeed it might have done had it been *theirs* instead of hers—

He had ordered breakfast and was in the bathroom, shaving. When he came into the parlor she was sitting at the table with the morning paper spread across her lap, and her face as white as chalk. She held the paper up for him to see the headlines, great black letters spread across the page: " 'S. S. Titanic' Lost." At first it hadn't registered—

"Uncle Elliott," she said.

"Good God!" He took the paper from her. The "Titanic" had collided with an iceberg off Newfoundland in the night—that night while they were sitting in the theater or the restaurant. It had sunk despite the fact that it was unsinkable, the final word in luxury, security, and speed, racing through the ice-encumbered ocean in the dark to break a record on its maiden voyage—to win a rag of bunting. It had gone to the bottom in two hours and a half. Two thousand people were on board her; no one could say as yet how many had been lost. Ships had been summoned by the wireless, and several had responded. The "Carpathia" had arrived upon the scene and rescued some survivors—

"Look here," he said and pointed to the line. "They'll be all right, Eileen."

She shook her head. She didn't cry—not then or afterwards.

He went on reading—the names of notables who had been among the passengers: Astor, Ismay, Widener, Guggenheim the copper king—like a page out of the peerage. Among the titans, lower down, was Wyatt. He felt a little thrill to see it in that list. He was deeply sympathetic and concerned, but on her account alone. Elliott and Daphne did not belong to him, had no claim on his emotions; he hardly knew them. He kept assuring her that they would be all right, reflecting to himself that people of importance always managed to be rescued, urging her to eat some breakfast. He was hungry but he felt that it would appear unfeeling if he ate his eggs and bacon in the face of her distress. He drank a cup of coffee and nibbled at the toast—

The telephone broke in—prelude to endless ringing. It was Wayne in

Highland Park. He had already talked with Neill in Florida; they were coming on at once, both he and Becky. He had also phoned to Wyattville and talked with Uncle Henry who was not well enough to make the trip; Wayne had advised him not to, for the present anyway. He, himself, and Cecily were leaving on the Century and would go straight to the Plaza where his father always kept a suite of rooms. He asked for Sam to keep in touch with White Star Line officials, and to wire to the Century any news that he could get—

"Why yes, of course—" he said.

He had gone down on the subway, eager to escape the bleakness of the room, repeatedly assuring her that it would be all right, that disasters of this sort were always magnified—

"Don't you worry, dear," he said. "I'll have good news for you. I'll stay there till I get it."

There was a crowd outside the White Star office, and a long line to the door with all kinds of people in it—shabby and well dressed, men and women, even children, and many foreign faces—with nothing common to them except the haunting fear that filled their eyes. They were silent for the most part, like people at a funeral. And there were policemen moving back and forth, keeping the sidewalk clear, being kind but firm about it. He waited for a while but the line seemed not to move; it appeared they were not letting people in. They were posting bulletins inside the windows and the news was whispered back along the line: " 'Carpathia' proceeding to New York with rescued passengers. List of names not yet complete." He stepped out of the line and started toward the door, but a policeman stopped him—

"Wyatt" he said. "I want to go in there."

The policeman shook his head, but then a man came up, who had overheard his words, an employee of the company—

"Mr. Wyatt?" he inquired. "Yes certainly, of course. Please come with me, sir." And the door had opened for them. And then he saw that there were others like himself, waiting in the room, leaning on the counter, pacing back and forth, sitting on some benches—men with anxious eyes, women with tearstained faces; and the clerks behind the counter, not doing anything. Now and then a name was called—familiar names they were—and the person would go back into a private office, and would presently emerge with relief upon his face or a dead look in his eyes. One woman who had fainted, was carried from the room—

· The man came back to him. There was no news as yet, but when his name was called, he could go into the office—

He waited a long time. It was after noon before his summons came. A haggard looking man, seated at a desk, asked him to sit down—

"Mr. Wyatt?" he inquired.

"Braden is the name. My wife—"

"Oh yes," the man had politely interrupted explanation. "Well, Mr. Braden, I have good news for you. Mr. Elliott Wyatt is on board the Carpathia."

"Thank God," he said, realizing now the strain he had been under. "And Mrs. Wyatt?"

"I regret to say we have as yet no news of Mrs. Wyatt."

"You mean—" He hesitated. "You mean she may be on the ship with Mr. Wyatt?"

"She is not on the 'Carpathia,' Mr. Braden."

"Oh—"

"But possibly some ship without a wireless—" It was plain to see he did not think so.

"There is no other inquiry to make?"

"I'm afraid not at the moment."

And he had left the office, passing by the silent people still waiting in the street; had sent a telegram to Wayne and telephoned Eileen: Elliott was safe and sound on the "Carpathia," but there was no news of Daphne yet. But this didn't mean a thing: the lists were not complete, and likely as not she was on another ship which did not have a wireless.

But he was certain then that she was lost; and he was right, for Daphne Wyatt—born Daphne Wayne of Boston—had gone down with the "Titanic."

She had run back from the lifeboat to which she had been assigned, and in which she had a place—a boat which had been saved, into which she had been tricked, being told that her husband was to join her. But there were not boats enough. And she had realized the kindly meant deception before the boat was lowered, seeing in it with her only women and children and some members of the crew; and had sprung back to the deck, though a steward tried to stop her, tearing from her shoulders the ermine wrap she wore. She had gone back to find him, in her flimsy evening gown and satin slippers, crawling on the deck which now was slanting steeply toward the bow, in darkness and confusion, for the lights had been extinguished and there were struggling people, mad with fear. And she had found him, standing with his back against the wall, outside the smoking room, his hands in the pockets of his English overcoat, a life belt on his shoulder which he had not strapped around him, a cigarette between his lips—Yes, he had mentioned that, that it had been the last one in his case, that he had smiled about it, thinking to himself he would never need another—

He had told them—pacing back and forth across the lovely room, the parlor of the suite they lived in at the Plaza, which looked across the park and was furnished with their things: rich oriental rugs, a grand piano, fine paintings on the walls, a portrait of his wife in a red hunting jacket, smiling from the canvas with cool, appraising eyes. And the room was filled with flowers; but it wasn't like a funeral, though that was what it was.

He had told them—smoking endless cigarettes, sitting down and getting up; not weeping, not depressed, but with funny little changes in his voice, and a kind of exaltation, though that might not be the word for it, which was *his* and like *himself*—like the white carnation in the lapel of his coat, like the way his clothes were cut, his hair was combed —like his hat, a little cocked—like he held his walking stick.

He had told them—all sitting there around him: Neill and Becky, Wayne and Cecily, and Eileen—and himself, Sam Braden, a Wyatt for the day and by the grace of God, sitting there among them, feeling awkward and uncomfortable; thinking what he'd say before he spoke; thinking of *his* sisters, *his* brother, and *his* father; conscious of the fact that he did not belong and never could, and that his wife was one of them—

He had told them from the start: how, at dinner with some friends, the ship had seemed to swerve, enough to slide the dishes on the table; and there had been the feeling that something brushed her side, from which she had been turned, but not quite soon enough. The contact had been gentle, not alarming in the least; and there had been a sound— like tearing cloth. They had gone on with their dinner: it was a gala evening and there were many parties; no one had been concerned. They were nearing the end of a record-breaking voyage to defeat the "Maure-tania," to win the championship of the Atlantic; and it seemed that they had done it on this day. There had been heavy gambling on the issue, and the winners were elated—champagne corks were popping, everyone was gay—

But later, in the lounge, one of the officers with whom he was acquainted, had caught his eye and motioned him to come out on the deck; and had confided to him that the accident was serious: the ship had brushed against the submerged shoulder of an iceberg. He pointed to it—looming like a mountain in the starlight, not far off and plainly visible. The ship's hull had been ripped, a long slit like a knife wound; and the sea was pouring into her. They were pumping and had hope that the water would not gain, if the bulkheads, which confined the damaged section, could withstand the pressure on them. Signals of distress had been sent by wireless; the "Carpathia" was close by and coming to the scene, and there were other ships not far away. He was notifying some of the passengers he knew, on whom he felt he could rely, asking them to use their efforts to avert alarm or panic, to minimize the matter. He called attention to the deck which was slanting slightly toward the bow—to the fact that the engines had been stopped, that the lights were dimmed a little. It would be enough to say that the ship had grazed some object in the water: a propeller had been damaged, and repairs were being made—

It was near midnight then. Of course he had agreed to do anything he could. He had rejoined his party, repeating what he had been asked to say, managing to circulate the story. He had not told anybody what he knew, not even Daphne, but she had been quick to note a change in his demeanor. Perhaps he had appeared overconfident about it, making light of something that was obviously alarming, for the slanting of the deck was very noticeable now. Still the gaiety went on—orchestras and dancing, and the champagne corks kept popping. Daphne had been wonderful, taking side with him at once, not asking any questions, pretending unconcern, reassuring other women. He had never seen her cooler or more sure of herself; and he knew now that she knew, and that this was her response—

He paused for a moment, fingering a button on his coat, buttoning it, unbuttoning it. "You would have been proud of her," he said.

Many of the passengers had already gone to bed when the alarm was sounded: shrill electric bells ringing everywhere; a voice that spoke through some kind of megaphone, saying that the ship would be abandoned, telling people what to do and where to go—half heard, not understood; and stewards running here and there, trying to explain to confused and frightened questioners what they did not really know. In the midst of this commotion he had met his friend, the officer; and the man had told him frankly that the ship could not survive, and there were not boats enough for more than half the passengers. "Women and children first" would be the rule of course, and the rest must take their chances. "Rather slim ones," he remarked. "And thank you, Mr. Wyatt, for lending us a hand,"—taking time to mention that, and the time was growing short—

He had told Daphne then, but not mentioning the fact that the boats were insufficient. And she had answered him that she knew it all along, from when he first came back after being called away, had read it in his face, in every word he uttered. She had laughed about it, saying, "If the brokers on the stock exchange knew you as well as I do, you would never make a penny."

They had gone down to their cabins which were on the deck below, to change to other clothes and to pack some things to take; and had found their steward there, as polite and calm as ever—a little cockney fellow they had traveled with before. He had urged them not to spend any time about their clothes, but to take warm wraps with them, not to bother with their luggage. The deck was slanting then so it was hard to stand without holding onto something. The steward volunteered to show them to their boat, but discreetly winked his eye when he was saying it—

He had understood the wink, but not knowing what to do, how to contrive the matter—being sure in his mind that if he told the truth, she would refuse to leave him. Yet how could he deceive her at a moment of this kind?—not even with a chance to say good-by. He had kept his face averted lest she should see the anguish in his eyes, kept silent lest his voice betray him. In the end he left his overcoat, pretending to remember it when they were on the deck: "I've come without my coat, dear. I'll just run back and get it."

"No, please!" She held his arm. "Let the steward get it for you."

But the steward knew his business. "Very sorry, ma'am," he said, "but my station's at the boat. Mr. Wyatt can go back; it'll only take a minute." And he pointed out the boat—where it would be on the boat deck overhead.

"Then I'll go too," she said.

But he had persuaded her—that the boats might well be crowded, and if she were on hand she could hold a place for him which might otherwise be taken. She had hesitated then, and the steward had cut in—

"That's a very good idea, sir."

And she had yielded to it, urging him to hurry, going with the steward who took her arm to help her climb the slanting deck, disappearing in the darkness among distracted figures running aimlessly around. He had not expected to see her after that—

He paused again, feeling the flower in his coat lapel, turning his head to smell it.

There was confusion now, the edge of panic—people swarming on the deck, in evening dress, in night clothes, as they had got out of bed;

cursing, praying, weeping, or silent with despair; women looking for their husbands, children wakened from their sleep and dragged crying from the cabins; officers and sailors rushing here and there, trying to maintain discipline and order, pleading, shouting, threatening—

He had gone back to the cabin and got his overcoat, and a life belt which he hung across his shoulder. And coming from the cabin he had run into the steward—

"I was looking for you, sir," the little cockney said. "I thought you'd like to know I put her in the boat. They'll be lowering it away any minute now."

"Why, thank you," he had answered, reaching in his pocket for some change to fee the man, finding it was empty—

"It'll do another time, sir," the steward had said, smiling.

He had gone back to the deck, making his way—out of custom probably, for he had not thought about it—to the place where they had had their deck chairs, where they had sat together through the voyage, warmly wrapped in steamer blankets, reading, chatting with their neighbors. He had stood there with his back against the cabin wall, in the dark, out of the way; and had lit a cigarette, the last one in his case—

And then—well, there she was—

"Did you think I'd go without you?" That was what she said. "Oh, Elliott, how stupid!—after all these years!—Did you think I would go back to Neill and Wayne, and tell them that I left you on a sinking ship? Elliott! Elliott!"

He stopped talking for a moment, standing at the window, looking out across the park. It was beginning to be dusk. Cecily was crying but none of the others were. And then he turned to look at the portrait of her; his lip was quivering, but, as he looked, the tremor passed away.

He had held her in his arms, so glad that she had come—not caring for their lives, so that they were together. He had taken off his overcoat and made her put it on, against her protest. And he had put the life belt on her shoulders, knotting the straps around her. Perhaps that had been wrong; the heavy coat from which she could not extricate herself, which would be very heavy in the water. He had found another life belt for himself, and she had tied it for him—

They had waited a long time, hands clasped, not talking, while the deck beneath their feet kept slanting more and more. Third class and steerage passengers had been assembled forward, but the bow was under water and the sea was eating at them. They came clambering aft at last in hideous panic, like frightened animals, breaking through the lines

« 223 »

which the sailors tried to hold. There was no order after that, no authority or discipline. And there were ugly scenes which he could not describe, wanted only to forget; and a few that he would treasure in his memory, of nobility and courage—

The sea had come to them, inch by inch along the deck. It was calm but with a swell, scarcely noticeable until it broke against the rail— breaking, washing back in foaming froth. And it was icy cold. He remembered how it felt when first it touched his ankles—like wading on the beach, not wanting to go in. They had not retreated from it, from the place where they were standing, near the middle of the ship; and at last they were alone there. And the water had come higher, to their knees and to their waists—like crawling ice—

They had gone together, hand in hand. But you couldn't swim that way. She had released her hand, saying they must swim to keep themselves from freezing, from becoming numb and helpless. She was the better swimmer. He had kept close beside her, kicking off his shoes, calling out to her—and then suddenly her voice was not so close. It was difficult to say what it was like, even to recall it: the darkness, and the swell which kept coming in between; and debris in the water, washing all around; and other swimmers too, fighting for their lives, crying out in strangling voices—

"Daphne, where are you?"

"I'm all right, dear. Go on."

"Daphne!" He had swum in the direction of her voice—of where she seemed to be. "Daphne!"

"I'm all right, dear." But her voice was fainter, farther off.

He had not heard it again—

He had kept on swimming, searching for her, calling, until he was exhausted—which perhaps had saved his life, had kept a spark of warmth alive inside him. He had not wanted to live; had tried, in his despair, to take his life belt off so that it might be ended, but his fingers were too numb to undo the canvas straps which she had tied—

The ship had sunk at last, sliding gently to its grave, belching clouds of sparks out of its funnels. There were no longer any voices in the water. He had lost track of time. Some sailors on a raft had dragged him out to safety. Then the "Carpathia" came—

It seemed that he had finished. He stood before the fireplace, looking at her portrait. It was quite dark in the room. Neill got up and went to him, and put his arm around his shoulders, affectionately—the way a man's son didn't do—

"It's all right, Father," he said gently. "That's the way she'd want it."

A dramatic, tragic story— Tragic, too, for *him*: end of a honeymoon, of one that never started. You couldn't make much love with that thing in between you. But Elliott survived. He had another wife now—young and beautiful and rich, and an office in New York, money pouring in. He had seen him not long since, walking down La Salle Street, as debonair as ever, carnation in his buttonhole, hat cocked jauntily, swinging his walking stick—

End of a honeymoon—of one that hadn't started, and never was to start, though he hadn't known that then; he had thought it was postponed, to be presently resumed when they got back to Chicago—when they were settled down—when this, when that—

The days had dragged away there in New York. She had spent much time with them—naturally enough—with her uncle and the boys, with Cecily and Becky. The telephone kept ringing, and it would be one of them—or she would be calling up. She would mention an engagement, apologetically: she had been so close to Elliott and Daphne ever since she was a child, like a member of their family—

"Why yes, of course," he said, "I understand."

"Won't you come to lunch with us, Sam, at the Plaza?"

But he would get out of it, alleging some excuse of business to attend to. And one day it was Nelly whom he said he must look up.

"Would you like me to go with you?"

"Well—" He hesitated. "—I guess right now you ought to be with them." And she hadn't urged the matter, as he had hoped she would.

He had gone to Nelly's address: a shabby boarding house in the thirties, west of Broadway—a neighborhood of tenements and decaying brownstone fronts, with ragged children playing in the gutters, and the smell of garbage from the cans along the sidewalk. He was glad he was alone, that Eileen had not come with him. The slatternly woman who responded to his ring, said Miss Braden didn't live there any more. She had moved away to Brooklyn; and she gave him the address on a mussy scrap of paper.

It proved to be remote and hard to find. He had gone in the subway, and finally in a cab, to a region not far from Coney Island—to another boarding house, as shabby as the first, but at least there was fresh air. He wished that he had written, or sent a telegram, for her to come and meet him in New York—

Yes, the woman told him, Miss Braden did live there. She was working for the movies out in Flatbush—the Vitagraph, they called it, or something of the kind. She told him how to get there, and he went on in the cab—

They came to it at last, over muddy, rutted roads, in the middle of a prairie, with a rough board fence around it—like a small-town county fair ground out of season. Grouped around the entrance gate were several shack-like buildings which appeared to be the offices; and in front of one of them, which was labeled "Casting," there were some signs of life—cheap-looking people hanging round, and going in and out—young men and girls. He went in and inquired of a youth who was lounging in a chair with his feet cocked on a desk—

"Braden?" The fellow took his feet down with an effort. "What does she do?"

"She's an actress, I believe."

"They all believe that, brother." He ran a grubby finger down a list. "Nope—no actress of that name is working here."

"I was told she was employed here."

"Would you know her if you saw her?"

"It's my sister."

"Oh, your sister, eh?" He lit a cigarette, scratching the match along the counter. "Well, go inside and have a look around." He motioned toward a door that stood open to the lot.

He went out into a cluttered and incredible confusion, a bad dream come to life: streets of canvas houses which had no backs to them; fragments of this and that, half torn down, like victims of an elfish cyclone; town streets with stores and lampposts, and woolly-Western ones with saloons and hitching rails—silent and deserted; stagecoaches without horses, streetcars without trolleys; rooms with two walls missing and no ceilings over them—a nightmare realized. But somewhere on beyond him he could hear sounds of life, voices shouting to each other.

He went on through the tawdry desolation, and at last came to the place—an oriental scene, a narrow teeming street of quaint bazaars, crowded with people, blacked up and wearing turbans: shopkeepers and street vendors, veiled ladies, dancing girls, beggars with wooden bowls, porters leading donkeys, children, even babies—all standing round and waiting, smoking cigarettes, laughing, cracking jokes. And at the end of it, where he had come upon it, were some cameras on a platform and young fellows in their shirt sleeves, and a man in golfing knickers on the platform with the cameras, sitting in a camp chair, shouting through a megaphone—

"Okay," he bellowed. "Go!"

The fellows at the cameras began to turn the cranks; and suddenly the scene began to move, everybody doing something: beggars begging, children playing, shopkeepers selling things, hucksters trotting with their poles, donkeys led along—as if you had been transported into another world. It was really amazing, and he had stood there watching, close beside the camera platform, forgetting for the moment the purpose of his visit—

The man with the megaphone kept shouting all the time with furious impatience: "You fellow in the silk shop, keep talking to that woman. You want to sell her something, understand?" —"Pick that baby up; his pants are coming off."—"Keep moving all of you."—"You beggar up in front, quit mugging at the camera."—"Keep that donkey moving."— "Keep moving, all of you, just the way I told you."—"Okay now, start the elephant."

And an elephant came lumbering down the street, right toward the camera platform. It was all done up in fancy trappings, and a fellow on its head was clawing at its ears with a kind of pointed stick, urging it along; and there was a howdah on it with a blonde girl sitting in it, looking beautiful and dumb; and a crowd rocking along on either side —dancing girls and beggar girls, and negroes carrying trays of fruit upon their heads—

They were coming right along, right at the camera, and one of the beggar girls who was dressed in tattered rags, with black smudges on her face, and her hair all in a tangle, kept running out in front, holding up her wooden bowl, begging for alms, salaaming, kneeling down— jumping up just in time to get out of the way. It was really pretty dangerous, for if she missed her footing or was a moment late, she ran a first-class chance of being stepped on—

He overheard the fellow with the megaphone, say to another, with weary irritation, "Look at that goddam woman, taking chances with her life!"

And the fellow laughed and answered, "What the hell does she care —if she gets a little footage."

And the man with the megaphone had shouted at her then, "Get away from that elephant, you fool!" And she had gone right on, as if she hadn't heard him, begging and salaaming, but minding what he said and not getting close again.

"Cut," the fellow yelled. The scene was ended; the cameramen stopped grinding, and a moment later everyone was back doing what he pleased—squatting in the street, smoking cigarettes, chatting with each other. The girl on the elephant, who was dressed up like a princess in a maze of beads and bangles, was coming down a ladder, being snooty and snappy with the men who tried to help her—

He had remembered then what he was doing there, and had been on the point of making inquiry of someone, when suddenly the beggar girl with the smudges on her face, came rushing up to him and threw her arms around him—

"Sam! Oh, Sam!" she cried. "I'm so glad you were here. Isn't it just wonderful!"

She called to a man who had led one of the donkeys, and he came over and was introduced as Pete—a big-boned, stalwart fellow with the figure of a life guard and a shock of curly hair, the kind that women fall for—the man she was to marry a few months later on, and from whom in due course would be divorced. He hadn't liked the fellow who was stupid and pretentious. There was something about him that suggested Wilfred Ashby.

He took them both to dinner at a place in Coney Island. And Nelly drank a cocktail—three in fact: three Martinis in a row, pouring them down as if accustomed to it. It had been startling to him, a little bit disturbing. And she smoked a cigarette, inhaling like a veteran. He hadn't liked it. And, too, he had been shocked at her appearance when he saw her in her street clothes with the makeup off: she was no longer young; her hair was black, but it had been different colors, streaks of which remained; the expression in her eyes held pain and hardness. She talked with animation as she always had, but when she wasn't talking she seemed not to be there, to go back into herself.

Mostly they had talked about themselves: happenings on the lot, the picture they were making, in the argot of show business, not always comprehensible; and they had attacked the food like people who were hungry. They were working as extras, she explained—five bucks a day when they were called—

"Just for a lark," Pete added.

She knew of course about his marriage, and had said some gushy things without real interest in them. And the "Titanic," too! Poor Daphne. What a tragedy! And she was back again in the world of make-believe and painted canvas—

"Did you see me, Sam?—flirting with the elephant?"

He nodded.

"I made it up myself. I guess they'll notice that."

"If it doesn't get cut out," Pete volunteered.

"Why would it?" she said angrily. "Can't I ever get a break?"

"I heard him call you down."

"I should worry. I got in ahead of him."

Pete took time to look around—at women whose attention his broad shoulders had attracted.

"Anyway my stuff was good. When the producer sees it, he won't let him cut it out."

"Sure," Pete agreed and changed the subject to a topic that involved himself—a long, dull story about a Broadway play in which he had had a part.

She wasn't listening now; her eyes were far away, or turned inward to herself. Once or twice he thought her lips moved, as if she were conversing with a hidden guest. They talked about the movies which had come to stay, she thought, might even make it tough for the theater after while. Pete laughed contemptuously.

"Go on and laugh," she said, "but pictures are okay. Sure they're cheap, just what the public wants; and they're run by pushcart Jews —I know all that. Don't let anybody kid you that those pantspressers aren't smart. Why, out in Hollywood—"

"Hollywood!" Pete snickered. "I'll stick to Broadway, baby."

"What for?" she said. "What's Broadway done for you—for either of us?"

"Oh well—" He winced and came up smiling. "Did I tell you that I had a call from Shubert?"

"Sure, you told me—everybody on the lot." She shrugged disparagement. "But I'll take my chance in pictures. I'll be in on the ground floor while the rest of you high-hat them. I'll be sitting pretty, see?—while you're sitting on your tail, waiting for some guy to call you up. I'd go to Hollywood—in a minute, any day."

And this was Nelly talking. It hurt him—hurt his pride and hurt his heart. He parted with them at the subway entrance; they would take a streetcar home. He suggested she come over and dine with them some night, and was secretly relieved when she said she couldn't promise, as much as she would love it. She had to stick around close to the phone, she said, and they often called you in the evening. She'd been working every day and hoped it would keep on, but still you never knew. She felt that at last she was really getting started, and it would be too bad to miss a chance. She knew he'd understand.

"Oh yes, of course," he said. "But phone us if you can."

"Give my love to Eileen, Sam."

"I will."

"And come out again if you get a chance."

"OK. So long—"

That was six years ago—April, 1912—and he had not seen her since. She had gone to Hollywood after the divorce, but nothing came of it. He had sent her the money to come back.

It had been close to midnight when he got to the hotel, heartsick and weary, to find a note from Eileen waiting for him: she was spending the evening with her uncle and the family; Neill or Wayne would bring her home. He had gone to bed and gone to sleep, and she did not wake him when she came—

End of a honeymoon—of one that never started.

They had gone back to Chicago on the day that he had planned, and had found the apartment ready for them: the maid in cap and apron, flowers in the vases, provisions in the icebox, everything complete. And the days and months and years had slipped away—

He had been very busy, leaving early in the morning before she would be up, getting home in time for dinner, sometimes working Sundays. The business kept on growing and the building on Canal Street was no longer equal to it. He was planning the new factory, absorbed in calculations, coming home with rolls of blueprints to decipher in his study—or sitting in the living room, when he had read the paper, figuring to himself, drumming on the chair arm. And she would read or sew, or go to the piano and play softly to herself, not to disturb his thought. They went sometimes to the theater, invited friends to dinner, or went to dine with them—a normal life in fact, on the surface anyway—

They didn't quarrel. But the gap between them, which never had been closed, kept getting steadily wider—so gradually of course that you didn't realize it except by looking back. In time he had quit trying to do anything about it, saying to himself that it was the normal course of married life, but never quite believing it. There was nothing to complain of, to put your finger on: his home was nicely ordered; his wife was beautiful, educated, cultured—complaisant to his marital attentions, unresisting, unprotesting. There was nothing to find fault with except —he was *alone*, separated from her by that enigmatic thing which you couldn't come to grips with, couldn't touch. And the fault he didn't find, and pretended wasn't there, was growing all the time into a deeply rooted sense of injury and resentment, which must break out some day —as in the end it did—

The twenty-third of June, 1915. But that was a coincidence. He had noticed the item in the paper in the morning, having breakfast by himself: Becky's suit for a divorce—a brief complaint which specified desertion, discreetly reported by the press. He was startled, not concerned—why should he be? He had not gone in to her with the paper in his hand, saying, "Look at this, Eileen!"—nor saying to the maid, "Show this to Mrs. Wyatt." He had left it on the table, not open at the place. And he had not thought about it through the day, having more important things with a claim to his attention—

But at dinner he had mentioned it: "Oh, by the way, did you see the morning paper?—about Neill and Becky?"

Yes, she nodded, she had seen it.

"Weren't you surprised?"

She hadn't said she was, or that she wasn't.

"Have you heard any rumors they were having trouble?"

She shook her head.

"Do you think there's someone else?"

"I have no notion, Sam."

"That she might be involved?"

She shrugged and spread her hands.

"Or he perhaps?"

"Possibly—" she said.

"You haven't heard from Neill?"

"Not lately."

"And no hint of any trouble?"

"No, nothing."

And that had been all of that—all that he remembered. The evening had been like any other one. They had sat in the living room; she had gone to the piano and played some old-time pieces—very lovely in the lamplight, in a filmy sort of house gown and her hair done some new way, piled high upon her head, invitingly exposing the whiteness of her neck, and the perfume that she used, which had its own seduction: an exquisite daintiness which was sometimes irresistible—

He had gone to her that night—waiting long after the light had been extinguished, debating with himself as he had often done, yielding at last to a kind of passionate loneliness, for the edge of his defeat was not yet completely blunted and he still sought to possess, in fullness and entirety, the woman he had married—

And then he had awakened, listening for her breathing, certain she was gone; and had got up to find her, with that panic feeling stirring, but with something else beside it: a burning sense of injury and resentment which could not any longer be suppressed—

She was sitting in the study with a white robe wrapped around her—sitting in the dark; she had not been quick enough to light the lamp before his finger pressed the button on the wall. There was something in her lap which she tucked from sight behind her. He spoke abruptly, irritably:

"What are you doing?"

"Nothing—" He thought that she looked startled, perhaps aware of something new in him.

"Why aren't you in bed?"

"I was restless—"

"Restless?—why?"

No answer.

"Why?—I'm asking you."

"I don't know, Sam."

"Are you sick? Is something wrong?"

She shook her head.

"Are you worried?—or unhappy?"

No answer.

"What about?" She kept looking at him steadily, but through him and beyond him, with a pucker in her forehead. He thought she had been crying, but she wasn't crying then. It was a warm still night. He sat down at the desk across from her, noticing the clock—a little after four. "What have you got there?"

"What?"

"Behind you?"

"Nothing—" Her hands were in her lap.

"But yes you have, Eileen. You had something in your hands when I came in."

No answer. He started to get up, to find out for himself.

"My gown," she said.

"Your gown?"

"My nightgown—" She took it from behind her—pink silk and lace, crumpled in a ball.

"But why?" He stared at it.

No answer.

"Why did you take it off?"

"It was mussed," she said a little desperately.

"Oh, mussed?" He nodded at her.—It was reasonable enough: quite possibly the gown had been uncomfortable—anyway she was fastidious about the things she wore. But resentment and injury were transported into fury, as any spark at all would have served to set them off.— "Mussed by *me*, you mean?"

She winced but kept on looking steadily at him.

And he had gone on talking, without any check upon him, goaded by her silence and enigmatic eyes into rash and bitter accusations—things that not till then had he even known he'd thought; really pleading with indictment for an answer, to sting her to denial, to defend herself, attack him—anything but silence which had become intolerable. He had raised his voice and shouted, beside himself with anger; had stamped across the room to take the nightgown from her lap and rip it into rags and fling it in the wastebasket—

"I have never had a wife," he said at last.

And she had answered now, her face as white as the robe around her shoulders: "Why are you doing this?—What is it that you want?"

"What do I want?" He leaned with his fists upon the desk. "I'll tell you what:" he said, "something I can't buy for a five dollar bill in any sporting house."

"Oh—" She had drawn in her breath, with a spasm in her face—as if she had been struck.

And that had been the end of it. Brutal, ugly words that could never be unsaid, no matter how you tried—and he *had* tried.

She had never worn her wedding ring again, and he had never seemed to notice that she didn't. He had never kissed her lips after that night. Funny she hadn't left him the next day, as he had been in terror that she would; but she was there when he came home that night. His things had been moved into the guest room, put away in perfect order; and he had accepted that, thankful at the moment that it was no worse. They had gone on together two more years, if you could call it that; though in fact not very different from the three that came before, except that now he had no hope about it. . . .

The story had run out, come back to where it started. He had been walking for an hour, and here was his hotel—comfortable and desolate. He crossed the empty lobby, with its chairs in summer slip covers, sticking up like tombstones, to the clerk behind the counter. There was a letter for him, a thick envelope from Madge. She wrote long detailed letters. "Any phone calls?"—"No, nothing, Mr. Braden." He took his key and went up in the elevator to a pleasant corner room which looked across the park. He had started with a suite, thinking to have people in sometimes, maybe little supper parties, intending to replace the hotel furnishings with things from the apartment, which had been put in storage, to have vases filled with flowers. But some cases of books were all he sent for; and he hadn't used the parlor, for guests or anything, and so after a time he gave it up. It was no use wasting money.

He sat down by the window and opened Madge's letter, skimming through it hastily: Father kept quite well though the heat had been severe. The town had made him *honorary* Marshal, which had pleased him very much, testifying to his faithful service for so many years. He would still receive his salary, in the nature of a pension, but would not be expected to take any active part. Young Henry and his wife had moved into the hotel, the new one on Main street which was opposite the bank—very startling to the neighbors. They had their house in Long Beach, Mrs. Henry said, and the big house was too big and hard to care for. The old place was already running down, the lawn was in a mess. Young Henry had tried to sell it to the town for a library or something, but the town had declined with carefully worded thanks. It was rumored that Young Henry had had losses. People said that a man couldn't run a bank and spend half his time in California. The old warehouse on the levee had come to grief again; the button factory had not been a success. People blamed it on the war. There was a lot of sickness, this awful influenza, everybody wearing masks to keep the germs out. She wished that he could see her garden which was at its best right now, petunias big as saucers— He skipped all that.—Oh yes, Cassie Cole was back in town— He frowned and read on carefully.—She had suddenly appeared, looking much the way she did when she was a girl—slim and brown and pretty. She was living with her mother, taking care of her, doing sewing and the like. Cora Lee had been so poorly since— But perhaps he hadn't heard: Peewee was dead in France, killed by a German bullet—

He put the letter down.—So Peewee Cole was dead—the funny little black boy, killed by a German bullet. Little Peewee Cole—running from the storm with his fish pole and the bullheads—playing in the yard—doing homework in the kitchen. He saw his face again, as he had seen it last, in the mirror of the bar, all the laughter faded out of it, furtive and ashamed, edging toward the door while that pig-eyed German fellow smashed the glasses on the floor—glasses that a black man's lips had touched—

It was still broad daylight—hot and muggy. He debated what to do —go down to the dreary dining room, eat by himself? He ordered some food sent to his room, not thinking what he wanted: a minute steak, iced coffee. And he took a shower and put on a lounging robe, over his naked body. The waiter came and put down the service table by the window. He sat down staring at it; it looked unappetizing. Anyway he wasn't hungry. Suddenly he flung his napkin down and pushed the table back—

The two of them!—Oysters and champagne—

He strode to the telephone and called a Hinsdale number—

"Hubert Baxter speaking."

"Hello, Hub. It's Sam."

"Yes, Sam. What's on your mind?"

"I've been thinking of our talk this afternoon. Maybe it would be as well to let it go. I mean, till she gets back."

"I think that's being smart."

"Well, suppose we leave it that way."

"Fine. Shall I write her that's the way you feel about it?"

"No, just let it go."

"Right. I'll mail her letter back to vou tomorrow."

"Okay, Hub. Thanks."

July, 1918.—A lot of Americans were summering in Europe, mostly young fellows who hadn't been before. They didn't like it, not the scenery nor the climate nor the people—not the British, who were snooty and superior, nor the French whose thriftiness seemed akin to picking pockets. You would think the amalgam from a melting pot should be comfortably at home most anywhere, but the fact remains— they didn't like it. Mike Hogan said one time, replying to a question, that of all the foreign people whom he had encountered, he had liked the Germans best, adding with a grin, from the corner of his mouth, "—because I seen less of 'em." A lot of other fellows felt like that. They wanted to come home; and some of them were coming—minus arms and legs, with lungs burned out by gas; and some of them would stay there, under rows of neat white crosses.—President Wilson had proclaimed his Fourteen Points. But the boys in the trenches were not paying much attention; they were out to make the world safe for democracy, and get it over with, and get back home again to their jobs and wives and sweethearts, some of whom no doubt were sleeping with civilians, for war and human nature go marching hand in hand.—Things were happening in their absence. The American Way had been greatly interfered with—at least the *Way* that Old Henry's feet had trod. Likely enough he was

« 235 »

writing in his grave, if he was aware of what was going on. The government was mixing into everybody's business, saying what they couldn't do, taxing them to death, spending money with both hands, simply throwing it away, lending it to people who would never pay it back, piling up a debt too stupendous to be counted; promising of course that when the war was over, everything would be the same—the way it always had been. But you can't unscramble eggs.—"Business as Usual" was the slogan for the country. But this was nonsense too. A lot of unknown people were getting very rich, but a lot of decent people were losing what they'd saved. And America, itself, was beginning to look shabby. The veneer was wearing off—it was never meant to last—and nobody seemed to care to patch it up; materials and labor were too high and hard to get, and you could rent the space no matter how it looked.—Chicago was a mess—buildings grimed with smoke, dirt blowing through the streets, shabby, running down, needing paint and wallpaper. There were no German names of hotels and restaurants, and there had been very many. The Bismarck Garden was now the Marigold. There had been talk of changing the name of Goethe street.

IX

TWO MONTHS LATER, IN SEPTEMBER, SAM WAS IN THE ARMY.
It was curious the way that came about. He was not drafted, nor was compulsion imminent. He volunteered as an officer candidate in the Field Artillery, and after some delay was duly notified that he had been accepted, with orders to report at Camp Taylor in Kentucky on the morning of September twenty-second. He had picked the Field Artillery with the idea that this service would not involve much walking: there would be horses, he supposed, and caissons to ride on. But on this score he would soon be disillusioned.

He broke the news to Jules on September twenty-first without preliminary warning, though he had had his orders for a week and a month had elapsed since he made his application. But he and Jules had barely spoken in that time. They had had a bitter row about the strike—a battle which the Frenchman believed that he had won. But he was wrong about it.

The strike was two months old. It had come a few days after his discussion with Hub Baxter, and had served to distract his attention from that matter—from all other matters really. It promised to be fatal unless it could be mended, and his efforts to mend it had met with no success. The Frenchman was determined not to compromise the issue, not to yield on any point to the *canaille*, as he called them. He stamped around the big skylighted studio where he had his office, gesticulating wildly, jabbering French and English—hysteric imprecations and theatrical allusions to the soldiers at Verdun whom no enemy should pass. It was childish and absurd, but Jules Tronchet was his partner, for better or for worse.

He had seen the trouble coming, had kept himself informed through some channels of his own. He knew very well what was going on: an agitator had been working on the job for several months—a shanty mick named Mooney, with a pair of shifty eyes and the pinched face of a thug. He had seen the man a time or two, loafing on the corner, craftily eying him, waiting for the workers to come out. The fellow was a drunk and had an itching palm, so his informants said. He was living in a cheap hotel with a peroxide blonde who was due to have a baby. It was here in this hotel that they held their meetings which were growing in attendance, so the informant said. Likely enough Mooney could have been bought off, but the Frenchman's thriftiness would not stomach the suggestion. He pooh-poohed the whole affair, insisting that his workers could not be seduced, that they were loyal to him.

He had let it go at that, though he was not deceived. The Frenchman was not popular; and, even though he were, it would not save his neck if they got their heels upon it. But it was up to Jules to run the plant; that was the agreement. One night in his hotel, a day or so before the lid blew off, he picked up the telephone in answer to a ring—

"Mr. Braden?" said a shanty Irish voice.

"Yes."

"My name is Mooney"—

"Yes?"

"J. D. Mooney. I've been staying down in Clearing for a bit."

"Yes?"

"I wonder, Mr. Braden, could we have a little chat?"

"What about?"

"Oh—" The voice laughed slickly. "—one thing or another."

"I guess you want to talk to Mr. Tronchet?"—This had been the time no doubt, but what good was it to talk if you couldn't follow through. His hands were tied.

"The Frenchman, d'ye mean?"

"That's right, my partner—the man who runs the factory."

"I don't think we'd get along—" He laughed again.

"Sorry, Mr. Mooney—"

"I'd sooner talk to you."

"I'm afraid I couldn't do that."

"The Irish and the French don't mix so well, but two guys like you and me could sit down and talk things over—maybe even have a drink."

"Thanks, but—"

"I could drop around and see you—"

"I think you better talk to Mr. Tronchet."

"Well, I'm sorry now—I am—" The voice sighed plaintively. "But nobody can say I didn't try. So long, Mr. Braden—"

"Good-by, Mr. Mooney." And he hung up the receiver.

And then it happened: a labored document in quasi-legal language, signed by a committee of employees—demands and grievances. More money and less work was the essence of the thing, but the shop was to be closed and the union recognized. Jules read it to him in a panting voice, tramping up and down the studio where the new line had been sampled—not just bread-and-butter merchandise, the kind they used to make, but a first-rate general line; the sampling of it cost near a hundred thousand dollars, and production had just started. The salesmen had gone out a week ago, fifty of them scattered from Maine to California. Orders were already pouring in. Mr. J. D. Mooney had carefully picked his time—

"*Canaille!*" stormed the Frenchman, and he tore up the document and flung it in the wastebasket, from which it must be rescued and with effort pieced together.

"Don't you think we better talk it over with them, Jules?"

"Never! I would not debase myself."

"Well, what are you going to do?"

"I will tell you, Sam: I am going to fire everyone who signed that thing." And he fished in the basket for the fragment with their names. There were about a dozen, haphazard through the plant, boys and girls and men. "I will fire them tonight at quitting time."

"Is that the only answer you intend to give?"

"That is my reply."

"Well, Jules, I think you're making a mistake."

"Mistake! But why?"

"You're stepping into something—"

"Bah! It's all a bluff."

"Suppose it isn't?"

"Why should I suppose? I know my business."

"Still, just suppose—"

"No, no, no!"

"We can lose a lot of money—and we haven't got it, Jules."

"I tell you it's a bluff."

"We could maybe patch it up, for the present anyway, with a little give and take, and then weed these people out one at a time—"

"I weed them out right now."

"They've got us with our pants down—"

"We will sink or swim that way."

"Take a day and think it over—"

"No, no, no!"

There was no use arguing with him.

Next morning about half of them were out—parading on the sidewalk, standing round in groups, shouting abuse at the "scabs" who were at work, but good-naturedly enough. And the workers in the factory would look out of the windows and shout things back at them. It seemed more like a picnic than a strike—like people on a holiday, elated with their freedom. Most of the girls had left off their working clothes and were dressed for the occasion in their Sunday best, the cheap finery of poverty. Twelve cents an hour they were asking, for standing on their feet ten hours in the day, sixty hours in the week, and would probably take less. Some of them were pretty. They skylarked with the boys —kids of high school age, for the older fellows had been drafted in the Army, except for a few with flat feet and other things. And there were the men of middle age, lounging against the building, with their hands in the pockets of their shabby jeans. They did not look dangerous— pathetic rather. Poor people, all of them—poor, as he had been—

They saw the Buick coming—the roadster that he used driving back and forth to town, which he did not drive too well—and lined along the curb with defiant, scowling eyes, or pretending not to see him, looking sheepish and unhappy. One group in the street made way slowly for him, holding up some crudely lettered banners: We Demand a Living Wage, and stuff like that; and there were some remarks, reflecting on his driving. But he was good-natured, too; he didn't blow the horn or shout at them, and they presently dissolved out of his path. He drove on slowly to the door where there was another group, and they made a path for him, with some jeering in the background. But most of them were smiling, seeming friendly and embarrassed; and a few called back, "Good morning," in answer to his greeting. They were familiar faces, but still he did not know them. He had not had much to do with the workers in the factory; that was up to Jules. Almost every day he would walk through the plant from one end to the other, nodding pleasantly to this one and that, pausing to chat with the heads of the departments, noting many things that he thought were inefficient, that might be better done; but he had long since despaired of effecting any change in his partner's methods. The Frenchman was as stubborn as a mule—

The office was as usual: typewriters clicking briskly, clerks bending over ledgers, executives busy at their desks. It was hard to believe that anything had changed until you stopped to listen to the throb of the machinery. The plant was running, yes, but—as he hung up his hat and went on into his office, he was calculating nicely—about half capacity, which would not earn a dime, for the profit that they made was dependent on production. They were losing money now, every time the clock ticked—at the rate of about a thousand dollars every day. He glanced at his mail and walked out into the factory—through the lofty basements, piled ceiling-high with raw stock, great webs of plain white paper not yet paid for—along the shipping floors, almost empty of merchandise—through the color-making section—on up to the machine floor. Half the machines were idle; he had guessed right from the sound—

He went down a flight of stairs into the studio. Jules was sitting at his desk, which was in its usual mess, figuring furiously and muttering to himself. He looked like a man who had been up all night.

"Well," Sam said, "it seems we have a strike."

The Frenchman laughed but there wasn't any laughter in his eyes. He said that it was nothing—in a week they'd all be back, all except the ones he'd fired, not one of whom would ever be permitted in the plant. Anyway it didn't matter: the ones who had gone out were the riffraff of the factory, troublemaking hoodlums. He was glad that they were gone, and it would be just as well if none of them came back; but they would be back all right when their belts began to tighten, crawling back to get their jobs like the *canaille* that they were—

"Half the machines are idle."

"Don't you worry about that, Sam." Jules jumped out of his chair and began to stamp around. It would only be this way for a day or two, he said. Some printers had gone out, but he had apprentices who were itching for their jobs and he'd break them in at once. They would be good printers, too, much better than the others. And the color mixers—well, he'd put on overalls and go back in there himself; he'd show these *scélérats* he could do more work than three of them. He'd have things running full—in a little while—

"Yes? When?"

He didn't answer that.

"At the rate we're running now, we are losing about a thousand dollars every day."

"What?" The Frenchman stared.

"A thousand a day, unless I miss my guess."

"You're crazy, Sam." He fingered his throat as if he might be choking.

"Well, I can't argue that. But don't you think we better call them in and talk it over?"

"No, no, no!" Jules shouted, pounding on the desk. "I could never show my face. I would be good for nothing."

"All right. It's up to you." He went back to his office, reflecting: there was a grain of truth in that apoplectic protest. Jules had stuck out his neck; it was *his* battle now. If they whipped him he was sunk. He could never run the factory after that. And suppose he couldn't run it, there were plenty more that could. You could hire men like that, better men than Jules; for ten thousand a year you could have your pick of them. But there seemed no path to that, unless—unless— He was thoughtful through the day, turning matters in his mind.

A month dragged by. A few of them came back, but more of them went out. They didn't hang around much any more; they soon got tired of that. August was brutally hot and there wasn't any shade unless you stood tight up against the building. The pickets did this, lounging against the wall with sullen, apathetic faces, a dozen at a time—girls and kids and men. They were there in the morning when he came, in the evening when he left; but there were no greetings now, no banter, no elation. They avoided looking at him. One day when he came out they were gathered in a group and he saw there was a girl lying stretched out on the sidewalk, and some of them were kneeling, fanning her with scraps of paper. He walked over and inquired. She had fainted from the heat, somebody told him. She was lying on her back—a pretty, dark-haired girl, maybe seventeen; but her face looked like a mask, chalk-white with beads of sweat and lipstick smeared across it. He noticed that her shoes were worn through, the heels run down to nothing. He suggested that they bring her in the office, that he would call a cab to take her home. But one of them answered roughly, "We can take care of her." He went back to the office and got a glass of water from the cooler by the door and brought it out to them. They took it without thanks.

He drove home feeling miserably depressed; he could not get the girl's face out of his mind. In some strange way, for there was no resemblance, she had made him think of Nelly. But there was something deeper gnawing at his heart, which he only partly sensed: he was really one of them, and he had been denied. He knew, he understood, he had been through all that—the broken shoes, the tightened belt, the agony of poverty. But there was a gulf between them; he could never be admitted to their fellowship again. He was terribly *alone*—

The strike went on—a tepid, shabby struggle. One night they broke some windows, but there was little violence you could put your finger on and there had been no occasion to call on the police. The apprentice printers hadn't done so well: two of them were in the hospital, suffering from contusions resulting from encounters outside of working hours. They said they didn't know who, or what, had hit them. The other apprentices had immediately resigned, and could not be prevailed on to go near a print machine. Jules had donned his overalls and was wading deep in color, but you couldn't mix colors for machines that didn't run. The plant was badly crippled—a thousand a day proved to be an excellent guess. But the strikers had no access to the balance sheet; they could only be sure they were hungry.

There was sabotage of course, but you couldn't pin that down; the waste was simply frightful, but this was partly due to inexperienced help. Jules would hire anybody—even taking kids below the legal age. If they said they were sixteen he'd take them on, though you knew by looking at them that they had lied about it—little fellows who belonged in grammar school, whose parents shut their eyes and took the money. Sam didn't like it. Walking through the plant one day he saw a little boy fast asleep on the floor beside a stick box, his head not six inches from an idling belt. He woke him with his toe.

"How old are you?" he said.

"Fourteen—" The boy was scrambling to his feet, rubbing his eyes. "Sixteen, I mean," he stammered.

"I heard you the first time," Sam said, smiling. "You go down to the cashier and get your check. Tell him Mr. Braden sent you." The boy backed away, tears welling in his eyes. He had a homely, freckled face and a cowlick in his hair. "Come back here, son." The boy came back a step, frightened and ashamed. Sam took a bill out of his pocket—a crisp five dollar note; and tucked it in the grimy little hand: "Don't feel bad because you're fired," he said gently. "It's not because you fell asleep." The child was staring at the bill, hardly daring to believe it. "You're too young to work up here; you'll have time enough for that. Now run along." The boy kited off, down the alleyway between the drying racks.

He spoke to Jules about it. "We can't do that," he said. "We can't have children working round machinery. Someday there'll be an accident."

"But how am I to know?" The Frenchman waved his arms. "If they say they are sixteen—"

"Hell," Sam said, "you can tell by looking at them. If there's any doubt about it, don't employ them. That's the law, and anyway it's only common sense."

But there were plenty more. He tried vainly not to see them.

The August days dragged on. The strikers could not close the plant, and the plant could not regain its schedule of production. The scales would tip a little up or down, but never far from balance. The matter was too small to occasion much attention in the industrial town, and public opinion was divided, apathetic. The strikers courted sympathy but without much success. If anything, it seemed that they were losing ground; some of them were drifting into other jobs. It began to look as though the Frenchman might win out—at a cost which only he and Sam could calculate. Even that, or most of it, might be recoverable if the battle should be won and the screws clamped down on things. And then something happened to tip the scales against him, to make that hopeful outlook exceedingly remote—

There were accidents of course, as there always were: fingers caught in cogs, rollers dropped on toes, bruises and sprains, rarely broken bones —not serious affairs. Making wallpaper was not a dangerous business, and the mill had never suffered a fatality.

It was in the afternoon, near quitting time. Sam was walking through the plant. He had come up the stairs at the end of the machine floor where the roller girls were working, and then along an alley between the drying racks, to the grounding machines which brushed on the background color. They were simple machines, easily operated, usually by boys. There was a row of them, five or six feet apart, behind the print machines. The place was a maze of belts and shafts and pulleys, with the paper from the printers running overhead, and the drying racks behind; and it was dimly lighted and deafeningly noisy.

He had come into the space between the grounders and the printers, about half of which were idle, when he saw, a machine or two away, something which at first he didn't grasp or understand—rags, or clothing, a shirt and jeans in fact, hanging in the air a foot or two above the floor. He stared for a moment before he realized that the jeans and the shirt were on a boy, and the boy was suspended in the air, apparently not struggling, and going slowly higher. But still he didn't grasp the situation which seemed to be an antic; there was no cry for help. He took a step or two and then he saw—

The boy was tangled in a belt, suspended from a line shaft, the shaft that drove the grounders. The machine that it belonged to was shut down, and it had been off its pulley with the loose loop of it idling on the floor. The boy had stepped into it and it had wrapped around him and twisted on the shaft. That was what had happened, as nearly as it could be constructed. What was happening now was all that mattered: the belt was winding up, coiling on the shaft like a python in a tree, with the boy all tangled in it—

His heart stood still with horror; he could hardly find the breath to shout a warning, and he ran toward the lever which controlled the shaft, which was beyond the boy, far off against the wall. He had passed by him, and the kicking feet were shoulder high, when he slipped and fell on the wet and mucky floor. Others had heard the shout, or had seen now what was happening; and he would have been too late even if he had not fallen, but perhaps not at the start, if he'd realized at first—

He had not regained his feet when he heard the scream—a sound that would linger in his ears for long to come, a sound that was not human, cut in two, divided between life and violent death. And then the hideous flap—flap—flap—as the body was whirled around the shaft, beaten into pulp against the steel I beam a few inches above it. Flap—flap—flap— And then at last it stopped.

A moment after that the quitting whistle blew.

Jules was on the job; he had been there on the floor, working in his overalls, his bare arms stained with color. There was nothing to be seen at first—a few rags hanging on the shaft in the knotted belt, a few more on the floor, a black splotch on the ceiling. The men came running up, not knowing what had happened—

"What?" they asked, then, "Who?"

Nobody knew; there was nothing to identify. And many had gone home when the whistle blew, running out before the news had got around. A Polish boy, some thought, whose name was unpronounceable. They called him Bojo. He had been in the plant only a day or two; he couldn't talk much English. He worked around the grounders, carrying pails of color. There was a bucket lying on its side in a pool of color. The boy didn't answer when they called him; his number on the time clock hadn't been punched out. Still, you couldn't say with certainty, and it wasn't a thing to speculate about—

One, more courageous than the rest, picked up a rag of clothing and felt inside the pocket. There was a nickel in it and a piece of chalk. Yes, Bojo, several said. He carried chalk around, trying to learn words by writing them, scribbling on the floor when he had an idle moment. He had been reprimanded—

Some girls had come back from the rolling room, not coming very close; and one of them called out she knew the boy. She lived next door to him; they were Polish people. Bojo was a kid; he played with her kid brother. She began to get hysterical—

Jules cleared them out. "Go home," he ordered. "All of you, go home." He kept three or four who volunteered to help him. And they did what must be done, gathering up the fragments in a sack—an arm, a leg; there were bits of rag and flesh fifty feet away. They worked on hands and knees, on ladders too, with color scoops and brooms and scrubbing brushes. The Frenchman didn't shirk, but led the way—crawling on the floor with a pocket flash, reaching under things, into dark corners. Sam stayed there to the end, but it took all that he had. Once he had gone back to the washroom and been sick—

The coroner came and asked the usual questions; and they reconstructed then what probably had happened. The boy had been careless, not looking where he stepped; contributory negligence would be their defense. They would have to fight a lawsuit, to keep from being robbed by shyster lawyers. An undertaker came and took the sack away—

It was near midnight when he got back to the city, heartsick, aching with weariness. The phone was ringing when he stepped into his room; he stretched out on the bed to answer it—

"Mr. Braden?— This is Mooney—J. D. Mooney."

"Yes?"

"I'm sorry to ring you up so late—"

"Oh, that's all right."

"I didn't wake you up now?"

"No."

"Well, that's good anyway." A pause. "I hear you had an accident—"

"That's right."

"Well, that's too bad—" The voice was slick as grease.

"Accidents will happen."

"Sure, don't I know it." Another pause. "A Polish kid, they tell me."

"So I understand."

"There's a lot of Polish people out in Clearing."

He made no comment.

"I was wondering, Mr. Braden, if we couldn't have a talk?"

"Mr. Tronchet is the man you want to see."

"Now what's the good of that, wasting time and money? You're not getting anywhere, and this accident today won't help you any."

"Accidents occur in every plant."

"Sure, I know that, and nobody to blame. It's just bad luck for you that the kid was underage."

He didn't answer that. But he had been waiting for it—waiting all the time since it had happened, not daring to suggest it by making inquiry; but he had been sure of it.

"Fourteen," the voice went on, "and that makes it pretty tough. They won't like it out in Clearing, Mr. Braden. They'll pass the word around that your factory is a deathtrap. And the law won't help you none, if the kid was underage. Public opinion will be pretty strong about it."

He took the only line there was to take: "We don't employ boys under sixteen years of age."

"I know that, Mr. Braden. This Polish kid was just a slip, I guess— or maybe you've got an affidavit?" The voice was laughing at him.

"We don't employ people under legal age."

"Well now, let's leave that be, for it's no affair of mine—not what I called about, only indirectly maybe. You've got a sweet, pretty business, Mr. Braden, and you're a smart guy too, from what I understand. What good is it to you to get yourself pulled down and a bad eye all around?"

"I'm sorry, Mr. Mooney—"

"And by God, you ought to be. But it's not too late right now to talk things over."

"It's outside of my discretion."

"Don't say that, Mr. Braden. For your own sake, don't say that—"

He hung up the receiver.—For his own sake—for his own sake— He had been thinking that; for a month conviction had been growing

« 246 »

that *he* would be the goat, that the burden of the thing, however it came out, would end up on his shoulders, be remembered against him, that ill will would cling around him and crop up in his path—that the strike was not an incident, but a measure of his skill in handling men and matters; and the way it had been handled was not his. There was a time to fight and a time to run away, and if you weren't a fool, you knew the difference—

Next morning the pickets stared at him with sullen eyes, and there were more of them. When he opened the door he was conscious of a change in the rhythm of the plant: more machines were down—two or three, he guessed. He found Jules in the studio, sitting at his desk, not in his overalls, looking haggard, old and sick, but the fire in his eye had not been quenched. Two more printers had gone out, he said, but they'd be back with their tails between their legs; they had families to support.

"They claim—" Sam lit a cigarette. "They claim the Polish boy was underage."

It was a lie, Jules said. He remembered the boy, had hired him, himself. He was sixteen at least, and maybe older.

"They'll believe his mother, Jules."

The Frenchman shrugged his shoulders.

"Anyway the thing won't do us any good. We ought to patch it up."

"Patch it? How?"

"Call them in and talk it over."

It was then that the Frenchman had gone into a tantrum, stamping up and down, shouting imprecations and allusions to Verdun which no enemy should pass, mixing French and English, incoherent, really mad. But there was something in it that evoked your admiration: the fellow with his back against the wall, beset on every side, with no support, but not giving in an inch—fantastic and absurd, but heroic in a way. He ran out of breath at last and came back to the desk, leaning on it with his fists, glaring at his partner—

"You would like to get rid of me," he said.

"Nonsense!"

"Why don't you buy me out?"

"I don't want to buy you out."

"I don't believe you, Sam."

He didn't answer that.

"You would like to buy me out, but not for a fair price. Well, let me tell you something: my interest is for sale, but I am not."

"All right. All right." Sam walked out of the studio. And a month went by, a month to a day, before he entered it again.

He left the plant at noon and drove to the city, to an office building in the Loop, and filed his application to be inducted in the Army, as an officer candidate in the Field Artillery. He had done some careful figuring since the previous night: it was time for him to bow out of the picture, and this was an excuse no one could criticize. Let the Frenchman take a beating, or win out if he could; he would have no part of it. The war was nearly finished—that's the way it looked; anyway he'd take the chance. And he needed a vacation; he had never had a vacation in his life.

A month went by. The strike dragged on with more fuel in its belly, but not winning and not losing. The plant kept running, hovering up and down around a third capacity. Order files were bulging, customers complaining; the people in the office were being driven mad. Notes were coming due and had to be renewed; in Stanley Adams' bank the atmosphere was frigid. A lawsuit had been filed by the Polish parents; they claimed ten thousand dollars. Hub Baxter hemmed and hawed, and took numerous depositions; he did not seem optimistic of the outcome. There were no more boys at work under sixteen years of age, but the stable had been locked too late to save the horse; and the news had spread around that the factory was a deathtrap with a callous, brutal management. The local paper printed a nasty editorial; in the shadow of an alley someone threw a brick at Jules.

They had never talked about the thing again—indeed, for a month, had barely spoken, until, late in the afternoon on September twenty-first, Sam walked into the studio. Jules was sitting at his desk, altering a design which was on a drawing board; he looked up, nodding coolly. Sam sat down in a chair across from him.

"I'm going away tonight," he said.

"Going?" The Frenchman went on tracing with his pencil. "Going where?"

"To Louisville."

"Oh—"

"I've enlisted."

"What?" He dropped the drawing board with a clatter on the desk.

"In the Army."

"In the Army? Are you crazy?"

"I don't think so." Sam laughed. "I could be drafted in a little while. This way I've got a chance to be an officer."

But the Frenchman was not listening. "You—you are joking me," he said.

"No, I'm not joking, Jules. I'm due at Camp Taylor first thing tomorrow morning."

"But no—" He got up, wobbly on his legs, looking stricken and bewildered. "How can you go away? Who will look after things?"

"There's nothing much to do, the way things are. The people in the office—Getz and Trask and Brown, they've got their hands on things—"

"Ah no! Please, Sam—" His voice was close to tears. "You wouldn't do that, Sam? You wouldn't go away?"

"We're in a war, you know. In another month or two I might not have a choice." But the man's distress was touching, worse than he had dreamed. "Come now, don't take it that way; after all it may not last long."

"You are serious? You mean, you couldn't change it now?"

"No chance." He laughed again. "I'd probably be court-martialed." He walked around the desk with the impulse to put his arm around the Frenchman's shoulders. After all, they'd been partners for six years—with disagreements certainly, but with big moments too, and they had been successful, had made a lot of money, though they hadn't much to show for it, at the present anyway; they had plowed back everything into the business. "Come now," he said again. "I didn't think you'd take it this way, Jules."

But the Frenchman drew back from him, the hollows in his cheeks puffing in and out. "You never told me anything. You never said a word."

"I didn't know for sure till just the other day—didn't know if they would take me."

"Why did you do it, Sam?"

"Why?" He looked away. "I owe something to my country."

"Bah!" Jules spat contemptuously. "It was a dirty trick—a dirty trick."

"Oh well, if that's the way you feel—" He turned on his heel, but then came back a step, holding out his hand. "Let's not part like this, Jules—"

But the Frenchman put his hands behind his back.

He went back to his office and sent for his executives, the department managers, Getz and Trask and Brown—credit, sales, accounting. He explained that he was leaving for the Army, would be away he could not say how long, Mr. Tronchet was in charge of everything, he would

« 249 »

like to have reports mailed to him once a week. He made it brief, shaking hands with them, cutting short their amazed, conventional words.

His secretary came and put a cable on his desk. He tore it open absently. "Please cable answer to my letter.—E." It seemed so long ago; he had almost forgotten. He brought his mind back to it with an effort: the letter she had written, asking his permission to secure a French divorce; he had never answered it.—He dictated an answer: "Think advisable await your return," signed "Sam." He shook hands with the girl and said good-by, but he did not stop to speak to anybody else; it would have meant to speak to everyone. The pickets on the sidewalk watched him with sullen eyes. Well, let them; it would be a while before they had a chance again. He was conscious of a deep sense of relief, almost of joy. He was out of it at last—

His room was in disorder, books sent back to storage, odds and ends of things—littered, ugly, naked. His army trunk was packed. He changed into another suit of clothes, an old one which he was ready to discard. And now what? His train would leave at ten, and it was six o'clock—four hours to dispose of. He was going off to war, from which he might not return, leaving one war for another—enemies in front of him and enemies behind. And no fanfare of trumpets; no genial party at the College Inn, like the one they'd given Mike; not a human being to say Godspeed to him. He paced the narrow room, the elation of his freedom taking flight. And then he had an idea: he went to the phone and called up Mama Kranz—

"It's Sam—"

"Oh, Sam! I have been wondering—"

"I know. It's been so long—"

"How are you, Sam?"

"Oh, I'm all right—"

"I'm glad. We have been worried."

"I'm going in the Army."

"Not really?"

"To Louisville, tonight."

"Oh dear!"

"I was wondering if you and Emilie could have dinner with me?"

"Of course we can."

"That's fine. Shall I come and pick you up?"

"No, don't you bother, Sam. We can meet you anywhere."

"Would the Congress be all right?"

"That would be lovely."

"At seven?"

"We'll be there, Sam."

It had been good to see them, like being home again. Mama Kranz was aging and her eyes looked very tired, but she was bright and cheerful. They had been taking lodgers, she explained—she and Emilie doubled up and there were three rooms to let; it had not been easy, but they could get along. Emilie was attending business college, learning stenography; she was proving very apt and would soon be prepared for a secretarial job—

"Oh no, Mama," Emilie protested. She was really very awkward, her shorthand was so bad, she could never read her notes. She blushed and looked away.

Sam laughed. He was thinking of the time when, as a little girl, she used to come at bedtime and cuddle on his lap, begging for a story. She was a woman now, twenty-two or three, yet still a little girl, unchanged, unspoiled—not the flapper type, with bobbed hair and painted lips and brazen manners. Mama Kranz had seen to that, or something had—

"How would you like to work for me?" he said.

"I'm sure I should never be good enough for that."

"We'll see—" He drank his cocktail; they had taken sherry. He had ordered the dinner and a bottle of wine. "When I come back from the war I mean to have an office here in town, on Michigan perhaps, looking out across the lake. And you shall come and be my secretary."

"You're only teasing me—"

He wasn't altogether. He was thinking of an office, like one that he had seen in the Stanley Adams' bank, with rich mahogany, oil paintings on the walls, thick carpet on the floor, and of Emilie sitting in it, coming in with letters, making his appointments—someone who would not be hired help, who would take an interest in him, in the things that he was doing. "You used to call me Uncle Sam," he said.

"Oh yes—" She was confused. "—when I was a child."

"She always calls you that," smiled Mama Kranz.

He frowned. "Well, am I Uncle Sam, or am I not?"

"But I couldn't call you that if I was your secretary."

"You can call me Uncle Sam anywhere and any time."

"Well—" She wasn't sure.

"Is it understood?"

"If you are not joking?"

"Let me hear you say it once."

"It's silly—"

"No, it isn't."

"Well then—Uncle Sam—" She was blushing furiously; her eyes were like deep pools, there was a glint of copper in her hair; beautiful was not the word—very lovely, very charming, rather fragile. The waiter intervened to cover her confusion.

They talked of other things. He told them of the strike; about his partner, Jules; the boy who had been killed. Matters were involved but they would be all right, once he was free to act. The business was a gold mine whose wealth was barely scratched. Stimulated by their interest he went on to trace its future, warming to the pictures which his eager fancy drew: a factory in the East, another farther west—kindred lines of merchandise: paint and varnish, for example—distributing houses in all important cities. There was nothing to prevent it, once he was free to move, to drive the thing ahead—

It was Mama Kranz who asked about Eileen. She knew of course that Eileen had gone to France, and no doubt she suspected that there was something wrong. He told them the truth—not any details, just that they had separated and there would be a divorce when Eileen came back from France. No, he did not have a wife—he paused and added slowly that he had never had one—

"Ah so," she sighed. "I was afraid, Sam."

"Were you?" He looked up quickly. "Why?"

"Because—" She spread her hands.

"Because she didn't love you," Emilie said.

"You didn't know her."

"I saw her at the wedding."

"You were a little girl."

"All the same I knew," Emilie answered firmly.

"Hum—" He changed the subject.

They went with him to the station. There were other fellows going off to war, and there were wives and sweethearts come to say good-by. He was glad he had not come alone. Mama Kranz was crying when she hugged him in her arms. "Come back soon and safely, Sam." He turned to Emilie; the train was moving. Suddenly, impulsively, he put his arms around her and kissed her on the cheek. "Good-by—good-by," he called. They kept waving to him as long as he could see them.

Sam loved the Army—the fifty fleeting days of his military life; loved being told when to get up and go to bed, what to eat and when to eat it; loved being relieved of all responsibility. Perhaps it would have palled if it had gone on much longer, but he loved it while it lasted. In later years he used to say, "The first vacation that I ever had." And he liked to talk about it: how smart he'd been, not rushing to the camp when he got off the train, as most of the others did, but going to the Seelbach for a hearty breakfast, and a bath and barber chair—how then he called a cab and continued on to war, like a banker to his office. Camp Taylor was some miles outside the town—a sprawling, dreary maze of rough, unpainted barracks, in a pleasant, rolling country whose roads were lined with graceful poplar trees. Coming to the edge of it they crossed a railroad siding where there were several freight cars from which soldiers were unloading wooden boxes which resembled coffins. He inquired of the driver what they were—

"Coffins," said the man.

"Oh, coffins?" He looked back at the boxes, piled up carelessly. "There's quite a lot of them."

"A lot ain't enough." The driver shook his head. "The place is full of flu."

That had been his introduction to the Army. But he didn't take the flu, though there were plenty did. Every morning two or three would not get up at reveille, but later they would stagger out for sick call—trembling with chills and flushed with fever. Some of them came back after a week or two, and some of them went home—packed in wooden boxes. No, he didn't take the flu, never thought he would, wasn't sick a day, had never felt so well.

He would go on from there: how, arriving at the camp, he had stood in line for hours—for a uniform that didn't fit and a campaign hat with a multicolored cord, badge of the candidate—he had a picture taken in the outfit, and in another war his son would smile at it—for shoes that were too big and woolen underwear that came down to his ankles; for a smallpox vaccination and a typhoid shot; for a noonday meal whose unaccustomed food he could not eat; for this and that, and nothing—

How, in the afternoon, which seemed like another day, they were herded in a barracks, which must be swept and scrubbed, and iron cots lugged in and set up in four rows, two head to head down the center of the room, and two against the wall—about a hundred of them; how then each man received a cotton bedtick, and must go a long way off and fill it full of straw and fetch it back again—

"Did you ever," he would ask, "tote a mattress for a mile?" There was no way to carry it; if you put it on your head, you couldn't see; it could not be folded underneath your arm; it would not stay on your shoulder or your back. He had made a roll of it and strapped his belt around it, but then he needed one hand to hold up his army pants which would slide to his feet if he let go. He had got back with it at last, panting and exhausted—

But it wasn't over yet: blankets must be issued and they stood in line for that; and then the beds were made—he had brought his sheets and a pneumatic pillow—while noncoms pushed around and showed them how, being pretty short and snappy and sarcastic; and the army trunks were set at the foot of every cot, and certain things were hung on certain hooks, on the walls and on the posts that lined the center of the room; and the mess kits must be polished and laid out on the beds, every item in its place. He had struck a quick acquaintance with his neighbors— a New York traffic cop and an auditor from Cleveland. They were mostly older men, in the middle thirties; the younger fellows had long since ʒotten in. And there were among them, it turned out, a Congressman, a judge, and an author of some note who had been the only one who seemed unhappy. He had liked them, liked the communal life: eating wedged among them, sleeping close together, washing in a trough— even the latrines which had no doors—

At the end, near suppertime, the job was done. But the orders were to keep off the beds, as the captain would be coming to inspect his new recruits. He sat down on his trunk, near the end of his resources, feeling that he could not do another thing or take another step. A pretty strenuous day for a young businessman of sedentary habits; he had almost forgotten the luxurious sensation of physical fatigue, when all you wanted was to rest your aching muscles, when just sitting down was wonderful—

"Attention," shouted someone.

He jumped to his feet and stood in the narrow way at the right side of his cot, facing the aisle which passed along the foot of it—palms spread against his trouser seams, eyes to the front, as he had been instructed. The long narrow room had suddenly gone silent; he could hear his neighbors breathing, footsteps coming up the stairs. But he did not look around. Eyes straight ahead—

They were coming, several of them, walking slowly through the aisles. From the corner of his eye he could see one out in front—that would be the captain; and the others behind him, the lieutenants probably. Now and then they paused, correcting something: the way a bed was made or something was hung up, or a man's coat was unbuttoned. He glanced down at his own to make sure it was right. His shoes were shined; he shifted the angle of his toes, and then shifted them again. He was conscious of a voice—the captain's, he supposed—sibilant and curt, somehow familiar. He wished he dared to look, to make sure of his bed, that his mess kit was arranged the way it should be, with the knife on the righthand of the folding dish, but it was too late for that.

He straightened up, pushing out his chest, hoisting his right shoulder which was inclined to sag. They were just a cot away. The auditor from Cleveland was being castigated: "Suck in that belly if you want to be a soldier." Very sibilant, familiar, but still he couldn't place it. He was nervous as a cat, certain in his soul that something was amiss with him or his equipment; he sucked in his belly as far as it would go; his hands were clammy—

Another pace and the captain stood before him. He caught his breath.

Mike Hogan in the flesh! Mike Hogan in a uniform that fitted like a glove, with artillery boots and spurs, silver bars pinned on his shoulders, a strip of colored ribbons on his breast, a wound stripe on his arm—black hair slicked on his forehead and some bubbles of saliva in the corner of his mouth, but big and tough and brawny—every inch a soldier. Mike Hogan looking at him without the slightest trace of recognition in his eyes.

And he was just as good, though for a moment he thought he might fall down; he didn't bat an eye. The captain passed along, two young lieutenants following at his heels; they looked like schoolboys. A sergeant, bringing up the rear, scowled at him and whispered, "Hands on your seams, you sap." He was standing with his hands behind his back, not along his trouser seams where they belonged. How had they got back there; he had not the faintest notion. He jerked them down, feeling like a fool. Good old Mike had pretended not to see it—or maybe hadn't wanted to bawl him out about it.

It was after suppertime—a supper which he ate without thinking what it was—when a noncom came up the stairs and called his name. He was wanted right away in the Orderly Room. He buttoned his coat and combed his hair, and went down to the cubbyhole which opened off the hall. The sergeant was typing at a table. "Braden?— The captain wants you. In there—" He pointed to a door behind him. Sam went in, standing at attention—or what he thought it was. Mike looked up from his desk, a slow, broad grin spreading on his lips—

"Well, Holy God," he said. "Old Sam—old Sam!" And he jumped out of his chair and grabbed him by the shoulders. "You could've knocked me over with a feather. Well now, by God—" He waved his arm. "Relax! Forget that stuff!" He kicked a chair across the room. "Sit down! Relax!" He went to the door and spoke crisply to the sergeant, "I'm busy for a while. Don't bother me." And he flung down in his chair with his feet cocked on the desk. "What the bloody hell are you doing in the Army?"

"Well," Sam smiled, "I thought I'd take a chance—"

"A guy like you." Mike shook his head. "A guy like me, that's different—with nothing behind me but the tax assessor's office. But a guy like you, a successful businessman! You ought to be in Washington, sitting at a desk, telling people what to do."

"Oh no," he deprecated.

"By God, I'm telling you. They need some guys with brains to run this war."

"Well anyway, I'm here."

"Holy Mother, so you are!" He couldn't seem to fathom it. "What made you pick the Field Artillery, Sam?"

"I thought there'd be less walking."

"Oh, you did?"

"We ride on horses, don't we?—or caissons or something?"

Mike shook with laughter. "There's not a bloody horse in the lousy camp," he said. "And the battery's got one gun which you wouldn't dare to shoot—left over from the Civil War, I guess. We take it apart and put it back again."

"But how do we learn about things?"

"You don't need to know much to get shot."

"It can't be that bad, Mike."

"Wait a bit and you'll find out."

He was exaggerating but not extravagantly. He was sore as a goat, it presently developed. He had been sent to France among the very first, and had risen like a shot from the ranks to a commission, and from that to be a captain, the commander of a battery—"The sweetest battery in the regiment," he said. And then, after a year, they had gone into action, and the very day it started the fragment of a shell had hit him in the arm—"Just my lousy luck," he groaned. It was nothing but a flesh wound, no worse than getting spiked in a baseball game— "But the bastards send me back here to teach school."

"Maybe because you were so good, Mike."

"Sure, I was good." He sighed and shook his head. "That's what they told me, too—they needed guys like me back home to train more officers. Soft-soaping sons of bitches!" He got up and paced about the tiny room. "And here I am, by God, diapering baby shavetails, cleaning out their noses. No horses, guns, or nothing but a lot of goddam flu. And the war'll be over maybe before I can get out of it, and where the hell will I be?—back, by God, in the tax assessor's office."

"Maybe—" Sam said thoughtfully, the vestige of an idea stirring in his mind, "—maybe something else will turn up, Mike."

"Tomcats don't have kittens," Mike said glumly. But then he laughed about it. "Now you know what's eating me. Anyway I'm glad you're here; it's like old times again."

"That's right, Mike." But the old times he referred to were very old indeed; he had not seen much of Mike since they were kids.

"If the war lasts four months longer you'll be getting your commission, and your ass will be a target for anybody's boots."

Sam laughed. They chatted on a while. When he was going out, Mike whispered confidentially from the corner of his mouth, "I won't know you outside, but I'll have an eye out for you. If anything goes wrong, just tip me off—" He winked suggestively. "The Army's no different from the City Hall."

"Thanks, Mike."

"These guys around here think I'm pretty tough. They step lively when I bark; they like it, too. I don't kid myself about my brains, but I can run a battery."

"I'll bet you can," Sam said.

He was thinking of that when he dropped off to sleep: Mike Hogan would be good at running things, if there was someone to tell him what to do; and he wouldn't balk at taking orders; he would want someone to tell him. And from there on you could trust him; he had loyalty, devotion, and he was not ambitious—he couldn't see that far—

The days slid by—warm, sunny days, beginning to get chilly in October. Every waking moment had its task: they took the gun apart and put it back again; they drilled; they marched—endless miles and hours every day, over hilly country roads, through meadows and woodland aflame with autumn colors, in a column of fours, with the baby-faced lieutenants pacing easily at the head or on the flanks, and the sergeant barking at them—"Close up! Close up! Close up!" And when they'd had a bellyful—"Double time," would be the order. And they would trot till they were soaked with sweat, till every whistling breath seemed like the last, resolving in their hearts to keep going till they dropped unconscious in their tracks, but nobody ever did. And then there'd be a rest and they'd fling down on the ground. And that was wonderful!

Mike Hogan looked them over on the drill ground, striding briskly through their ranks and nodding brusque approval. They were getting hard all right, getting hard and tough. "If you live another month or two," he said, "you may be soldiers." They were terribly set up— the Congressman, the judge, the author of importance, every man of them. They talked about it in the barracks afterwards; they loved and feared their captain, and his praise resembled God's.

After supper until bedtime, they struggled with mathematics. He had feared this would be hard since he had had no schooling. But geometry and algebra and problems of ballistics turned out, on close acquaintance, to be mostly common sense; and he was better at them than many of the others who had gone to college. And also he was quick to assimilate the technique of the professional soldier, which consisted in the main of staying out of sight, of being in the rear rank whenever it was possible, of never volunteering to do anything, never holding up your hand when they were asking questions, never sticking out your neck or stepping into things, being just as inconspicuous as you could—

He got on K.P. once for some infraction of the rules; and Mike would have got him off, but he wouldn't let him. The days were chilly then and the kitchen was a warm and cozy place. It was pleasant sitting there, peeling potatoes, listening to the grousing and chatter that went on—standing at mess time behind the service table, ladling out the food into the mess tins, picking out choice morsels for your friends who were most friendly at these moments, saving some tidbits for yourself—even scrubbing the grease-encrusted pans had its compensations—scouring them until they shone. And the cook would grin approval, and dig from its hiding place a goody of some sort reserved for such occasions; and they would share it, sitting on the meat block. He loved the Army.

In later years he would remember best the drill ground in the morning, when the rising sun would be behind him and the distant landscape shimmering in blue haze. At the far end of the field there was a hill, and on the summit of it was the flag—a huge one, flapping idly in the morning breeze, or spread against the turquoise sky like a cathedral window—the only vivid object in a wide perspective of softly blending colors.

In the gray dawn when the ground was white with frost, there came from every side, converging on the drill ground, columns of olive drab, winding through the hills, swinging jauntily in quick cadence, column after column, each led by its little band of field music, two or three fifes and drums, and everybody singing the camp songs of the day—

Yes, it was thrilling. It made you catch your breath, made you feel proud that you were one of them, that you were an American—

Madge wrote frequent letters: they had a service flag with one star in it, in the parlor window. Father called attention to it when anybody came, saying very proudly, "My boy, Sam, is in the Army." He kept quite well but did not go out much now. Tom had been in town, just passing through. He was out of a job, had gotten very fat, his color looked unhealthy; she feared that he was drinking rather heavily. He had said that the war interfered with race-track business and had asked for a small loan; she had helped him out a little— from some money she had saved to buy a winter coat, but her old one would do nicely with minor alterations which Cassie Cole could make. The flu had come to Wyattville and was proving very serious: people caught cold and the next day they were dead. George Wyatt had succumbed, and several other friends. They were still eating tomatoes from the garden, and she had put up a lot. She was sending him some peach preserves she knew that he was fond of—

Getz and Trask and Brown reported regularly. There was no change in things; the strike went on, one day a little better and the next a little worse. They were swamped with unfilled orders, and the shipping floor was bare; the stuff went out as fast as it was made, and there wasn't any way to accumulate a stock. Getz was forcing collections to the limit of persuasion, but it was nip and tuck to meet the pay rolls. In this connection he had done something rather smart— which he hoped Mr. Braden would approve: with the bait of extra discount he had gotten some old customers to sign advance acceptances, and they were borrowing on them, though the goods for which they paid had not yet been shipped or manufactured. Their comment on Jules was careful and reserved; they did not know what to say, how far they dared to go; but he read between the lines: the Frenchman was floundering, getting nowhere. Trask enclosed an editorial from the local paper which had changed its tune entirely. "Mr. Braden Goes to War" was the heading of the thing, and it went on with praise of his patriotic action, concluding with a slap at the striking workers who "—in times like these should forget their petty grievances, or emulate the owner of the factory."—He could not repress a smile of satisfaction—

The days slid by—the autumn foliage faded, the woods were deep in shriveled, crinkly leaves; the grass was turning brown. In the Army you never know what's happening in a war. There were rumors of all sorts and one night a false alarm; but the battle of Camp Taylor occupied their full attention.

The Armistice took them completely unaware. With rare exceptions they were not elated, though they made a pretense at it: they were caught out on a limb, hanging in the air—neither officers nor privates, soldiers nor civilians, not fish nor flesh nor fowl. They were going to a war and the war had let them down. Their morale melted away like a snowball in the sun; they began to grouse and grumble before the ink was dry.

Passing through the hall that morning Sam heard Mike's voice instructing his lieutenants. "Take 'em out," he said, "and march their bloody tails off. Don't let 'em have a minute. Run 'em ragged, understand?"

They marched that day until their tails were dragging, uphill and down, through meadowland and woods. "Close up! Close up! Close up!" and "Double time!" And they took it on the chin. They were hard and tough all right; but hard and tough—*for what?*—You couldn't make it *real* again, no matter what you did—

At attention on the drill ground they listened to their captain: "You're in the Army until you get discharged. We're going right ahead until we're told to stop—" a lot of stuff like that. They listened soberly but their attention wandered. They would have followed him— or so they thought—through shell-torn battlefields, through hell, itself; but this was different. It wasn't any use to kid yourself about it—

Late in the afternoon when he got back to the barracks, there were two letters for him: one from Madge, one from the factory. He opened that one first; it was from Trask. Mr. Tronchet had been taken ill, a heart attack perhaps, though they really didn't know. He had been found unconscious on the studio floor. A doctor had been summoned and had called an ambulance to take the sick man home, and the doctor had gone with him, all the way to Woodlawn. They had telephoned of course to Mrs. Tronchet. He was writing an hour after it had happened, so they had no further word. He was sorry to disturb him with bad news, but with Mr. Tronchet absent from the plant, there was no one in the place authorized to sign a check—

Poor Jules!—But he was not much surprised. He had foreseen something of the sort—not this of course, but something—

He opened Madge's letter, thinking what he'd do, that he'd go and talk with Mike: he must get back to Chicago, and quickly, too, if it were possible. He read the opening lines without attention— "Dear Sam: You will be shocked and grieved to learn—" A clipping dropped out of the envelope—she was always sending clippings from the Wyattville *Gazette*. He stooped to pick it up and the headline caught his eye:

"Neill Wyatt Killed in France." He sat down on his cot; his heart was pounding. "—son of Elliott Wyatt—whose mother lost her life in the wreck of the 'Titanic'—nephew of Henry Wyatt—well known in Wyattville—graduate of Harvard—tennis star and auto racer— flying ace—twice decorated for conspicuous gallantry, by the British and the French." He had been shot down in a battle in the sky, some- where in France. Particulars were lacking, but the fact had been con- firmed. "—will be mourned by countless friends on both sides of the Atlantic—"

"Bad news?" His neighbor, the traffic cop, stretched out on his cot, was looking at him.

"No—yes—" he said. He got up and went down the stairs, outside the barrack door. It was already dark.—Not the two of them—not any more.—He had always liked Neill Wyatt—really, in his heart. He saw himself a little boy again, playing on a log raft in the river— slipping, falling—coming up under the tangle, choking, badly scared. And he heard Neill Wyatt's voice—Neill who had come back when the others ran away (yes, even Mike had run), treading the rolling logs, not knowing they were dangerous, or not caring if they were— stuttering, as he did when he was excited: "You—you—you all right, Sam?"—clinging to his wrist, staring at the blood—

Neill Wyatt dead in France, in a war that was now over—to which *he* had come too late, while he was *playing* soldier—dying like his mother, for that's the way he would die, not caring much about it—

"Oh Christ! Oh hell!" Tears were running down his cheeks. He walked up and down in the frosty darkness; the stars were coming out. —How did Eileen feel? How much had she cared?—Well, it didn't matter now.—*Not* the two of them, not ever in this life.—He was crying for himself, for her, for Neill. He did not know why he cried—

After a while he went back into the barracks, to the Orderly Room, and asked to see the captain. Mike was sitting in his chair with his feet cocked on the desk, looking like the picture of a man without a country. He put the clipping on the desk—

"Neill Wyatt's dead," he said.

"Yeah?" Mike glanced at it. He didn't care; he had never liked Neill Wyatt. There was no use going on with that. He remembered suddenly why he had come;—he had the other letter in his hand—

"Mike," he said, "I'm in a jam. My partner's had a heart attack, or something. There's no one in the plant to sign a check. I ought to get back there—if it's possible?"

"I'll get a furlough for you."

"Yes, but can you?"

"I'll get it in the morning if I have to shred their guts." He slouched down in his chair. "Before it runs out, you'll maybe be discharged."

"Thanks, Mike."

"We were kids together, weren't we?"

"Say, Mike, in case I don't come back—"

"Yeah?"

"Before you take a job or begin to look around, come in and see me—"

"Sure, I'll do that."

The next night he was on the train, with a ten-day furlough in his pocket. He had said good-by to his closest friends—the traffic cop, the auditor, half a dozen others—saying he'd be back. But he did not go back. Before the expiration of the furlough, he had been discharged.

It was lonely on the train.

It was lonely in Chicago in the morning. The civilian population was still suffering from a hangover—from the headache of its recent celebration. He checked his baggage in the station and drove to the factory in a taxi—in his baggy uniform and battered campaign hat with its multicolored cord; they had looked all right in camp, but were suddenly become a little silly. He felt self-conscious in them. Still, he thought, it might not do any harm if they saw him in his uniform—just once.

It was a cold, bleak day. The pickets were outside the door—in overcoats and sweaters, with their hands deep in their pockets, looking poor and dejected and forlorn. They recognized him when he got out of the cab; he could see them nudging one another. And a girl called out to him—a red-cheeked girl in a tam o'shanter hat, "Hello, Mr.

Braden." He felt a change in them—that they were more friendly, less hostile anyway.

The office was unchanged: typewriters clicking busily, clerks bending over ledgers. The throb of the machinery seemed about the same. Getz and Trask and Brown sprang up to welcome him with appropriate words of greeting, suitably restrained; they said the Army had agreed with him. He did look well, brown and hard and tough. They had not much to add to what Trask had written; they had talked with Mrs. Tronchet on the phone, but she had not told them much beyond that her husband was seriously ill.

Toward noon, when he had got his breath, he called the Woodlawn number. He barely knew her—a nervous little woman who spoke English very badly; he had never been inside the Tronchet home— the French were clannish. He had driven past it once, out of curiosity —a modest wooden house in a decent neighborhood—

"Mrs. Tronchet?—This is Sam Braden—"

"Oh, Mr. Braden—yes—"

"I just got back this morning—" He explained that he had come as quickly as he could. "But tell me, how is Jules?"

He was very ill, she said.

"Nothing serious, I hope?"

She didn't answer that. He thought that she was crying.

"Have you got a good physician?"

"Oh yes—" She named the man and spelled it, and he wrote it on a scratch pad.

"Would Jules like me to come out?"

She hesitated. He was so ill, she said.

"You think perhaps it would be better if I didn't?"

She spoke confusedly; it was hard to understand her.

"Please be quite frank," he said. "Do you mean that Jules wouldn't want to see me?"

She admitted that was it.

"Well, of course then— I'm so sorry— But tell me, Mrs. Tronchet, is there anything that I can do?"

Yes, there was—she stammered over it: she did not have money for necessary things—

"Why certainly," he said. "How much do you need?"

A hundred dollars if that would be convenient—

"I'll mail you a check this afternoon."

"Oh, thank you, Mr. Braden—"

"I hope that everything will be all right."

He phoned the doctor who made his home in Woodlawn but also had an office in the Loop. He introduced himself and explained the relationship between himself and Tronchet, mentioning that he had just spoken with the sick man's wife, rather intimating he had been referred to him for further information, but not saying so exactly—

"Mr. Tronchet is very ill—" The doctor hesitated.

"Not critically, I hope?"

"Not in immediate danger."

"Then, with good luck, he'll be back with us soon?"

"I'm afraid not, Mr. Braden—"

"But what—"

The doctor told him: Jules had had a stroke. His right side was paralyzed—the face, the arm, the leg; he could speak but it was difficult to understand his words. In time some recovery might be possible, but, too, there was the danger of another stroke. It was unlikely he would ever be able to resume an active occupation.

"I see. I'm dreadfully sorry. Well, thank you very much."

He checked on Jules' account which was not overdrawn—they drew equal sums, sufficient for their living; everything else had gone back into the plant. He was certain that the Frenchman didn't have a dime outside his modest home and his interest in the business.—Yes, he'd sell out all right—at a *reasonable* price. Just let the thing alone and give it time—

He remained at the factory until ten o'clock that night, with a sandwich for his supper, working with Getz—with balance sheets and statements, unfilled orders, inventories, receivables and payables. When he left he had a picture of the business in his pocket, and its history reduced to a paragraph of figures, and its future clear as crystal, ready to be phrased. In the morning he intended to call on Stanley Adams, whom he had never met—and to see him personally, if it should be possible; and, owing what they did, he suspected that it would be. Anyway he was prepared. In the taxi he went over and over it again.

He had sent a boy to take his baggage home, had phoned the hotel to have his room for him, his things unpacked, his clothing put away—to have the valet press the dark blue suit he would be wanting in the morning. When he came up to the desk the clerk held out his key with a lukewarm smile of welcome—"Glad to see you, Mr. Braden."

He glanced around the dim, deserted lobby. "A man was asking for you about an hour ago. I think he said he'd wait. Yes, there he is."

A figure rose from a deep upholstered chair—a short, squat man with the features of a thug. He shambled toward the desk, sticking out his hand—

"J. D. Mooney, Mr. Braden—"

"Oh, how are you, Mr. Mooney—" They shook hands.

"I was in your neighborhood, calling on a friend, and I thought I'd just drop by. I heard today that you were back." He was a little drunk, and the smell of whisky hung around him.

"I just got in this morning—" Sam was leaning on the desk, calculating swiftly: the dirty little bum had overplayed his hand; he had come around *too* quickly—

"I was thinking maybe we might have a chat?"

"It's pretty late tonight—" He wasn't going to show any interest in the matter.

"That's a way of looking at it," Mooney grinned. "But it ain't as late as it'll be tomorrow."

"Well—" He hesitated, laughing. "—come on up."

They went up to his room. He lighted the lamps, got a bottle of scotch out of his suitcase, poured out two drinks—a big one for his guest, a short one for himself. It was getting close to midnight, but he wasn't tired.

"Very sociable and friendly," Mooney chuckled. "Just to think, Mr. Braden, we could've done this long ago and saved a lot of grief."

"Well, I don't know," he answered carelessly. "Things take their time." He was thinking intently; he had a hunch that Mooney was out to save his face—

"You're a smart guy, Mr. Braden. I take my hat off to you."

He laughed.

"Here's bottoms up to you." Mooney drained his glass. "Pretty goddam smart, I mean; and I ain't kidding either. Say, you and me together would be a winning team. We could organize the country and clean up." (

"That's an idea," he said, smiling. The man was pretty drunk; the thing to do was let him talk.

"I had you on the skids—" Mooney winked his eye. "—had you whipped, by God. And you outsmarted me—pretty goddam smart it was—going off to war. Yes, by God, that was a good one, and I take my hat off to it.—Could I have another drink?"

"Sure, help yourself." He pushed the bottle to him.

"Thanks—" He poured himself a drink. "It's no good, Mr. Braden, you and me to kid each other; we're both too smart for that. With the Frenchman out of things, there's just you and me to talk. Am I right or wrong about it?"

"Right, I guess," he said.

"Well then, here's the way it stands—and I'm laying down my cards face up here on the table: we ain't whipped, and that's a fact; but we ain't whipped you either. Oh, you've lost a lot of money; I know that. And you'll keep on losing it every day that it goes on—" He paused to drink. "But we ain't done so well—four months the boys been out, and it's been tough on them. We're suckers to go on, just to cut each other's throats. Well, there it is." He leaned back in his chair with a sly grin on his lips. "I'm ready to talk business—reasonably, you understand."

He nodded. It was plain enough: Mooney was out to save his face. The bargain wouldn't be too hard: some crumbs of victory to compensate the strikers, to let them kid themselves that they had won. "Shoot," he said. "What's your proposition?"

It was settled in an hour: everybody could go back to work, including those whom Jules had fired; there were to be some minor wage adjustments; anyone could join the union, but the shop would not be closed; collective bargaining was not mentioned. Five hundred dollars was suggested and accepted—to be paid in currency when the men went back to work—

"It's cost me more than that." Mooney shook his head. "I swear to God, I haven't made a dime." He had a final drink to seal the bargain; the bottle was half empty and the man was really drunk. "Sam," he said, "you're a goddam smart guy, see? I like you, Sam. You and me, we could go places. You got the front, my boy, and the big stuff in the bean. And I got the inside angle on these working suckers. I can tie 'em up in knots; they eat out of my hand. You and me, Sam,— if you ever take a notion—" He wove out of the room.

It was nearly three o'clock. Sam went to bed—taking off, for the last time, his country's uniform.

At noon next day—clean-shaven and conservatively dressed—he was sitting in Stanley Adams' office—an office he had seen in the absence of its owner, exhibited with pride by one of the vice-presidents who was sitting near him now, looking nervous and depressed—rich mahogany, oil paintings on the walls, thick carpet on the floor. It was a large room. Stanley Adams sat with his back to the window. He was a tall, gaunt man, with short white hair, parted in the middle—with a thin, ascetic face, as unchanging in expression as a mask. And he did not look at you after he had looked at first, but at a little penknife along whose open blade he slid his thumb, half closing it and opening it.

He had thought there might be some words of conversation, such as businessmen engage in before they come to grips, but Stanley Adams' eyes did not invite amenities. He acknowledged the vice-president's introduction with a nod, not offering to shake hands nor rising from his seat. He did not speak; he waited.

Sam told his story, and he told it well. He wanted assurance that the loans would be renewed, and an additional credit of a hundred thousand dollars to cover the amount the strike had cost, which he promised to clean up in six months time. He wanted in addition, when occasion should arise, a personal loan of fifty thousand dollars with which he proposed to buy his partner's half interest in the business, and which he would presently secure by collateral in the form of stock to be issued when the business should be incorporated, following acquisition of his partner's interest. He proposed to incorporate for half a million dollars—book value of the plant. The fifty thousand loan would therefore be secured by collateral in a sum ten times as great. He felt that he could clear it in a year—

Mr. Adams asked a question—the first words he had uttered: "Have you an option on your partner's interest, at the figure you have named?"

"No sir, I haven't."

"What reason have you to suppose that your price will be accepted?"

"I believe, in the circumstances, that the price is fair."

"You have not answered my question."

"No, well—" His hands were sweating. "I will buy it at that price or not at all."

"I see. Go on."

He went on into the future: the history of the business from the time of his association with it was a reasonable clue to what one might expect; and he sketched these expectations, not too extravagantly. The country had gone shabby in this period of war—he nodded toward the window which looked out on soot-grimed buildings; it was dirty and run-down, crying out to be cleaned up. Business would be good for years to come. There was a time to finish what he had to say, and he finished on the dot. It had taken thirty minutes.

"Mr. Calkins—" Mr. Adams was addressing his vice-president. "—we will go along with Mr. Braden, in the way he has proposed." The penknife blade snapped shut and he put it in his pocket. "Submit the details to a memorandum."

"Yes sir."

Sam stood up. "Thank you, Mr. Adams."

"Good day, Mr. Braden—"

"Good day, sir."

And a good day it was. He walked out of the bank treading on the air. He had gotten what he wanted—everything. But what else could they do? They were in too deep to quit; they had to play along. And the old man was smart enough to know they'd get their money; he wasn't taking chances. As for the Frenchman—that could ride along a while; there wasn't any hurry. Sooner or later he would buy Jules Tronchet's interest for fifty thousand dollars, not a penny more or less. The thing was in the bag; the business was *his*.

He plunged into his job with all his heart and soul, with strength and confidence, with nimble wits. He was at the factory at seven in the morning, and seldom left his desk before six o'clock at night. In a week the plant was running at full capacity—running like a watch, better than it had when Jules was there. The stock pile on the shipping floor expanded magically, and strings of loaded freight cars were shuttled from the siding. The people in the office began to smile again.

A few days before Christmas, Mitch Ballou phoned from New York—charges collect.

"Sam?—Mitch Ballou."

"Hello, Mitch."

"How are you, Sam? How's tricks?"

"Okay. I thought you were in Russia."

"I was. I'm back. I heard you were in the Army."

"I was. I'm out. Who told you?"

"Nelly."

"Oh!" He had a sudden feeling that something bad was coming. He hadn't heard from her for several months, though he had written. "Where did you see her?"

"In a drugstore on Sixth Avenue. Just happened to run into her."

"How is she?"

"Well—" He hesitated. "—she didn't look too good. I guess perhaps the sledding's been a little tough."

"Yeh?"

"I gave her a card with my name and address on it; suggested she call me up sometime—"

"Yeh? Well?" He was sure of it now.

"Well, a doctor at Bellevue called me up this morning—"

"Bellevue?"

"The hospital, you know—"

"Oh yeh. Well, what?"

"Nelly's in a ward there—the Observation Ward—"

"What's wrong with her?"

"I don't know exactly. I went over right away, but it wasn't visiting hours and they wouldn't let me see her."

"Did you see the doctor?"

"Yeh—"

"What did he say?"

"I couldn't make much out of it."

"Is she very ill?"

"No, no, not dangerously at all."

"Oh!—How come they called you up?"

"Well, they found my card in her pocketbook—"

"You mean, she was alone?"

"It was on the street somewhere—"

"I see—" He had an inkling now, something he had feared.

"I think, if you can, you better come on down. That's why I called you up."

"I'll be there in the morning. I'll go to the McAlpin."

"Okay. I'll phone you, Sam. Oh, by the way, the doctor's name is Goldsmith—the man you want to see."

"Thanks, Mitch."

He caught the Century. The hotel valet packed his bag and brought it to the station. Before noon the following day he was at the hospital, in Dr. Goldsmith's office. The doctor was a young man—a psychiatrist, he said—

"But why—" Sam stared.

"Routine," the doctor smiled. He went on to explain, reading from a card: she had been picked up by the police—it was at night, somewhere on the West Side—with what they mistook for alcoholic symptoms—

« 269 »

"Mistook?"

Yes, that was a mistake. Alcohol perhaps was in the background of the matter, but at the moment of being taken ill, she was suffering from the use of drugs—

"Of drugs?"

"Cocaine." It was recognized at once when the patient was admitted to the hospital.

"You mean that she's an addict?"

Addict was a word that he could not subscribe to, on the evidence he had. She had been taking drugs; that was a fact. To what extent and over what period of time— He shrugged his shoulders. She was not in good physical condition, very thin, badly run-down. She was not communicative—

"But a habit of this kind?—it can be cured?"

"Oh yes, Mr. Braden." He mentioned Bloomingdale, a sanitarium he could highly recommend. "Oh yes, these things are curable, but—" He hesitated, fingering some object on his desk. "—but the problem is not solved until the source is found."

"The source?"

"The thing from which the patient is trying to escape."

"I see."

"I have seen your sister several times. I have been interested in the case." Again he hesitated, as if to choose his words. "There are, I think, incipient signs of some deterioration—in her psychology."

"What do you mean?"

"It's like this, Mr. Braden: when reality becomes too painful to endure, there is one sure method of escape; and that is to deny it— to take refuge in a world which one makes to suit oneself. Daydreaming is the common, harmless form of it. But if one embarks too far, comes finally to exchange the fact for the illusion, then reality is lost; there is no contact with it. The dreamer cannot—will not—be awakened."

"Yes, I understand."

"Your sister has suffered some bitter deprivation, deep wounding of the psyche—one time or many, what or when, I have no means of knowing."

"I know," Sam said.

"Yes, well—" Dr. Goldsmith spread his hands. He was a Jew, with a narrow, sensitive face—very young to be so wise. "Nor can I tell you what to do—" He shrugged and smiled. "A normal, healthy life, with someone closely bound to her by a strong emotional tie—" He paused, drumming with his fingers on the desk.

"Not an easy prescription," Sam said grimly.

"No, not easy, Mr. Braden. Perhaps not possible." He went with him to the door. "If you decide on Bloomingdale, I shall be glad to make arrangements."

Nelly was in a ward, lying quietly with half-closed eyes. A nurse had pointed out her bed, and as he came close to it he thought that the woman had misdirected him, so greatly had she changed since he had seen her last—two or three years ago, when she passed through Chicago coming back from Hollywood. But then he saw that it was Nelly—very thin and white, with bluish circles underneath her eyes, her hair once more its natural color but there was a lot of gray in it. Her hands were open limply on the covers.

He spoke to her, and spoke her name again before she turned her head; and then for a moment she seemed not to recognize him—as if association functioned slowly. Perhaps, he thought, the result of sedatives. But then she smiled, not seemingly surprised or very glad to see him. She didn't ask him anything: how he happened to be there or who had told him.

"Well, Nelly—" He was being brisk and hearty, as healthy men incline to be in the presence of the sick. He stooped and kissed her forehead, and sat uncomfortably on a chair beside the bed. The adjoining beds were occupied; there was no privacy. "How you feeling, Nelly?" She shook her head, not in complaint, but as if to indicate she hadn't thought about it. He talked at random in the ritual of the sickroom: bits of news and gossip Madge had written, anecdotes about his army life, and—perhaps she hadn't heard—about Neill Wyatt being killed. It was a monologue which he could not maintain; he would start off bravely and it would peter out. She asked no questions, evidenced no interest, yet he couldn't say she wasn't listening.

He tried another tack: he had talked with Dr. Goldsmith and been much impressed with him; the doctor had in view a sanitarium— a delightful place close to the city, run like a fine hotel, with the best of food and service—where she could get her health back, really get to feeling well, tiptop and full of pep. She shook her head, but he didn't stop to argue. When she was herself again they could plan about the future; maybe she might feel like going home to Wyattville —just for a visit. She shook her head.

"Sam—" He would never have recognized her voice—a rasping whisper. She motioned him closer, and he drew his chair against the bed. "I got a cold," she said. "I can't talk very loud." He nodded sympathetically. "You understand me, Sam?"

"Yes, Nelly." He took her hand; there was no feeling in it.

"I'm whipped, Sam."

"Now, don't say that. It's just because you're sick and tired out."

"No—" She shook her head.

"We'll have you stepping out again."

"No—"

"Why not?"

"Because I'm whipped."

"Nonsense!"

"I was always kidding you, writing cheerful letters—kidding myself too. But I never got a break—not ever once. I've been whipped for a long time—maybe back in Muscatine. I was awful young and green—"

"Both of us, Nelly." He pressed her hand.

"Show business—and actors—" She made a sound that might have been a laugh.

"We'll get a fresh start, Nelly."

"No, it's too late."

"You'll feel different in a month."

She turned her face away. He went on talking for a while, venturing this and that, but then he couldn't stand it any longer. "I guess I better run along and let you get some rest." Her eyes were open but she didn't answer. "I'll drop in again tomorrow. And don't you worry, Nelly; everything will be all right."

He went back to Dr. Goldsmith. He had decided on Bloomingdale, he said. He waited while the doctor telephoned and made arrangements. There were different rates, depending on the type of room. Perhaps Mr. Braden would like to see the place, select a room himself? Yes, he would like to do that, but he was pressed for time, must return to Chicago not later than tomorrow. The doctor concluded the arrangement, selecting a room of medium price. In a day or two she could be moved—

"Could you," he inquired, "continue in some way to supervise the case?"

"Yes, certainly," the doctor said. He had other patients there and would see her regularly. He thought she should remain about three months. "And then—" He spread his hands.

"And then we'll see," Sam said. He explained that he would take care of all expense, and that he would attend to the packing of her things and have them sent to her—he had the address of the place she had been living—

Dr. Goldsmith nodded.

"Well, thank you very much for your interest in the matter. And you'll keep me posted, doctor?"

"Yes, fully, Mr. Braden."

It was snowing when he left the hospital. He took a cab to the address —another brownstone house in the west thirties, smelly and forbidding. And another slattern woman, of a piece with those he had interviewed before, answered his ring. She listened with suspicious eyes, but impressed with his appearance and with the waiting cab. She didn't know, she said; she ought to have an order, she didn't have a right to let anybody in to go through a person's things; she might get into trouble. She didn't know a thing about it; sometimes Miss Braden went away, and was gone for several days. She might be in the hospital, and then again she mightn't. Anyway she owed three weeks, and her things would have to stay there until the bill was paid—

"I'll take care of that," he said.

"Well—" But it seemed to dispose of any scruples that she had. She changed her tune: she was sorry to hear that Miss Braden had been sick; she guessed things hadn't been so easy for her; the theater season hadn't been a good one—several of her lodgers had been out of jobs and got behind on paying—

She led him up three flights of dark and dirty stairs, thick with the musty smell of greasy cooking, into a small bare room with a window that looked out on a brick wall—a room that never knew a ray of sunlight. It was in disorder, and the bed had not been made since it had been slept in. The woman said, apologizing for it, "I was waiting to change it till I knew if she'd be back."

He nodded. He wanted to get rid of her, refusing her offer of assistance. He could manage by himself. He paid her what she said was owing to her; it wasn't much.

And there wasn't much to pack: poor, shabby garments, the only kind that she had ever had; pink underthings, worn out and faded, washed till they were ragged, dried on the looking glass; some toilet articles, a book or two, letters in a drawer—he thumbed them through

—some from him, from Madge, others that he didn't know—clippings in an envelope, old theater programs. On the dresser was a photograph in a tarnished silver frame: the actor she had married—handsome and no good. You could guess by looking at him what had happened. All that there was he packed into two bags—a cardboard suitcase and an old valise that seemed familiar to him: the one she had brought when she came to Muscatine, nearly twenty years ago—

He was glad that the woman had gone out, that there was no one to intrude upon his memories. Poor little Nelly—waiting in that room, or others like it, for a break that never came; listening for the phone at the bottom of the stairs, praying that the call might be for her—waiting through the years, while youth and beauty faded, while Hope gave up the ghost—sitting there at night beneath the naked light bulb, patching up her clothes so she might be ready when Fortune glanced her way—going to bed and getting up again, never having anything, always being poor—pinching, scraping, waiting—

He heard again his mother's voice speaking to him from her deathbed; and Dr. Bentley urging her, translating what she said—"Now, Sarah, just a little louder. Try real hard.—She wants you to be a good man, Sam. Not great, but good, she says.—You understand that, Sam?—She says, take care of Nelly—of Nelly, Sam."—Hot tears came to his eyes.—Take care of Nelly, yes. But what more could he have done? He had always sent her money, even when it meant giving up things that he needed. What more could he have done?—what else?

The door stood ajar. He heard a telephone ringing remotely, and then the woman's voice calling up the stair well, and a girl's voice answer her, and the sound of clattering slippers on the stairs—then dragging up again. He waited by the door, not wanting to encounter anyone. From the landing underneath he caught scraps of conversation: "Any luck, kid?"—"Naw." The voice was weary, listless. "My brother down in Jersey." A door banged petulantly. He went quickly down the stairs, hurrying to get out into the open air.

He left the bags at an express office. It was near five o'clock when he got back to the hotel. He stopped in the flower shop and sent some roses to the hospital. The floor clerk handed him a message and a telegram: the message was from Mitch, naming a number where he could be reached; the wire?—from the factory, he assumed. He didn't open it until he was in his room—and then at first he didn't understand—

Am at the Waldorf. Could you possibly arrange to come and see me?—E.

Eileen come back from France?—here in New York?—He read it again, turned it in his hands.—And how could she have known that he was in New York?—even his hotel?—But then he saw: the message had been filed that morning, sent to him at the factory, and relayed back again. It was funny: there he was a block away, when she was telegraphing to Chicago.—"Could you possibly arrange to come and see me?"—And that was funny, too.—See her?—about what?—Why was she stopping in New York? Why hadn't she come home? And why would she suggest that he go a thousand miles to see her about something?—The divorce, no doubt; but that was not a matter to justify the trip; it could wait a day or two till she got home.—Was it something else perhaps?—"Could you possibly arrange to come and see me?"— Strangely phrased, he thought—a hint of desperation, an appeal that wasn't like her. Could it be that she was ill?

He picked up the telephone but changed his mind before the operator answered. It was only a step down Thirty-fourth Street. Why not go and see? He was curious, intrigued—conscious, too, of a quickening of his pulse at the bare idea of seeing her.—"Could you possibly arrange—" She had never said a thing like that before.— What was it anyway?—He went into the bathroom and carefully combed his hair and set his necktie straight. Going through the lobby he stopped in the flower shop and bought a box of violets arranged in a corsage with a fragrant gardenia in the center—flowers she had liked to wear. There could be no harm in that, no matter what she wanted. The girl behind the counter tucked a white carnation in his buttonhole, but in the street he took it out and put it in his pocket.

It was dark now and still snowing. He walked the long block briskly, thinking of the past, his honeymoon: a little way down Fifth, was the old Holland House, if it was still there—he didn't know; he had never been inside the place again. He passed a shop where they had gone for tea. It was all remote, like something in a dream, ended and forgotten; still, not entirely—else why would he have bought the box of violets, be walking toward the Waldorf, be thinking of the past, be conscious of his pulses?—It would certainly surprise her. "Could you possibly arrange—" Wiring to Chicago at ten o'clock this morning, and having him walk in a little after five. Perhaps they would have dinner, if she was not engaged; and, if she was—well, she might even break it. There must be something that she wanted to discuss. He could see Mitch tomorrow—have lunch with him perhaps. It popped into his head—possibly the snow, but there it was: a ragged little boy dragging his broken sled with Mrs. Henry's dress—the iron fence—the snow man by the walk—the two of them—

He came into the Waldorf, to the desk. "Mrs. Braden?" he inquired. The clerk glanced at the room chart and reached for a telephone. It flashed through his mind that this would rather spoil it—he would like to see her face when she found that he was there. "You needn't phone," he said. "I'm Mr. Braden."—"Oh, excuse me, Mr. Braden." He named the number of the room. "Shall I send a boy to show you?" —"No thanks, I'll find the way."

In the elevator with him was a nursemaid with a baby—a very tiny baby, he suspected, from the way it was wrapped up. Probably it had been out, trundling in its cab, for the woman had a fur robe on her arm—a foreign-looking nursemaid in a cap with big starched bows. Apparently she knew no English, for she had some trouble to indicate her floor. And she left the car when he did. When he saw that she was leaving, he stepped back to let her pass, and he caught a fleeting glimpse of the baby's face—pink and puckered from the cold—too tiny to be going out in the winter snow. He was thinking of this as he walked along the corridor, glancing at the doors for the number that he sought, watching the nursemaid who was walking on before him—thinking that the Waldorf was a poor place for a baby. She stopped before a door, knocked lightly and went in. He went on around a corner of the hall, and then he saw that the numbers were too high. Watching the nursemaid he had missed the one he wanted. He retraced his steps—there it was, as big as life. But he could have sworn that it was the door on which the woman knocked, through which she had gone. Mistake of course. There was another door a few steps farther on—

He knocked and a voice said to come in—her voice, he thought; and so it proved to be. She was alone, sitting on a couch beside the fireplace in which there was a fire, glowing coals—and there was a table with some tea things on it. She had thought it was the waiter and she didn't look around; her back was to the door. Standing in the doorway he had time for observation: the room was a parlor, part of a suite, old-fashioned, very comfortable, probably expensive. Her hair was bobbed—and this was startling—cut off to brush her shoulders, as beautiful as ever, but straight and severe. He couldn't see her face. She was wearing a negligee, creamy and soft—elegant as ever—

"You can take the tray," she said.

"Yes, madam—" And he laughed. Now she was on her feet and staring at him. "Service," he said lightly, still standing by the door. "Service, madam. You press a button and I come on a magic carpet."

She didn't speak. He had really startled her—too much perhaps. He saw that she was thinner; still, she looked very fit. He closed the door, put down his hat and coat. "In fact," he said, "I happened to be here. Your wire was sent back; I got it half an hour ago."

"Oh—" She nodded.

"Well—" He came over to the couch which was between them. "You're looking fine. You've been all right, I hope?"

She didn't offer to shake hands; and that would have been stupid. But he was self-conscious now, the excitement wearing off. It wasn't any different—anything about it—just where it had left off.

"I'm sorry—" she said half to herself, and added quickly, as if in explanation, "I didn't dream—"

"Of course." He laughed, wishing now that he had telephoned. Surprising people wasn't very safe. But it hadn't crossed his mind that she would take it this way—be so upset about it. "Some violets, Eileen—" He handed her the box.

"Thank you, Sam—" But she didn't open it. She sat down on the couch—abruptly, he thought, as though she might feel giddy.

He selected an easy chair, with the fireplace between them. "Nice old hotel," he said. "I didn't know you ever stopped here?"

"I never have before—" She kept looking at him in a way to add to his discomfort—not the old way that he knew, but quite apart from that. He couldn't analyze it. "Would you like a cup of tea, Sam?"

"No thanks." He lit a cigarette. "When did you get in?"

"Yesterday—"

"Oh, yesterday?" He was thinking: she hadn't lost much time in sending him that wire—"Could you possibly arrange"— But she didn't seem eager to develop what she wanted. "Pleasant trip?" he asked.

"Not very—"

"Oh! Well, that's too bad." He searched his mind for something else to say, but nothing seemed to fit: he couldn't mention Neill, nor yet ignore him. Had she seen her Uncle Elliott? But that was a question which would lead straight to the other. Or "Tell me, Eileen, about

« 277 »

your life in France—" Even that was tricky ground. His hands were sweating—

"Funny thing," he said, with affected heartiness, "I couldn't find the room. I must have walked right past it, down the corridor, around the corner—" He motioned with his hand. "I was watching a nurse-maid with a baby in her arms—a foreign-looking woman with a big, white, starchy cap. And I walked right by the door. I would have sworn that she—"

He was suddenly aware that she was not attending, that her attention was directed elsewhere—toward a door that was behind her, which led perhaps to a connecting room. Her head was half turned toward it. The expression in her eyes, which he hadn't understood, was now revealed and unmistakable: anxiety, expectancy—anxious expectancy. Yes, that was it: not fright or fear, but consuming apprehension. She was listening to something—for which she had been waiting—which at first he didn't hear. And then he did—muffled, scarcely audible—the wailing of a tiny baby—

And suddenly he knew, knew everything: that the nursemaid and the baby had come into this room—that the baby was hers, hers and Neill Wyatt's.

And she knew that he knew, read it in his face as he stumbled to his feet—that there was nothing now to conceal or to explain. She stood up facing him, apprehension fading from her eyes, giving place to something else—

"I didn't mean for it to be this way—"

No, naturally, of course. But he didn't say the words; he was choking with humiliation. The box of violets unopened on the table, the elation he had felt, the quickening of his pulse in response to her appeal—"Could you possibly arrange—" A calculated decoy—

"I'm dreadfully sorry, Sam—"

That's what her eyes were saying, that she was sorry for him—sorry like a girl who jilts a man—like a woman confessing that she has a lover—no, worse than that: a woman surprised in the act of infidelity. His sense of injury blinded him: in fact she owed him nothing; she was not his wife in anything but name, and she had pleaded to be free of that—

"I couldn't write about it. I meant to meet you somewhere and—"

"I should have telephoned," he said between his teeth.—Well, she was square with him—square now for everything: for tearing her nightgown, for saying those things that couldn't be unsaid—

"I don't mean that. It was kind of you to come—just the way you did. It's only that I'm sorry—"

"I understand."—He understood all right: she had never loved him; she had been in love with Neill, always, from the start; she had gone to France to find him, and she had found him, too—made love to him no doubt—to Neill who would be generous with his favors, who would take it in his stride, who loved everything too well to love one woman much or very long. No matter about that, she had gotten what she wanted—

"When I wrote to you last summer—"

"I'm sorry too," he said.—But was he? Was there any reason why she should be spared?—her sin absolved? Certainly it would have been convenient: a French divorce, no questions to be asked—being decently, or legally, bedded with her partner—not bringing a nameless child into the world. The outraged Puritan rose in him—the heritage of Puritans: his wounded and humiliated ego.—Yes, he was sorry, but sorry for himself.

"It's my fault, Sam. I should have told you then—"

He didn't answer that, edging around her, toward his hat and coat. He wanted to get out—out into the air. She followed him a step, pleading with her eyes—like the words she had written in the telegram—"Could you possibly arrange—"

"We must do something, Sam—"

"Yes, well—" He fumbled with his coat.—We?—what did she mean by that?—Why had she sent for him?—what did she want?— Was she asking for the shelter of his name?—that the child should be protected—

But it wasn't that, not anything like that. She must have read the question in his face, for she winced as if he'd struck her; and she stood between him and the door, flushed, with blazing eyes, angry and hurt—as he had never seen her, not even that last night that they were man and wife—

"No, no," she cried. "How could you think that I—"

He was searching for his muffler in the pockets of his coat—searching with averted eyes. He was ashamed—

"His name is Neill," she said, "Neill Wyatt—his father's name and mine."

He nodded, sick of it, frantic to be gone.

She went on passionately: she wanted a divorce and that was all. She had come under compulsion, because he would not give consent unless, or till, she did. Well, she was here. It must be settled now. She wanted to return to France at once, to carry out the plan she had proposed—a French divorce. There would be no publicity; no one need ever know the date of it. It could be assumed to have happened long ago, that she and Neill were legally man and wife. And she would remain in France until any question of it was forgotten—

She had never said so much within his hearing—perhaps had never had so good a reason; she was pleading for her child, that he might never suffer the handicap of knowing—

"Certainly," he mumbled. "Anything you wish—"

And then at last he was outside in the hall, almost running to be gone, passing by another door through whose open transom he could hear the puny wailing—

Neill Wyatt come back from the grave.—The two of them *again*—the two of them—

X

SAM MARRIED EMILIE KRANZ — HURRIEDLY AND RASHLY — IN September, 1919. He used to say, with a twinkle in his eye, "The only hasty thing I ever did." And, he might have added with some degree of truth, the only one he never had occasion to regret.

He was thirty-five years old and she was twenty-three. She had been working for him, as his secretary, in an office on Michigan which looked across the lake—not a very big office and not at all pretentious. The furniture was mahogany veneer, manufactured in Grand Rapids; there were no oil paintings on the walls and your feet did not sink into the carpet. These things would come later, when he moved the office force into the city—Getz and Trask and Brown and all of them—to occupy the whole of a lofty tower floor in a new expensive building. It was good publicity, and anyway he wanted things where he had his fingers on them.

But to begin with there were only three of them—himself and Mike and Emilie. And Mike was on the go most of the time, running back and forth to Clearing, learning about wallpaper, poking into corners, conducting liaison, transmitting orders, word for word, in a confidential whisper from the corner of his mouth through bubbles of saliva—stupid but devoted, a good staff officer; in time he came to be invaluable. If you told him what to do, and were careful what you said—to cross all your *t*'s and dot your *i*'s—you could count on the result. Like that legendary hero with his "Message to Garcia," Mike would keep going till he got there.

Emilie was not a very good stenographer; she had trouble with her notes. Often enough she would come into his office, which was partitioned off in a corner of the room, with her notebook in her hand, standing near the door, dreading to disturb him. And when he looked up—

"I'm sorry, Uncle Sam—" He had insisted on it at the start, and she had made a way of saying it which didn't sound like that, which no one who overheard it could possibly interpret. "Unkam," it sounded like, and later came to be. "I hate to bother you—"

"Yes? What?"

"I don't think I've got this right—" And she would read her notes up to the fatal point: "—re ream basis: indicated weight reduction will not affect eye value and should not endanger—" She would pause, blushing like a rose. It looks like "toothless," but of course it isn't—"

"Tensile," he would smile. "—the tensile strength."

"Oh yes, that's what it is. Tensile—tensile—" And she would back away, terribly embarrassed. She hadn't bobbed her hair as so many of them had. It was piled up on her head, full of the glint of copper, above the deep brown eyes in the sensitive oval face. Her skin was smooth and dark; she didn't use cosmetics—didn't even paint her lips which had color of their own—which made you think of velvet. Very feminine. A slender, graceful figure—almost fragile—

"That's all right, Emilie." But he had thought at first he would have to get another secretary, someone more experienced; not letting Emilie go, but pretending there was too much work for her to do alone. But then she had improved, after a month or two; she was quick and deft and willing.

She always kept a flower on his desk—a rose or a sprig of heliotrope, some dainty, fragrant blossom; she had thought of that herself and had bought a little vase, and when she went to lunch she would bring back something for it. He had tried to reimburse her for the money that she spent, but she had seemed so hurt that he had not insisted—

"That would spoil it, Uncle Sam. It's because I want to do it."

"All right." He let it go. Now and then he gave her something: a box of candy or a book—tickets for a concert once or twice, saying carelessly that she could take her mother. Her face had lighted up—she was fond of music, a good musician too; but he had cut short her blushing, stammered thanks, pretending that the tickets had been given to him, that he wouldn't use them anyway, wouldn't sit through such a thing—

He was careful not to overdo it. He never asked her to have dinner with him, not even when he kept her, finishing her letters, until after six or seven—and they were alone, just the two of them. And he always remained until she left. When the letters had been sealed and stamped and dropped into the chute, she would come to his door—she would have her hat on now—

"I guess that's all tonight?"

"That's all."

"Good night, Uncle Sam."

"Good night, Emilie."

He would wait a while before he left, not wanting to catch up with her at the elevator. A time or two, on stormy nights, he had been tempted to suggest that he would take her home—take her in a cab, so she wouldn't have to wedge into a crowded streetcar, maybe hanging on a strap—it was in the same direction, though Deming Court was farther; and it would be nice to be sitting by her side, going nome together. But he never did it.

He took a cab alone. Sometimes he'd have dinner in a restaurant in the Loop—nearly always by himself unless he kept Mike with him to discuss some business matter. And more than once he thought that it would be very pleasant if Emilie were sitting across the table from him, but—business was business, and it didn't do to mix things. He could look around and pick the men dining with their secretaries, who were out for what was in it, or didn't dare refuse. They didn't act like wives, or like sweethearts either; they were too eager, putting on the stuff, being terribly absorbed, laughing when they should, coy when it was time—anything to please the boss. The men were middle-aged, prosperous-looking fellows; they didn't act like husbands or like lovers, but as if they were accustomed to pay for what they wanted—and to get it, too. The girls were young and pretty; they looked all right if you didn't look too close, and then you saw that the fur was artificial and the jewelry was by Woolworth. They'd start off with a cocktail; likely as not, when they got to the dessert, they would be rubbing knees underneath the table—

Emilie was like his sister, almost like a daughter: she couldn't be subjected to anything like that—being stared at in a restaurant and smirkingly appraised. No, it wouldn't do at all; it would not be fair to her, and he would feel uncomfortable—self-conscious—

He didn't know he was becoming fond of her in the way in which he was. The idea hadn't crossed his mind—or, if it had, he had rejected it. That would be nonsense. There were twelve years between them—or was it eleven?—No matter which, he had been a grown man while she was still a baby, when she used to cuddle in his lap and beg him for a story, when she found that funny name for him— made it up herself, though she could hardly say it—Uncle Sam, when he used to take her to the zoo on Sunday afternoons, and she never got enough of staring at the bears—the big white one was her favorite —"Will he bite me, Uncle Sam?"—"He might."—"But he doesn't look cross at me."—and they'd buy a bag of popcorn or a box of Crackerjack—Well, of course, it was ridiculous—

And how did she think of him?—Probably as an old family friend, a sort of relative—an uncle naturally, almost like a father, old enough to be; a man who had been married—married and divorced, of tarnished experience, verging on middle-age—not a romantic figure. Yes, that would be the way he must appear to her. Perhaps she had a sweetheart, a young fellow who came calling, but she'd never mentioned one; he didn't think she had. Anyway it was absurd—

It was at the end of August—a sultry, sticky day with the promise of a thunderstorm that wouldn't seem to jell, and an irritating matter to add to his discomfort. In the morning Hub Baxter had called up: Mrs. Tronchet had phoned him and wanted him to call; she had not said what about and had been, as usual, hard to understand. He wanted to discuss the thing again before he went—

And this was irritating. There was nothing to discuss. The Tronchet matter remained in *status quo*; although eight months had passed, not a thing had been accomplished. Hub Baxter had made several trips to Woodlawn—he was acting for them both, a role involving a point of legal ethics which he and Sam had carefully ignored. But he hadn't closed a deal, nor even got in shouting distance of it. Jules would sell all right, but he wanted book value for his half—or, the way he figured it, two hundred thousand dollars—four times what Sam had offered. And the Frenchman hadn't given in a penny, stubborn as a mule, acting exactly as he acted with the strike: whipped but not admitting it.

He was flat on his back, one side of him dead. He couldn't talk so you could understand him; you wrote down on a tablet what you thought he said, and then held it up for him to read, and with a lot of struggle you would get it straightened out. Hub had described his visits, which he had not enjoyed, and for which he was charging a pretty handsome fee. It took half a day, he said, to get anywhere at all.

But this morning he spoke cheerfully: her sending for him now made it look as though the Frenchman might be coming to his senses, as though a deal of some sort might be closed, though he greatly doubted that the figure Sam had set—

Sam interrupted him. "That's the limit," he said briefly. "Fifty thousand dollars." It was really irritating; they had been over that a dozen times. Fifty thousand was the figure he had named to Stanley Adams, and the limit he could borrow; there wasn't any more. Anyway it was annoying: you hired a lawyer to do something that you wanted, and the first thing that he thought of was to compromise the issue—

"Are you serious about it?"

"I'm serious about it." Sooner or later the Frenchman had to sell. The partnership agreement was that they should draw in equal sums while *active* in the business, aside from distribution of the profits. Jules was no longer active, and there were no profits; the business was in debt—would be for some time—*could be* indefinitely—

"You wouldn't raise the ante?—just a little anyway?"

"Not one cent." He had been sending money when she asked—a hundred at a time. But that was charity; he could stop it any moment that he liked—

"It isn't very much, if you take the balance sheet—"

"That's a matter of opinion. Anyway that's up to me." It was like a lawyer, free and openhanded with his client's money—

"Well, I'll do the best I can. I'll give you a ring when I get back."

"All right," he said and hung up the receiver.

Mike had gone to Clearing. The day wore on, getting heavier and hotter; the thunderstorm was lurking in the southern sky, not coming any nearer; the lake looked like a sheet of molten lead. It was terribly oppressive. After lunch he called Emilie for dictation—long letters, rather technical, and copious memoranda for Getz and Trask and Brown; the selling season was commencing.

He dictated pretty fast, faster than usual. He knew that she was having trouble, sitting close beside him at the desk leaf—looking cool and comfortable in a thin white frock fitted snugly to her slender figure, cut low around the neck and without sleeves. There were no damp spots of perspiration on it. Ordinarily he would have slowed or asked her to read back, but he was in an irritable and sadistic mood; his Palm Beach suit was wet and sticking to the chair. Once she broke her pencil point, but he didn't even pause; she grabbed another quickly. She didn't ask for mercy, didn't look up from her book. He was wishing that she would—maybe trying to compel it. It was after four o'clock when he let her go.

It was five when Hub called back. His voice was far from cheerful: Jules had had another stroke, the night before. He couldn't talk at all now, or even nod his head. He seemed to be all dead—all except his eyes which were blazing with defiance.

"Yeh?" He thought a moment. "What did she want of you?"

"Well—" Hub seemed vague about it. "—I guess she's up against it, doesn't know which way to turn. Poor woman—" You could feel him shake his head. "I felt sorry for her."

"Yeh, sure," he said drily. Sorry was all right, but *he* would get the bill. He turned the matter in his mind. "Where do we go from here?"

"I don't know, Sam. I've been thinking about that—"

"Humph!" And that was like a lawyer—waiting for you to tell them what to do, and then picking holes in it.

"They go on living for years sometimes, I guess."

He didn't answer that.

"I suppose—" Hub hesitated. "—in a case involving total incapacity, some form of guardianship might be indicated."

"Would the court come in on that?"

"Yes. Yes, it would."

"All right, scratch that one."

"Yes," Hub agreed, "that's what I thought. I don't believe the court would authorize a sale at the price we've offered—"

"No matter," he said testily. "We'll keep out of court."

"Well, what—"

"I'll tell you what," he said, and he was sure now. "Just nothing for the present, not a thing. Lay off. Forget it. If she sends for you again, don't go—unless you want to pay a social visit. Understood?"

"Check," Hub said, and added, "Oh, by the way, Sam—"

"Yeh?"

"A cable came this afternoon from Paris—"

"Yeh?"

"Well, that thing's all cleaned up. The decree was granted yesterday."

"You mean, I'm a free man?" He smiled ironically.

"Well—free in France."

And that was like a lawyer—hedging to the last. "Okay," he said. "So long—"

He sat there, drumming with his fingers on the desk. It was as hot as ever, but the sky had darkened; the thunderstorm was coming—its fleecy harbingers scudding high above the lake.

Free.—There was no elation in the idea. He had not been thinking in other terms than that, not for a long time; it served no purpose now to be reminded of it, except to increase his sense of irritation. He had been saying, when people asked about Eileen, as they sometimes did: "Eileen?—She's still in France, I think." And he would add, as if it were a thing of common knowledge, "You know, we're not together any more." And if they looked embarrassed or astonished—"Yes, we've been separated quite a while." He never spoke of a divorce; yet, from what he said, a divorce could be implied. He had protected her.

He had told the truth to Madge, one week end that he spent at home—not to anybody else, not even Mama Kranz. He had told Madge because he thought she ought to be prepared for gossip that was certain to arise in Wyattville. It was in the spring, after Sunday dinner. They were sitting on the porch behind the honeysuckle vine, and Jim was in the house, taking his midday nap. Madge had been horrified; she had cried about it—

"Oh Sam—" She couldn't look at him. She was a small-town woman, prim and a little prudish. "—why should such a dreadful thing come into your life?"

"Things happen, Madge."

"Well, they ·shouldn't—not to *you*—" Her chin set firmly. "—you who are so kind, so good to everybody."

"Oh well—" He shrugged.

It was a shame, she said, a disgraceful, wicked thing. No good would come to Eileen Wyatt from it. Sooner or later people suffered for their sins. The neighbors might forget, but God remembered—

He wasn't listening. He was thinking of Neill Wyatt playing in the yard, swinging in a hammock, drinking lemonade; and Eileen running back and forth from the house across the Square. He could see the iron fence through the honeysuckle vine, through the cottonwoods which were not fully out—the old brick house with its crazy cupola, pretty shabby and run-down, empty and deserted—

He changed the subject. "How's your garden, Madge?"

They went to look at it. The lilac was in bloom, and things were coming up out of the ground—tiny little shoots of this and that. She explained them eagerly, but his thought was far away—

Afterwards she wrote him that rumors were about: it was whispered that Eileen had a child, that Neill Wyatt was the father, that she had not been married to him, perhaps not yet divorced—nobody seemed to know. Anyway it just confirmed what they had always said: that Eileen would get Neill Wyatt in the end, one way or another; they seemed rather pleased about it. The Henry Wyatts had not returned from Long Beach at their usual time, were not coming back this summer; Young Henry had been ill, so Mrs. Henry wrote. When people questioned Madge, or poked around the subject, she handled the matter as he had asked her to, saying that she really didn't know a thing about it beyond the fact that her brother and Eileen had parted long ago. She didn't give them any satisfaction.

Free.—Far off thunder rumbled; the stagnant air stirred restlessly and then lay still again—like a sodden blanket wrapped around your head.—Free—both of them. And he had protected her—alleging, or admitting, nothing—her and her child who should have been *his* son, whose name *was* Braden, no matter what she called him. Yes, he had protected them—and, in a way, himself. It was not a situation one would choose to advertise—

He was drumming with his fingers on the desk. He could hear the clicking of the typewriter; and through the open door he could see his secretary, sitting trim and straight at her machine. It would race along a while—she was a rapid typist: line after line, with the tinkle of the bell, and the bang of the carriage jerked back to the start. And then there'd be a pause. He knew that she was having trouble, knew it all the time he was thinking other things, as a sort of an accompaniment—aware when she was struggling, staring at her notebook, leafing through the pages of the dictionary, searching for some word that might prove to be a clue to the pothooks which defied interpretation. And then she would go on: click click click, tinkle bell and carriage bang; and the platen would spin as she jerked the letter out. One more gone anyway. And then the rustle of another letterhead and second sheet and carbon, and the tapping of the edges, evening them upon the desk, and the sound of them whirling into place. Click click click, tinkle bell and carriage bang—away she'd go again for half a dozen lines; and then another pause—irritating interruption of the rhythm, like waiting for the fellow to drop the other shoe. He knew if she was stopping to erase; that was quickly done and the clicking would resume. But if in a moment it didn't start again, he knew she was in trouble.

And she was in trouble now. It was almost quitting time, and there she was, staring at her notebook. For several minutes there hadn't been a sound—just the rustling of the dictionary pages, and now not even that. He might have called to her, as he often did, "In trouble, Emilie?"—Or she might come in and ask; she could see that he was sitting there, not doing anything. Well, let her struggle—

But the matter took possession of his fretful mind—like a buzzing fly in the lamp shade when you're reading: what was she puzzling over? Some silly, trifling thing. He walked out to the cooler for a glass of water, appraising, from the corner of his eye, the letters in the basket: not more than half, he thought; there remained a solid hour's work of typing. How the devil could she sit there doing nothing?—did she think the notebook might begin to talk?—He dawdled by the cooler, rinsing out the glass, fuming with impatience; and then he started back, determined not to help her, not even glancing at her, though he knew she had looked up, that she was watching him. He had almost reached the door—

"I hate—" she ventured timidly.

"Yes? What?" He snapped

"I hate to bother you. I know you've been upset—"

"Nonsense," he said. "What is it?"

"A word I can't—"

"What does it look like?"

"If I read the sentence to you—"

"No, don't." She might as well learn to use imagination. "Just tell me what it looks like."

"It looks like 'selfish,' but—"

"*Selvage*." He took a chance.

"Oh yes! Yes, that's it. Thank you very much—"

He turned on his heel. "It's getting late," he said.

"Yes. Yes, I know. I'm awfully sorry—"

"Humph!" He went on toward the door.

"Perhaps—" There was something in the word, or in the way she said it, that raked across his nerves—that made him jerk around, half aware of what was coming. She was blushing and confused, biting her lip. But he waited, glaring at her. "Perhaps you ought to get another secretary?"

"What?"

"I mean, I know I'm not competent enough—"

"You mean you want to quit?—walk out on me?"

"Oh no. I'd stay of course, till you found another girl—"

"I see." He came back to her desk, furious and hurt. "Till I found, another girl, eh?"

She nodded, staring at him.

"I'm not looking for another girl—not now or any time."

"I—I only meant—" she stammered.

"I don't care what you meant." He was leaning with his knuckles on her desk. "I'm not looking for another girl. You understand that, Emilie?"

"Yes—" she gulped, not knowing what he meant. Nor did he know, himself, until that moment.

"You're the girl I want—always—*always.*" She was sitting with her hands spread limply on the keyboard, and the desk between them—funny how there always was a desk—staring at him in amazement, wide-eyed, a little frightened. "I'm in love with you. I love you." He almost shouted it, angrily in fact.

"Oh—" she said, and that was all. There was no way of telling what the exclamation meant.

He stood there for a moment with the desk between them, not adding anything, not another word; and then he turned and stared toward the outer door. But outside in the hall he came back and opened it. She hadn't moved; her eyes were on the door through which he had vanished and now had reappeared.

"Don't go till I come back." And he was gone again.

In the elevator he kept repeating it beneath his breath: "Don't go till I come back."—Stupid admonition. Probably she thought he had gone crazy. Possibly he had. Of course she wouldn't go, not with those unfinished letters. She'd be at them for an hour, and she'd be stuck again: "selfish" or "selvage"—some damn word or other—

The elevator starter looked at him in surprise, suggesting politely, "Your hat, Mr. Braden?"—thinking he'd forgotten it.

He laughed. "I'm coming back."

Spaulding's jewelry store was on the corner. The thunderstorm was almost overhead; the sky was black, and big wet raindrops were splashing on the sidewalk. He went into the store. They were putting things away, spreading dust covers on the counters. He didn't notice any other customers. A salesman whom he knew, came hurrying toward him—

"Closing up?" he asked.

"Beginning to get ready—"

"Too late to make a purchase?"

"No indeed, Mr. Braden." The salesman smiled. "Never too late for that. What have you in mind?"

"Diamonds."

"Something in a ring?"

"That's right."

"For a lady?"

"Yes."

"A solitaire perhaps?"

"Perhaps.—Let's see."

He was looking at a tray of them, spread out on the counter, when he heard a voice beside him, light and gay and mocking—

"Well, well, well, if it isn't Uncle Sam!"

For a moment he didn't recognize her—it had been seven years; that time at the Plaza was the last, in the parlor full of flowers, listening to the story of how Daphne met her death. But then she turned her head and he saw the scar—there was no veil to hide it—the livid welt across her cheek; that hadn't changed. Nor had she much; it was the changing fashions that made women look so different. She was smiling at him—kidding, the way she always did, head cocked impudently, smart and chic as ever.

"Hello," he said, "how are you?"

"I'm raising beagles."

"What?"

"Kennels, darling—out in Lake Forest, with the horsy set."

"Oh, dogs—" It was as hard as ever to keep track of what she meant.

"It's easier," she said, "less trying on the nerves. How's everything with you, Sam?"

"Fine, Becky."

"Getting what you want?"

"Well—" He laughed evasively. He had turned his back a little to the counter, edging in between so she wouldn't see what he had been looking at. He noticed a ring that she was wearing—a pale blue stone, and when she moved her hand there were soft white lines in it, radiating from the center like a star—the only ring she wore. Very stunning on her hand—

"And how is dear Eileen?" There was mockery in the question, but he came back with his formula—

"Eileen?—She's still in France, I think." A decent pause. "You know, we're not together any more—"

"Oh really? What a lark!" She was giggling, laughing at him. He was no match for her—no more than he had ever been. Her eyes had gone beyond him, to the rings spread on the counter, which he hadn't managed to conceal—eyes dancing with mischief, and they came back to his. "Better luck next time," she said, stepping back to go, pausing to call breezily, "If you ever need a dog—"

"Yes, I'll remember, Becky—"

"You can count on a dog. There's nothing like a beagle—not for steady company. And the bitches are delightful." She tripped away— jaunty, cocky, brittle. He didn't like her. He saw a sporty roadster standing at the curb, and a chauffeur waiting for her—

He turned back to the counter, shuffling the rings around, his interest in them staled a little. All diamonds looked alike, but that ring she was wearing—

"Oh yes," the salesman said, "the star sapphire, you mean. Exquisite piece." He leaned across the counter. "Confidentially, Mr. Braden, that was her engagement ring. Neill Wyatt gave it to her. I made the sale, myself."

"That right?" He poked around a moment. "Have you got another like it?"

"Why yes, I think we have—very close to it, in fact." He found it in the showcase. It looked about the same, with small diamonds set around it, and the soft, white, starlike lines when you held it to the light—

"How much?" he asked.

"Twenty-three hundred."

"Humph!" He had thought, if he had thought at all, to spend a fourth of that.

"It's our own work, Mr. Braden—designed and made here in our shop. You'll never see another one exactly like it. The color is exceptional and it has a perfect star."

"Yeh—" He hesitated. "Do you happen to remember what the other cost?"

"Yes, about the same—possibly a hundred one way or the other."

"All right," he said, "I'll take it. Don't bother wrapping it." He put it in his pocket. "If I should change my mind—"

"Of course, Mr. Braden; I'll mark it 'on approval.' And thank you very much."

"Okay—"

Lightning split the sky and a thunderbolt seemed to shatter in the street. The rain came in a torrent with gusts of cool, fresh air, beating on the pavement, bouncing up like buckshot. It was quite dark. The Avenue, deserted for a moment, looked like a muddy river. Old memories stirred. He ran the half block to his building— thinking of the time he had run along the levee from that other storm, drenched to the skin, certain that the lightning was snapping at his heels, the crashing sycamore, the smell of sulphur—running to the shelter of the dark and littered warehouse—to the end of childhood—

The lobby was empty; it was after six o'clock, everybody had gone home. The elevator operator looked at him and grinned. "You got wet, Mr. Braden."

"Yeh—did I?" He felt the shoulders of his coat. Yes, he was wet all right. He laughed; he hadn't noticed it.

Along the corridor the offices were dark—all but his own. He could see the light through the panel of the door, but he didn't hear the clicking of the typewriter, and he thought with consternation: perhaps she had gone home, scared out of her wits. My God, he wouldn't blame her—behaving as he had, that cave man stuff, she would think that he was crazy—saying what he said, and then rushing out and buying a two thousand dollar ring—imagining she could have any interest in a man old enough to be her father. He had acted like a lunatic, and running into Becky didn't make it seem more sensible. He paused outside the door, almost afraid to try it; but then he did—

She was still there—sitting at her desk, with the notebook on the leaf and the dictionary open and a letter sticking out of the machine. His heart leaped up again. Madness it might be, but a madness that he didn't want to part with—anyway you couldn't stop it; it was too late for that—

She looked up like a shot when the door latch clicked, so she was looking at him when he came into the room—straight at his eyes— anxiously, he thought, perhaps a little frightened, wondering what he would be up to now. But he stopped to get a towel from the cupboard by the cooler, to dry his face and hair—

"Got a little wet," he said.

"Oh, that's too bad—" She waited till he'd finished. "I'm afraid I'm stuck again—"

"That right?" He strolled over to the desk, standing beside her, looking at the letter, at the line where she had stopped, but not noticing the words—thinking how desirable she was, how very lovable, how wonderful it would be if she cared—how the pale blue stone would look on the slender, dark-skinned hand which had no ring on it—

"I'm awfully sorry—"

He laughed—thinking of her hair, so close now to his hand, closer than it had been since he had used to tweak it when she was a little girl—thinking of the joy of buying things for her: dresses, jewelry, furs, anything she wanted—all the things she'd never had—

"I know it's stupid of me—" She looked up questioningly, and then quickly looked away.

"Hum, well—" Thinking of her eyes—dark brown eyes they were, like deep still pools, serious and honest. What they told you would be true—

"It's this word, here—" She pointed with her pencil to a pothook in the notebook.

"Oh, that one, eh? What does it look like?"

"Not like anything—"

He laughed again, beginning, for no reason he could put his finger on, to feel confident and safe.

" 'Conditions are improving.' " She was reading from the letter. " 'We can now supply, for immediate delivery, in any quantity—' But what can we supply? That's the word I missed."

"I see." He nodded gravely. "And you haven't any idea?"

"No, I haven't, Uncle Sam."

"Looks fairly simple." He pretended to consider, trying hard to keep his face straight—wondering if she heard the beating of his heart. "Show it to me in your notebook." She held the book for him to see. "Put your finger on it." She did that. "Why, I can read that word and I don't know any shorthand."

"You can?" She didn't know—didn't quite believe it.

"Yes sir, I've got it. And it's the only word that'll finish out that sentence. 'We can now supply, for immediate delivery, in any quantity—' Don't you see it now?"

"No, I'm afraid I don't—"

"One four letter word?"

She shook her head, eyes on the notebook.

"Love," he said. "That does it."

"Love?" She looked up, trembling and confused.

"Why certainly, of course. 'For immediate delivery, in any quantity—' What else could it be?"

"Are you—" She stood up suddenly, the chair between them. "Are you teasing me?"

"No, Emilie."

"You—you really meant what you said when you went out?"

"Every word of it."

"Because—" She stopped, searching his eyes.

"Because what, Emilie?"

"It wouldn't be a joke—"

"I love you," he said. "I'm asking you to marry me."

"Oh—" She nodded slowly.

"If—if you could love me?"

"Yes—" she whispered.

"You mean, you think you could?"

"I *know*," she said. But it didn't need her words for he had read the answer in her eyes. "I do. I always have."

"My dear, my dear—" He took her in his arms, knowing she would fit against his body as she fitted in his heart, that he had come home at last—that no matter where life led she would be beside him, that nothing ever could get in between. And of that, for twenty years, he never had a doubt—that she was happy, that he had made her so, that he had not left a single stone unturned. He gave her everything—everything except— But that comes later.

Lightning streaked across the windowpanes, thunder crashed and echoed, wind howled in the street, the rain poured down. They didn't notice it.

They were married in the house on Deming Court, where they meant to make their home, for the present anyway—and they were to live there for ten years, half their life together. It had been home to both of them, and Mama Kranz was like *their* mother; they couldn't leave her, and Sam had no wish to do so. In time the house would be remodeled and enlarged: a nursery, a garage, extra rooms for servants; and it would be refurnished in the prevailing fashion. But Mama Kranz' room was never changed; she wanted it the way it was, and it stayed so while she lived.

There were no guests at the wedding. A Lutheran clergyman performed the ceremony, and the neighbors from next door came in to be the witnesses. He hadn't wanted any fuss about it, and Emilie didn't care. She wore some orchids that he brought; she had the others still, pressed between the pages of a book. She didn't care about anything at all—anything but him.

Jules Tronchet died that day, but it was three weeks later when he learned the fact. He had said to Mike, "Don't bother me with business matters." And he had been obeyed.

They went to California on their honeymoon. He had taken three weeks off—more than he could spare, but he meant to look things over on the Coast, where he felt they were not getting the volume that they should—three weeks packed with delight, with unending revelation, with love that seemed to flow out of the fabled pitcher: the more you poured out of it, the more it would run over. It was wonderful to have her, more wonderful than he had dreamed it could be— to waken in the night and find her close to him, to hear her breathing softly, to reach out his hand and touch her—

They did everything there was to do. In the morning he would ask: "What will it be today?"—"Anything you like, dear."—"Shall we go and see a moving picture studio?"—"That would be fun."—"Or shall we rent a car and drive to Tia Juana?"—"Yes, let's do that."—"Shall we have dinner here in the hotel?"—"I'll wear the dress you bought me yesterday."—"Suppose we prowl around and find some little place?" —"I'd love it. Let's do that."—She didn't care; if she was with him, she was happy. If he gave her orchids, she was pleased—just as pleased with a bunch of violets; if the dinner was elaborate and expensive, she enjoyed it—and with equal relish, a tamale at a lunch counter. She loved her ring—would have loved it just as much if it had cost ten dollars. *Things* meant little to her, only the thought that lay behind them was important. She adored her husband, worshiped him; she believed that everything he did was perfect. And he—

But why go on?—Writer's despair!—What is one to say about people who are happy?

Driving one day in a big touring car through a shabby section of sprawling Hollywood, his attention was arrested by a tumble-down old house—a poor, unpainted place with a patch of sun-baked lawn, and a sign above the door with the gilt flaked off the letters. He was holding her hand, and perhaps she felt a change in the pressure of his fingers; anyway she looked up anxiously—

"What, Unkam?" Her name for him had finally crystallized.

"Nothing, darling—" He put his arm around her and drew her close to him. He had read upon the sign: WILFRED ASHBY—SCHOOL OF ACTING.

A fleeting shadow crossed the sun.—Poor little Nelly.—He wished he might give some of his happiness to her, feeling guilty for a moment at the wealth of his contentment. She had left the sanitarium several months ago. Dr. Goldsmith had written quite fully at the time: her health had been restored and the drug addiction cured; her morale was much improved, though restoration of it to a normal point would only come with time, and—he had added, underlined—a *favorable environment*. She would not consider going back to Wyattville, and he had not urged it; indeed, he didn't recommend it: association with the past would not be beneficial; a new attack on life was what she needed. He was trying to stimulate her interest in some sort of social work, without much success as yet, but he was hopeful of it. In the meantime she was living with a family whom he knew, a pleasant, cheerful place where he sometimes placed a convalescent patient. He was keeping a close eye on her. What she really needed was to *belong to someone*—he had underlined that too, but not added anything—

Belong to someone.—Yes, of course, but you couldn't pick that out of a hat. Nelly had written, too, quite like herself again, eager and affectionate, thanking him for all that he had done—Dr. Goldsmith was so kind; they were talking over things but she hadn't made her mind up—the people where she lived were very nice to her; they had a little boy who seemed quite fond of her, and sometimes they went walking in the park—it was a pleasant neighborhood, not like the places she had lived. And—oh yes—she had been to the theater for the first time in so long, and had seen a splendid play, but the leading actress hadn't been so good, though the critics raved about her; she was certain she, herself, could have done more with the part—

"What are you thinking, dear?"

"Nothing—" He smiled and took her hand again. He had never told her much about his family: things about his mother, a little about Madge, not even much of Nelly—nothing of their troubles.

The shadow blew away; the sun came out again. He was sending Nelly a hundred every month, and paying for the doctor—doing everything he could, that anybody could—

Something else occurred, in Tia Juana. They had gone into a gambling place, just to look around—a big room with a bar along one side, and all kinds of games of chance: faro, dice, roulette, and twenty-one; and in the back were tables where men were playing poker, rough-looking fellows, most of them, distinct from the tourists who were wandering about—the kind of men you saw in moving picture Westerns, and the place was like that, too, like an old frontier saloon.

They bought a stack of chips and he was showing Emilie how to play roulette, when there was an altercation at a poker table in the back part of the room—someone accused of cheating, and some pretty ugly words which seemed about to resolve into a fight. Everybody heard the row and edged around to see what was going on, from a respectful distance. For a moment or two the air was pretty tense. But a fellow at the table, who was playing for the house, told the cheater off and made him quit the game, being calm and cool about it, but with something in his eye that didn't look like bluffing—

"Go on, get out!" he said. And when the fellow tried to argue with him, "You heard me. Get."

The man got up, scowling and ugly, gathering up some silver he had left, cursing underneath his breath—a big broad-shouldered fellow, fat and paunchy, a man who had been handsome, but his face was coarse and bloated. He walked away, unsteady in his footing, passing close to them, almost brushing against Emilie, and went over to the bar and threw some money on it, ordering a drink of whisky.

"Let's get out of here," Sam said.

"What was it, dear?" she asked when they were in the street.

"Nothing—" He shrugged, tossing in the gutter a few chips they hadn't played.

"Did you know that man?"

He shook his head. But he had recognized his brother, Tom. "Stuffy in there," he said. He didn't talk much driving back to San Diego.

Shadows on the sun, but they were little ones, not lingering very long—only long enough to act as a reminder, to keep you from forgetting the measure of your blessings.

In May the following year, almost nine months to a day from the day that they were married, Hathaway was born. Hath he was called—Hath Braden—

But stop a bit. There is something to be told about success, with which Sam Braden's life was so terribly concerned; and the time has come to tell it: the mechanics of the matter, a dull subject at the best, for who cares about success, except it be his own?

He bought Jules Tronchet's interest for fifty thousand dollars, the figure he had set—bought it from the widow who was very glad to get it, to whom it was a godsend. The question of its value is not worth while debating: without *him* it was worthless, if you want to view it that way. No doubt he could have bought it for considerably less, since there was no other market and the widow had to sell. But this is not the history of a rascal—

Anyway he owned it, except directors' shares issued to Hub and Mike; and owned these too, in fact, since they were reposing in his safe-deposit box, endorsed in blank. He owned it all.

Think back a moment to the day, about ten years before, when, noticing the sign—alert to things—he had climbed three flights of stairs to the Canal Street loft, in search of a customer for Acme—to the day when Lubin sent him, and he had found the Frenchman walled up in merchandise, busted, being smothered. And he had dug him out, working nights and Sundays, with a line he didn't know, discovering incidentally a market for the stuff—cheap stuff that other people didn't want to make, that the Frenchman, himself, only made because he had to, because he lacked the money and equipment to do better, not seeing in the least the advantage of fortuitous monopoly. And then it was the Frenchman who wouldn't let him go, who insisted on his staying, and finally sold him half of a gamble that was nothing if he played his hand alone. And then go on from there—step after step: there is nothing anywhere to criticize, unless one proposes to condemn some cardinal virtues: vision, enterprise, determination—

"Tron-shay," in later years the radio announcers would invitingly intone, "Say Tronshay." But that was long after Sam was through with it, when he no longer owned a penny of its stock or had the slightest interest, not even sentimental, in what became of it. He was never a producer, never in his heart a manufacturer. He was a *businessman*. He had no interest in machinery, no affection for it. He had never in his life had very much, and after the day the

Polish boy was killed—well, he simply kept away from the machine floor unless he had to go there.

You could, he always said, hire people to produce. That was not the problem. The problem was to sell the stuff they made, and to get your money for it, and to see that you got more than it cost to make it. The problem was to plan what these fellows were to do—like designs for wallpaper: they were always making things because they liked them, and if you didn't watch they would slip a lemon in—just because they thought that it was pretty. But that was not the way to do the thing. What you liked and what you didn't were no part of the affair; you were not in the game to please yourself, and the stuff you made was not for your personal use. You were making it *to sell*. If people had bad taste, it wasn't up to you. Will it sell or won't it?— at the price we've got to get?—And he was good at that. He could run through a line, almost as fast as a man could turn the sheets, pulling out the patterns that he didn't think would sell. "Tear it out," he'd say. "I wouldn't waste the cost to set it up." And designers and colorists would stand by silently, no matter what they thought.

He didn't change the name; it had a good will value, though he carried it at nothing on the balance sheet—until about the time the Elliott Wyatt Company came into the picture, in 1928, when Elliott wrote to him from his office in New York:—"Dear Sam: I expect to be in Chicago Tuesday. Could you have lunch with me at the Athletic Club—say one o'clock? I hear fine things of the way you're getting on, and there's something I'd like to talk with you about, which might be in our mutual interest.—Sincerely—" He read it with a smile; he knew pretty well what it would be about. In a way he had been waiting for it—from Elliott, or someone.—"Could you have lunch with me—" said the spider to the fly.—"Could you *possibly arrange*—" Not that of course, but it flashed into his mind.—The letterhead was rich and plain, deeply embossed—ELLIOTT WYATT COMPANY. MEMBERS, NEW YORK STOCK EXCHANGE, CHICAGO BOARD OF TRADE, etc., etc.—BRANCH OFFICES—" there was a column of them.

So what?—Tronchet had branches in every major city in the United States; factories in Clearing, New Jersey, Kansas City; wallpaper— not just cheap stuff but the best that could be made, paint and brushes, wood molding, window shades; half a million balance in Stanley Adams' bank.—He dictated a note: "Dear Mr. Wyatt:" He could never call him Elliott. "I shall be glad to meet you at the Athletic Club at one o'clock on Tuesday.—Sincerely—"

"Tronchet Corporation"—that was the new name for it; and it still had that name when he slid out of it in 1929—when its stock was selling on the curb for five times the price at which, the year before, it had been subscribed, and which he had thought then was too daring to consider, the limit of impertinence. But Elliott had smiled. The public, he remarked, was in a buying mood.

They had got down to business after lunch, sitting in the big room at a window table which had been reserved, waiters and captains hovering round—Mr. Wyatt this, and Mr. Wyatt that; half the people in the room had looked up when he came in, anxious for a chance to catch his eye, to let other people know they were on familiar terms. And he had smiled and nodded passing by them, walking with his quick and jaunty step, slim-waisted, trim as ever, carnation in the lapel of his coat. His hair had turned to silver, but his face was young and bronzed—like a tennis player's. He had another wife, acquired recently, the third—beautiful of course; and a big place on Long Island, and another at Palm Beach, an apartment at the Plaza. He must be close to seventy, but you would never guess it watching him or listening to his pleasant, casual voice. Amazing man—balancing half a billion dollars worth of public-service stocks, or a coffee spoon, with the same indifferent certainty.

He had been thinking that, thinking many things, eating shad roe for the first time in his life, feeling self-conscious, not quite comfortable, as he had always felt with any Wyatt—remembering a young man with a shiny walking stick who had been kind to him, who had set his broken sled back on the path and tucked a big half dollar in his mittened hand—more money than he'd ever had till then. And now he was a big boy—big enough for Wall Street to make love to him, but he still felt like a little one, sitting there across from Elliott—

Elliott kept chatting about one thing and another, making conversation easily, speaking of his place out on Long Island, of some flowers that he grew which had taken several prizes—

—Thinking that a place on Long Island would be nice—ground that was your own, and raising something on it, not flowers certainly, but dogs or horses—maybe blooded cattle, fine, prize-winning stock. It would be nice for Hath when he was old enough to go away to school and came home for vacations; and maybe they'd go hunting quail or rabbits, and the boy could have a pony. And it needn't be Long Island where you might not quite belong; it could be somewhere in the Middle West—the heart of America, not the ritzy fringe of it, and where you would have room to turn around: broad rolling acres and pleasant shady woodland. It would be good to have a river near it. The idea wasn't new; he had thought of it sometimes: of what he'd do with money when he had enough of it. But perhaps this was the time when decision crystallized, when he first really saw it—saw the river as the Mississippi, and the rolling meadows spread out along the bluff surrounding Beaton's woods; and saw a house, a home there —white-pillared, in Colonial style, roomy, comfortable, set deeply in the woods at the end of a long avenue, looking toward the river to the shore of Illinois. And the name of it came to him, as if it had been waiting for a chance to say itself: "Glencoe" of course, the name of the place where his mother had been born, which he had dreamed of longingly when he was a child—

Elliott was talking about Wayne who was in charge of the Chicago office, of everything in fact west of the Alleghenies, doing very well indeed. He spoke about his grandchildren: there were two or three of them—

—Wondering if he'd mention that other one in France, or wherever he might be; how much he really knew, and what he thought about it?—Had he accepted it? Would the boy some day inherit what would have gone to Neill? Had Neill confided in his father? Had he acknowledged his paternity and left a will providing for his son?—It wasn't likely that he had—that he'd ever thought about it.—And how did Wayne feel? Wouldn't he resent an acceptance of the matter which would deprive his children of a fortune?—He saw Wayne now and then, when he dropped in at the board room on La Salle Street to make a modest bet or just to notice what was going on. But no hint of anything was ever mentioned.—The Wyatts were a funny lot: you couldn't tell about them.—He had never seen Eileen after that day. But he had seen the child, not knowing who it was until Madge whispered to him. It was in Wyattville, three or four years ago, the year before his father died. He had driven down to spend the day, and the child was on the sidewalk, riding a velocipede, and had pedaled over to him, looking at the car—cute-looking youngster, dressed in foreign fashion with his short pants much too short, bare legs and socks: and the child had spoken with a foreign accent, very nicely mannered, different, rather quaint.—A little of that stuff didn't hurt a boy, so long as he remembered he was an American—might be good for Hath sometime.—His hair was like his mother's, but he looked like Neill. Still, he hadn't thought of that, or noted the resemblance, until later when Madge told him. Eileen had come for a visit with her parents; she had brought a lot of luggage and an English governess; they had gone to the hotel where Young Henry and his wife now made their home; there were rumors that she had come to stay, to settle down in Wyattville, that the old house might be opened and completely renovated. But of course that was absurd. She had stayed for a few weeks and had then gone back to France—somewhere anyway, and she had not returned. Mrs. Wyatt was her name, Mrs. Neill Wyatt; and that had been accepted in the town, so Madge reported to him in a letter. There hadn't been much talk: people had forgotten, or they took it at face value; and the Wyatts were important no matter what they did. Eileen had seemed unchanged, gracious but reserved. She still looked young, Madge said—

Elliott leaned back; the table had been cleared, the crumbs swept up. "I dare say you're a very busy man?"

"Well—" He sat straighter in his chair. It was time to be alert, cautious and on guard, not thinking about water that had run under the bridge.

"It was good of you to come, to spare the time—"

"Not at all," he murmured. All this was fencing, getting into place.

"I've kept an eye on you for several years—" Elliott cocked his head, quizzical and jaunty, explaining carelessly that, as a director in Stanley Adams' bank, he was not unfamiliar with the Tronchet picture —or a banker's picture of it—and it had intrigued his interest. "Frankly," he said, "my respect and admiration."

"Thank you, Mr. Wyatt—" High praise from a high source. His hands were moist and he rubbed them with his napkin.

"You've gone a long way, Sam, for a young man."

"I started pretty young."

"So you did," Elliott agreed. "The early bird, Sam."

He nodded, waiting, every ounce of him intent.

"However that may be, you have built a splendid business of which you may feel proud. And you are, I believe, sole owner of it?"

"That's right," he said.

"Yes, well—" Elliott tapped a cigarette into an ivory holder. "—that brings me to the point."

And the point was the point he had foreseen: that the public be invited to participate in Tronchet, through the medium, of course, of the Elliott Wyatt Company, which would effect the matter for a normal

brokerage profit from such an underwriting, plus a bonus in the form
of a block of common stock to compensate the job of exploitation.

"I see." He nodded.

Elliott went on: there were several aspects worthy of attention, but
the first and most important was not open to debate: the public was
in a buying mood.

He nodded.

Others he could mention depended more or less upon a point of
view: life was mutable, uncertain: however good the eggs and however
good the basket, it was doubtful policy to keep them all together.

He nodded.

There was, indeed, an altruistic angle: the sharing of good fortune
with thousands of investors, who, incidentally, immediately became
customers and friends, who could be counted on to advertise the
product. And there was a corporate dignity that derived from fiscal
bigness, from listing on the curb, possibly preliminary to ultimate
inclusion on the big exchange—an adventure into channels which
might make important contacts, might lead to many things not
apparent at the moment.

He nodded.

Elliott concluded: it had been his observation that it was distinctly
possible, though generally denied, to have your cake and eat it—at
all events, in corporate matters. In his opinion a handsome sum might
now be realized from an offering to the public—without in any
way affecting the control, the actual ownership.

"Yes," Sam said, "I see." He was silent for a moment, penciling
figures on the cloth. "It seems like small potatoes for you to bother
with—chicken feed, I mean."

Elliott laughed lightly. "It all adds up," he said, "and—well, I've had
my eye on you: I think I can depend on what I'm selling to my
customers—that you won't let me down."

"Yeh—" He smiled.—The wolves of Wall Street.

They talked all afternoon.

That's the way it happened.

Sam never felt the same about the business afterwards. He didn't
own it all.

In 1933 Tronchet went broke, died and was reborn—reorganized,
they call it, which means that everybody lost their shirts. The Stanley
Adams bank took a licking at that time, but, as usual, they were in
too deep to quit. They wrote off their losses and started in again:

bonds, preference debentures: "Class A, whereas—"; "Class B, and when—"; "Class C., convertible—"; and a million common shares of no par value—or any value really—as a bait for hopeful suckers.

They offered Sam—it was in the fall of '33, when he had come back from Europe after being gone three years—they offered him a million in bonds, debentures, stock, and a fifty thousand salary, if he would come back and run it.

But he refused politely, alleging that his health would not permit. He was in excellent health, but completely absorbed in the development of Glencoe. He had five million dollars, and it was safe and sound—in governments, municipals, nearly all in tax exempts. No, he wasn't interested. Anyway the business, though at heart it was as sound as it had ever been, could never overcome the rigging it had suffered, never hope to liquidate the burdens piled upon it. At the top of its capacity, under favorable conditions, with keen and skillful management, it might at best meet the interest charges on its funded debt.—No, he couldn't see his way to undertake it—

The business failed again in '39. But the Adams bank was out and another crowd was in. The new crowd gathered up the pieces and pasted them together—reorganized again: stock, debentures, bonds. It was too big to die. And it didn't matter much whom it belonged to, or whether they got back anything they spent. Mitch Ballou said humorously that it was a perfect model for a Communistic enterprise, since nobody but the workers ever got a dime.

It is still running now, in 1943. You can find it, if you look, listed on the curb; it never gained the dignity of the big exchange, but you will find it: "Tronshay" is the name—TRN in curb abbreviation. It is not often traded, so not always in the paper; but there was a sale the other day: one hundred shares at fifteen cents a share. A year or two ago it took a little spurt and got up to fifty cents, and a few smart people sold. But most of them hung on, as the suckers always do, figuring they'd get more if they held out a while.

But the outlook is not hopeful: what with the war—priorities and labor and materials getting scarce, and people only buying what they have to have—no, it isn't hopeful. If you ask your broker what he thinks about the prospects, he will likely hem and haw and hedge around. "Well," he may say, "if you're figuring on a long pull, Tronshay might be all right, but—" and he'll name some other things he would sooner see you buy.

Or if you ask Mike Hogan, sitting at Old Henry's desk in the Bank of Wyattville—a banker now, in fact, since 1934 when Sam sent for him to come out from Chicago, and asked him casually, with a twinkle in his eye:

"Say, Mike, how would you like to be a banker?"

"Jesus, Sam," Mike said, "I think that would be fine. I'd get even with those bastards who were always riding me."

"Okay," Sam said, "you're a banker now." And he made him a present of the Bank of Wyattville, or what was left of it. He had bought it out of the receivership in which Young Henry left it when he died—bought it because there were a lot of frozen mortgages on rolling meadowland spreading out from Beaton's woods. But he didn't exactly make Mike a present of it; he kept control, himself. Still, it was a break for Mike—son of the man who had driven Birney's hack. And Sam was glad to do it: Mike had served him faithfully for a lot of years; and he wanted Mike around, where he could see him every day or so, commission his assistance—someone he could trust, whose devotion he knew he could rely on. There were times when it was lonely in the country—

So if you should ask Mike a question about Tronshay, as a customer did the other day—if he thought it would be a good investment?— Mike was home for a few days, sitting at Old Henry's desk in his colonel's uniform, checking up on things—

"Tronshay?" Mike laughed. "Why, I used to work for Tronshay when Mr. Braden had it."

"Well, you ought to know a lot about it."

"I'll say I do."

"I was thinking I might buy a little stock. It's pretty cheap right now."

"Uh-huh—" Mike nodded, swinging in his swivel chair. "The sweetest running business in the world—"

"That right?" the customer edged closer to the desk: he was in the stable, getting feedbox information.

"Yes sir, you bet—a gold mine—"

"Yeh?" The man was drooling.

"There's just one trouble with it—" Mike cocked his head with warning in his eye. "—just one little trouble that makes me hesitate to advise you to go out and fill your pockets."

"Yeh? What?"

"It isn't much," Mike hastened to assure him. "Maybe when I tell you, you'll decide to go ahead—"

"Well, what?" The man was wriggling with impatience.

But you couldn't hurry Mike; he took his time about it, enjoying every moment. "Yes sir, just one little thing that might not be worth mentioning. It's a big concern, you know—half a dozen factories, fine stores everywhere. Why, they've even got a place in Muscatine—"

"Sure, I know. I bought stuff there for years—"

Mike held up his finger. "Say, you ought to see the way that outfit runs—like an airplane motor. Ever hear of Leonard Trask, chairman of the board? Mr. Braden taught him his job, and you can believe he knows it. They make good merchandise, and they know how to sell it. Ever hear their radio programs?—every Wednesday night?—symphony orchestras, actors from Hollywood—"

"Yeh, that's one thing got me thinking—"

" 'Say Tronshay,' you know—"

"Yeh, sure—"

"There's a business for you—" Mike waved his hand. "—around the clock, from coast to coast—"

"I thought I'd take a flyer and buy ten thousand shares—"

"You bet. But wait a moment: there's just that one small thing I was about to mention—"

"Oh yeh? Well what?"

"You know Lem Richards?"

"Yeh—"

"You know Lem's got a cow?"

"Say, what's this all about?"

"Anyway he's got a cow. Well, the other day I was at his house and he pointed out this cow, eating grass out in the yard. And he says to me—'Mike,' he says, 'that's the best looking cow I ever had.' She was good looking, too—sleek and fat and clean—looked like a cow a feller'd want to own.—'Yes,' I says, 'that's some cow, Lem.'— 'Yeh,' he says, 'that's right, Mike. But there's just one thing about her—just one little thing. You might not believe it, looking at her, Mike, but that brindle bitch won't give a drop of milk.' "

"Oh yeh?" The fellow looked a little sick.

"That's all." Mike laughed till the tears ran down his cheeks. "And that's all that's wrong with Tronshay: she won't give a drop of milk— not if you were dying. The bankers milked her dry, and they did a swell job of it. She'll still be dry when Gabriel blows his horn."

A more comprehensive comment on the subject of Tronshay has not been formulated.

Perhaps if Sam had stayed—if he hadn't gone to Europe at the end of '29, and left the job to Trask, who was good but not that good—possibly the wreck might have been averted. But it is by no means certain, for his interest was detached, and the driving force behind it was decelerating. He was through with Tronshay—through as he had been with Clem Wyatt's general store, with the Rock Island Railroad, with the Acme Paper Company. And he was very tired; he had been on the job for thirty years. But even had none of this been true, had he been on his toes, at the top of his capacity, the issue of the matter would be doubtful: the impending times were *new*; there were scarcely any precedents for able men to follow.

Nor could it be truthfully said, however it might look to an observer, that he, the captain of the ship, deserted it in time of peril, and left his crew and passengers to perish. That was not true. He was carrying out a plan which had been in his mind when he sat that day at lunch in the Athletic Club—when Elliott had said: "I think I can depend on what I'm selling to my customers—that you won't let me down." And he had smiled—smiling to himself: the wolves of Wall Street, talking like the players on a college football team; it was naïve. Did Elliott suppose he was in business for his health?—that his purpose in life was to benefit the public?—And there was then no vestige of a warning. Nor was there in the spring of '29 when he began to ease out of the picture—no inkling of disaster, nor had he foreseen it. No subtle intuition motivated what he did. He was carrying out a plan: if the public was to share, then they could have it all—if they would pay the price. He had not dreamed of the price that they would pay— nor, for that matter, had anybody else.

He had read a book that spring, by a man named Daniel Price, Ph.D., Economist—*Mr*. Daniel Price—had seen it in a shop and picked it up. It was socialistic stuff, predicting a disaster from the speculative madness that was sweeping through the country, and a new kind of a world. He had read it with some interest; it seemed reasonable enough in its diagnostic aspects, though he could not subscribe to its radical ideas. But it did not influence him; he was not alarmed. He belonged to the vast and comfortable majority who believed in America—believed things would go on, with minor ups and downs—on and on and on. He sent the book to Madge who wrote that she found it rather dull—

He began to unload in the spring of '29, cautiously at first. He opened a small office in New York, with no name on the door, and sent Mike there to carry out his orders. At first he sold and bought, through a dozen different brokers, under different trading names; he would sell a thousand shares in hundred lots, and buy half of them himself, or if quickly taken, none at all; and he would offer lots above the market and then bid up to them but not high enough to take them. There were several other dodges that he worked, all aimed to make a market for the stock.

But in the summertime the market ran away, and Tronshay with it. You could sell anything. It was no longer necessary to obscure your operations: nobody was watching, no one cared. And then he really started to clean house, at prices that kept jumping every day, indignant at the paltry sums he took the week before, unable to believe what the fools were paying—wondering if, after all, they might not be right: that there was no end to it, no ceiling to the thing. But still he kept on selling—it was too late to stop—until he had sold out, every share he owned. It was early in September. He was worth five million dollars, as near as he could figure it; you can never tell exactly when you get into those sums—

And he had been figuring it, in the office, late one night, with Mike across the desk—nobody but Mike knew what he had been up to—both of them in their shirt sleeves, for the night was hot and close, and the big desk strewn with ledgers and scraps of figured paper. They had gone out to get a bite to eat when the office crowd went home, and had come back to work when they could be alone and undisturbed. He had been doing this for months, all through the long hot summer. It was getting close to midnight when he dropped his pencil on the desk and leaned back in his chair.

"About five million, Mike—"

"Jesus, Sam, that's money." Mike seemed as happy as if it were his own. He didn't have a dime except his salary, as treasurer of the company; he didn't seem to care. That's why he was valuable.

"That's the end of it. I'm through with Tronshay."

Mike nodded solemnly. "What will you do now, Sam?"

"Well, the first thing that I want is a vacation—"

"You've sure earned it."

"And then—" He tipped back further in the swivel chair with his eyes upon the ceiling. "And then I think I'd like to have a home—a big place in the country, with woods and farming land, maybe blooded cattle."

"Yeh—" Mike nodded doubtfully. "That wouldn't take the place of Tronshay, Sam."

"Maybe not—" He shrugged. "With five million dollars you can do a lot of things—"

"No more penny-pushing stuff?"

"No." He shook his head. "Motors, aviation, radio: they're all good bets."

"I guess they are," Mike said.

"I'd like to take a year and think it over. Maybe go to Europe—"

"That would be swell."

"Yeh—" He had been thinking about that for a long time. He had never been to Europe, nor had Emilie; he knew it to be one of the great dreams of her life. And it would be good for Hath—that funny little boy whom he sometimes felt he hardly knew, whom he almost never saw; it would give them a chance to really get acquainted. And Hath was at an age to derive advantage from it—to learn a foreign language and get a sort of finish that children got abroad. He had been thinking of it for a year, but he hadn't mentioned it. Mama Kranz had not been well; she had had an operation and had not seemed to recover, though she was better now—

"But say—" Mike hesitated, "—who'll look after things?"

"Trask can run the business."

"Well," Mike said, "I guess so."

"It's running like a watch."

"While you're here, Sam."

"Hell!" He laughed. "They might as well learn now to get along without me. The public owns the business and it's up to them to run it."

"Sure," Mike agreed. He always agreed with anything Sam said. "And what'll I do, Sam?"

"Stick around and draw your salary until we look things over."

"Okay," Mike grinned.

"If anyone had told me—" He was deadly tired but there was exultation in his voice. "If anyone had told me thirty years ago—or twenty years, or ten, that I'd live to see the day when I had five million dollars—"

"Yeh—" Mike gloated with him. "Elliott Wyatt never turned a neater trick."

"Humph!" He swung back to the desk, something wincing deep inside him and the keen edge of his triumph dulled a little.

It was then the phone rang. The switchboard operator left his phone connected, but Emilie was the only one who ever called at night—

"Yes dear?" he answered before he heard her voice, and then when he knew that she was crying, "Emilie, what is it?—Is Hath all right?"

No, it wasn't Hath; his pulse began to steady. "Mama—" she said. "But what?"

"She—she's gone—"

"Oh, Emilie—" He couldn't realize it for a moment: it was so tangled up with figures. He kept on asking questions. It had happened in ten minutes—perhaps since he had dropped his pencil on the desk. She had been in Mama's bedroom, reading to her. At first she thought that Mama had dozed off, but then she realized her eyes were open—

"Yes, dear?" he urged. A doctor in the block had come at once. But she was—gone. The doctor was still there, but she was gone—

"I'll come right home," he said, and hung up the receiver.

"Something wrong?" Mike asked.

"Mrs. Kranz—she's dead, Mike." He was putting on his coat, reaching for his hat. "Just now while we were talking—"

"Holy God, I can't believe it. Can I do anything?"

"No, thanks. Put away the books."

"Yeh, sure, Sam. Do you want me to come up there?"

He shook his head, standing at the door. "I'll see you in the morning."

Well, death is like that, coming where and when you least expect it. A lot of people die, are dying all the time, though you rarely think about it; and a lot of them had died within those last ten years: his father in 1924, peacefully in his bed, aged eighty-four—not exerting any effort in the matter, not taking any trouble, nor suffering in the least—dying in the end as he had lived, with complete regard for his comfort and convenience. He had gone to the funeral and had taken Emilie—the first time she had been to Wyattville. He had meant to take her long before, but first she had been pregnant, and then Hath had been a baby, and then—well, Cassie Cole. Of course that was absurd, but he kept postponing it. It was Cassie who had met them at the door—slender and comely, respectful and inscrutable. And there was his father in his coffin in the parlor, old and shriveled up, in his best blue coat, with the nickel-plated star pinned on his breast above the folded hands, the rolling thumbs forever still. It had not moved him much.

Madge had come to visit them, but she hadn't stayed long. And

then she had gone on to be with Nelly. Nelly had been ill again—
"ill" was what they called it when they spoke about it. But Madge
had not been happy in New York; she missed her garden. It was *too
late* for that: when ruts got deeply worn it was better to stay in them—
Outside the door, on Michigan, he hailed a cruising taxi.

And Tom was dead—killed in '26, in a gambling brawl in Memphis.
The news had come to Madge who had phoned him at the office. And
he had gone by train that night, and had stood in a dimly lighted
morgue beside a concrete slab on which his brother lay, with a white
sheet drawn back to show his face, not far enough to disclose the
bullet wound which had gone through his heart—a face he hardly
knew, that life had disfigured and death had not restored.

"Yes," he said, "my brother." He was not deeply moved. He had
seen Tom half a dozen times in twenty years, the last time in that
place in Tia Juana when he had not spoken to him or admitted who
it was. Perhaps he should have done so—

He had sent the body home to Wyattville and paid the expenses
of the funeral, but he hadn't gone, himself—simply couldn't spare
the time. A man had been arrested and there had been a trial, but
not much publicity—no mention of the thing in the Chicago papers,
and the Wyattville *Gazette* had been discreet and kind. A woman
had turned up who claimed to be Tom's wife—by common law, she
said; and there was a child she claimed was his—a drab and vulgar
woman, neither young nor pretty. She had come to the office and
he had been forced to see her in the fear she'd make a scene, but
she didn't seem that kind—

She didn't know, she said, if she had something coming. She had
been a waitress in a restaurant when she first knew Tom, and she
had loved him. She had a husband then, but they were separated,
though they hadn't been divorced; afterwards they were, but then
she and Tom had drifted on, intending to get married but not getting
round to it. She could get along, she said; it wasn't that she wanted
something for herself, but there was the child; she didn't know if that
was up to her. She had taken care of Tom for a long time, and it had
not been easy—

"I took care of him," she kept repeating. "I took care of him the
best I could—"

He had sent her to Hub Baxter who had advised a settlement: the
woman might make trouble and get into the papers. She had no
case, no claim on anybody, but it might be wise to spend a small

amount to dispose of her for good. And he had settled for a thousand dollars.

She had written to him, thanking him—a misspelled, ignorant letter. She had asked to bring the child, suggesting that perhaps he'd like to see her—a little girl of four. But he hadn't answered that—

The parallel had haunted him: the woman and Eileen, the child without a father, the sordid circumstances far removed from those other ones—yet, who could say how far? She had loved him, so she said, had taken care of him—

Well, his son had a father, and no blot on his escutcheon to cast a shadow sometime. He wished they were closer to each other, more companionable—the sort of thing you read about but didn't often see. The boy was like his mother: serious and earnest—too serious sometimes. And he resembled her; he was slender and small-boned—a little fragile looking, becoming in a woman, but not the sort of thing with which to buck the world, though he, himself, had been skinny as a child—

In truth the boy was much more like his father than his father knew. He did look like his mother—his hair and big brown eyes, deep, thoughtful pools; and he had her loyalty, her quiet strength, her unswerving sense of *right*. But also he was very like his father—what his father *had been* when he was a child. But he had changed, and he had forgotten.

He wished that Hath were more robust and athletic. He had done his best to stimulate his interest in such things. A year or two ago at Charlevoix, when he would run up for week ends, he had almost drowned the child, teaching him to swim, had really worn him out so he had to stay in bed the following day. But that was the way you learned—

The taxi dove into the dark, deserted park.—And *it* had changed— not the comfortable, roomy place it had been thirty years ago, when they used to come on Sundays for a picnic—almost like going to the country. It was too crowded now, motorcars and people—and all cut up with roads. They were passing by the zoo and some animals were barking. It made him think of something:

Hath had not begun to talk at the time most children do; and when he did begin he sometimes talked of things which had occurred before. One day he said abruptly, apropos of nothing, "I don' wike the bears."

"What bears?" his mother asked.

"The big bears in the park."

"But last summer when you used to go with papa to the zoo, he always said when he came home, that you had watched the bears."

"I wike the otter."

"But if you like the otter why did you watch the bears?"

"Papa wikes the bears."

They had laughed about it. He did prefer the bears and had insisted on them, bored with the otter, waiting for the creature to swim across its pool; the bears were more exciting. But Hath had "wiked" the otter, with no words to state his case, but he had remembered it. Hath knew what he liked, and that was something; and he knew what he didn't like, and that was something, too—

Other people died in those ten years: the Hogans, both of them, Annie and old Mike; Clem Wyatt, close to ninety; Dr. Bentley, Grover's father, long since retired from practice in favor of his son; and Mitchell J. Ballou, preserved in alcohol right to the end, at least so people said. Mitch had turned up to claim his patrimony—the house in Wyattville, sole residue of Mitchell J.'s estate. The *Gazette* went to Young Henry on a note, no doubt to his disgust—

Mitch had called up one day, a year or so ago, passing through Chicago—

"Sam?—This is Mitch."

"Well, Mitch—"

"How's tricks?"

"Okay.—Say, Mitch, come out to dinner, eh?"

"Can I bring a friend?"

"Of course. Who is it?"

"My wife."

"Your wife?—On the level, Mitch?"

"So far as I know."

"Why say, that's great—"

"We also have a child."

"You have?—Bring him."

"It's *her.*"

"Well, bring them all."

And he had come—a little older, very much the same, cuffs as frayed as ever, quick-witted, sharp of tongue. He had made an instantaneous hit with Hath, taking out his eye and handing it to him. "Take this my son," he said, "and look around."

The wife was young—not pretty, but interesting looking: black hair, high cheekbones with the skin drawn over them like parchment, rather Jewish features. Her eyes were bright and restless—almost feverish in the way they took things in. She looked as though she had been ill, and she had a little cough—tubercular perhaps. Jewish, he felt sure, the moment that he saw her. But Mitch had settled that—

"She's Jewish," he announced. "But don't restrain yourself: she doesn't savvy English, anyway not much, not enough to be insulted. I found her in Odessa; she was starving at the time, and she hasn't gotten over it." Bugs he called her—"Because," he said, "I can't pronounce her name."

The child's name was Natasha—Nat for short, and she looked Jewish, too: black hair like her mother's, and an olive skin. Eight she might have been, a year younger than Hath, but she seemed quite grown up—shaking hands with everybody like an adult—"How do you do"—"Oh, thank you very much"—the way foreign children speak, with a funny little accent—and not sitting down till the older people did—

"She can cook," Mitch said. "She can also speak four languages: Russian, English, German, French." There was proud affection in his eye.

"Can she drive an automobile?" Hath asked with bated breath.

"Well—" Mitch laughed, "—if she can't, it's because she hasn't tried."

Their clothes were poor and shabby. Funny that Mitch should have kept the thing a secret, never mentioning them in the hurried letters which infrequently he wrote. He answered the question before it had been asked—

"I kept them up my sleeve for a surprise, thinking any time I might come back." They'd been living in Berlin. Bugs could speak German. Mama Kranz and Emilie had taken her upstairs, chatting with her in that language.

He and Mitch had gone out with the children to the yard where there was a swing. And a neighbor boy had joined them and had shinnied up the swing rope, showing off, a good stiff climb, hand over hand. He had wanted Hath to do it—

"Can you do that, Hath?" he said.

"I don't know. I never tried."

"Well, let's see what you can do."

"I don't want to."

"I'll bet you could."

Hath edged away.

"I'll tell you what: I'll give you a quarter if you make it."

"Un-huh—" Hath shook his head.

"That's pretty easy money," he had urged. He felt a little miffed with Mitch there looking on, wishing now he hadn't started it. "Mr. Ballou would like to see you do it."

"That's a lie," Mitch said. "Don't you climb that rope for me, Hath. I don't give a damn about it. I'd leave that to the monkeys."

"Oh, well—" He laughed it off, not thinking it was funny.

"And by the way," Mitch added, grinning at him meanly, "I don't remember you ever climbing any ropes."

Old Mitch, not changed a bit.—After dinner he had talked, pacing up and down the room, cynical and caustic; international politics, places, names, and people—London, Paris, Moscow—talking so fast it was hard to follow him.—Yes, Mitch had been around, had seen the world, but it hadn't got him anywhere. At the end of twenty years he was right where he had started, working for a salary—and, judging by appearances, not a very good one. They had kicked him out of Russia, as he put it, for some reason not quite clear—something he had said that the big shots didn't like. But he didn't seem to bear a grudge about it—

"They're tough," he said. "I guess they have to be with the whole damn world against them. But I'll go back to Moscow if they ever let me in."

"But why?" he demanded. "I should think you'd had enough."

"I'll tell you why," Mitch said, leaning with his elbow on the mantel and a highball in his hand. "I'll tell you why, Sam: I saw a thing in Russia that I've seen nowhere else. I saw a lot of people working for an idea. Not every stupid pirate working for himself, not repeating like a litany, 'What do I get out of it?,' but a lot of people working for an *idea*—understand?—Maybe a good idea, or maybe bad —I'm not sure about that; that's why I'd like to go and take another look—but anyway an *idea*."

Yes, he remembered that. Out of all the talk it had stuck fast in his memory—that and a name. "There's a bird named Adolf Hitler, in Germany," Mitch said. "Probably he's crazy, but crazy like a fox. Keep your eye on him." He had never heard the fellow mentioned since.—An idea.—But what idea exactly? They never told you that; even Mitch was vague about it, wanting to go back and have another look. Well, he'd only waste his time—running away from the only big idea that had ever proved itself, had really worked: the American idea, toe the line together and let the best man win. The race was to the swift, and so it ought to be—a premium on endurance, industry, and thrift; that was the way to get ahead and there'd never be another. And Mitch, himself, had better watch his step; he was pretty radical, getting kind of pink if not actually red. If he kept on that way he might find it hard to hold a job. The American people weren't friendly to that stuff; they were smart enough to know where their bread was buttered—

The taxi emerged out of the park and turned west onto Deming. And *it* had changed. The neighborhood had cheapened and was getting shabby. There were few private houses left; the street was lined with flat buildings, not very good ones—milk bottles on the window sills. No suggestion of that pleasant old world atmosphere remained. The war had finished that; and the good German people who had brought it from their homeland, had nearly all passed on—

He had deliberately avoided dwelling on the fact, thinking rather of the past; but there it was—Mama Kranz was gone. She wasn't very old, sixty-five perhaps; she might have lived another twenty years; still, she belonged to another generation—one you must expect to part with, soon or late. He would miss Mama Kranz, but she wasn't indispensable—like Emilie or Hath, not really part of him. Death had struck closer than it had since his mother died, but then he was a child and death meant something else—had struck now close enough to let you know its sting, but the wound was not a deep one and it would quickly heal. It was Emilie's wound that he would feel, her grief that he would grieve for—

The cab stopped at the door. The windows were alight. He paid the man and hurried up the steps. Across the street a girl was calling from the window of a flat to a fellow in a car, kidding back and forth.

Yes, the neighborhood was second-rate. Funny how a thing like that went on, and suddenly one day you realized it. The house was never much. Papa Kranz had bought it more than thirty years ago, and though they had remodeled it and spent a lot of money, it was not much of a place—not suitable at all—

While he was fumbling with his latchkey a frightened, tearful maid opened the door. The doctor was coming down the stairs—

"Too bad," the doctor said. "Probably an embolism. She was dead when I arrived."

He nodded. "And Mrs. Braden?"

"Your wife is upstairs in her mother's room."

"Oh—" He started toward the stairs.

"By the way, Mr. Braden, I was waiting to ask you about an undertaker. There's Kramer on Clark Street?"

"Yes, Kramer—" he agreed.

"Would you like me to arrange?"

"Please do—"

"Well, good night, Mr. Braden—"

"Good night—" And that was the way it was—all in a day's work, happening all the time; but you didn't think about it.

He found her sitting by her mother's bed, and took her in his arms and held her tenderly, with soothing, loving words, and hot tears in his eyes. And it came into his mind, then, at that very moment: there was nothing in the way now—

In the following week, one evening after dinner, he said abruptly, "How would you like to go to Europe, Emilie?"

"Unkam! Do you mean it?"

"I do."

"But when?"

"Right now—next month."

"Oh—" She was breathless. "To Paris and to London?"

"Anywhere you like."

"What would we do about the house?"

"Close it up."

"And the servants?"

"Let them go."

"But—when we came back?"

"We won't come back."

"Unkam! What do you mean?"

He laughed. "We'll stay a year."

"A year?" She stared. "But who will run the business?"

"I don't care," he said.

"Why, what—"

"I'm out of Tronshay, Emilie." He had never told her anything.

"Out?—Out of the business?" He thought that she looked startled; it was actually dismay.

« 317 »

"I've sold, lock, stock and barrel—for a lot of money, too, more than we'll ever need."

"Oh—" She nodded slowly. "But now—what will you do?"

"Now?" He laughed and took her in his arms. "I'll be with you. And we'll see Europe first; and then—" He glanced at Hath, who was curled up with a book, watching from the corner of his eye, as he always watched when his father put his arms around his mother, with a queer look in his eyes, almost resentful. He loved his kind, cruel father, but he adored his mother. "Well, Hath, what do you think about it, eh?"

"I would rather go to Wyattville," Hath said. He had spent a summer there with Aunt Madge and Cassie Cole, and he had liked it.

"Well—" His father smiled, feeling a bit let down, as he often did with Hath. "—perhaps we'll do that, too, when we come back."

"Probably I'll be too old then," Hath said with resignation.

"Nonsense! Perhaps we'll build a house there—out in the country. Did your Aunt Madge ever take you out to Beaton's woods?"

"I think so, yes—" Hath nodded. "On a picnic once."

"Well, how would you like to live there?"

"In the woods?"

"In Beaton's woods."

"I wouldn't like it—much."

"Why not?"

"It's gloomy."

"Gloomy? Nonsense!" He was irritated now. Hath always said the things that you hoped he wouldn't say.

"Why, Hath," his mother said reprovingly.

"Well—" Hath considered resolutely. "—it was gloomy to me."

"Nonsense!" he said again. "It's a beautiful place—the big trees, and the river, and the fields—"

Hath went back to his book.

There were some futile warnings in September, murmurings in the engine, of bearings running hot, of a flywheel speeded up beyond endurance; but they went unnoticed, disregarded. And then, in sound and fury, the golden bubble of the twenties burst—

But who knew that it had burst?—or that it was a bubble?—Not Sam Braden certainly; scarcely anyone in fact. A full year later, when the holocaust was fairly in its stride, they were still buying stocks at what they thought were bargain-counter prices. And ten years later there were still a lot of them waiting patiently for the return of something that they called "the good old days." Ideas are hard to kill, particularly those that promise profits.

When the crash came, in October, he was in New York, with Emilie and Hath, staying at the Plaza—he had been stopping there in recent years—in a suite of rooms which looked across the park, exciting in the evening when the lights came on. The house on Deming Court was closed, packed away in moth balls. He had a feeling on the day he left it that he would never live in it again; and he was right about it. Passports had been got, and steamship reservations—de luxe accommodations on a Cunard liner. They had come some days ahead of sailing time: he wanted Hath to get acquainted with New York, and to visit Nelly. She had been ill again, was in a sanitarium—a new one in Connecticut, which Dr. Goldsmith thought more adapted to her needs—

Sitting in the Oak Room at his lunch he could hear the clicking ticker, could almost see the blackboard in the neighboring broker's office. In one day Tronshay dove to the prices of last spring. In a week he could have bought back every share he'd sold, with most of his five million still intact.

That's what other people did—those who were sitting pretty with money in their pockets, who hadn't been washed out by the first blast—jumped back in to make another killing, to fatten on disaster, and finally lose their shirts. But he was smart; he didn't buy a thing. And "smart" is not the word; it was not a reasoned matter, not the product of special acumen. It was simply not his nature to go back. He was through with Tronshay; he was going to Europe for a holiday, with his wife and son—

Mike phoned him from Chicago, sputtering with excitement—
"We could buy it back for next to nothing—"
"No."
"But, Holy God—"
"I'm going to Europe, Mike."
"You could put it off a while—"
"Not a single day."
"You're passing up a fortune—"
"I'm satisfied."
"But Tronshay, Sam—"
"I wouldn't touch it with a ten foot pole."
And that was that. Emilie asked with anxious eyes—
"Do you think you ought to go?"

"Why not?"

"But—perhaps it will be serious?"

"Not for us," he said.

"But, Unkam, are you sure that it's not on my account?—I wouldn't want to go if I thought you ought to stay."

"Nonsense!" He laughed. "It's a stock market panic, gamblers getting trimmed. The country's sound as ever. America's all right, and it'll still be here when we get back."

He had no inkling of it—no more than you and I, or anybody else.

The day before they sailed he went to visit Nelly, and took Hath with him. Dr. Goldsmith had suggested that he do so, that seeing her nephew might stimulate her interest. He had not been encouraging: they had now to reckon with another factor—the climacteric period, or menopause, a difficult ordeal under normal circumstances. He looked up from the record card which he had been consulting. "In the past ten years she has been hospitalized four times. I'm afraid, Mr. Braden—" He put the card back on the desk. "—I'm afraid we must face the fact that your sister has become an institutional case."

"You mean she will have to be confined?"

"Cared for is the term," the doctor said.

"But—" He found nothing to say. The verdict was not wholly unexpected.

"I am sorry I have not been more successful. But—" The doctor shrugged and spread his thin white hands. "—our therapy is a poor and fumbling one. Perhaps some day it will be better."

The trip to Connecticut would take all day, and they would not be back until quite late at night. Hath was disappointed; he had counted on the Hippodrome, but he made the best of it. On the way to the station they stopped and bought some flowers, and a box of candy for Hath to give Aunt Nelly—

"Is she very sick?" he asked. He had never heard her mentioned until the day before.

"No, not very sick."

"What's the matter with her?"

"Well—" He hesitated. "—she was tired and she's resting."

"Oh!" Hath was silent for a moment. "Who does she live with?"

"Just by herself—alone."

"Hasn't she any children?"

"No."

"She could come and live with us."

He didn't answer that.

The sanitarium was a pleasant place on the edge of a small town, in a park with trees and lawns—not like a hospital; it was expensive, too. A nurse came to conduct them. Going through the halls they passed through several doors whose panels were of wired glass. The nurse unlocked them with a latchkey, so deftly that you hardly noticed what she did. Walking along he asked her—

"How is Miss Braden getting on?"

"She's comfortable, I think," the nurse said noncommittally.

"Taking more interest now?"

"Well, some days, Mr. Braden—" She came to a door and opened it and left them.

The room was of good size, nicely furnished, homelike: pictures on the wall, knickknacks on the dresser. The afternoon sun was streaming through the window and she was sitting near it in a dressing gown. She didn't look around when they came in. He waited for a moment, Hath standing there beside him, and then he spoke her name. She didn't turn her head or give any sign of hearing—

"It's Sam," he said, coming closer to her, holding Hath's hand. "I've brought your nephew, Nelly. I brought Hath with me." He put the box of flowers on a table, moving so that he could see her face. She was looking through the window on which there was a screen, not the ordinary kind but made of thick, strong wire—looking through it but not seeing; you could tell that from her eyes. Her hair had turned quite gray and it wasn't as tidy as she had used to keep it. Her face was grayish too, with no cosmetics on it, but she did not look sick—quite well in fact. She was smiling—not at him, not at what he'd said, not at anything *outside*.—"Nelly—" he raised his voice, and then he touched her arm—

She turned her head. There was no recognition in her eyes, no spark of anything—

"It's Sam," he said, "Sam, Nelly. And this is Hath—" Her eyes followed his and rested on the child, and Hath was frightened and drew back. "Come now," he said sharply, "give Aunt Nelly the present that you brought." Hath held it out. "Put it on her lap." He did it gingerly, keeping at arm's length. She had turned back to the window, the expression on her face unchanged—empty and smiling, smiling at something invisible to them. He got a chair, rattling it briskly on the floor; it seemed to him that he must rouse her that way, by talking loudly, making noise. Hath backed away behind him—

"Papa, let's go," he whispered.

"Yes, in a little while—"

"No, now."

"Hath, please—"

"I want to go—" His voice was close to tears. "I think she's crazy, Papa."

"Hush! Be still!" He waited.

The nurse came back, standing in the door, competent and cheerful. "Now, that's too bad," she said. "But I'm afraid it isn't any use today."

"No—" He got up wearily. Nelly moved and the box of candy slid onto the floor. The nurse picked it up and put it on the table.

"She'll enjoy that, Mr. Braden." She waited for them at the door. "She eats well, sleeps well, hasn't any aches or pains. She's really very happy."

"Yes—" he said. "Yes, I suppose so."

They went back down the hall, the latchkey clicking softly through the woven wire doors. In a room they passed he heard a woman sobbing.

The train was late and crowded. The clicking of the wheels was like that clicking key.—Confined.—"Cared for was the term," as Dr. Goldsmith put it.—Cared for. Cared for.—His mother's words came back: "Take care of Nelly, Sam."—Well, he'd taken care of her, taken care of all of them, carried them on his shoulders all his life.—"Don't do that, Hath," he said. He was tired and depressed, and Hath was fidgety.

They had dinner in the diner. At New Haven a boy came through the car with late editions of the New York evening papers. He bought one to see what the market had been doing; the day before had been a bad one. The headline, bannered clear across the page, drove every other thought out of his mind—ELLIOTT WYATT FAILS.

"Good God!" he said.

"What, Papa?"

"Nothing. Never mind." He was running down the column; there wasn't much of it except the headline: the market had had the worst day yet—a few minutes before closing the announcement had been made on the floor of the exchange—the Elliott Wyatt Company had failed to meet commitments—trading was suspended—liabilities rumored to reach fifty million dollars—company had branches in every city in the country—lately identified with big-scale promotion of

« 322 »

public-service enterprises whose securities had crumbled in the panic—Elliott Wyatt, financier and sportsman—racing stable, yacht—show place on Long Island—

"Yeh—" he said, noting that his fingers had torn through the paper.

"What, Papa?"

"Nothing—"

"Can I see the funnies, Papa?"

"Yeh. Here, take it."

Elliott Wyatt busted, down and out at last—the wolves of Wall Street snared in their own traps. It was incredible—as if the house of Morgan had gone bankrupt, or Gibraltar had succumbed to an invader.—Fifty million dollars. No penny-pushing stuff about those fellows: they gathered it in chunks and dropped it the same way. Easy come and easy go.—Racing stable, yacht, show place on Long Island—the crown jewels staked and lost. No kingdom to be split among inheritors—of authentic, or of *doubtful*, origin. The dynasty was ended.

Yes, but was it?—People who could fail for fifty million dollars were seldom really broke—only *relatively* so. They had something tucked away out of sight of prying creditors, a million or two, a comfortable nest egg; and they'd compromise their debts for a fraction on the dollar and start in fresh again. They were never really hungry; they managed to hang onto the price of theater tickets and a flower for their buttonholes—

Elliott Wyatt—God fallen out of heaven.—He wouldn't be so jaunty now perhaps—so sure he could count on what he sold his customers—cricket stuff and tennis.—But then he had a vision of a ragged little boy standing in the snow beside a broken sled, and a pleasant-faced young man with a shiny walking stick— Good fellow, Elliott—no matter what they'd say about him now, and they'd probably say plenty. Too bad—

He was sorry; he was glad: he did not know what he felt. Hath dropped off to sleep curled up in his seat with the paper spread across him.

It was after eleven when they got out of their cab at the Fifty-ninth Street entrance of the Plaza. He was paying the driver when a big, black Lincoln car drew up close behind him, and he heard the doorman's voice—the doorman who had left him in a hurry—

"Good evening, Mr. Wyatt—"

He turned and there was Elliott—topcoat on his arm, spotless yellow gloves, shiny walking stick, hat cocked same as ever, white carnation in his coat lapel—but it looked a little wilted. And the man looked wilted, too—very, very tired, but not tired in his heart, not broken or afraid.

"Why, Sam—" he said, holding out his hand, "—this is a surprise. It's nice to see you."

"How are you, Mr. Wyatt—" He was conscious of a thrill of admiration, of something else that made him feel embarrassed, ill at ease. Hath was tugging at his sleeve—

"Is that your son?"

"Yes—yes, this is Hath." He introduced the boy, but Hath was unimpressed, and he was tired and sleepy; he hung back childishly.

"Reminds me of you, Sam, when you were a youngster."

He mumbled something, and then he said, not knowing what to say, "I'm awfully sorry, Mr. Wyatt—"

"Thank you, Sam." He dropped his cigarette and flicked it with his stick into the gutter. "Well, that's the way things happen; you have to take the good ones with the bad." His shoulders were drooping with fatigue but he straightened them. "You young fellows will have to carry on—chaps like you and Wayne—"

They were at the door when two cabs came dashing up and men spilled out of them, men with cameras and without—near a dozen of them. And flashlights started popping before he realized what was going on—

"Mr. Wyatt! Mr. Wyatt!" they were calling. "Just one minute, Mr. Wyatt.—Just a minute, please." But Elliott walked on, not pausing and not hurrying, concluding his remark which had become inaudible. "Mr. Wyatt, have a heart. We been on your heels all the way uptown." And then in a moment they were in the lobby, crowding close around him, blocking his way to the waiting elevator—rough fellows, not unfriendly but determined.

"Well, good night, Sam—"

"Good night, Mr. Wyatt—" He pushed through them toward the elevator, holding Hath's hand.

"Mr. Wyatt, please. Just a couple of pictures and then we'll let you go."

"I'm pretty tired, boys—"

"Sure, we know you are." They seemed to like him, to want to be as quick and painless as they could. "We're pretty tired, too," one of

them said. "We been trailing you since three o'clock this afternoon."
The flashlights kept on popping. "Mr. Wyatt, please look here—over
this way, just a second."

He lingered by the elevator door. Hath was wide awake now—

"What are they doing, Papa?"

"Wait—"

"But, Papa, will they hurt him?"

"No, no, they're taking pictures."

"Taking pictures?—why?"

"Hush now. Be still."

"Mr. Wyatt, would you give us just a line—something to quote?"

"I'm sorry, boys, I can't do that tonight."

"A word about your plans?—what you're going to do?"

"I haven't any idea."

"Are you going to raise some more of those prize flowers on your
Long Island place?"

Elliott Wyatt laughed.

"Won't you have to sell it, Mr. Wyatt?"

"Yes, it will be sold."

"What about the yacht?" Five or six of them were asking questions.
"Your racing stables?—The Palm Beach house?"

"They will all be sold," he said. "You may say that."

"Mr. Wyatt, how much money do you really owe?"

"I don't know that."

"As much as fifty millions?"

"I don't know."

"I'll bet it's plenty though," somebody said. "Elliott Wyatt wouldn't
do it cheap." A laugh ran through them.

"What're you going to do about it, Mr. Wyatt?"

"What do you mean?" he said.

"About the money that you owe the public?"

"I'm going to pay it back."

"When, Mr. Wyatt?"

"I can't say when." He stood with his back against a table on which
there was a vase filled with tall white flowers reaching high above
his head. And he raised his voice a little with a new note sounding
in it. "But they'll get their money back if it takes a hundred years."

"Do you think you'll live that long?" somebody asked.

"No, I don't." He smiled. "But there will be other Wyatts."

« 325 »

The flashlights were still popping. "Come, Hath," he said and stepped into the waiting elevator.

1929—end of an epoch, and beginning of another. Ten years had slid away since the boys came marching home—up Broadway mid the blare of welcoming bands, through snowstorms of confetti ticker tape which would ultimately strangle plenty of them.—Democracy had triumphed, and the next thing on the program was to "turn the rascals out." Woodrow Wilson was repudiated, along with everything the boys had fought for, if indeed they'd fought for anything at all; on this point they had doubts which would grow into conviction that they'd been a lot of suckers. "A martyred President, gentlemen—as truly martyred as the Great Emancipator," some Congressman has said, or may say now. "The great somnambulist," as Hugo called Napoleon—an heroic figure walking in a dream. He knew history well enough, having read and taught it; he did not know how to make it—perhaps because he visioned his electorate as composed of eager youths in caps and gowns.—Harding—Teapot Dome.—Coolidge—"What this country needs is a good five cent cigar."—The greatest Secretary of the Treasury since Alexander Hamilton.—Hoover.—It was in the air again in 1929: "Turn the rascals out." Democracy still functioned in America.—Women had got the vote, but had not done much about it; surprisingly enough they acted like the men. Another experiment had not turned out so well: the country had gone dry, and people who had never done much drinking in the past, now got regularly drunk—to testify perhaps to their constitutional rights.—Bootleggers, hijackers, gangsters, dives.—But the country was all right: the train was on the track, going straight ahead, a mile a minute—everybody making money, back to earth again. A journalist named Brisbane had the right idea: "Don't sell America short" and "Two cars in every family." That was something like it, good old common sense that a man could get a grip on.—Chicago was still shabby. But when business is good you don't have to doll things up.—In Wyattville things were much as usual. A new three lane highway had recently been opened, coming down from Muscatine and on to Burlington; and the interurban railway which succeeded the Rock Island, was pretty much discouraged about the trucks and buses. They were talking about tearing up their tracks which were grown up with weeds and getting rusty. Some folks in Wyattville were dabbling in the stock market—in a dingy bucket shop behind Nick's Barber

Parlor. Even Young Henry had been fooling with the thing—making piker bets through a fellow that he knew, so it wouldn't get around. A day or two before the crash he bought a hundred shares of Tronshay at the highest price it ever reached.

XI

TWELVE YEARS WENT BY BEFORE DEATH STRUCK AGAIN, BUT HE MADE amends for the delay, striking quick and hard and deep—

Emilie Braden died in the summer of 1941—at Glencoe, in her beautiful big room with Colonial furniture, with windows which looked out through the foliage of tall trees to the river and the shore of Illinois. The sun came in these windows very early in the morning, the moment that it rose above the distant edge of earth and sky, but softly filtered by the leafy branches, making pretty patterns on the wall.

She was forty-five years old—too young to die. But that's an idle comment: people are dying all the time, at every age, every milestone on the path. Still, he had never thought of such a thing. The disparity of age—he was fifty-seven—was an actuarial factor in his favor, but mortality tables are based on averages: the chances were he would not survive his wife, but they were only chances—the kind of chance an even money favorite has to win a race, but favorites often lose. He had never thought of losing. Sometime *he* would die, but Emilie would be there—with him to the end—

Lately he had given thought to the eventuality: what would Emilie do when he was gone?—what would become of Glencoe?—Hath was a boy, though in years he was a man, in his senior year at Harvard; but he hadn't settled down to a career, rejecting, or evading, the suggestions he had offered, such as medicine or law. The boy was a good student, serious and earnest, but he had some funny notions about things. He didn't feel that he knew Hath very well, not at all the way that Mitch did, which he secretly resented. When the boy was coming home for a vacation—well, he was glad of course, but apprehensive, too.—How could he best protect his wife and son?—Six million dollars, even after taxes, would take looking after—

The previous winter, living in Chicago at the Drake, he had spent a lot of time going over things with Hub, and had drawn a new will which provided that the Adams bank should function as trustee for Emilie and Hath after his death. And there were provisions about Glencoe, in the nature of entailment—the British method of protect· ing property against the whims of inexperienced heirs. He felt, at the end, that he had things in good shape; and the job had served to pass the winter months which were sometimes rather tedious. That last day in Hub's office he had asked, with the pen poised in his hand—

"Sure we haven't overlooked a single thing?"

"Not a comma, Sam."

"Glencoe—"

"No one can touch it."

"And Emilie—"

"Residuary income for her life."

She was ill only five days—pneumonia, the ordinary sort of thing so many people have—have and get over. And it was in July—hot, sunny days when life was at its flood, the lawns like velvet, the cutting gardens massed with color—days when no one dies. Yes, but they do, in summer, too; there is no rule about it. She was never very strong— there had been, since Hath was born, a little murmur in her heart; that's why he hadn't wanted her to have another child—but wiry, he believed, perhaps because she did not admit fatigue, nor ever that she wasn't feeling well. And Glencoe was not an easy job: the house took several servants and they were hard to get and hard to keep, and coming and going in the spring and in the fall meant adjustments and replacements; and then there were the gardens which were her responsibility to plan and to direct; and finally there was Sam, a dynamic, restless man, tender and devoted, but generally impatient and often irritable, for getting what you want at the moment that you want it gets to be a habit. Even in Europe it had not been easy. It was never easy after Deming Court.

Hath said to her one time—he was ten that winter, on his Christ· mas holiday, they were in St. Moritz at a fashionable hotel, and his father had been angry because he had been clumsy at his skiing lesson; his mother had defended him, and his father had been cross with her and had stamped out of the room—and then he had said, frowning seriously, talking like an English boy—

"Why don't you chuck it, Mother?"

"Chuck it?" she repeated.

"I mean, why can't we go and live together by ourselves?"

"Oh, Hath—" She sat down on a chair and laughed until she cried. "But I love your father, dear."

"Even when he's cross?"

"Even when he's cross."

"Well—" He shook his head. "—I don't see why."

She had a cold, as anyone might have; and then she had gone out into the pouring rain, at night, alone, in a summer frock and thin white slippers—had gone to look for Hath, to bring him home. The next day she was ill, as anyone might be; but it was more than that, for she was sick at heart. She had gotten up as usual in the morning— he had heard her moving in her room when he went down to breakfast, but then she hadn't come and he had sent the maid who had come flying back—

"Mr. Braden, please come quickly—"

He had run into the hall—the beautiful, big hall which visitors raved about, with wide arched doors at either end, toward the river and the woods—up the circling staircase for which an architect had searched New England—across the upper hall, past Hath's door and his own. She was lying on the floor beside her dressing table, half dressed, the hairbrush fallen from her hand—

"Phone Dr. Bentley," he commanded. "Tell him to come at once." And then he picked her up—she wasn't much to lift, and put her on the bed, and held and chafed her hands which were burning up with fever. "Emilie, my darling—Emilie—" A maid had wet a towel and put it on her head. And then her eyes had opened and she had looked around, as if she didn't quite know where she was—

"Why, what—"

"Emilie! What is it, darling?"

"Oh—" And then she smiled. "I think I must have fainted."

"Fainted?—But why?"

"I can't imagine, Unkam. But don't you worry, dear. I'll be all right in a little while."

Grover had come immediately, and later Madge had come. Madge came every day, wanting to bring her things and stay at night, but he had urged her not to, feeling that her staying would confirm a situation which he did not want to face—

The day that Emilie died a specialist had flown from Chicago, in a chartered plane to Muscatine, and he had sent the Cadillac to bring him on to Glencoe. Grover had suggested it, saying that he thought

Sam might feel more comfortable, though he had no doubt of what was being done. The man had come in the afternoon and had stayed about an hour. He saw the patient briefly and had some talk with Grover. Later, in the library, he had refused refreshment or a glass of sherry. He must get back, he said, as quickly as he could—

He concurred completely in the diagnosis; the treatment was classical; he had nothing to suggest beyond what was being done; the patient's heart was under heavy strain; if weakness should develop in this quarter, Dr. Bentley would know what to do about it. He glanced around the room while he was speaking, through the open windows across a bed of brilliant cannas, down the long straight avenue through the heart of Beaton's woods—

"Charming place you have here, Mr. Braden—"

"Yes—" he said. Funny how far away from things those fellows kept themselves.

"Interesting—" The doctor was looking at her portrait, framed in the paneling of the wall opposite his mother's. It was a full-length figure, done in Paris by a painter of some note. She wore a soft, white gown, *Directoire* style, swinging in her hand a straw bonnet with blue ribbons—coming directly toward you, almost dancing from the wall. The man had caught the copper-tinted hair, and the deep pools of her eyes, and the music of her smile. It was very lightly painted—almost impressionistic, but it was like her—like her soul.—The doctor looked at it, turning his head the way a connoisseur does. "Yes, interesting—" He waited for a moment, seeming to reflect, to make sure there was nothing he had overlooked. "Oh yes, I meant to ask: has anything been troubling Mrs. Braden?"

He didn't answer quickly, moistening his lips.

"I mean, her mind?—has she been disturbed?"

"Yes," he said.

"She keeps calling for someone—"

"Her son—our son."

"Hm—" The doctor pressed out his cigarette. "It might be helpful if she could be reassured—if your son could come."

"Yes, I know."

"I believe I have nothing further to suggest—"

"Thank you," he said.

"Good day, Mr. Braden—"

"Good day, doctor—" Grover went with him to the door.

He had been trying to find Hath, almost from the start, phoning every place he thought the boy might be. He had sent a dozen wires; he had even tried to locate Mitch Ballou, calling Chicago and New York. But there had been no answer—

The last words Emilie Braden spoke were these: "Poor Uncle Sam—" She had not called him that for twenty years.

It was late that night, but not yet midnight. Madge had gone home; she had wanted to stay, but he had insisted. Her efforts to divert his mind were futile, and her presence was prophetic—a mourner in advance. They had dinner in the big white room with its high glass doors opening on the terrace above the cutting gardens, looking southward through a twilit wooded vista to immaculate great barns and lofty silos, and cattle grazing in wide meadowland—like little wooden toys. The doors were open to the summer evening, and the air was heavy with the scent of stock and jasmine. There was larkspur on the table, a bowl of purple blossoms—white linen, glistening silver, shimmering glass; and there was—the vacant chair opposite his own; Madge sat at his side.

She said, making conversation: someone had had a letter from Eileen. She had managed to get out of France, among the very last, and was living in New York. She had had a dreadful time of it, according to her letter, losing everything she had—her car and household things. "Has she any money, Sam?"

"What?" He wasn't listening.

"Has Eileen any means?"

"Eileen?—means" He forced himself to think about it. "Something, I suppose. Enough, I guess."

"But her father didn't leave—"

"Nothing," he said. "The house in Long Beach where her mother lives, and a little life insurance."

"But the old home place?"

"Yes, it belongs to her. It was in the trust Old Henry left her."

"Maybe that's the reason Young Henry wouldn't live there after his father died?"

"Maybe—"

"Anyway it's just a ruin."

"Yes, a ruin," he agreed.

She went on talking: Eileen's son was in the Army, she had heard —a pilot in the Air Force, she believed,—following in his father's footsteps, though he hadn't hurried off to help the British. Still, it did seem strange, the way things were repeated—

« 331 »

"What?"

"Eileen's son in the Army, in the Air Force."

"Oh!—Oh yes—" he said.

After dinner he had sent a car to take her home. He couldn't listen any more, simply couldn't stand it. He had walked out with her to the car, standing in the driveway, with the cannas in the center, looking across them down the tree-lined avenue—half a mile of it. It was not yet dark; the first stars were coming out—

"Dear Sam—" Her voice was choked; her eyes were brimming. "—you mustn't be discouraged. You've been so good to everyone. God wouldn't hurt you, Sam; you must have faith in Him. She'll be better in the morning. I *know* she will."

"Yes. Yes, of course," he said, calling after the departing car, "Good night—" He turned back to the house—the imposing portico with its white wooden pillars, the low wing at his left where the guest rooms were, rooms so seldom tenanted—well, they had been enough, just the three of them. The white walls of the house caught the dying light through their coverlet of vines—ivy, Virginia creeper; seven years they had been growing, spreading on the walls, climbing up the broad brick chimneys—

In the hall the nurse was going up the stairs. He thought that she was hurrying to avoid his questions. He didn't ask her anything—

He had gone into the library. There were flowers in the room—on the table in the center, on the ends of the marble mantel shelf. It was his favorite room—heavy, rather somber with its dark oak-paneled walls and the long sides of it lined with books from floor to ceiling. He had turned the radio on and turned it off, picked up a book and put it down—as he had been doing all day long. A little after nine Grover had come back.—Perhaps the nurse had called him? But there was no reason to imagine that. He had been coming every night about that time. When he was leaving he would look in at the door, saying, "See you tomorrow, Sam" or something of that sort, in a reassuring way. And he would ask the question: "How is she tonight?"—"Fairly comfortable, I think," Grover would say cheerfully —but not any more than that, though he held his breath to hear it. Grover had gotten heavy and quite gray—an old familar friend; and no doubt he knew his business as well as any of them—

Waiting, he got out some snapshot albums from the drawer of the big table—from his chair he could see through the open door into the hall, would see Grover coming down the stairs. He fluttered through the pages, stirring memories here and there: pictures of Hath from the time he was a baby, in the yard on Deming Court, in Lincoln Park, gazing at the bears, with his nose pressed to the netting of the otter's cage. Hath in Paris, in shorts which were too short, which he hadn't liked to wear, bare legs and socks—spindly little legs. The Rolls Royce car he had rented in London for a month, and had kept for three full years, in which they had junketed through Europe, every corner of it. The funny Cockney chauffeur with a mustache like a walrus— Orlick was his name, or perhaps it had been Horlick—honest and efficient, with a fine contempt for foreign places. He had been a sailor once and had sailed the seven seas; there were anchors and things tattooed on his hands. He would never ask directions however badly lost; he distrusted foreigners. He was not impressed with scenery. Of Mont Blanc he had remarked, "Bit ragged, sir." The cathedral at Chartres had inspired him to say, "Too 'igh for comfort, sir." Morocco he dismissed as, "Niggers." But "niggers" for the man began at Calais—

Europe—*ses plages, ses monuments, ses* this and that: they had done it thoroughly. They hadn't gone to Russia; Mitch had been there then, reinstated for the moment in the Bolshevik good graces, and he had written him, suggesting they might come. But Mitch had not encouraged it, and the Rolls Royce couldn't take them since there were not any roads. "You wouldn't like it," Mitch wrote briefly in reply. "It's poor and rough and ugly, like Shanty Town on a colossal scale. Trains are bad, hotels are worse, food not fit to eat. All the people in the street look like factory workers, and they are, but the factory is their own—anyway they think it is. You wouldn't like it, Sam. It stinks. It only has one virtue: *it's alive.*"

No, they hadn't gone to Russia, but the rest of it they'd seen, every capital of Europe, crisscrossing here and there with the mood of the moment or the season of the year, with pleasant, restful pauses at the Dorchester in London, the apartment in Paris—visiting *couturiers,* buying things for Emilie; going to the seashore or to Switzerland for Hath's vacation times. You got into the rhythm of it afterwhile, but there were times, of course, when it was dull and lonely.—Decadent and dying Europe, poor and down at heel, not adapted in the least to modern life—political confusion, Communists and Fascists, bedlam of disunion. "Sure," Mitch had sneered one day when they were talking, "but how the hell do you know? You can't see anything out of the window of a Rolls; the glass is shatter-proof and it's *opaque.*

You're completely insulated; by the time a club gets through to you, the wood has turned to feathers."—Old Mitch getting bitter with the years—as edgy as his ragged cuffs. They had never been in agreement about things—still, who could have foreseen it would come to where it did—

Pictures—the little town near Munich where Mama Kranz was born. Emilie had discovered some distant relatives—humble, kindly people, asking endless questions about America.—Three years.—He had meant to stay a year at most, but the time had slid away; and there wasn't any reason to go back—things were in a mess at home, the depression dragging on. He had ideas in his head: motors, aviation, radio; but this was no time to be fooling with a buzz saw. It could wait until the country got straightened out again. And Hath was doing well in the German school in Spetzgart—

Pictures—with neatly lettered captions she had written for them, and phrases to bring back amusing memories: the time he had tried to learn to ski—half buried in a snowbank, looking pretty grim.—Pictures, pictures—the history of a lifetime, of more than twenty years of it, of all of it that mattered.—He started, thinking he had heard Grover's footstep on the stairs, but it was nothing. He glanced at the clock, a little after ten—Grover had been up there quite a while—

Pictures—of Hath at that first school in Switzerland, the one he didn't like, or didn't like at first, though he had protested leaving it for the other one at Spetzgart. Mostly French and English boys—unkind or snooty, Hath reported. He had written painfully scrawled and tearful letters to his mother, pleading for release. Emilie had been sick about it; she had wanted to go back—all the way back from Berlin—

"Nonsense!" he had said. "He'll come out of it all right."

"But he's such a little fellow—only ten years old."

"When I was ten—" and he had gone over that.

"I know," she said, "but I don't want Hath to be unhappy, Unkam. I can't believe that will do him any good, that it ever could be good for anyone."

"We can't back down." He had been firm—well, somebody had to be. "I'll tell you what: we'll try it for the term. We've got to give the boy a chance to whip it."

He had written Hath a letter, and had it typed so there would be no chance he couldn't read it, being kind but very firm: the boy must see it through to the Christmas holidays, and then they'd talk it over; there was no alternative, so the thing for him to do was make the best of it. Some day he would be glad that he had won the fight. And he must not write begging letters to his mother, which made her very sad and could do no good for him. He must learn to play the game—"With much love—Papa."

And in fact the situation had immediately improved: there were no more tearful letters, and, in a month or two, indications of adjustment. Hath had made a friend whom he wrote about with great enthusiasm: a boy a little older than himself, bigger and stronger too, and a year ahead in school, but "not stuck up about it." They hadn't got acquainted till quite lately. He had thought the boy was French until one day some French boys got him cornered in the yard and were hitting him with switches because he'd accidentally kicked some marbles they were playing, and his friend had come along and scattered them, "made them run like scary cats," and this was the way they got acquainted. And it turned out that the boy wasn't French at all, but "American like me," although he lived in France and had not been to America since he was a baby, but he wanted to go back there, and he would when he grew up. He was "sure good at things," soccer and hockey games, and he could "lick a French kid with both hands tied behind him." His name was "Neel. I guess that's how you spell it". He didn't know his last name—

He had looked in the catalogue, the list of pupils in the back, which he had barely glanced at, and there it was: "Neill Wyatt—Paris."—Anyway the school had not been satisfactory—too many English boys, no chance to learn a language—

Pictures—Hath at the Unknown Soldier's grave. It was that summer day, strolling back along the Champs Élysées—

"Papa! There he is."

"What?—Who?"

"My friend—the boy I knew in school in Switzerland."

"Where?"

"Coming, don't you see?" He pointed eagerly. "In the taxi with that lady." They were passing as he spoke—the taxi top was down—a boy in Eton collar with blond hair brushed straight back—Eileen, erect and smart; she hadn't changed much, not that you could see at a distance, in a moment. "Papa! Stop him, please."

He had stood there with Hath tugging at his sleeve—

"Hi, Neill!" But the taxi had passed by and the childish voice was lost in the rumble of the traffic. "You could've stopped him, Papa."

"Well, I—"

"Yes, you could, and you didn't even try." They walked in silence for a while. "Papa—"

"Yes?"

"If he lives in Paris, don't you think that we could find him?"

"Well, maybe so. We'll see about it." A few days later they had gone to Brittany—

Pictures—pictures—

There was a footstep on the stair—Grover coming down. He came into the doorway, looking grave—or perhaps it was the shadow—

"Sam, I think you better come now."

"Oh—" He stood up quickly, putting the album on the table.

"She's asking for you."

"Oh—asking for me—" he repeated.

"She's conscious; her temperature has dropped—"

"You mean—" His heart leapt up. "—you mean, she's better, Grover?"

"No, I'm sorry, Sam—she isn't any better."

"Oh—" He went into the hall whose doors stood open to the starlit summer night; he could hear frogs croaking, the chirping of a cricket, the murmur of the river—up the circling stairs, his hand upon the rail, like a man who drags himself, his heart turned suddenly to lead, weighting his feet so he could hardly raise them—across the upper hall, past Hath's door and his own—

There was a light beside the big four poster bed, next the side of it on which she always lay, so small and fragile underneath the covers —"Like a wrinkle in the blanket," he had told her once. He had used to joke about it, coming in the dark to find her, pretending that he thought she wasn't there—

He stood beside the bed. Her face was very white with the flush of fever gone, her hair spread on the pillow, coppery glinting in the light. Her eyes were open—looking *for* him—looking *at* him now that he was there, relieved, smiling a little. He knelt beside her, but her eyes bade him come closer and he sat on the bed so that she could feel his nearness. Her hands were moving, fingers pinching at the sheet; he held them tight in his—not hot and dry but cold now. For five endless days she had not spoken to him, knowing what she said, but she knew now—

"Poor Uncle Sam—" That was what she said. She had not called him that for twenty years, not since they were married, longer than that. "Poor Uncle Sam—" He could never say the full of *how* she said it: as if she were so very sorry for him, as if she knew how much he needed her, as if she understood everything about him—with loving tenderness, with deep compassion—as if she were a little girl again—but, too, as if she had gone on, far, far away, and was already looking back from a high and distant place—

"Poor Uncle Sam—" That was all she said.—He didn't see death coming, didn't notice any change, but suddenly Grover spoke sharply to the nurse, commanding something which she put into his hand, which was prepared and waiting, and came quickly to the bed, pushing him aside almost roughly in his haste, throwing back the sheet, feeling with his hands, driving a long needle deep into her breast, pressing on it with his weight—

And that was the way that people died—but always in your thought, if you ever thought about it, the other fellow's wife—

It was an hour later that the telephone had rung and a servant had come to him in the library—

"It's Mr. Hath, sir, on the phone—" The man was struggling to control his voice. "He's asking for his mother."

"All right," he said. He spoke into the phone on the table at his elbow, quietly and calmly, "It's Father, Hath."

The voice that answered him was cold and defiant. "I want to speak to Mother."

"Where are you, Hath?"

"I want to speak to Mother."

"I've been trying to find you, phoning everywhere—"

"I want to speak to Mother."

"Hath, please—"

"I *asked* to speak to Mother."

"Your mother has been ill, Hath."

"Ill?" The voice was startled but suspicious. "Well, she can tall to me; there's a phone beside her bed—"

"No, Hath, she can't—"

"I want to tell her something."

"Very, very ill," he said.

"What?" The voice was frightened now. "What do you mean by that?"

"Your mother—" But he had gone the limit of it. He put his hand over the receiver. "Grover, please—" holding out the phone to him. "Tell him, Grover. I—I can't—"

He had gone out of the room, stumbling blindly through the hall, through the screen doors to the terrace, into the warm, still night—the scent of stock and jasmine, the frogs still croaking, the murmur of the river, not arrested for a moment, the blackness of it glimpsed through the foliage of the trees—

Grover had come to find him, pacing at his side up and down the terrace, not saying very much, or much that he remembered, but once out of the darkness: "That's the way things happen, Sam. You've got to take it."

And he had taken it, with his back against the wall—not against a table with a vase of tall white flowers, but backed against the wall—

And again, when he was leaving, when the dawn was in the sky: "You've been very lucky, Sam, to have so much to lose."

Yes, he'd been lucky, too, for more than twenty years—the kind of luck few people ever had, or if they did, something happened to it. And it wasn't only death which was terrible but clean; there were cheap and ugly happenings: look at Nelly. Or nothing ever happened: look at Madge. Yes, he had been very lucky. But you paid for your luck as you paid for everything, one way or another, in the end—

That was in July, and now it was December.

The trees were bare, the lawns turned brown, the cutting garden empty, the muddy river high and sullen—a wintry Sunday morning, bleak and overcast. And Sunday was a day he dreaded: no work to be inspected, no orders to be given, no one to give them to—lately there had not been very many; some of the younger farm hands had been drafted, and others had deserted for higher factory wages. They were making planes in Wyattville, bombers and pursuit planes. They had started in the old abandoned warehouse on the levee and had spread through half a mile of concrete buildings; and they were building more of them, tearing up the earth and pouring concrete. On week days you could hear the shovels and the mixers as far away as Glencoe. Wyattville was booming, humming with activity, and the river was alive with tugs and barges—

He pushed back his breakfast tray, sitting by the window of his room, in the brocaded robe Emilie had given him last Christmas. It had been a merry Christmas, the three of them and Madge, and Mitch and Nat—the big tree in the hall in the circle of the stairs, where they always had it—the wreaths and holly berries, and the yule log in the library. Mitch had been unusually agreeable, in an expansive mood; and he hadn't drunk too much, as he nearly always did. After dinner Hath and Nat had slipped away. Hath had asked to use a car—his own car was in Cambridge—

"Why, sure," he had said, "take the Packard if you like," inquiringly carelessly where they were going.

"Just for a ride."

"Yeh?" He hadn't thought a thing about it then, but afterwards remembering, or imagining that he did: an expression on their faces as they looked at one another—

Perhaps that was the start of it?—But the start of it was far, far back of that. It was like a powder train, twisting on the ground, disappearing here and there till you picked it up again on the other side of something, but burning all the time and always coming closer.—Perhaps that rainy evening in the spring of '33, almost nine years ago, when they were coming home, waiting in London for the "Berengaria," a day or two before they were to sail—when he had said to Orlick, pressing a button and speaking through the tube which was close to Orlick's ear, "Drive back through the Strand."—Yes, then perhaps—if there was any point where anything *began*?—He had been to his tailor, to the steamship office—"Drive back through the Strand"—for no reason other than he liked the bustle of it, the lights and crowded pavements that made him think of home.—Or if at the moment he had not glanced through the window, or had glanced through the one on the traffic side?—Yes, that must be the start of it—

But the start of it was far, far back of that.

A servant came to get the breakfast tray. It was late, close to eleven. On Sunday there was little reason to get up—and he slept so badly, often reading until daybreak. But today there was something that he had in mind to do. The phone rang and the servant answered it—

"Miss Braden, sir." The man was new, awkward with the tray, looking like a hostler despite his service jacket. Good help was hard to get, and getting harder. It was lonely in the country; they didn't like it much. He hadn't meant to stay there through the winter, but where was he to go?—where else on earth could he occupy himself?

"Yes, Madge?"

"How are you, Sam?"

"All right," he answered cheerfully.

"It's such a dreary day—" She was going to church, would he care to go with her?—No, not today, he thought. She asked him every Sunday and he never went.—Well, would he come to dinner?—Cassie's chicken and hot biscuits—

"I've just had breakfast, Madge."

"Oh—" She was disappointed. Would he like her to come over in the afternoon?

"Well—" He hesitated. "—I've got some letters that I ought to write—"

"Oh—" She sighed. "Well, call me if you're lonely."

"Thanks, Madge." He smiled, thinking of himself calling Madge when he was lonely, calling all day long and in the night, calling anybody whom his voice could reach—

Thinking while he shaved: Madge had been wonderful, coming every day, asking him to dinner, telephoning. She had wanted to bring Cassie and keep house for him, but he had avoided that: she had her life in Wyattville, her friends—or wanted him to come and live with them. But he was waiting, undecided; had been waiting through the months—for what, he didn't know—for something to emerge out of the wreckage of his life, for a voice within himself that would tell him what to do—

People had been kind. But aside from Mike and Grover he had no friends in Wyattville. Acquaintances, of course, who spoke to him on the street, but not the way they did to one another. They came to Glencoe when they were invited, but not the way they visited their friends; they put on their Sunday clothes and stood around, and were careful to agree with what he said. They didn't really know him, or he them. He had given Wyattville a country club—bought the land and built the clubhouse, soon after he came, in the depth of the depression when things were pretty cheap. He had liked doing it, and he had done it right. But he never went there. If he came up on the porch or into the locker room, into a group of men, they would greet him pleasantly, a little deferentially, but they wouldn't go on talking as they did among themselves. He had mentioned it to Mitch—

"Hell!" Mitch grinned. "They hate you, Sam."

"Hate me?—Why?"

"Home-town boy makes good. They can't stand that; it burns them up."

"Nonsense!" He laughed uncomfortably.

"Look!" Mitch said. "Try and get it through your head: *you can't have everything.*"

Of course it wasn't true: people didn't hate him. They really hated Mitch—anyway, the ones you'd see around the country club—

He finished dressing and went into Emilie's room, as he did every morning, looking to see that it was quite in order—fresh flowers in the vases, from the greenhouse now. The room was as she left it: books on the table, magazines of last July; her desk with the calendar arrested on the date, a letter she had written which had not been mailed, a memo of the things she had to do that day, a market list. Her dresses were hanging in the closets; things on the dressing table— toilet pieces, perfume bottles. He had not known what to do with anything—and then he couldn't—

He opened her jewel case and took out the sapphire ring, turning it to see the star, thinking of the day he bought it, of running through the storm back to the office. There was something he had in mind to do, but not today—at Christmas time, he hoped. He put the ring away, studying himself in the dressing table mirror—his clothes: brown flannel slacks, a jacket of corduroy, loose and soft as velvet, a tan silk shirt, open at the neck. His hair was getting thin, too thin for any cowlick, and it had turned quite white around his ears. His face was tanned from being out all day; it looked a little gaunt and—rather sad. He hadn't gotten heavy, but neither was he trim—certainly not jaunty, though his clothes were smartly tailored.—No, he wasn't old, but neither was he young. His health was good enough. Grover couldn't find much the matter with him—heart sound, arteries still all right. He got a little stiff if he sat for a long time, but that could be expected. He might live twenty years—

He went down the circling stairs. The man was waiting for him in the hall with his hat and walking stick—a hat of brown velour, a thick Malacca stick—

"Will you want a coat, sir?"

"No," he said. "I'm going over to the other house. I shan't want any lunch."

"Yes sir. In case someone should phone?"

"I don't want to be disturbed."

He went out across the terrace. The air was raw and chilly, and a blanket of white mist was rising from the river, climbing up the bluff and spreading through the trees. He walked a little way, perhaps a hundred yards, along a winding path through a grove of sycamores, to the house in which he had been born—

Yes, to that very house, the house in Shanty Town, moved—no, not moved, for, in its decrepitude, it would not suffer moving, nor could it have been moved down the drive and through the woods— but cut in many pieces, marked and numbered, and all put back together, faultlessly restored. A straw that he had clutched at in those first torturing weeks; and Madge and Mike had encouraged him to do it. But he had thought about it long before. He had a deep attachment to the house; he didn't like to see it neglected, falling down, the shingles off the roof and the glass gone from the windows. He had mentioned it to Emilie one day when they were driving by the place—

"A kind of monument," he said. She seemed a little doubtful. "I mean—" He had explained: of interest to his son, to his grandchildren perhaps—the old house and the new one, showing what a man could do, how he could get along—

"Why, yes—" she said, adding with a smile, "and if we should lose our money we could come and live in it."

"Live in it?" He laughed. He meant to use it as an office, a place to keep his letter files and ledgers, where the foremen would come to get their orders.

"Oh—" She nodded. And then she had said, jokingly of course, but now that he remembered it, perhaps a little wistfully, "Sometime, just for fun, we might pretend that we were poor."

And he had laughed at that: it wasn't a thing he'd be likely to pretend—

Had she been happy?—He stood still in the path. The question had never occurred to him before. Of course those last few months, when his quarrel with Mitch had shadowed things, when the rift was widening between himself and Hath—but that was a matter which could not have been averted, in which he had no option. And that wasn't what he meant: had her life run in the channels of her choice?— Had she really wanted Glencoe?—She had never said she didn't, but only that she hoped it wouldn't be too large. Two thousand acres was the figure he had set, and the figure that it was. But she had been speaking of the house—urging that it shouldn't be elaborate or pretentious—

"I mean—" She had pushed back the blueprints which he had been explaining. "—well, Unkam, don't you see: if it gets to be too big it won't belong to us; we'll just be working there like all the other people."

And he had laughed at that. But to please her he had modified the plans, lopping off the whole south wing which was to have contained a billiard room and bar, and a sort of recreation hall where he had thought some day Hath might entertain his friends. He had cut down the greenhouses, cut the swimming pool in two, given up the idea of a boathouse on the river—

Had she been happy?—not with Glencoe or without it, but—*with him?*—Well, of course, the question was absurd. Their life together had been perfect; they had never really had a disagreement—until just at the end. He had wanted her to have everything she wanted; and she had said to him so many times: "My dearest wish is that you should be happy." And he had been happy, in all that pertained to her—loyalty, devotion, and companionship. Yes, they had both been happy—

He walked on slowly toward the house. They had picked the site together, among the sycamores, close to the bluff, the porch faced toward the river as it had in Shanty Town; and then he had been busy doing other things, and had almost forgotten it—

But there it was—even the lilac bushes which the gardeners had maintained could not be moved. But they had been moved and would live to tell about it, though now in December they did look black and dead. The clapboards and the shingles were as paintless as they had been when he was a child, but they had been carefully oiled; and where new ones were needed the wood had been antiqued so you couldn't tell the difference. It had taken nearly four months; the last of the workmen had finished yesterday. And Madge had been there all day long, putting things away: things she had saved and resurrected from the attic—almost everything, she said. There had not been very much—

He walked on around the house, past the windows of the parlor where, one Christmas day, he had made a fire in the stove for Mr. Daniel Price—Mr. Daniel Price who had not come back, who was now in Washington, a familiar in the White House, adviser to the President on economic matters—anyway, so he had read.—The girls' room overhead where Madge no doubt had wept bitter tears into her pillow at parting with her lover. His mother's room to which he had been summoned in the night—"Not great but good, she says." Yes, he remembered that, as if it had been yesterday.—Had he been *good?*—and how was one to tell?—Well, he had tried, had done the best he could.—The room above where he and Tom had lived, where he had gone to sleep thinking of Eileen, of being rich some day—

The pump outside the summer kitchen; the shed at the back with the chopping block, or one that looked just like it, where he had sat beside his broken sled while Nelly tried to comfort him, where he had gone to read his first letter from Eileen, from which one night the Pope-Toledo vanished—

He turned the corner of the house, went up the steps, across the narrow porch, and through the door. The room was as it had been in his childhood: the table in the center which would serve him as a desk, his father's chair, his mother's rocker, the stool he had sat on when she read to him, her workbasket—Madge had even found the thimble he had given her that Christmas, the Christmas that he didn't get the sled. The cook stove and the sink where he had pumped and scrubbed, with the mirror hanging over it—he had had to stand on tiptoe to comb his cowlick flat; the old clock ticking on its shelf, and the shelf with dishes on it—amazing, all the things Madge had dug up. And there was nothing new, not a thing that hadn't been there, except his files and ledgers. The old oil lamps were wired, and there were electric heaters hidden in the wall—he held his hand close to a metal grille and felt the warmth. But the room seemed rather chilly, and it had the musty odor of disuse—

Yes, a kind of monument—

He sat down in his father's chair, at the end of the table which had been his mother's place. There was a blotting pad with silver corners, his fountain pen, stationery in a rack; he took a sheet of it—fine white bond with "Glencoe" at the top, picked up the pen and wrote in his small and careful hand, "Dear boy—" but then he tore it up and took another sheet—

Dear Hath—

Winter has come to Glencoe. It is quite cold and raw. Today the sky is gray, as if there might be snow; and there is a thick white mist rising from the river, climbing up the bluff and spreading through the woods, like a London fog.

He leaned back in his chair.—Yes, that's where it had started, if things started anywhere—when he had said to Orlick, pressing a button and speaking through the tube—"Drive back through the Strand"—in the spring of '33, a day or two before they sailed for home. Hitler had come to power, and Emilie was determined that Hath should not continue in a German school. He had thought she was unreasonable about it, that it could do no harm for a few months anyway; but she had stood her ground, had been almost sick about it, emotional and upset. And then the banks had closed and he had been really frightened, thinking that he'd better look after his investments, though he was pretty sure they were sound, if anything was sound. And so in a moment the decision had been made: Hath had been sent for in the middle of his term, and the Rolls had brought them racing back from Cannes—

"Drive back through the Strand."—He was looking through the window at the people on the sidewalk, hurrying homeward through the rain, when suddenly—"Orlick, stop!" he cried; and Orlick pulled up sharp against the curb—

"Hi, Mitch!" And it was Mitch, plodding through the rain with his hands deep in the pockets of a shabby overcoat, and a rusty looking hat pulled down over his eyes. He paused and looked around. "Mitch! Here!" he called, leaning out the open door. "My God!" He gripped his hand. "I thought you were in Russia."

"I was," Mitch grinned. "They kicked me out again."

"What're you doing here?"

"Looking for a job."

"Where you going now?"

"Where I live."

"Get in. I'll take you."

"Yeh?" Mitch hesitated. "I'll get your jewel box muddy."

"Oh hell! Get in." And Mitch had gotten in, giving Orlick an address which Orlick didn't know, though he'd lived his life in London.

"It's in the slums," Mitch said. They got it straightened out.

"How's Bugs?" he asked, once they were started.

"She's dead," Mitch said, as he might have said, "She's fine."

"Dead?—No."

"She died last year in Moscow. The winter got her."

"Why, Mitch—" He did not know what to say.

"That's all right—" Mitch shrugged. "She's been dying all the time, ever since I married her."

"And your daughter, Mitch?"

"Okay."

"With you here in London?"

"Cooking supper for me now. We got one of these dumps they call 'housekeeping flats'—a gas plate and a sink. But, hell, she's used to that; we came from Russia. She can poach an egg the way you never tasted one, if—" he chuckled dryly, "—if she has an egg."

"But who looks after her?"

"I do," he said defiantly, and then he changed the subject. They had kicked him out of Moscow for something he had written: a famine in the Ukraine; the peasants had rebelled against collective farming, and the government had cleaned them out of everything they had and was leaving them to starve. They had censored his story and he had telephoned it—

"But you must have known they'd kick you out for that?"

"So what?" Mitch said. "It's their job to keep it quiet, and mine to tell the truth—when I can find it." The peasants were, in fact, a lot of stupid fools, but—they were *starving*. He'd been hunting for another berth but jobs were hard to get. The Reds didn't want him; they thought he was a Tory, and the Tories were convinced he was a Red. "I'm Mitch Ballou," he said, "a sucker with a passion for the facts." He had had a chance today to go back to Berlin, but he wouldn't take Nat there—

"Why not?"

"Because her mother was a Jewess."

"Oh!— Oh yes—" They stopped before a shabby house in a wretched neighborhood.

"Say, Sam—"

"What?"

"I'm flat on my uppers. Could you lend me—say, ten pounds?"

"Why, of course—" He was feeling in his pocket. "Let's say twenty, Mitch—"

"No, ten's enough. And I'll never pay it back."

"Well—" He shoved the note into his hand. "Say, wait a minute: I'm not going to leave you this way. Get Nat and come along. We'll have dinner at the Dorchester with Emilie and Hath."

"No thanks." Mitch had gotten out onto the sidewalk, with Orlick standing at the door. "She'll have my supper cooking—"

"Oh, come along. It'll be a treat for her." He could see that Mitch was wavering.

"No. I haven't even got a dinner jacket."

"We'll have dinner in our rooms, just the way we are."

"Well—"

"Go and get her. Hurry up." Waiting, he had gone across the street into a pub, and had telephoned to Emilie, explaining the encounter and the facts as he had learned them. Mitch had come back with the child who could not have been more than twelve years old, but strangely like an adult, sitting straight between them, hands folded in her lap, not self-conscious or impressed. Her coat was clean but threadbare; her thick black hair bobbed at her shoulders, severe and unbecoming; her white pinched face and Jewish features—not pretty in the least, but there was something arresting and appealing, wistful and pathetic: a child who seemed at once both an adult and an orphan—

"Sausages," Mitch said. "Sausages and mustard greens; and I'll bet they don't have 'em at the Dorchester—not the way that Nat can cook 'em."

And the child had said with her very English accent, "Oh, it doesn't matter, Father. They'll be quite good tomorrow."

They had not had sausages or mustard greens—he did not remember what: possibly a pheasant and a bottle of choice wine, served by a man in livery in the parlor of their suite. The little girl had eaten as if she were half starved, but with perfect table manners, listening like an adult to the conversation, smiling appreciation of her father's caustic humor, adoring him completely. They understood each other. And his own boy sitting there—still in shorts, the way German boys were dressed, but not caring any more—in his Bond Street jacket and white starched Eton collar, with his coppery tinted hair brushed back from his forehead, and his mother's deep brown eyes in the eager, thoughtful face—

He had shaken hands with Nat, stiffly clicking heels, like a German boy. They had been polite to one another, not any more than that. It was Mitch who captured his attention—

After dinner Mitch had paced and talked as usual, emptying glass after glass of Scotch and soda, prowling up and down the room like a creature in a cage, seedy looking and unkempt, but with fire in his eye and passion in his voice which would suddenly dissolve into bitter cynicism. It was mostly about Russia—

The hope of the world was there, he said—a hope which might remain no more than that, which might never be fulfilled, and which was not apparent on the surface, not easily recognized in what they did, had done yesterday, would do tomorrow. The hope was in the idea which lay behind their effort—not a new one to be sure, but an old one lifted out of the fog of mysticism, resolved from superstitious into practical attack—an idea which might never be achieved, which might suffer defeat from without or from within, which might be modified or compromised and ultimately lost, which might fail, as Christ had failed, to change the hearts of men. It was much too soon to tell, but the hope of the world was in the idea—in an extension of it, in the leveling of frontiers, of nationalistic lines and racial boundaries, to the end that men and women, and the products of their toil, .

might flow freely and unchallenged over all the lands and seas. It was possible perhaps to visualize a day when a man, if asked his nationality and residence, might answer in reply: "I am a member of the human family, and my home is in the world."

Old Mitch and his ideas! No wonder he had trouble holding jobs. "A sucker," he had said, "with a passion for the facts." And a lot of good the *facts* had done for him—busted, on his uppers, and not getting any younger. But he had predicted something that had actually occurred; he had said there would be another war—

"Oh, not another war, Mitch," Emilie had protested.

"No, not another one." Mitch paused to fill his glass. "But the same one going on—on and on and on till the issue shall be clear, clear to all the peoples of the earth."

He had laughed at the idea: the world still bankrupt from the wastage of the last one, broke and disillusioned. No, it wasn't likely. It was then that Mitch had said what he said about the Rolls, that the windows were opaque; and he had turned to Hath who was hanging on his words—

"What do you think, Hath?—Will there be another war?"

"Yes, I think there will," Hath said, flushed with pleasure at the compliment of being treated like a man; and he had gone on talking, answering Mitch's questions about his German school.

It was in the course of this that Emilie caught his eye, motioning him to come into the other room, wanting to talk to him about the child. It was heartbreaking, she said, to see the little thing in that hideous, unbecoming dress, with her hair done like an Indian; and to think of her being dragged about, motherless, uncared for, waiting in the evening for her father to come home, cooking supper for him —a child who should be playing with her dolls—

"Yes, dear—" he agreed.

"But can't we do something for her?"

"Well, I don't know," he said. "What would you suggest?"

"I've been thinking, Unkam, from the moment that I saw her—" She hesitated, looking straight into his eyes, and her own were moist with tears. "—Can't we take her home with us?"

"Home?—with us?" It was a little startling.

"For a visit, dear, I mean." She went on eagerly. "We could send her to school, and see that she had things that children ought to have, and make a home for her. And Mitch could take his Berlin job; and then later on when he gets settled somewhere, we could send her back to him, whenever he was ready and able to take care of her."

"Yes, well—" He was thinking that it might be good for Hath if there was another child about his age, particularly living in the country; and it might help him, too, to keep up his languages. "I don't know," he said, "how Mitch would feel about it. He and Nat are pretty close, and Mitch is proud."

"If you'll let me do it, Unkam?" She took hold of his hand. "I can talk to him about it so he won't be offended, so it won't seem like charity but because I really want her."

"And do you, Emilie?"

"With all my heart," she said.

"All right," he smiled and kissed her. "You talk it over with him. I'll send him in to you."

That's where it had started—

And Mitch had come back with her, after half an hour, with a suspicious look around his eyes, blowing his nose, saying he was catching cold; and he hadn't wasted words or time about it—

"Nat!"

"Yes, Father?"

"How would you like to go back to America?"

"I'd like it very much if you would, Father."

"I mean, without me?"

"Without you, Father?" The little girl looked startled and incredulous, searching his face to see if he were joking.

"With us, dear," Emilie said. "Just for a visit. Until your father—"

"Till I get back on my feet again," Mitch interrupted roughly. "Let's let it go at that."

"Oh—" The child nodded very seriously, looking from one to the other of them; her lip was quivering but she steadied it. "Would you like me to go, Father?"

"Yes, I would—" he said, pouring a stiff drink into his glass, "—if it's all right with you, Nat?"

"Yes, Father, it's all right." He had watched her swallow hard, but there were not any tears—sitting like a soldier, hands folded in her lap, smiling bravely at her father—

Mitch had ridden with them to Southampton in the Rolls, a little drunk already, though it was in the morning, and morose and disagreeable—impossible in fact—

« 349 »

"I'm not indebted to you—not for this," he said. "If there's any debt between us, it's a debt you owe to me."

He had paced up and down the dock, walking with the child, holding her hand; and suddenly, when he was close to them, had whisked her up onto a wardrobe trunk, so that her face was level with his own; and he had said things to her that he wanted *them* to hear—roughly, almost brutally—

"Listen to me, Nat, and remember what I say—"

"Yes, Father." Sitting like a soldier on the trunk, with her feet high off the planking of the dock, and people hurrying by and porters carrying luggage, looking already less like a little waif, for Emilie had been shopping and the child was nicely dressed.

"Your mother was a Jewess," Mitch said harshly, "—a Russian Jewess, born in Odessa, and a Bolshevik to boot. Well, she believed in *something*, and, in a way, she died for it. But that's another matter."

"Yes, Father."

"And you're a Jewess too—if, according to the Nazi, one drop of Jewish blood is enough to make a Jew; anyway, *half* Jewess, Nat."

"I know that, Father."

"Don't interrupt me." Hath was listening with a queer look on his face; and perhaps it was Hath to whom he was really talking, not knowing what the boy already knew or had been told, and not taking any chances that he shouldn't know the facts, for he kept glancing at him from the corner of his eye, and once when the boy, embarrassed by his violence, had made a move to go, Mitch had motioned him to stay. "Half Jewess," he repeated. "It's nothing to be proud of, or to be ashamed of either."

"Yes, Father."

"If anybody asks you, you tell 'em what you are."

"I will, Father."

"Half Jewess, see?"

"Yes, Father."

"And the other half of you—" He laughed hysterically. "Well, by God, I wouldn't know." And suddenly he swept her off the trunk into his arms, hugging her against his breast, choking with sobs, tears running down his cheeks—

A painful and unnecessary scene, but of course he had been drunk—

He was standing on the stringpiece of the dock as the ship was easing out, not in the crowd of people who were calling last farewells to relatives and friends, but conspicuously alone; not waving back to them, nor to the child whose head barely reached above the rail, but his hands shoved in the pockets of his shabby overcoat, and his weather-beaten hat pulled down over his eyes. It was a drizzly day and in a little while they couldn't see him—

Yes, that's where it began—

He rubbed his hands: the room was rather chilly. And he picked up his pen and began to write again, commencing a new paragraph—

Wyattville is booming. It is really quite amazing. Mike said the other day that he thought the population had doubled in a year, which would mean about ten thousand. People come flocking in from everywhere, tempted by the wages at the airplane factory which is growing like a weed. Shanty Town is full of trailers with whole families living in them, and there are trailer camps on the outskirts of the town. Until it got too cold many people lived in tents. The government is starting some sort of housing project. They've condemned the country club, though of course they'll pay for it; and they're cutting up the golf course, running broad paved roads through it. I hear that the clubhouse will be used as a commissary. The old Rock Island line from Muscatine is humming with activity; and they've run a spur track from the north edge of the town, down the bluff along the levee to the factory. It seems as though something happens every day. You would hardly know the place, even since these last few months.

Yes, the room was chilly. He got up and walked around, feeling with his hand again to make sure that the heaters were turned on. Perhaps he should have ordered more of them. Something caught his eye, in a corner on the floor, glistening in the light—a pair of big glass jars. He recognized them: the jars he'd used for batteries when he learned telegraphy, that Clem Wyatt got for him; and Madge had found them somewhere. He prodded with his toe: behind them was the instrument that he had used for practice. He picked it up and put it on the table, thinking of the hours he had sat there in the evening, and on Sundays, struggling with it, making Nelly help him when she didn't want to do it, urging her to keep on just a little longer—

Another memory stirred—

He was sitting at a table in a New York speak-easy, in that spring of '33 when they had come home from Europe, with an architect whom he had been consulting, discussing plans for Glencoe. The man had an office on the Avenue, and, finishing their conference late in the afternoon, had suggested that they have a drink together. They had walked around the corner, somewhere in the fifties, into this basement room—a stuffy little place with closely crowded tables but not many people in it—

They were sitting at a table, talking matters over, when a fellow came in selling apples—one of the unemployed you ran into everywhere, with a tray with apples on it and a strap around his neck. He had hardly noticed him, except that he had on a derby hat which seemed strangely out of place with the apples and the strap. The fellow didn't ask anyone to buy an apple or approach the tables where the guests were sitting, but sort of hung around as if he hoped someone would notice him. And no one did—

He was talking to the architect, describing Beaton's woods, the nature of the ground where he meant to put the house, intent upon the subject, when he became aware of the clicking of a wire—not aware of it at first; it went on a little while. But he'd never lost the knack: the dot and dash of Morse was as clear to him as speech; and presently, in a corner of his brain reserved for them, the sounds began to register—

"plg—plg" it tapped insistently—the old code for the Plug. He thought he must be dreaming, misinterpreting some sound like the ticking of a clock. —"plg—plg—plg"— He turned his head. There was no clock in sight, and there was no one behind him except the apple seller, standing with his back against the wall—

But the tapping went right on—"plg—plg"—and then suddenly it changed—"clg wyvil"—calling Wyattville. There was no mistake about it. He jerked around again, staring at the man—a derelict, ragged, dirty, with the battered derby hat. And he saw that the fellow had a pencil in his hand and was tapping with it on the wooden tray—

"O'Gara!" he exclaimed. And so it proved to be. He had heard the name of Braden, heard them mention Wyattville—

"And so," he grinned, "I thought it might be you."

"Well, by God, O'Gara!" The boy he'd known so well and never seen—old and wizened and unshaved—a devil with the girls—and still a little cocky. He asked him to sit down and have a drink, not caring very much what the architect might think. Shortly afterward the man excused himself and they had gone on talking, with the tray of apples on the chair between them—

Just a bum: that was his history, and he made no bones about it. He'd spent his life, he said, getting jobs and losing them, but he'd never had one yet that he wasn't glad to part with. And he'd had a lot of fun, one way and another; but it hadn't been so easy since the country went to hell. Soup kitchens were his restaurants, and a flophouse his hotel—

"And I guess you're rich," he said, not enviously at all.

"Oh, I've done pretty well—"

"No monkey business, eh?"

He laughed. They sat there for an hour talking of the past: Rooney, Bullock, Mr. Butts with his curly black toupee, and the girls in Muscatine whom he had never met. He emptied out his pocket when they parted—perhaps a hundred dollars—

"Thanks—" O'Gara grinned, nodding toward the tray. "Do you want the apples, Sam?"

He smiled and shook his head.

"Okay." O'Gara sighed. "I've had 'em for a week. They buy one now and then, but nobody ever takes 'em."

Pretty tough.—But there were decent men who had worked hard all their lives, selling apples in that year of '33—that is to say, begging on the street. Something had gone wrong. The America to which he had returned was not the one he'd left, nor one that Old Henry would have recognized at all—

The room seemed warmer now and he sat down again, but he did not at once begin to write. His thought kept drifting back—

Nat had been sent home from that first summer camp—the one they had selected in the Adirondacks, though Emilie had been doubtful, saying that she thought it too elaborate and expensive; but he had wanted Nat to have the best—the same that he would give her if she had belonged to him. Hath, too, had gone to camp, a neighboring one for boys, but they wouldn't see each other. Hath hadn't liked it much, complaining in his letters that the boys were rough and noisy, and always breaking rules, and not kind to one another like the German boys at Spetzgart where the big ones always helped the little fellows. It had taken him a while to get back into things—

And Nat had been sent home within a week, all the way back to Chicago, preceded by a letter with a check enclosed—a letter which he did not understand.—"Natasha does not seem quite adapted to our group," so the letter read. "We feel she might be happier in some other camp." He had carried it to Emilie—

"What do you make of this?"

"I can't imagine, Unkam." She pondered for a moment. "You don't suppose it could be—"

"Nonsense!" he exclaimed.

"Did you mention it to them?"

He hadn't mentioned it. And he had questioned Nat when she arrived, on the Century in care of the conductor. The thing was most annoying; they were living at the Drake and he was very busy, running back and forth to Wyattville, closing up the options which Hub Baxter had arranged, getting ready to begin to build the house. There was no time for children or their problems, and he needed Emilie's help and her advice—

"Did you like the camp?" he asked.

"Oh yes," she said, sitting stiffly in her chair, hands folded in her lap—like a little adult.

"And did you like the girls?"

"They were very nice to me."

"And the teachers, Nat?"

"I liked them, too."

"Well then—" He hesitated. "—why did they send you home?"

"They didn't say. We were going out in some canoes, and then Miss Thomas called me and said I needn't go, but that I should pack my things."

"She didn't tell you why?"

"No, she didn't tell me why. She only said that I was going home."

"Can you think of any reason?"

"I don't know—" She thought about it, soberly but not resentfully. "Perhaps because I'm Jewish?"

"Did you tell them that you were?"

"Yes, I did."

"Did they ask you?"

"No. But the other girls were telling what they were, so I said what I was, too—half Russian Jewess."

"But you needn't have done that."

"Oh yes." She looked at him so steadily that he felt uncomfortable. "Father told me to."

"Well—" There was no use arguing with a child, not with that child anyway. Her calm, unflinching gaze was disconcerting; her eyes contained no hint of compromise, nor of resignation either, nothing as soft as that, nor of injury, nor of pride, It was hard to put a name to something that went back through two thousand years of history—

Of course such things did happen, were happening every day. But he hadn't been aware what the problem could be like—not that aspect of it. It was bad enough to have a door slammed in your face, your money tossed back across the counter; but suppose the child were *his*, how would he feel about it?—That would be worse than Shanty Town, than poverty—like Peewee Cole and the broken cocktail glasses—

And perhaps *that* was the start of it—the start of it for *him*.—He picked up his pen and put it down again—

They had found another camp, but this time they were careful; and careful in the fall when a school had been selected. And nothing else had happened, not the slightest thing; but they had been *careful*—

The children had got on well enough together, but they hadn't seen very much of one another until that second summer when the house was partly finished—enough so they could live there. And then they had been like a brother and a sister, swimming in the pool, riding horseback, playing tennis, fishing in the river, all the things that youngsters do; and they had their disagreements—

"What's wrong between you two?" Emilie would ask, noticing their silence across the dinner table.

"Nothing, Mother," Hath would answer with his eyes upon his plate.

"What is it, Nat?"

And she would say, whatever it might be, but not looking for redress or bearing tales—just a statement of the facts. "He wouldn't take me with him on a log raft on the river."

"No, I wouldn't." Hath glared at her. "And you know the reason why: you can't swim well enough."

"I can swim as well as you can." Which was true.

"Anyway it isn't safe and it's no place for a girl."

"I can do what you can do."

"No, you can't."

He had put an end to that, admonishing them both to stay off of the rafts.

Or it would be something else. Once, in defiance of his orders, she had tried to jump a horse across a fallen log, and the horse had balked and thrown her. She had come down pretty hard, not breaking any bones but scratched and stunned. And Hath had carried her half a mile back to the house, storming at her furiously, and crying, too, with exertion and alarm—

"You silly little fool, I told you not to do it." And shouting for his mother, "Mother! Quick!"

There had been a great to-do, and Grover had been sent for, but before he had arrived she had regained her senses, lying in a porch swing on the terrace, with her face still pretty chalky, but the glimmer of a smile of triumph on it—

"I did it, Hath."

"No, you didn't," Hath retorted, his cheeks still wet with tears. "You never jumped an inch. The horse just balked and threw you on your silly little head—like a sack of barley."

"Oh—" She sighed. "Well anyway I tried."

Yes, they had their disagreements, usually resulting from some masculine assertion of superiority which she was never willing to accept. But the next day they'd be friends, as good as ever. And before another summer came Mitch had cabled for her. He had a job in Paris. And they had sent her back, interrupting her school in the middle of the term although it had been paid for—not the child that they had taken, but well and strong and happy, and beginning to be pretty in a way that was her own; she didn't look like anybody else. They had put her on the boat with an outfit of new clothes and money in her purse, arranging with a stewardess to keep an eye on her, but she didn't need much looking after.

Hath came down from his prep school in New England to say good-by to her—a slender, gangling youth in the awkward age when his clothes never fitted and he hadn't learned to tie his necktie right, when his voice would break in the middle of a sentence: neither child nor man, but that agonizing period between. He had hardly said a word, standing with them in the stateroom, a little one she had all to herself—

"Will you miss us, Nat?" his mother asked.

"Yes, I will, Aunt Emilie."

"You must come back sometime."

"I hope I can."

"You must try to bring your father home to stay."

"I will, Aunt Emilie." And she had thanked them, not effusively at all but simply and sincerely. She was sad at parting from them, but there were not any tears; there never were with her—

It was time to say good-by and they went back to the deck. Emilie embraced the child, almost clinging to her; and he had hugged her for a moment in his arms, suddenly aware that he would miss her, that next summer would be different with her gone. "Good-by, my dear, good-by—" They were loosening the ropes that held the gang-plank. Hath held out his hand—

She looked him in the eye. "Aren't you going to kiss me, Hath?"

And Hath had kissed her, with his face as red as fire—"Good-by, Nat."

"Good-by, Hath."

"Come back sometime."

"I will."

Walking back along the pier his mother said, watching the boy from the corner of her eye, "You'll miss her, Hath."

"Oh, I don't know—" Hath shrugged.

And that was that. They had corresponded for a while, but even that had stopped. And Hath had finished prep school and started in at Harvard where he didn't want to go, protesting against being parted from his friends, most of whom, he said, would go to Amherst. But he had wanted Hath to go to Harvard, had never considered any other college. He felt that Harvard had a certain prestige—

"I don't know what," Hath wrote after a month or two. "It's cliquy and snooty, and unless your father went here they've got no use for you." But shortly after that his attitude had changed: he had found a long lost friend—"remember, Father, the boy I knew in Switzerland?" —He could see the letter now as he had seen it then, the emotions crowding back.—"He's a year ahead of me, just the way he was in Switzerland, and just as nice as ever. He's introduced me to a lot of fellows, and they aren't half bad, once you get to know them, not really snooty underneath. But the funny thing about it—and I can't figure out why you didn't know unless perhaps I didn't have the name right—his mother was your wife."

Remembering again that sick and helpless feeling, old resentments welling up out of the past, things that wouldn't die however deep you buried them, but would creep out of their graves and come knocking at your door; and you couldn't put an end to them—

The letter had gone on: "His mother lives in Paris and he goes there for vacation in the summer, but he's just as American as I am. His father was a flyer in the war and was killed in combat soon after Neill was born, but of course you know all that as well as I do. And about the family, too: they were very very rich, but his grandfather lost every penny in the panic and had to start all over from the bottom, he and his other son whose name is Wayne. And they paid every

« 357 »

nickel that they owed. It took them seven years, and his grandfather lived to see it done; and then he died, just a month or two ago."

And that was true: Elliott Wyatt died on the floor of the exchange at the age of eighty-one. Died as he had lived, so the papers said—no doubt with a carnation in his buttonhole, though they hadn't mentioned that—smiling and unfrightened, thanking a fellow broker who had brought a glass of water, asking the last quotation on some item on the board—

The letter had continued: "The firm of Elliott Wyatt is going strong again, and when Neill gets through college he intends to go into it with his Uncle Wayne and to get to be a partner. I know you'd like him, Father. He's about my size and build, but more athletic—a perfect whiz at tennis, though he never seems to care, just takes it in his stride. He'll hit a ball as if he wasn't looking. I was wondering if you'd mind if I asked him home for Christmas?"

Wondering if he'd mind.—He had struggled with the question for a week, not mentioning it to Emilie; and then he couldn't do it. It was too much to ask. He had written Hath evasively, with some pretext of postponement; but Hath had understood. "Of course," he wrote back curtly, "if that's the way you feel—" offended naturally, thinking that his father was intolerant and unkind—widening the gap between them. And Hath had never mentioned Neill again—

The months and years slid by, and then one day in the fall of '39, soon after war began, a servant came to find him in the garden—

"Long distance, sir," he said. "A Mr. Ballou calling from New York, charges collect."

Old Mitch!—He hurried to the house, eager and elated. "Well, Mitch! How are you?"

"Okay.—How's the country gentleman?"

"Fine.—Say, it's good to hear your voice. When did you arrive?"

"About an hour ago."

"Where's Nat?"

"Right here."

"That's great. What are you up to in New York?"

"Damned if I know."

"Oh!—Well what—"

And Mitch had told his story: he hadn't lost his job; this time he'd quit. The Nazi war machine would go through France, he said, like a dose of salts, like maggots through a hunk of rotten cheese; and he wouldn't take a chance on being there with Nat.

« 358 »

"Have you anything in sight?"

"No, not a thing." Anyway, he said, he was sick and tired of it—of telling the truth to people who didn't want to hear it, of reporting facts which were distorted or suppressed. He'd spent his whole life at it and he was bloody sick of it—

"What have you in mind?"

"I don't know, Sam. I'd like to write a book, but we've got to eat."

"Well, hell—"

"Now wait! I'm not panhandling. I'm not a beggar—yet."

"All right." He laughed. "I'm listening."

"Well, it just occurred to me, if I could settle down in some small place and make enough to live on—"

"Yeh?"

"I own a house in Wyattville, you know—"

"Yeh sure, Mitch, I know."—His father's house, a paintless, run-down cottage on the north side of the Square, rented since old Mitchell J. had died.

"Well, it occurred to me we could live there pretty cheap, for next to nothing; and if I could get a job on the Wyattville *Gazette*—enough for bread and butter—"

"Yes, Mitch, I see." He thought for a moment, smiling to himself: the *Gazette* belonged to the Bank of Wyattville, and the bank belonged to him, though Mike was nominal owner. They had sold the paper to a man who hadn't made a go of it, and were on the point of getting it back for the notes he couldn't meet. Mike had talked to him about it just the other day, asking what to do; and he had said to let it string along, that he'd sooner have the notes, as worthless as they were, than to have the *Gazette* back on their hands. "I'm thinking, Mitch," he said. And he was thinking, too, that it would be very nice to have Old Mitch around, living there in Wyattville, coming out to Glencoe, chatting on the terrace or around the library fire—someone with a stimulating mind, no matter if his ideas were a little cockeyed—a friend whose friendship had endured since they were children. Yes, that would be very nice.—"How would you like to own the paper, Mitch?"

"Own it?" Mitch laughed grimly. "I haven't got a dime."

"Well, I'll tell you what I'll do, Mitch: I'll take your note for it." He had been about to say, "I'll give it to you." But Mitch might be offended, and perhaps it would be as well to see how things turned out. In a year or two—maybe some Christmas day—he'd give him back his notes. He'd have them in an envelope hanging on the tree, with a little card of greeting: "Merry Christmas, Mitch—from Sam." He had had a picture of it in his mind—

The sun was breaking through the fog, the thick trunks of the sycamores looming gaunt and sleek against the muddy river. The room seemed comfortable; no doubt it was warmer out of doors. He took up his pen and began another paragraph—

It is quite a job now to keep Glencoe going. We have such difficulty keeping help. Of course we can't compete with the industrial wages: a dollar an hour and even more than that, and a forty hour week seems to be the rule—quite a contrast with the world in which my life began, when fifteen cents an hour was the price for common labor, and a sixty hour week was the normal working time. But I doubt the working people are much better off, for the cost of things has risen to about the same extent. Wages and prices are like growing children, one a little taller and then the other one, but always keeping pretty close together. Politicians never seem to understand this. At all events the problem is becoming serious, and added to it is the question of supplies: wire for the fences, already hard to get; and many tools and implements which are scarcer every day. It distresses me to see Glencoe running down, in need of things which I cannot supply; but I fear the situation will grow worse instead of better. I have only a couple in the house, not very satisfactory; and it would not surprise me if they left at any moment. Ben, my driver, has been drafted, and so I drive myself when I go to town which is not very often.

He had come to the bottom of the page and he took another sheet out of the rack—

So many of the young men are being drafted now. One of Mike's boys went away to camp last week, and Grover's son has enlisted in the Navy. But I cannot feel that we need to be involved in the misery and disaster of this war, though perhaps the preparations which are being undertaken could not safely be ignored. Yet, I am not sure about that, remembering a phrase credited to Talleyrand: that one could do anything with bayonets except to sit on them. And so it seems to me that, once we are prepared, we may have to go to war to justify the effort. And that would be a very dreadful thing. The staggering cost of intervention in this European conflict, so remote from our shores and from our natural interests, would mean the end, I fear, of my America, of what I have understood to be the American way of life. And, too, having lived through

the war which was to end wars, which was to make the world safe
for democracy, I may be excused for having doubts—doubts that we
Americans are specially qualified to reorganize the world, to furnish
a solution of its problems in political science or economic principle.
I think—

He paused and read what he had written, slowly and carefully, and
then he tore it up and took another sheet. He did not know what he
thought. His world had run away from him; the ground beneath his
feet had turned to quicksand—

Quicksand.—He leaned back in his chair looking through the window, through the naked sycamores, seeing in his memory the broad
brick terrace on a summer evening—in June it was, not yet six
months ago—the warm glow of the house lights spilling out across it,
the porch swings with their gay striped canopies, big cushioned chairs,
a table with ice cubes and half-empty decanter, though he had hardly
touched it—the terrace awning rolled back, and the stars and fireflies.
And the moon creeping up out of the fields of Illinois; and a sand bar
in the river, sprawling flatly from the bottom of the bluff, shining
whitely in the moonlight. And then at last the voices for which they
had been waiting, coming up the winding path through the ravine—

"Hath?" Emilie calling from the terrace edge.

"Yes, Mother?"

"Where have you two been?"

"Walking on a sand bar—" And he laughed.

And Mitch getting up abruptly from the porch swing where he had
been sitting glum and silent, stumbling as he strode across the terrace,
for he had been drinking, and he had been angry too, calling irritably,
"Nat!"

"Yes, Father?"

"I've been waiting. Hurry up!"

But they had not hurried much, strolling up the path, conversing
gaily, glimpsed through the foliage of the trees, silhouetted in the
moonlight. He could see them from his chair—the tall, slender figure
of his son, and the girl who walked beside him, whose head reached
to his shoulder, picturing her straight black hair, features too angular
for beauty and not exactly pretty, but arresting and intriguing, foreign
looking—rather Jewish. And their voices: Hath's was laughing, and
the other soft and deep, like a musical accompaniment—not an
ordinary voice nor one that you'd forget. Figures coming up the path,

in and out among the trees, seen and then not seen, heard and then not heard—his son and a girl—*half* Russian Jewess—

It was then the idea struck him, at that very moment: suppose that Hath should fall in love with her. Funny he hadn't thought of it before—perhaps because it seemed so utterly impossible, and thinking of them still as being children, not really thinking anything, but thinking *now*—watching them come along the terrace side by side, as if their arms were locked or hands were clasped, or *had been*. Thinking of himself and Cassie Cole—of broken cocktail glasses—of a letter from a summer camp, with check enclosed—

"I'm sorry, Father," Nat was saying. "We were walking on the sand bar—"

"She insisted," Hath explained.

"I took off my shoes and stockings." Her thin white skirt was wet and clinging to her legs. "It was exciting in the dark."

"I told her we'd get lost."

"And so we did," she said. "When we started to come back we couldn't find our way, and no matter where we turned we came to quicksand. We'd be in up to our knees before we knew it."

"To our necks if we'd gone on." Hath laughed, glancing ruefully at his slacks which were rolled above his knees and thick with sand. "We had to wait until the moon came up." They had come into the light spilling through an open door—

"Quicksand—" Emilie said to break a silence, "—that could be dangerous, Nat."

"Yes, dangerous," Mitch said harshly. "And we're all wading in it." He stamped across the terrace toward the hall. "Come on, Nat, let's go home."

And Nat had followed him, calling back good night, Hath walking at her side, both of them aware by now that something had gone wrong, but not thinking much about it, for Mitch was easily angered when he'd had a drink or two, and then he would be rude or glum and surly. And Emilie had gone with them, chatting pleasantly, pouring oil on troubled waters. But Mitch had not called back or turned his head. No doubt if he had acted as he had so many times, getting up and going with them to the door, laughing matters off, saying, "Come to dinner Sunday" or something of the sort—

But he hadn't stirred out of his chair, not thinking of the row that they had had, which was like so many others, on the surface anyway; but thinking of his son and Nat Ballou—of the lifetime he had spent to be free of handicap, to free his son from any chance of it.—Hearing the voices going through the hall, but not catching what they said. —Thinking of Glencoe, of his son who would inherit all that he had won with long and patient effort, and would use it and conserve it and one day pass it on to a son that he would have.—Hearing the motor of the rattletrap old Ford Mitch couldn't drive, never having owned a car until six months ago—and good thing he couldn't drive it, drinking as he did.—Thinking it was easy to take a chance on things if you had nothing to lose—politics, ideas, almost anything in fact; from the bottom of the ladder you could safely risk a fall, but the higher that you climbed the more cautious you must be.—Hearing voices call good night, but not hearing Mitch's voice—and then the car receding down the drive.—Thinking of a world whose future was obscure, in which dreadful things were happening—*might* happen anywhere; thinking of a grandson with black hair and Jewish features—

Glass tinkled on the bricks: the tumbler in his hand had broken like an egg, and a fragment of the glass had cut his finger. He wrapped his handkerchief around it—

"Why, Unkam, what's the matter?"

"I broke a glass."

"You've cut yourself."

"It's nothing."

She looked and let it go, sitting down near by in the swing where Mitch had sat. And Hath came out again, saying he was wet and thought he'd go to bed, kissing his mother and bidding them good night, pausing at the door—

"You and Mitch been having trouble, Father?"

"The usual thing," he said. But suddenly he knew it was much more than that.

"Oh well—" Hath laughed, going on into the house.

"Poor Mitch—" And Emilie sighed.

He didn't answer.—Thinking of his son and Nat Ballou: what he could remember since Mitch and Nat had come to Wyattville in the fall of '39, almost two years ago. They hadn't seen very much of one another; that first Christmas they had met at Glencoe, but not as if they had been friends before, like strangers really, very formal with each other. And the following summer Hath had been away most of the time, visiting schoolmates in the East; and then there was last Christmas when they had seemed more friendly—he suddenly remembered a look they had exchanged, which he hadn't analyzed, and couldn't now—the Christmas he had thought to give Mitch back his notes, to have them in an envelope hanging on the tree, but he had put it off—

"I feel so sorry for him."

"Do you?"—Thinking: Nat didn't have much time to devote to social matters; she was busy all day long, working in the office, or collecting local news, subscriptions, advertising—though lately there had not been much of that. And in the evening they had a kind of group, as Hath described it—young people in the town who came to Mitch's house, and he would talk to them and answer questions. He had cautioned Hath about it, that Mitch Ballou's ideas should not be taken seriously. But perhaps it wasn't politics—

"I'm afraid, dear, you can't change him."

"No, probably."—Thinking, with a start: why had Hath come home so quickly? That hadn't been the plan. Emilie had gone to Cambridge, to the graduation. She had wanted him to go, but he hadn't felt that he could get away: June was a busy month; and there was the mess Mitch had gotten into, and the question of what to do about it. So she had gone alone, planning that she and Hath would drive home in his car, taking their time about it, going up to Montreal and back through Canada. And he had encouraged it, thinking she looked tired and run down, and that it would do her good—

"One has to take one's friends the way they are."

He nodded.—But they hadn't gone to Canada or anywhere at all. They had left the car in Cambridge and come home on the train. Emilie had not explained their change of plan beyond that she had caught a little cold—and indeed she had it still, though they had been home a week—and that Hath had been anxious to come back—

"Does it really matter, Unkam, what he prints in the *Gazette?*"

"Yes," he answered sharply. "Yes, of course."—Hath hadn't been so anxious other years; and the trip they hadn't taken was one he had suggested and urged upon his mother; and it wasn't one that she would be likely to give up because she had a cold—

"But why, dear?"

"Why?" He forced himself to think about it. "He'll go broke if he goes on antagonizing people."

"But if he'd rather say what he believes than to make money—"

"That's not the point."

"You mean—the money that you've loaned him?"

"No, certainly." He shrugged impatiently.

"Then what?"

"I can't afford to be involved."

"Involved?—But how?"

"It's very simple, Emilie—" And suddenly it was. "—everybody knows it's my money that he's using; and so, in a way, I am sponsoring what he says."

"But that's not true."

"They think it is."

"Does it matter what they think?"

"Yes, it matters," he said grimly. "This is my home; I live here."

"Is it worth a friendship, Unkam?"

But he evaded that. "I'm only asking him—" He hesitated for the word, and she completed it—

"For everything he has."

"A lot of cockeyed notions."

"Perhaps, but they are *his*."

"Nonsense."

"Is it worth that much to you?"

He didn't answer that, fingering the handkerchief tied around his hand; and she came and sat on the low arm of his chair, with her cheek against his head—

"You've known Mitch all your life, and you're fond of one another, no matter what you think about politics and things. It would be such a pity if anything went wrong—such a pity for you both." He didn't answer, hearing the radio in Hath's room playing softly—dance music from Chicago. "You make things so dreadfully hard, dear—so hard for yourself." She sighed, and then she shivered, saying it was getting chilly. And he had reminded her to do something for her cold—to take an aspirin—

"Yes, dear—" She smiled and kissed him. "Are you coming soon?"

"In a little while—"

"It's such a lovely night—" She went on toward the door.

"Emilie—"

"Yes, dear?"

"You don't suppose that Hath—" He stopped.

"Suppose that Hath?—What, dear?"

"Nothing," he said. "Good night."

He had sat there till the moon was risen high, with his eyes upon the sand bar spread flatly in the river, reaching out into the current

« 365 »

like the fingers of a hand—feeling quicksand in the bricks beneath his feet, but debating and deciding—

The picture vanished, dissolving back into the winter landscape: the gaunt, bare trees; the muddy, swollen river—no hint of any sand bar showing on its surface. He turned back to the table and picked up his pen again, smoothing the sheet of paper, fingering an edge of it, like a person unsure what to say, or how to say it. And then at last he wrote—

It has been called to my attention that the checks which have been sent you regularly every month, have not been cashed. I have hesitated to inquire why, but uneasiness impels me now to ask you. You have mentioned that you were at work, but your earnings must be small—I know, when I began, how difficult it was to make ends meet; and it grieves me that you should deprive yourself of my assistance, or feel compelled to adopt an occupation unsuited to your background and advantages, to the position in the world for which your endowments and training qualify you, and to which I have looked forward and endeavored to prepare you through so many years. If the money I have made is not to benefit my son, it would seem to have no purpose. I do not condemn your pride, if that is what it is, but I wonder if you have foreseen the anxiety and grief which has come to me by reason of it, and which I cannot feel was your intention. And so I would suggest that you look closely at your motives—the motives which prompt you to reject your father's help, for motives are not always what they seem.

He read the paragraph: it sounded stiff and formal—not the way he meant it should; but it would do, he thought. And he read again, aloud, the closing words: "—look closely at your motives—for motives are not always what they seem."—Yes, motives were important, the things that really mattered—not *what* you did, but *why*. And perhaps there had been times when he hadn't looked very closely at his own, or had looked the other way—

It was a thread he didn't want to follow. His thought went back to Mitch—

Wyattville had welcomed Mitch with open arms, and had been flattered, too: a foreign correspondent who had spent most of his life in the capitals of Europe, who had been around and seen things, hobnobbing with the great and aware of secret matters which ordinary people didn't know; and the son of Mitchell J. who, drunkard though he was, still lingered in the memory of the older generation as a citizen of parts and a "literary figure." Yes, the town was pleased and flattered that Mitch should have come home, ignoring the temptations of Chicago and New York, coming back to Wyattville, to the house on Second Street in which he had been born, to the *Gazette* which his father had founded and conducted with a competent, if alcoholic, pen for nearly half a century.

The Rotary Club held a luncheon in his honor, and Mitch had made a speech which was humorously received. He'd been a news reporter all his life, he said, but he'd never had a chance to tell the truth—(laughter and applause).—Mike, reporting the affair in the library at Glencoe, thought he might have had a drink or two. But Mike was not fond of Mitch who commonly ignored him, and had once referred to him as "Braden's Friday"; and it was likely, too, that he was a little jealous—

Mitch had gone on: he had come to Wyattville at the invitation of his friend, Sam Braden, who had made it possible for him to acquire the *Gazette*—(applause)—

"Did he say that?"

"That's what he said."

He and his daughter would constitute the staff and business office, anyway to start—

"Was she there?"

"Sitting right beside him."

"Did she say anything?"

"He asked her to stand up and take a bow, so they'd know her when she came around to get their advertisements. They laughed at that." Mike frowned. "She looks a little Jewish."

"Yeh?" He didn't comment. Mike didn't like the Jews, and there were other people in the town who were prejudiced about them. "What else?" he asked.

The *Gazette* would print the local news as nearly as the facts could be determined. If they stank, you were free to hold your nose (laughter). He could not hope, in a small-town weekly paper, to chronicle the news of world events, but he could comment on the facts, interpret them correctly and disclose their inner meaning, and he would reserve a column for that purpose—a column in which he proposed to tell the truth, whatever it might be, and no matter how unpleasant, nor whom the telling hurt (applause).

"I don't know—" Mike shook his head, "—what that'll get him."

There hadn't been much more. Mitch had told some funny stories, concluding with his favorite description of himself: "—a sucker with a passion for the facts." And they had laughed at that. But it had turned out to be no laughing matter—

Still, the *Gazette* had started with a bang, had actually made money for a while. Everybody read it, and people had fun with other peoples' hurts until they, themselves got pinched, which in time most of them did—that is, the ones that mattered, the people who had anything to lose. But Mitch went right ahead chopping things to pieces, not caring where the chips fell; and not only local matters: he was for Roosevelt, for the New Deal, complaining only that it had no teeth; for the WPA, for higher income taxes in the upper brackets; for the workingman and labor unions; for intervention in the war; for the Russian Bolsheviks—and that was hard to take in the fall of '39 when the ink was hardly dry on the Berlin-Moscow nonaggression pact—

Dr. Bunting, the pastor of the Congregational Church, preached a sermon on the subject, denouncing the *Gazette* as un-American; to which Mitch had replied with scathing brevity: "Whether or not the *Gazette* is un-American may remain an open question, but the fact is now established that the Reverend Dr. Bunting is no Christian." This had pleased the Catholics; even Mike had smiled. But Madge was shocked—

"You don't suppose," she said, "that Mitch could be a Communist?"

"No, of course not."

"Well, a lot of people say he is."

"Nonsense." He laughed. "Old Mitch—"

But in sober truth he didn't know what Mitch was—hadn't then and didn't now, except that he was full of cockeyed notions which could do no good for him or anybody else. He had tried to argue with him many times, pointing out the folly of antagonizing people whose friendship and support were essential to success, whose help you had to have to pay your bills—decent, law-abiding citizens, raising families, paying taxes, playing golf on Sunday, minding their own business, working hard to make a living and to get ahead a little, not wanting to be changed or interfered with, not caring what the Russians did or thought, not interested in foreigners or things in foreign places—good Americans, in fact, following the traditions of their country—

And Mitch had gotten angry, as he nearly always did, and had spoken of his country with contempt, calling it a nation of sentimental morons, who would stab you in the back and send flowers to your funeral—whose national anthem should be "Mammy"—

Of course he hadn't meant that: when he lost his temper he was likely to say anything that came into his head. Perhaps he'd been away too long to understand America; and never having had anything that was his own—dollars in the bank or a little patch of ground—perhaps that was the reason he couldn't understand—

Still, people kept on laughing for a while, being friendly and good-natured—after all, Mitch was a home-town boy, no matter if he was a little crazy; and they would smile and nod to the now familiar figures: the girl with straight black hair and uncompromising manner, hurrying in and out of Main Street shops for advertising copy, waiting patiently if need be, hands folded in her lap, earnest and efficient; and Mitch Ballou striding down the street in search of news, unkempt, with tousled hair which was white around his temples, and late in the day not too sure of his step, but his one eye keen and watchful and defiance burning in it. "How are you, Mitch?" they'd wave, or maybe stop to chat—

But Wyattville was changing after all its sleepy years. The old families had died off or sunk out of sight in the flood of the depression—there were scarcely any Wyatts left and none of consequence. Another group had taken over things: the Birney boys who had the Ford garage, sons of Dave Birney who had run the livery stable, but had never been admitted to the houses on the Square; and some of the Hogan clan had been doing very well, contracting and the like; and there were numerous others with unfamiliar names who had come in off the farms and whose children were in business—tradesmen, chain-store managers, and some professional men. And the town was growing, too, since the airplane factory started, and the tempo of it quickening with industrial undertaking—

And so, beneath the surface, there was real trouble brewing, for Mitch had found a tender spot at last, and sympathetic ears among the factory workers; and he was harping steadily on that string—complaining of the housing, demanding higher wages, anything he could discover in the nature of a grievance—stirring up dissension which was bitterly resented by the factory management and the townspeople as well, who saw expanding profits being threatened. Every ninety days Mike would raise the question—

"What about that note of Mitch Ballou's—it's coming due tomorrow."

"Renew it."

"Well—" Across the telephone he could feel Mike wince, sitting in his office in the Bank of Wyattville. "—if you say so, Sam. But—"

"But what?"

And Mike would recount the latest offense of the *Gazette,* which might be nothing more than opposition to a filling station which Ned Birney was trying to install in a corner of the Square, or something more important relating to the workers in the factory—

And he would laugh and say, "Well, that's up to Mitch, I guess."

"But the boys don't like it, Sam.—By "boys" he meant the fellows who belonged to Rotary, the Chamber of Commerce, and the Legion, of all of which he was a member.—"They're sore as a goat."

"Let them fight it out with Mitch."

"They're crabbing because we let him have the money—"

"He's paying interest, isn't he?"

"Yeh, sure, but it makes it tough for me. Some of them are threatening to take their business elsewhere—"

"Yeh?" He laughed at that. There was no other bank in Wyattville; and even if there had been, he would not have cared. It was penny-pushing stuff in which he had no interest. "I guess they'll have to wait till Mitch goes broke."

"That's what I keep telling 'em, but they're getting tired waiting." —The *Gazette,* though no longer making money as it had for a few months, was still managing to stay out of the red, making up for shrinking advertising columns by expanding circulation which was growing with the town—every airplane worker was a reader. —"Say, Sam, can't you have a talk with him and get him to lay off?"

"You know old Mitch—" He'd laugh.

"Yeh, I know him," Mike would groan. "And you want I should renew his note?"

"Certainly, of course."

"Okay, Sam."

And that would end the matter for another ninety days. But he had talked to Mitch, had done his level best, getting pretty close to quarreling once or twice—not because he cared about the "boys" in Wyattville, who were old enough to take care of themselves, nor the penny-pushing bank and its chicken-feed affairs; but because Mitch was his friend, and he wanted to help him and see him get along and make something of his life. And it was nice for him, having Mitch in Wyattville, coming out to Glencoe in the evening and on Sunday—

And so things had gone on through a winter and a summer and

another winter—but in the winter months he and Emilie were away, living at the Drake, from the New Year until April—had gone on until last May. And then something really happened, which you couldn't laugh about, which had been a front-page story in the Chicago papers—

Negroes had been coming up the river in the spring, coming up from Memphis, attracted by the wages they had heard about, flocking into Wyattville, working as stevedores, shovel men and laborers for the airplane factory which was starting to spread out and was hiring everybody it could get. There wasn't any place for them to live except along the levee where they had a kind of camp, building shacks with scraps of driftwood, tents made out of rags, even dugouts in the bluff. Of course it had been bad: no water but the river, no proper sanitation —a lot of them were sick. And Mitch had sailed into the mess, confirming his description with a page of photographs which Nat had taken, proclaiming the conditions outrageous and disgraceful, and denouncing the authorities for permitting their existence.

And Mitch had good grounds to kick, though it wasn't anybody's fault and there wasn't much anyone could do about it, except to clear them out and ship them back to Memphis. But the factory needed labor and the town was after business: the groceries that they bought —pay roll money circulating; and so things slid along, though Mitch kept right on howling with the biggest type he had.

The negroes made the next move and the one that caused the trouble; they hadn't been complaining, but, reading the *Gazette*, they began to feel abused. And suddenly one day five families of them, nearly twenty counting children, turned up in a house in Shanty Town —a house that they had rented, nobody knew how, but it was said Mitch had a hand in it—in Shanty Town where, save for the Coles, who had lived there longer than anyone remembered and were not thought of as "black," no negro had presumed to make a home.

They were ordered out at once by the owner of the property; and perhaps they would have gone. But in the midst of this the *Gazette* came out again, championing their cause, defending their right to live anywhere they pleased, if they could pay the rent—"on Second Street," Mitch wrote, which was the street he lived on, across from the homes of Ned Birney and his brother, "if they can stand the neighbors."

And then there had been trouble, as might have been expected. At night a gang of men had gone to Shanty Town and cleaned the negroes out and burned the house down, too; and in the excitement, had

« 371 »

burned down several others, including the Cole house where Cora Lee still lived—an accident of course, for Cora Lee was beloved of everybody, white and black. But however that might be, the house was burned to ashes, and the kind old woman who was well into her eighties, passed away a few days later in a white neighbor's home—from shock and exposure, people said. Almost everyone in town went to her funeral.

He had driven by the place the day after the fire. There was nothing left except the picket fence, and some odds and ends of things that had been saved; among them, propped against the pickets, was the picture of King Cole in the funny looking hat with feathers in it, and the broad red sash and shiny sword. The old Braden house had not been harmed: that's why he had come, to make certain about that. The lilacs were in bloom, not withered by the fire—

"Race riot," the Chicago papers called it. But it was scarcely that: nobody had been killed or seriously injured. The sheriff had arrived with a swarm of deputies, and the negroes on the levee had been shipped back to Memphis, and their wretched camp destroyed. As for the self-appointed vigilantes, nothing had been done; the sheriff had gone home, and the state's attorney said the members of the mob could not be identified and the incident was closed.

And so it would have been, for there were other matters to occupy attention: the German armies were marching into Russia which everyone in Wyattville expected to collapse like a rotten watermelon. Yes, that would have been the end of it if Mitch Ballou had been content to let it rest. But Mitch kept right on howling, demanding apprehension of the vigilantes, threatening toward the last: if the state's attorney persisted in refusing to investigate the case, he would publish the names of "these lawless desperadoes who are known to everybody but the public prosecutor."

Mike had come to Glencoe in a panic. It was possible some Hogans were mixed up in the affair, but he didn't mention that. The boys were wild, he said; if Mitch didn't keep his mouth shut they would tar and feather him and run him out of town.

"I guess that's up to them—" He smiled, but it was past the point of being funny.

"We got to stop him, Sam."

"What would you suggest?"

"His note is due next week; we can close him up."

"I don't want to do that, Mike."

"Ned Birney'll buy the paper and give us cash for it. He told me so today."

He shook his head.

"Well, Jesus, Sam—" Mike groaned, "—why should we sit by and let him wreck the town?"

"I'll have a talk with him."

"You've talked to him before."

"Yeh, this is different—"

"But if he won't behave?"

"I don't know, Mike. We'll see—"

But he had put it off from day to day. Emilie and Hath had suddenly returned from the trip they hadn't taken, and it was good to have them home again; he dreaded a discussion of the matter: an unpleasant undertaking of whose outcome he was doubtful, which was no affair of his. If Mitch was determined to go on exposing things which everybody knew, and, if they were smart, pretended not to see, it was not his job to stop him; or if the "boys" in Wyattville could run Mitch out of town, it was up to them to do it without any help from him. He saw no reason why he should be mixed up in it, or have a row with Mitch—

Then Mike had telephoned: "Say, Sam, have you had that talk with Mitch?"

"Not yet."

"Well, holy God," Mike sputtered, "tomorrow is the day his note is coming due. You don't want I should renew it until we get things settled?"

"No, of course," he said impatiently. "I'll talk to him tonight. Call me in the morning."

And Mitch had come to dinner—Mitch and Nat: one of so many dinners, and the last—

Again he saw the terrace on that summer evening, not yet six months ago, but remembered like something at the far end of a lifetime: stars and fireflies, and the moon creeping up from the fields of Illinois, silvering the riffles of the sand bar in the river—and Mitch in the porch swing where you couldn't see his face, sitting glum and silent with a highball in his hand. But that was at the end when he had had his say, when he had finished tramping up and down, had finished shouting. There had been a long, long silence—and Emilie had come out; she had left them after dinner, after coffee on the terrace, knowing they had things to talk about. And she wasn't feeling

« 373 »

well; her cold was bothering her, possibly she had a little fever even then; but she had been gay and cheerful at the dinner table—

It was twilight when she left them. Hath and Nat had disappeared; he hadn't noticed where. He had opened the subject as discreetly as he could, trying to be casual—

"What about that book, Mitch?"

"What book?" He was pouring a drink from the decanter.

"The book you meant to write when you came to Wyattville?"

"Oh that!" Suspiciously, "What of it?"

"Why don't you take the time and write it?"

"I'm gathering the material," Mitch said dryly.

"I should think you'd have enough to fill a book by now."

"Yeh?" Suspicion mounting, "What're you driving at?"

"Why nothing, Mitch, except—"

That's how it began; and then it had gone on until the sky was dark and the stars had all come out—perhaps not much they hadn't said before, but now there was an issue you could put your finger on, and he had been more determined and Mitch had been more violent. It was completely futile: there was no common ground, no point where they could see eye to eye with one another. And Mitch had lost his temper almost at the start, and then it was no use, because he wouldn't listen to anything you said. He had stopped trying then, but Mitch had gone right on, stamping up and down the terrace, a little drunk by now, gesticulating, shouting—

He'd print their names—as many as he knew, and he knew a lot of them, and no matter who they were or who got hurt. There were no strings on him and none on the *Gazette*. He'd say what he damn pleased as long as he could punch the keyboard of a typewriter and had a press to run it. He was not for sale, and he was not afraid of that gang in Wyattville—not afraid of anybody who couldn't face the truth, who didn't have the guts to call a spade a spade—

"I'm not solving problems," he shouted near the end. "I don't know the answers for the niggers or the Jews, or you or me. But I know damn well we'll never find 'em with our heads stuck in the ground like a lot of bloody ostriches. I want to know the facts, and that's my job—to dig them out and print them. And, by God, I'll keep on doing it while I've got the strength."

It was then he'd flung himself down in the porch swing, hoarse from shouting and exhausted. And there had been a silence. There was nothing to be said in answer to his ranting; no practical reply that could be made. And then Emilie had come out, saying something pleasant, remarking on the beauty of the night, sitting in a deck chair in the darkness. But Mitch had only grunted, and the silence had gone on until he said abruptly in a vicious, sneering way—

"The boys from Wyattville: you and me, and Mike and Hub and Grover—cross section of America, beginning to get old and damn near finished with it.—A small-town doctor—came home and settled down, as you might have known he would when he was a kid, sleepy and good-natured; I don't know if he wanted anything or ever thought about it; decent guy—the medical journal and the *Readers' Digest*— plays a little bridge, a little golf.—Hub Baxter, corporation lawyer, onto all the tricks, slippery as an eel—how to get around things, wriggling like a snake—how to keep rich clients out of jail; not are you right?—but have you got it? Smart guy, they say.—And Mike, the perfect yes man—crawling up his master's pole, keeping close to his behind; you can put him in a nutshell: I'd sooner have them with me than against me—And me—what would you say I was?"

He didn't answer. He knew the line—provocative, to stir things up again.

"Mitch Ballou, the dirty Red." He laughed. "I'm not a Communist. I wish to God I was, but I'm not even sure about that. Anyway, that's what they call me: 'Mitch Ballou, the dirty Red.' They don't know what it means, but that don't matter—anything at all they think might hit their pockets. 'A drunkard, too—' they're beginning to say that '—following in the footsteps of his father.'—And you?—How would you describe yourself?"

No answer.

"Well, I'll tell you, Sam: the hero of the boys in Wyattville, in every Wyattville across the land, of every little fellow, of every good American—the guy that went and got it, got it for *himself*—no matter *how*; we won't go into that. But the guy that brought the bacon, got what he went after; and if it wasn't money, what the hell else would it be?—Five million smackers, wasn't it?"

No answer.

"And boy, that's dough—stuff worth going after. They'd sell their souls to stand in your shoes, Sam; they sell 'em every day for dimes and nickels. A big shot—not the biggest, not big enough to make 'em feel they haven't got a chance—and not like Elliott Wyatt, when he was in his prime; that's something else entirely—it's got a sporting element they don't even understand, any more than you do, although you've tried like hell—been trying all your life. But you—that's something they can get their teeth in, can dream about without it's being funny: five million bucks and a hunk of Iowa—two thousand acres, isn't it?"

No answer.

"You've done everything the copybooks advise, everything the kids are taught to think. You should be immortalized, for the story of your life is, in a way, the story of America—a statement of its *values*.—And now, from where you're sitting, what do you think about it?—What do you really think about yourself?"

No answer.

"I'll tell you, Sam,—I'll tell you how you look to me: the loneliest man I've ever known; and I've been lonely, too, but not like you."

He moved uncomfortably; he was getting tired of it.

"A lonely man, going nowhere, in the dark—"

And again there had been silence—just the tinkle of the ice in Mitch's glass. The moon was coming up now, shining on the sand bar, making lines of black and silver in the riffles. He was thinking what to do?—what to say to Mike when he called up in the morning?—half deciding that he'd wash his hands of it: give Mitch back his note or tear it up, as he had meant to do last Christmas day. Let Mike and his friends wriggle out the best they could; that was no concern of his. But he had not decided. He was hurt and angry at the things that Mitch had said—drunken words of course, but that did not excuse them—

And then there were the voices coming up the path—his son and Nat Ballou. And Mitch had gone, not calling out good night or looking back—

The moon was overhead when he came to a decision.

In the morning Mike had phoned and he had told him curtly, not wasting any words: "Go ahead and close him up."

"Jesus, Sam, that's swell! The boys'll certainly be grateful."

"Yeh," he said and hung up the receiver.

And the day had dragged away—a hot and sultry day with a brewing thunderstorm. He had gone about the things he had to do, but uncomfortably expectant—still, he didn't think Mitch would make a scene; he'd be too proud for that, to plead or to protest. And yet he had the feeling of some dire thing impending; he couldn't shake it off all through the day—

It was at dinnertime and they were at the table, himself and Hath and Emilie. He could even remember what they had to eat: jellied consommé, cold meat and salad, tall glasses of iced tea—not the dessert, for they had not come to that. He had been questioning Hath, trying to find out what the boy intended doing—he was twenty-one years old and through with college, the age that he had been when he traveled Illinois for Acme Paper. But Hath had been evasive, as he often was—

He didn't know, he said. It was likely he'd be drafted, though his number was not close; still, it would come up in time. He had no interest in military matters, but of course he'd have to go—

"Yeh—" He nodded, thinking that the "boys" in Wyattville, some of whom were on the draft board, might show their gratitude by arranging Hath's exemption; but he didn't mention that. Instead he said, "Maybe you could help me here at Glencoe?"

It was then, before Hath answered, that he heard the car coming down the drive, and was sure that he recognized the bang and rattle of it. And Hath had listened, too, and said that it was Mitch. And then the man had come—a comparatively new one—addressing him and saying, as he understood it, "Mr. Ballou is calling."

"Ask him to come in," Emilie had suggested. But he had gotten up and started toward the door. "Bring him in," she said, "to have dessert with us."

"Yes. Yes, I will." And he had gone into the hall and found Nat standing there—standing near the door, waiting rigidly. "Oh—" he said. "I thought it was your father. Won't you come into the dining room and have dessert with us?"

She shook her head.

"You wanted to see *me*, Nat?"

"Yes."

"Well—" He motioned her to go into the library and closed the door behind them. It crossed his mind, in the moment that it took: perhaps he could make a bargain with her, perhaps that was the reason for her coming. But he knew this wasn't true, that she would not be one to compromise an issue, whatever it might be. And perhaps there was no issue in the realm of his suspicion; the fact that she was there suggested that. These things he was thinking while she stepped into the room, and crossed beyond the table, and turned around to face him. "Won't you sit down?" he said.

She shook her head.

"No?—Well—" He waited, across the table from her. It was beginning to be dusk; and the storm which had been threatening all day long, seemed to be coming now: there was faint stirring in the sultry air, little puffs of coolness through the screens of the tall windows, and a whirl of dust above the bed of cannas. His palms were wet and he rubbed them with his fingers. "What is it, Nat?"

"I came to ask you why you did it." Her face looked very white—perhaps it was the contrast with the cannas which were behind her profile—and very Jewish: like a picture he remembered having seen in some gallery in Europe. Her lips were tight, eyes fixed on his—not afraid and not resigned—

"You mean, about your father's note?" he said.

She nodded.

"That's a business matter—" His shoulders moved. "—a matter for the bank."

"No." She shook her head.

"If there was any question, your father should have come."

"My father is not fit to come," she said.

"Oh! I'm sorry, Nat.—But I'm afraid there's nothing to be done." He looked away and went on in broken sentences: "The pressure on the bank—disturbance of the public interest—menacing the good of the community—constant irritation.—I assure you I have tried to make your father see the importance of conforming, within reasonable limits. —And there is the money, which of course the bank doesn't feel like losing. Mr. Hogan has been very patient in the matter.—Embarrassing for me, and painful, too; but I cannot support your father's attitude further than I have. He has had ample warning—" It came to an end, what he had to say, which he had said much better a dozen times that day—but he had not dreamed it would be said to her, and so his preparation did not serve him very well.

But still she waited.

"I'm very sorry, Nat." He spread his hands.

"I came," she said, "to find out *why* you did it."

"I've explained as best I can—"

"No, it isn't that." She moved toward the table, coming closer to him, looking at him steadily, disconcertingly. "You wouldn't care that much—not about a little money, because now you've got so much and a little doesn't matter. You wouldn't care at all if we could never pay it—"

He didn't answer.

"And you wouldn't care what Ned Birney said or thought, nor any of those men, because you know they can't do anything to you—hurt

« 378 »

you or take away anything you've got. You don't care about them—

"I live here," he said. "I belong to the community."

"No," she said, "you don't. You don't belong to anything. Things belong to you."

"Nonsense." He felt the pulses pounding in his temples, blood rushing to his head. "It's simply that I can't support subversive undertakings which attack the institutions I believe in. Well, I have certain principles—" He shrugged impatiently.

"No," she said, "you haven't."

"Really—" He stepped back from the table, holding down his anger. "Really, I'm afraid there's nothing else to say." And she said, evenly and quietly—

"It's because I'm Jewish, isn't it?"

He heard the door latch click, but he didn't turn his head.

"Because you were afraid that Hath and I—" She stopped. And he saw in her eyes that he had been right about it, that she was in love with Hath. And then he heard Hath's voice, but still he didn't look—

"What's the matter, Nat?"

"Nothing," he said thickly. "Wait outside a moment." But Hath ignored him, repeating what he'd asked—

"What's the matter, Nat?" A man's voice, not a boy's—something that was not to be commanded. And she answered him, as she always answered questions, not mincing words about it—

"Your father has taken the *Gazette* away from us."

"Taken the *Gazette*?"

"He told Mike Hogan not to renew our note, and there's a chattel mortgage on everything we have."

"But why?" Hath said.

And he had spoken then, fury surging in him, being spoken of, hearing the thing discussed as if he were not there. "I'll tell you why," he said. "Because the paper has become intolerable, because I can't subscribe—"

"No," she interrupted. "Because I'm Jewish, Hath."

"What?" Hath said.

"Because he was afraid you were in love with me.—I thought that must be it, but I wanted to be sure." And then she crossed between them toward the door.

"Wait, Nat!" Hath tried to stop her, but she went around him, out into the hall. And he heard Emilie's voice call a greeting to her, heard the screen door close, and the motor of the car. And Hath stood staring at him—

"All right," he said. "Maybe that's part of it—"

"By God!" Hath said, and that was all—staring at him, with a look in his eyes which would be hard to forget—bitter and contemptuous. And then Emilie came into the doorway, looking at them anxiously, asking what was wrong—

He didn't remember very clearly after that—beside himself with rage and injury, and the sense of being cornered, that whatever he had done, and for whatever reason, he would not profit by it. Like that night in the apartment—saying to Eileen those things that couldn't be unsaid, ripping her nightgown into rags, seeing her face through an intervening curtain—out of reach, beyond control. Seeing Hath's face then—disdainful and defiant, goading fury higher; and Emilie's frightened eyes. Seeing through a curtain—alone, detached from them; shouting down her protests, not hearing what she said. Commanding what he'd have: a return, some compensation for the lifetime that he'd spent to make the future safe and clean of handicap—obedience to his will.—"That Jew girl," he had called her. But he'd known in his heart that he was whipped—

And Hath had gone. He had kissed his mother, saying to her not to worry, that it would be all right. He hadn't tried to stop him—not to stop him with his hands. He had thought of doing that, and had thought better of it—

"Look!" he said. "If you go, then don't come back."

And Hath had gone, not even glancing at him.

"No!" Emilie cried. "You don't mean that." She took hold of his arm, pulling at his sleeve. "Think what you're saying. You can't do things like that. You can't make people's lives for them. You can't. You can't." She stamped her foot. "Go quickly, bring him back. Tell him that you're sorry, that you didn't mean it."

"No." He undid her fingers from his sleeve, holding her wrists. "No," he said, "I mean it."

"Oh—" She pulled away from him, looking at him strangely—a desperate, hunted look. And then suddenly she turned and ran into the hall; and again he heard the door, and, looking through the window, saw her running down the drive, around the bed of cannas—

He had felt sick and dizzy, and had gone into the dining room to get a drink of brandy, noticing the table not yet cleared and the man

« 380 »

still fussing with it, hovering about uncertainly, aware of course that there had been a row, inquiring awkwardly if he would have dessert—

"No," he said. "No, nothing." He had gone to the sideboard and poured a good stiff drink, thinking of the things that could happen in a moment, between courses of a meal; struggling already with the sickness of remorse—that empty, hollow feeling which had no bottom to it, which was, itself, *defeat*—

And then the storm had burst with a splitting crash of thunder and jagged streaks of lightning stabbing at the river. And he had got a flash and gone running down the drive, stumbling in the darkness, calling out to her; finding her at last when he was in a panic, drenched and shivering underneath a tree. She had seen Hath far ahead but she couldn't overtake him, and he hadn't heard her voice, and then the storm had come. And he had carried her in his arms back to the house, reassuring her anxiety: there was a service station close by on the highway where the boy could call a taxi—

And in fact, a little later, Hath had phoned and talked to her. He did not know what was said, but she had packed some clothes and sent them by the driver. He hadn't interfered or asked a question. He had gone into her room before he went to bed. The storm was over and the moon was coming up; from her window he could see the sand bar in the river—

"Tomorrow, dear?" she questioned, clinging to his hand as he stood beside the bed. "Please bring him home tomorrow. He's hurt and angry, too; you're very much alike. Don't let it wait. A family is so precious— the most precious thing on earth."

He hadn't answered yes or no, but had bent to kiss her, remembering afterwards that her face was hot and flushed, not thinking of it then—

And the next day she was ill; and the day after that Hath could not be found, and the house on Second Street was empty—

And then, and then—

He winked the tears out of his eyes, stiffening his shoulders, picking up his pen again, writing rapidly, careless of his words—

Please come home for Christmas—you and Nat. There are things I want to talk to you about—to both of you: things which I doubt you understand and which are too involved and difficult to write. And I *need* to see you. I have been very lonely. So come and we will try to have a happy time—a tree and Christmas cheer. Please let me know as quickly as you can. I shall be waiting anxiously to hear.—Love to you both.—Your father.

He turned his head to listen, thinking he heard a car coming down the drive. Madge perhaps, he thought, though he had suggested that he would be busy. He wasn't in a mood to see her now, nor anyone; he hoped the servant would be firm about it—

He read the letter from the start, but his thought ran on behind it: he had seen Hath only once, the day of Emilie's funeral; Hath had come alone and stayed the day and gone. But the day was blurred beyond clear seeing of it. He had put his arms around his son, groping blindly in his grief; but there had been no response—only the gesture of it, awkward and perfunctory; and nothing in Hath's eyes—no hint of understanding. It was too late to say, "I'm sorry"—as if you'd overturned a cup of coffee—too late and too soon. And so nothing had been said. He had written regularly, as he had been writing now; and Hath had answered him—friendly letters, brief and empty. He had never mentioned Nat—

But now he knew, thinking through the months, that being sorry wasn't what was needed. It was too big for that. It must be *understood* —how, step by step, you came to something that couldn't be averted; and the steps went far back, out of sight of everyone, most of all yourself. Yet still, they must be there; and if you told about them, everything you could remember, being very honest, not concealing anything, though it might not seem important, then perhaps it would be clear— anyway, to someone else—someone like your son—

He came to the final paragraph, the only one that mattered—which he had been phrasing in his thought for weeks; and which had now been written in a moment, with his heart— "Please come home for Christmas—you and Nat.—There are things I want to talk to you about—to both of you.—I *need* to see you.—Love to you both. —Your father."

He folded the pages and put them in an envelope and addressed it to a town in Massachusetts, and fixed an air-mail stamp in the corner of it. And then he listened, thinking that he heard somebody call; and he got up from his chair to look out of the window, moving a little stiffly, cramped from sitting there so long. A man was coming toward the house, striding along the path between the sycamores. He recognized Mike Hogan, and he opened the door and stepped out onto the porch.

"Hi, Sam!" Mike hurried toward the steps. "The fellow at the house said you weren't to be disturbed, but I thought perhaps you hadn't heard the news."

"What news?"

"You didn't hear the radio?"

"No, I've been out here—"

"It's war."

"War?"

"Yeh, war, by God!" He came puffing up the steps, aquiver with excitement. "It's on the radio, all the stations, all the time. We're in it, Sam."

"In it?—How?"

"Up to our necks, I guess—" Mike paused to get his breath. "The dirty Japs! They bombed Pearl Harbor, Sam—"

"Bombed?—Pearl Harbor?"

"Caught us with our pants down—bombed hell out of us."

"Oh—" he said. He felt confused and sick.

XII

THERE ARE EVENTS WHICH HAVE AN INEXORABLE QUALITY—WHICH, though unforeseen, and regardless if they be malignant or benign, yet seem completely *right*—a fulfillment of design, without alternative.

Glencoe was destroyed by fire, in December '42—"a total loss" according to the account in the *Gazette*, which added paradoxically, "fully covered by insurance."

The origin of the fire was unknown. The house had been unoccupied for several months, save for a caretaker, who, a few days previously, had quit his job; and a new one had not yet been obtained. There was electric current in the house, needed to operate the automatic furnace which must be kept going in the winter months to prevent the pipes from freezing and damage to the furnishings. Possibly a faulty connection was to blame, though the wiring was a type approved by underwriters; or a spark from the motor operating the oil burner, though everything nearby was fireproof. Still, the oil line could have sprung a leak, and a pool of oil have formed, reaching back to some partitions; but the oil was not inflammable until it was vaporized, and so this explanation seemed unlikely.

There were numerous other theories, variously held: spontaneous combustion from drawers and shelves of linen and closets filled with clothing; oil-soaked rags left carelessly about by the departing caretaker, though the man maintained that this was not the case; mice igniting matches, some older people said, thinking of the matches of another day; and there was the chance that entry had been forced by thieves or vandals, bad characters among the migrant population whose shacks and trailer camps had spread along the levee and the bluff to the edge of Beaton's woods, and who might have set the fire to cover up their tracks; or neckers, young fellows and their girls in search of warm soft quarters, dropping cigarette butts on the rugs, not thinking and not caring.

Even sabotage had been suggested, though it was hard to see what the burning of Glencoe could contribute to the enemy, unless the saboteurs had hoped to start a fire which would spread through Beaton's woods to the hangars and the barracks which were then under construction on the broad rich meadowland, now known as Wyatt Field. Proponents of this theory called attention to the fact that a strong north wind was blowing, and, had the fire spread, there would have been real danger to the half-completed buildings of the camp. And no doubt this was true, for some trees on the south side of the house were badly burned, though on the northern side, no damage had been done. But the sabotage theory was a very tenuous one, defended by a handful of the fearful, who were likely to see parachutes in flapping sheets on clotheslines. The truth was that the fire was a mystery, and remained a mystery now after six months.

It was at night. The blaze had been discovered by a sentry, walking post at the north boundary line of Wyatt Field, just beyond the barns and silos which were empty and abandoned. The boy had called the guard and pointed out the sparks blowing high above the trees; and there had been delay, in the military fashion, for the matter was outside their reservation. In the end they had done no more than phone an alarm to Wyattville; and the fire company had immediately responded, though the house was far outside the corporate limits of the town. But the men were unfamiliar with the place and there was no one to guide them. Glencoe was equipped with great storage tanks of water, fire lines and pressure pumps; but the firemen had no knowledge of the premises, and so they wasted time running lines into the river, only to discover that the engine would not pump the water to the bluff. And then it was too late—if it had not been too late even at the start.

Sam had had a strange reaction to the fire: as if he had expected it or known it in advance, which of course he hadn't; it was hard to put it into words: as if it was a necessary part of an incompleted pattern whose end was dissolution, final and complete—as if it *should have* burned—*must* be destroyed. Perhaps the mystery of it contributed to that. Yet even at the time, when in the night Madge came knocking on his door, telling him in horrified excitement: someone had telephoned that Glencoe was on fire—no, even then, he hadn't felt surprised, not surprised or grieved—looking at his sister standing in the doorway in her faded dressing gown, with her gray hair done in curlers, thinking: poor old Madge!—plain and getting old.

"What time is it?" he said.

"A little after two."

"Yeh—" He lay back on the bed—his father's bed.

"But, Sam—" She started incredulously. "Aren't you going to get up? Aren't you going out there?"

"No," he said. "What for?"

"Don't you understand: Glencoe is burning, Sam."

"I can't put it out, Madge."

"But—"

"And I don't want to watch it."

"Oh dear—" She went to the window and looked out across the Square, exclaiming tearfully, "Why, Sam, the sky is red!"

"Is it?" he said. He had not gotten up to look. And suddenly he'd realized, as he had not done before, that he was through with Glencoe—as through as he had been with Clem Wyatt's general store, with the Rock Island Railroad, with the Acme Paper Company, with Tronshay—that in no circumstances would he ever have gone back there, to the place or to the life for which it stood, which had never been what he had thought it would be—never had and never could. And the fire was no more than a punctuation point at the end of something that was finished—had been finished long ago.

He had driven out next day, anxious for the safety of the *old* house. It was unharmed; the sycamores around it were not even scorched. Fortunate that the wind had been the other way. But of Glencoe there was nothing—a heap of smoldering ashes, with jagged ends of chimneys sticking up like rotten teeth. The fire engine was still there, water from the hose sizzling in the ruin, clouding it with steam.

Nothing had been saved: the portraits of his mother and his wife, his books, most of his clothing which he had left there when he moved to town, not feeling sure that he would remain; all of Emilie's things, even her jewelry in the wall safe in her room, which he had meant to put in the safe deposit box—every piece except the sapphire ring which he had given Nat on Christmas day—the Christmas day before, when she and Hath came home.

The safe was never found, though the ashes had been sifted and resifted. It had either been destroyed, which its makers claimed impossible—or it had been stolen. The insurance company had acted on this theory, employing detectives, combing pawnshops in St. Louis and Chicago; but their search had come to nothing, and a few days ago they had paid the claim. The wall safe and its contents remained part of the mystery: the wiping out of things by unseen hands—a house that you had built, a birthday gift, or the labor of a lifetime—reduced at last to figures on a check—

He moved uncomfortably, listening to sounds which came in the open window, and which perhaps had waked him; and he raised on his elbow, glancing at his watch on the table by the bed. It was near nine o'clock, later than he'd thought. He pushed a button on the wall—a bell which had been put there for his father. And he went into the bathroom, slipping on a dressing gown over his pajamas, thinking he would go downstairs to breakfast, but he felt a little giddy and wobbly on his feet; and so he got back into bed again. He had had a touch of flu, so Grover said—nothing serious at all. The unaccustomed business of standing on his feet for eight hours at a stretch, and working in the garden in his leisure time, spading, bending over—perhaps a bit too much for a man approaching sixty.

Grover had advised him to take a few days rest, and so he'd stayed in bed; and Madge had babied him. She had telephoned the factory, explaining he was ill and couldn't come to work. She had had a time, she said, to make them understand. They kept asking for his number and to repeat the name. "As if you weren't—" she said, "—well, who you are." He smiled about it now, thinking of himself as a number on a list—a long list, too. But Madge would never be convinced that he was not important.

The pounding was disturbing—and workmen's voices shouting, somewhere across the Square. The shades were partly up but he couldn't see through the foliage of the trees. There were other windows at the side, which looked across the garden—a victory garden now with scarcely any flowers, but long neat rows of vegetables, easily confused with weeds. He couldn't see the garden from his bed—just the vine-clad walls of the old Bentley place where Grover had lived since his father's death; a comfortable house like the one that he was in, built back in the eighties or the nineties when there was space in which to spread things out—when lumber had been cheap and you could hire labor for fifteen cents an hour.

His room was comfortable: spacious and high-ceilinged, with those plaster curlicues where the chandelier had been; and rather nice old pieces of antique furniture: a table with a marble top, a dresser and a highboy, things Madge had picked up—and room to walk around them. And there was a Morris chair which had been his father's— where the old man had sat when he had passed the point of going down the stairs—had sat and rolled his thumbs.

He had often wondered whose room it had been when the house belonged to Elliott—in the days of his childhood when he had used to pass it in search of Mitch or Grover, pretending not to be aware that it was there, kicking rocks along the unpaved sidewalk, but seeing from the corner of his eye if there were any of them sitting on the porch, peeking cautiously through the shrubbery toward the hammock, listening for their voices and the tinkling sound of ice in lemonade, hoping they'd notice him and call out to him to join them, hoping that they wouldn't.—Whose room had it been then?—Elliott's or Daphne's?—or maybe both of them had lived together in it?—Funny he should live in a room which had been theirs—and yet it wasn't strange, seeing how the Wyatts had been mixed up in his life.

Old Henry and Elliott had had their troubles, too. He smiled to himself thinking of the time Elliott had started for Chicago in Birney's hack with old Hogan on the box, and Jim had tricked him into stopping for a drink. But afterwards he went; and then he had come home and the hatchet had been buried.

Well, Hath had come home, too, and that hatchet had been buried —buried deeper than he'd dreamed or dared to hope—

They had come on Christmas day, eighteen months ago. Madge had gone to meet them, and he had waited for them, pacing the drive in a fever of impatience. And at last the car had come; and his son had waved to him and called a cheery greeting, as he had used to do coming home from school in his vacation times. And Nat had shaken hands, smiling with level eyes.

They had been very kind, friendly and polite, trying to act as though nothing had occurred, but not fooling anybody. They had gone into the house, exclaiming at the tree which he and Madge had trimmed the night before, which stood as high as ever in the circle of the stairs, resplendent in its tinsel, but in its heart as bleak as the sycamores outside, for the soul of it was missing.

And then there had been dinner—an ordeal of make-believe, the conversation like an ebbing tide, breaking and receding. They told him of their work in a defense plant where guns were being made— hard manual work, but they enjoyed it. They spoke of Mitch who had gone back to London as a correspondent. They talked about the war, being careful what they said, uncertain of each other's points of view. Madge had been helpful, bridging awkward gaps, chatting of the changes going on in Wyattville: new names and faces and the old ones disappearing; the town, she thought, would never be again the pleasant, easygoing place it had been; the shops were filled with grimy factory workers buying everything in sight, no matter what it cost; you couldn't find parking space on Main Street. They talked of Glencoe—mostly about things that had happened long ago, when Nat had been there as a child.

After dinner Madge had gone to some function at the church, and he was alone with them: his son and his son's wife, more strange to him than strangers—with the yule log on the hearth and the portraits on the wall. It had seemed hopeless then. His heart had been like lead; but still he had gone on, suggesting there was something he would like to show them. And he had led the way across the terrace, along the path among the trees.

"Hello!" Hath exclaimed. "You've been building something, father."

"No, not *building*, Hath." He smiled. "A kind of monument—"

"Monument?" They stared.

"Well, yes—" he said, "—the house where I was born."

But first he wanted them to walk around it, remarking that he knew Hath had seen it many times when it stood in Shanty Town, but he had never told him much about it, nor anything to Nat—so, if they didn't mind? And of course they said they didn't. It was a clear cold day, with patches of snow in the shadows of the trees. He led the way, pointing with his cane in the manner of a guide, talking volubly and nervously, as if he were unsure what came next—in fact, not like a guide, but rather like a man with an overwhelming stake in the issue of his task.

He called attention to the heavy sills and timbers, some of them hand-hewn: there had been, he admitted, minor restoration, but the building was substantial; it had stood the test of time, for it was already old, or so he understood, when the Bradens had moved in. And it had survived through all the years, the product of a period when craftsmanship was valued and things once joined together had a way of staying put.

He pointed out the window of the room that had been his, which he had shared with Tom—his brother who was dead; and the girls' room next to it—his sisters, Madge and Nelly. But Nelly was not dead, as most people thought who remembered her at all; she was in that sanitarium where Hath had gone to see her—had been there all these years. Her health was good: she ate and slept, sat in a chair or lay upon her bed. What was passing in her mind no one could say, but she did not seem unhappy. She had escaped out of a world which had been very cruel to her, and had gone so far away that she couldn't be recalled. And if she could, what was there to come back to? Perhaps it was better as it was.

He changed the subject, pointing out his mother's room which had also been his father's, but he had always thought of it as hers; and next to it the parlor which they seldom used—his mother's coffin had been put there. It was a day, he said, when things were done at home —important things like being born and dying.

Not a bad house to have lived in as a child, and it was always kept neat and clean inside, though there was never much in the way of things to keep: just what you had to have, and food enough to eat, not fancy things of course; but he could not recall ever being hungry —anyway, not very hungry. Their situation hadn't been unique, but like countless other families. He did not mean to depict it otherwise, nor himself as an undernourished waif, for indeed he had been nothing of the sort, but a boy like other boys in Wyattville and everywhere— not so well off as some and better off than others. But poverty it was —the shabby genteel sort, perhaps the most degrading.

He pointed with his cane: that was the woodshed, and there had been a manger for a cow. He led them on around the house: there were the lilac bushes—the same that had been in Shanty Town; when they were in bloom the whole house was fragrant with them. There had been an apple tree, but it was dead—anyway, it couldn't have been moved. He went on up the steps, across the porch, into the house. This was the room in which they'd lived, he said, which now he was using as an office; and he added with a smile, not wanting them to think he'd been serious about it, that the *monument* was not without utility. But aside from a shelf of files and ledgers the room was as it had been in his childhood.

He was silent, giving them a chance to look around, watching the expressions on their faces: they were being polite; not much interested, he thought—all this talk about the house, relics of a past in which they had no part. He had wanted them to get the feeling of the place, thinking it would help them understand, but now it all seemed futile. They glanced at things and asked some casual questions. The atmosphere was heavy with constraint.

"But please sit down," he said. And they sat at the ends of the long table—his son uneasily, avoiding looking at him; and the girl with Jewish features and disconcerting eyes, in his mother's chair, hands folded in her lap. She was looking at the workbasket on the table at her elbow. And suddenly he said in desperation, not knowing what to say, "That was my mother's, Nat."

"Oh—" she said, and took the basket in her hands.

"My mother was a seamstress—" His voice was hard, almost aggressive. "—a very good one, too, luckily for us. She made dresses for the ladies of the town, Mrs. Henry Wyatt and her friends—made them in her leisure when she wasn't nursing children, waiting on my father, cooking, scrubbing, washing dishes. She was a lady born, a gentlewoman, Nat; and my father was a shiftless, good-for-nothing man."

She had found the thimble in the basket.

"That was her thimble. I gave it to her for a Christmas present when I was nine years old—a little fellow, about as high as that—" He indicated with his hand. "I hid it in her stocking and then I helped her find it. It was way down in the bottom of the toe, but it wasn't hard to find, for there was nothing else."

She held the thimble to the light.

"It sparkles, doesn't it? I was sure they were diamonds, and Clem Wyatt said they might be; he didn't lie about it. I bought the thimble in Clem's store. Nelly was with me. I think Clem cut the price to help me out; anyway, fifty cents was what I paid—all the money that I had, and the most I'd ever had or ever seen—a big, shiny half dollar that Elliott Wyatt gave me."

"Elliott Wyatt?" Hath exclaimed.

"Yes, Elliott," he said.

"But why, Father?"

"Why?" He turned the matter in his mind. "Because I was a little boy in trouble—because Elliott Wyatt was that kind of a man."

"Go on," Nat said.

"On?" He turned his head, looking at her doubtfully.

"What trouble were you in?"

"Oh that!" He smiled apologetically. "The trouble of a child. I don't know if you'd care—" It didn't seem important.

"Yes, tell us," she insisted.

And through the hours of that Christmas afternoon, pacing back and forth across the room, sitting down sometimes and getting up again, watching their faces till he could no longer see them in the deepening winter twilight, he told them the story which began on another winter day nearly fifty years ago—the story of a broken sled, a little girl with flaxen curls, and a boy in sailor pants.

The story you have read, if you have read this far. And he told it very much as it has been written, though not always in that sequence of events; and some things he omitted, which had escaped his memory, but none that were important. He didn't undertake to justify himself, or interpret what he said: that this was good or bad, and this was wise or foolish. He was too confused for that; he didn't know. And so he was content to tell them what had happened, hoping they would see how one step led to another and could hardly be averted—the steps of that ladder which he had so painfully climbed, and which now it seemed had no more rungs, leaving him suspended helpless in the air no closer to the stars than he had been at the start.

And he did not spare himself or modify the facts, though parts of it were hard to tell to your own son: for example, what pertained to Cassie Cole, though he was careful not to name her; and his wedding night, that first one with Eileen; and those things he'd said to her which could never be unsaid; and the wailing of the infant in the other room—shabby, shameful things, no worse perhaps than others, but harder to repeat.

It was quite dark when he finished. He couldn't see their faces. He was conscious of a sound, as if Nat might be crying; but he thought that wasn't likely because she never cried, and he wasn't sure what there was to cry about. And then his son had come to him and put his arm around his shoulders—a thing he had never done before; and he had said in a way that settled everything, that left no shred of doubt—

"It's all right, Father—"

He started, sitting straighter in his bed, remembering something long forgotten: the words that Hath had said were like an echo, for they were the very same that Neill had said to Elliott, in that beautiful big room with vases filled with flowers, when Elliott had finished explaining to his sons—yes, and to *him* who had no business there, who had somehow crashed the gate and was conscious that he didn't have a seat stub in his pocket and fearful lest an usher should demand to see his ticket—Elliott explaining to his sons how it was he had come home without their mother. Not defending himself, there was nothing to defend; nor explaining really, just telling them the story, being sure of himself and of them, too. And at the end of it Neill had gone to him and put his arm around his shoulders—the way a man's son didn't do—

"It's all right, Father—" That's what he had said, just as Hath had said it. And you knew that it was true.—Funny he hadn't thought of that before.

"Come in," he said in answer to a knock. It was his breakfast tray. "Good morning, Cassie."

"Good morning—" She never spoke his name if she could help it, but he was used to that. She put the tray down on the bed, smiling pleasantly, remotely and detached. "You feeling better?"

"Fine," he said. "I'm going to get up."

"That's good." Her voice was soft and musical and she drawled her words, but not at all like the negroes on the levee; you felt she was removed from what she said, not much concerned about it. She went to the windows, raising the shades higher. "Your sister's gone to market. She said to tell you she'd be back in a little while."

"Yeh—" He nodded, toying with his grapefruit, watching her move about the room—trim and graceful still, though she was in her sixties; no wrinkles in her face, no signs of age; hair as black as ever, not kinky like a negro's, smoothed back on her head, with a white flower in it; ankles peeping out beneath her crisp white dress—seeing her again: a boyish, naked figure, brown like the color of the hogshead at her back, slim and brown and beautiful—wonderful and terrifying. Always seeing her like that and uncomfortable about it, not wanting to remember and not able to forget—

"It's a lovely day," she said.

"Is it?" He poured coffee in his cup. The morning sun streamed in but there was a gentle breeze; it wouldn't be too hot. He caught the scent from the honeysuckle vine wreathed around the window.—June again—another June, another summer—

"You could sit on the porch when you get up." She arranged the window curtains, running her fingers down the pleats. "The sun'll do you good."

"That's right," he said.—What did *she* remember?—what did she think about it?—what had it meant to her?—And suppose she had been white—just a little difference in the color of her skin, what would have happened then?—what *had* happened in her life?—in those years that she was missing, visiting Grandma Cole in St. Louis, so they said.—*Why* was she sent away?—Had she ever had a husband?—or a *child*?—any other lover than himself?—What did she have to remember besides that: the warehouse and the soft warm earth between tall rows of corn and snug places in the woods out of sight of prying eyes?—He said, not looking at her, busy with his breakast:

"Are you fond of children, Cassie?"

"Children?" She turned her head

"Little ones, I mean."

"Oh, babies?"

"Yes, little babies."

"I don't know." She laughed softly, straightening objects on the dresser. "I guess I would be." She moved the photograph of Hath in its leather frame—Hath in his uniform. "Why did you ask me that?"

"Why?" He could see her looking at him in the mirror of the dresser. "I just wondered, Cassie."

"Oh—"

"You see, Miss Nat is coming home, coming with the baby—"

"Yes, I know." She looked away, smoothing with her toe a wrinkle in the rug. "Your sister told me."

"Coming here to live with us."

"It'll be nice," she said, "to have a baby in the house." She stooped to pick up something from the floor. "Nice for you, having someone that belongs to you."

"Yes, nice," He nodded, eyes upon his plate.—Unanswered questions, never to be answered.—He said abruptly:

"What's going on out in the street?"

"In the street?" She looked up, languidly indulgent, as one who humors the notions of an invalid. "There's nothing going on."

"Yes, there is," he said with a note of irritation. "Don't you hear that racket, Cassie?"

"Oh, that's what you mean." She turned back to the window.

"They've been at it for an hour."

"Have they? I didn't notice."

"Banging things around—"

"Workingmen, I guess—" She was trying to see through the branches of the trees. "Over by the Wyatt place—"

"What're they up to, Cassie?"

"I can't see very good." She went to the window which looked across the Square. "Well, I declare—" she said with mild surprise.

"What?"

"Looks like they're tearing down the big old iron fence."

"The iron fence?—What for?"

"I wouldn't know." She shrugged. "Maybe scrap—to melt it up for bullets."

"Oh!—Oh yes—" He nodded.

"It's no good any more, just standing there." She chuckled softly, moving toward the door. "Nobody to keep in and nobody to keep out." She glanced at his tray. "You finished with your breakfast?"

"Yes, thank you, Cassie."

"You didn't eat much." She took the tray and went into the hall, closing the door noiselessly behind her.

He lay back on his pillows, listening to the clang of hammers striking iron and workmen's voices calling to each other.—So they were tearing down Old Henry's iron fence. Old Henry wouldn't like that if he knew about it—wouldn't understand or tolerate it.—Fences coming down.—The world he'd lived in had been built of fences. Whatever way you turned you were face to face with one. Some you could climb over or crawl under or break down, but there were a lot of them that defied your strength and patience. The thing to do of course was to build one of your own, high enough and strong enough to keep everybody out. And when you got it built—well then you were alone—

Fences coming down.—Bombers flying the Atlantic in four hundred minutes, going anywhere on earth in no more than sixty hours; voices talking to you from Moscow or Chungking. A shrinking world, getting smaller every day: no room for fences—the kind of thing that Mitch had talked about and it had seemed pretty crazy, but now he didn't feel so sure about that.—Little fences coming down, right here in Wyattville: going to a movie, waiting to get in, standing in the line with everybody else—no chance to peel a ten spot from your roll and slip it to a scalper for two good ones on the aisle. Or like that road-house where they sometimes went for dinner, which wasn't far from town and didn't take much gas; it had always been expensive, cater-ing to the few, but now it was packed with factory workers in their shirt sleeves and women carrying babies in their arms—people drink-ing cocktails at sixty cents a throw and eating sirloin steaks that cost four dollars. People doing everything that anybody else did, going anywhere there was to go, buying anything there was to buy. Money in their pockets, and little books of tickets that entitled them to have neither more nor less than anybody else. And the boys in uniform—no matter where they came from, no matter who they were.—Fences coming down—*just for the duration*, a lot of people said. But things did not go back.

That's what Hath had meant, standing by the window in the old house on that Christmas evening, looking at the big one looming in the twilight, speaking gently, rather sadly.

"I'm afraid it's finished, Father—finished in the world."

At the time he hadn't understood; even now he wasn't sure that he did. He had been telling them how difficult it was to keep things going, hinting hopefully at the idea that they would come home to live, to make their home with him and help him with the place; and he thought Hath was talking about Glencoe. And so of course he was, but he had meant more than that—not the house and acres, but some-thing vastly bigger of which they were a symbol: a way of life, an attitude of mind, a set of values—fences around things—

But there was another reason why his son could not come home, which then he didn't know. Later, in the library, with the yule log still smoldering on the hearth and the portraits smiling at them, Hath told him: he was in the army, on his way to a training camp in Texas, and Nat was going with him and would live somewhere nearby.

"In the army?" He hadn't heard the rest of it. "But you're not in uniform."

"Not yet," Hath smiled, "but they've got one waiting for me."

"You mean that you've been drafted?" It flashed through his mind that if he'd known about it—that the "boys" in Wyattville—

"No, I enlisted."

"Enlisted?" He looked at Nat, seeing in her eyes that she had no part in it, that she had neither urged him nor attempted to dissuade him, that she never would for a purpose of her own.

"In the Air Force, Father."

"The Air Force," he repeated, conscious of a tightening in his heart —mingled fear and pride. "But I didn't know—"

"Nor I." Hath laughed. "But the army seems to think they can make a flyer of me; it was their idea, not mine."

"Oh—" He nodded vaguely.

"Of course I may wash out."

"Of course," he agreed, but he knew that wouldn't happen. He couldn't seem to get a grip on the idea and kept asking silly questions, as: "Why did you enlist?"

"It's hard," Hath said, "to put that in a sentence."

"Six months ago you didn't think—"

"It's different now."

"Yes, different," he admitted.

"It's our world, Father, and we have to live in it, and some of my crowd may be here quite a while."

He nodded, but the matter wasn't clear. "Do—do you want to go to war, Hath?"

"*Want* to go to war?" Hath laughed. "No, I don't suppose I do. I'm not a warlike person, not an advocate of violence. I don't like killing things, not even ducks or rabbits. I love my wife and I don't want to leave her, and it's pretty soon for that." He went and sat beside her on the couch, and she smiled and put her hand upon his wrist. "No, I don't want to go to war, and among my friends I know very few that do, but—" He hesitated, careful of his words. "—but I don't want the war to go without me."

"What?" he asked, not understanding.

"Let's put it this way, Father: the war belongs to us, my generation; we're the ones that have to fight it; we didn't make it, but it always works like that. Well, I wouldn't be content to be left out of it. I want my share of it, however good or bad. I don't want to be shot at, certainly not killed—maybe by a boy who roomed with me at Spetzgart, of whom I was fond, and will be again if I ever get a chance." He reflected for a moment. "I don't hate anybody, and I don't believe they can make me feel that way, or that it's necessary to feel that way to win, or that winning wouldn't be defeated by it. And I think most of my friends feel about the same as I do—the boys I knew at Harvard and the fellows in the factory making guns."

"Yes," he said, "I see." But he had not seen very well, his attention so engrossed in listening to his son who had never talked to him, who had always been evasive and defensive, to whom he had never listened, whom he had never tried to understand, whom he had never known—this fine young man, his son.

"I don't know how to put it any better, Father." He took Nat's hand in his, the one on which she wore the sapphire ring, which he had taken from the tree a little while ago, giving it to Hath to give to her; and Hath had slipped it on above the plain gold band which was her wedding ring. "Maybe you can say it, Nat? You're pretty good at getting to the bottom of a thing."

"What, Hath?" She looked up at him.

"*Why* I have to go to war."

"I'll try—" She smiled. "For your soul's sake, isn't it?"

"Why yes," Hath said, "of course. That's it exactly: for my soul's sake, Father."

"Oh—" He nodded, but it wasn't very clear. And then he asked, dreading to hear the answer to his question: "When must you go?"

"Tomorrow morning, Father."

"Tomorrow—oh—"

"That's why I didn't tell you right away."

"Yes—" He nodded dully. Nothing to do about a thing like that; war went its way, and you went with it, or you stood on the sidewalk with the crowd and watched the boys march by.

"And now," Hath said, "Let's not talk about the war, nor anything unpleasant or important. Let's have a little fun. We'll make a night of it, if you don't mind sitting up?"

"Oh no, I don't," he said.

"Fine." Hath grinned. "We won't go to bed at all; we can do that any time."

"Yes, any time," he echoed, and he jumped out of his chair, excited and elated. "Yes, a night of it, of course. We'll do that, Hath. We'll open up some wine." He started toward the bell, to ring it for the man.

"Wait a moment, Father." Hath was at his elbow in a stride. "No use to ring the bell; they've gone to bed. And it's no good wasting time to chill the wine. Brandy would be better, don't you think?"

"Yes, brandy," he agreed—would have agreed to anything.

"A bottle of your best—" Hath winked his eye.

"The old Napoleon, Hath?"

"That's the ticket, Father. And a kettle from the kitchen, and lemons and sugar; and I'll brew a punch for you here on the hearth— the kind Mitch used to make. Nat knows how to do it."

"The very thing," he said.

And they had gone, the three of them, to the kitchen and the cellar, laughing and stumbling in the dark, feeling for the unfamiliar switches, opening the iron door into the vault where the wines were kept, searching the shelves until at last they found it: a cobwebbed bottle coated thick with clay.

"That's what we want." Hath peered into the bin. "And it seems to be the last. Do you want to save it, Father?"

"Save it?" He laughed. There would never be a better time, nor one of greater moment in his life—

And Hath had brewed the punch, kicking the smoldering yule log into blaze, filling the same thick glasses they had always used. And when they were filled he had proposed a toast, raising his glass to the portraits on the wall, to one and then the other—

"To those gallant ladies, Father: your mother and mine." And they had clinked their glasses.

And the hours of the night had slipped away into the winter dawn; strange hours they had been: sad and happy, gay and deeply moving, warm and chill—joy and fear and pride inextricably mixed. And they had gone, leaving the empty bottle and the embers on the hearth and the portraits on the wall smiling their approval—

Clang—bang— Fences coming down.—He got up and tried his legs. They did not feel wobbly now, and he went to the window and looked out across the Square, but he couldn't see through the foliage of the trees, except that there were workmen doing something. He went into the bathroom, deciding he would shave and dress himself. Planes were droning overhead, as they did the whole day long: bombers from the factory, trying out their wings; boys from Wyatt Field, learning how to kill—boys who hadn't been a party to the quarrel, whose fathers were to blame or someone more remote, but whoever they might be they were safely in their graves or retired to the bench, unfit for active service. Even a perennial warrior like Mike Hogan. He smiled, remembering—

Mike had been in the reserve and had applied at once for active service, waiting with impatience for his orders to arrive, doing daily calisthenics to flatten out his belly, barking at the bank clerks in military fashion, whispering confidentially from the corner of his mouth to customers and friends: "Yeah, any day now.—Artillery, that's my branch.— No, I don't know where; maybe England or Australia.— I'd like to get a crack at those dirty little Japs.—You bet.—Well, thanks a million, brother." And then—

One day he had gone into the bank to find Mike slouched down in his chair with his feet cocked on the desk, scowling darkly at a letter he was reading. He said, by way of greeting, in a sepulchral voice—

"From the War Department, Sam."

"Bad news, Mike?"

"Yeah, bad."

"Don't they want you?"

"Sure, they want me." He laughed with a very hollow sound. "I've been promoted, Sam; I'm a lieutenant colonel."

"Congratulations."

"Congratulations hell! They've put me into ordnance."

"Ordnance, oh—"

"I'd sooner be a private in the field artillery." There were tears in his eyes. "Stupid brass hat bastards! Last time I was too good, and now I'm too damn old."

"Perhaps they thought you'd be more useful there?"

"Sure, I know." Mike groaned. "Sitting at a desk, keeping bloody books, counting G I junk—like the tax assessor's office."

"When do you go?"

"I don't know when or where. It don't say in the letter. I'll get my orders later."

"Maybe—" he had said, trying to cheer him up, "—maybe they'll send you overseas."

"Overseas?" Mike looked up hopefully. "You really think they might, Sam?"

"Why not?"

"Yeah, maybe—"

But it hadn't worked like that. A month or two went by and then one day Mike came tearing out to Glencoe in his colonel's uniform, with all the stripes and ribbons from that other war, erect and fit, looking every inch a soldier, but the hair slicked on his forehead getting pretty gray, and his face bleak with despair.

"I got my orders, Sam."

"You have?"

"I got to go next week."

"Where, Mike?"

"By God, you'd never guess."

"Overseas?" he ventured, but he knew the news was bad.

"No." Mike shook his head. "Rock Island, Sam."

"Rock Island?"

"Rock Island, Illinois, so help me Christ!"

"Well," he smiled, "that's close to home."

"Yeah, too damn close."

"You can keep an eye on things."

"To hell with that!" He stamped across the room. "A war going on and me sitting on my arse in the arsenal at Rock Island! By God, I got to see what I can do about it. I got to pull some wires."

And he had pulled all the wires he could reach, but the "boys" in Wyattville couldn't help him out of that. To the arsenal at Rock Island he had gone, and there he had remained, champing at the bit in furious resentment, coming home to Wyattville every other week or so, keeping track of matters at the bank, barking orders at his wife, snapping at his grandchildren to suck their bellies in.

Poor old Mike, spoiling for a fight, no matter what the issue, certainly not wanting to pull down any fences, staunch disciple of an age that had built a lot of them.

It was not long after this visit with Mike Hogan that the young man came to call on him at Glencoe—a comparatively young man, not a soldier, for he wore civilian clothes, though he came in a military car with a soldier at the wheel; but he hadn't seen the car and the soldier until later. He was sitting at the table in the old house, going over some accounts, when, looking up in answer to a knock, he saw the young man standing on the porch, with a brief case underneath his arm, looking rather like a salesman, though there were not many now with anything to sell. It must have been in May, for the lilacs were in bloom.

He had been carrying on, not knowing what to do, the problem getting tougher every day. He had sold most of the stock because he lacked the help to raise and harvest feed; half the cultivated fields were lying fallow. His superintendent had resigned the week before, apologizing for it, but refusing to remain at a big increase in salary, because, as he put it, he couldn't do the work, and couldn't just stand by and watch things go to hell: fences and equipment which they couldn't keep repaired without labor and materials which were not to be obtained. The garden was a wreck, with one old man left to do the work of six: greenhouses empty, hedges and shrubs unpruned, scarcely any flowers; weeds growing from the cracks between the terrace bricks and sprouting from the pavement around the swimming pool. The inside of the house was not much better: no one could be found to wash the windows; awnings rotted out couldn't be renewed; the silver went unpolished, flower vases empty; dust lay thick on everything. There was another couple, slothful and incompetent, and it seemed unlikely they would stay. Already, in a month, they were complaining that it was too lonely in the country.

He had been going over the accounts. Glencoe was in the red. This was not surprising, for it had always been a losing proposition, and he had no expectation of a profit. But that was unimportant. The point was that the place was running down, that no effort of his will or expenditure of money seemed able to arrest the course of its decline. Glencoe was a failure, and the bare idea of failure was intolerable. He had been thinking this, remembering suddenly what Hath had said— "I'm afraid it's finished, Father"—not thinking then what Hath had really meant, not seeing Glencoe's failure as the failure of an idea, but only in the literal sense of a physical machine which wouldn't run. And then he'd heard the knock and had looked up from his figures to see the young man standing on the porch—a salesman, he supposed—

"Mr. Braden?" A brisk young man with a brief case in his hand.

He nodded, impatient of the interruption.

"I'm sorry to disturb you. I'm from Washington, from the War Department."

"The War Department?"

"Yes sir." He presented his card and a letter of credential.

"Will you come in?"

"Thank you." He sat down at the table and opened up his brief case. "I won't beat around the bush, sir, for I happen to know that you're a businessman."

He nodded, wondering what this could be about.

"Well, sir, in a word then—" The young man smiled. "—we want your property."

"*What?*" He stared. "What property?"

"Glencoe, Mr. Braden." He took a map and some papers from his brief case, explaining crisply: an army project, flying field and training school—the location was suited to their needs and surveys had confirmed its adaptability to the desired purpose—extensive frontage on the river offered opportunity for amphibian operations—the broad fields to the south could be readily converted into runways—in short, the situation was ideal. There was other land which might be utilized, but all of it was held in modest parcels, requiring multiple negotiations, which would involve delay; and time, of course, was the essence

« 401 »

of the matter. He pointed with a pencil— "This is a map of Glencoe, Mr. Braden. The red lines indicate the property we need—everything in fact except the house and the park in which it stands, which, I believe, is known as Beaton's woods."

He nodded.

"The balance of the place—some eighteen hundred acres, according to my figures, we are prepared to purchase."

"To purchase—" he repeated.

"At a reasonable price, including the improvements on the premises: farm buildings and the like."

"I see."

"Everything except your home."

"And what would you suggest that I should do with that?"

"Really, Mr. Braden—" The young man spread his hands. "Your country is at war."

"Yeh," he said, "I know."

"We are prepared to pay a reasonable price, one we have determined to be fair, and which—"

"How much?" He interrupted.

The young man found a memorandum in his brief case and handed it across the table. He glanced at it and put it down, no expression on his face, calculating shrewdly: the price was fair enough, much more than he had paid in those dark foreclosure days of '33 and '34— more than all of it had cost, including Beaton's woods. There was a handsome profit in the deal. But no hint of this escaped him.

"Yeh—" He nodded, drumming with his fingers on the table, looking through the window at the white and purple lilac whose fragrance filled the room, studying his visitor's face from the corner of his eye: this young man was smart, but also he was young, a novice at the game; he was too eager and too anxious. They would go higher— enough perhaps to amortize the house and all that it contained. He had only to sit tight, to shake his head. Business was business—anyway, it always had been.—He picked up the scrap of paper and glanced at it again: a row of penciled figures.—His country was at war, and *time* was the essence of the matter, and his son— "For my soul's sake, Father."

"All right," he said, "you've bought it."

"Why, thank you, Mr. Braden—" The young man caught his breath. "Thank you very much." He fumbled through his papers. "People as a rule want to put things off; they don't like to make decisions. It's been a pleasure, sir, to deal with you. The government, I'm sure, will appreciate your attitude." He found what he was seeking. "Could I trouble you to sign this, Mr. Braden?—an agreement to sell at the figure I have named."

He signed and pushed it back across the table.

"Thank you, sir." The young man strapped his brief case and stood up. "There is nothing else, I think, except the question of when we might take over."

"Take over?" He smiled. "Tomorrow if you like."

"Tomorrow?" The young man stared. "Really, Mr. Braden, we don't want to inconvenience you."

"No," he said, "you won't."

He had walked out with his visitor, along the path among the sycamores; and then he had seen the military car with the soldier at the wheel, waiting in the drive beside the canna bed, but there were no cannas now.

"By the way—" The young man paused with his foot upon the step. "—it might be of interest to you, Mr. Braden: this cantonment will be known as Wyatt Field."

"Oh, Wyatt Field—" He nodded.

"Yes sir. I believe they're naming it for one of our ace flyers who lost his life in the other war, and whose family, I understand, came from Wyattville. Perhaps you knew him, sir?"

"Yes," he said, "I did."

"Well, good-by, Mr. Braden, and thank you again."

"That's all right. Good-by."

And when the car had gone he had stood there in the drive for a long time, gazing through the tangle of the woods to the broad rich meadows and cultivated fields—seeing Glencoe's fences coming down —seeing geometric runways as level as your hand, barrack buildings, hangars, a military camp—not Glencoe but an unfamiliar landscape known as Wyatt Field, named with a name dug out of a grave, and which would not stay buried.—No matter, he was through with it, and at a profit too.

Next morning he had gone, moving into town, taking almost nothing with him, not certain that he'd stay; coming to live with Madge and Cassie Cole—to live in this house which had once belonged to Elliott, in this room which had been his—or perhaps it had been Daphne's.

He finished dressing, in comfortable old clothes which he wore to putter in the garden; and he stood at the mirror, combing back his hair to cover a bald spot which he couldn't see but which he knew was there. He looked his age, he thought—not as young as Mike, younger perhaps than Mitch, about like Hub or Grover. The exertion of his toilet had fatigued him, and he sat down in the Morris chair—

Until a year ago, when he moved to town, he'd hardly had an idle moment in his life. Making money had been a full time occupation; and once you got it made, it wanted looking after, though lately he had given little thought to his investments, for with taxes what they were, there wasn't much inducement to add to what you had—no use shifting things around for speculative profits; it had been enough to know that the principal was safe, in tax exempts and governments and strictly high-grade bonds—as safe as money could be in a very unsafe world. The bank looked after details and kept his books for him, clipping coupons and the like; and so, aside from general supervision, his wealth made few demands upon his time. It reposed in the dark depths of a massive vault, packed tightly in the drawers of strong steel cabinets, themselves securely locked. The vault was not unlike a mortuary chamber, and the cabinets, in size and shape, were suggestive of a casket. He had remarked the fact one day, and since then seldom went to look at his possessions of which there was careful record in a padlocked ledger on his desk downstairs.

But running Glencoe had been a busy job, and when he came to town he did not know what to do. For a month he had tried loafing— getting up late in the morning, going for a stroll, sitting on the porch, puttering in the garden; but it wouldn't do. He must have employment to occupy his mind, and one day he mentioned it.

"Of course you should," Madge said. "And it's your duty, Sam."

"What would you suggest?"

"Washington. They need you."

"For what?"

"Why, everything—"

He laughed.

"Yes, but they do. They need businessmen to run things. They'd be glad to get you, Sam."

"Maybe," he agreed, but he was doubtful of it. "Anyway, I don't want to go to Washington; I'm no hand at politics. Something closer home would suit me better."

"Well—" She thought about it. "—why not the airplane factory?"

"Yeh—" He nodded; he had thought of that, himself.

"You could telephone the manager—"

"No," he said, "I'll go just like anybody else."

And he had gone. He smiled to himself remembering that visit: the wilderness of wire fence and closely guarded gates, acres of parked cars, long low concrete buildings, planes taking off and landing on a strip of narrow runway, others screened from view with sandbag walls, workmen hurrying here and there, the machine-gun sound of riveting and the roar of airplane motors. He had got in at last, directed to a building marked EMPLOYMENT OFFICE, which he thought he recognized as the old original warehouse, but he wasn't sure of it. The room was full of people— men and women sitting around on benches or waiting in line to interview the clerks behind the counters. And he had waited, too, amused and curious.

"I want to see about a job," he said.

"What can you do?"

"I've been a businessman."

"Oh!" The girl seemed puzzled. She produced a questionnaire. "If you will check these items, the things that you can do?"

His eye ran down the columns: all the trades and crafts that he had ever heard of and many that he hadn't, but nothing, not one question to which he could answer yes. "I'm afraid," he smiled, "I can't do any of them."

"Oh!" She looked surprised and disappointed. "Something clerical, perhaps?"

"For example?" he inquired.

"Typing, comptometer—" She rattled off the list.

"No," he said, "I'm sorry."

"But—" She seemed incredulous. "—you have done something?"

"I've made a lot of money."

"Oh, money—" She nodded vaguely; and then suddenly she pointed to a man who was passing through the room, walking briskly, not looking to the right or left—a comparatively young man. "That's Mr. Gray," she said, "manager of personnel. You go and speak to him because I don't really know—"

"Thank you." He hurried to overtake the man before he disappeared into a private office, and caught him at the door. "Excuse me. Mr. Gray?"

"Yes." The man was in a hurry.

"My name is Braden—"

"Oh, Mr. Braden—" His manner changed to one of decent cordiality. "What can I do for you?"

"I came to see about a job."

"A job?—for someone else?"

"No, for myself."

"Oh, for yourself?" Mr. Gray looked at him, a quick appraising glance.

"I haven't had occasion to look for a job for more than forty years, but now—" He shrugged, still amused and curious but not quite comfortable, half wishing he had telephoned or written them a letter. "I'm not looking for a salary. Just something where I could be of service."

"Yes, I understand." Mr. Gray opened the door into the office. "Come in, Mr. Braden, and let's see what we can do." He nodded toward a chair and sat down at his desk. "Of course I know your name—" He meant to be polite. "—but excuse me if I ask: what have you done?"

"I have been a businessman."

"Yes, naturally—" Mr. Gray swung in his chair, his eyes straying to the papers on his desk. "But more specifically?"

"Specifically?" he said, a little nettled. "Well, I've been a salesman and a manufacturer. Perhaps you've heard of the Tronshay Corporation?"

"Oh yes."

"I organized it, built it, ran it for many years."

"You're familiar with machinery, Mr. Braden?"

"No, I'm not," he said. "I hired men for that. Making money was my job." And he added rather testily, feeling strangely out of place on the wrong side of a desk. "I've been pretty good at that, starting out from scratch."

"Yes, I know." Mr. Gray was apologetic. "Please don't misunderstand me, Mr. Braden. I know you are a wealthy and successful man. That's not the point. The question is: what can you do for us?"

"I don't know," he said. "That's what I came to ask."

"Yes, well—" Mr. Gray leaned back in his chair. "You have been a salesman, Mr. Braden. Unfortunately we have nothing to sell. Our problem is production. You have been an executive, but we do not need executives. Sometimes I think we have too many now." He paused, considering. "We do need men to tell others what to do, to instruct and direct them in the doing of things they, themselves, know

« 406 »

how to do: foreman, superintendents, in all departments of this plant. But making money isn't on the list."

"Yeh—" He smiled. "I noticed that."

"So you see—"

"You mean there's nothing?"

"I wouldn't say that, Mr. Braden. With a little training you could be taught to do something useful with your hands."

"What, for example?"

"Riveting, welding, to operate a lathe—"

"I'm pretty old to learn new tricks."

"We have many older men."

"Yeh?" he was still amused and curious. "How would I learn?"

"They have classes in the high school."

"Oh, the high school?" That was funny, too: the high school that he'd quit in his first year, when he was fifteen, when he'd had to go to work to help Madge make ends meet. "And then?" he asked.

"Why then, Mr. Braden, we'd be very glad to have you." They laughed together, and Mr. Gray walked with him to the door.

"I may be back," he said, not thinking that he would.

But in five months he was back, with a letter from the high school certifying to the fact that he had satisfactorily completed four hundred hours of machine-shop training, that he was competent to operate a lathe—not very well of course, not like those fellows who had been garage mechanics, and some of the girls were pretty handy, too. Still, he hadn't done so badly, once he'd overcome his fear of the machines, had ceased to see in every idling belt the helpless figure of the Polish boy winding upward toward the shaft. He made mistakes, of course, did stupid things; and on more than one occasion the instructor had lost patience. Once he had said—

"The trouble with you, Sam—" He called them all by their first names, no matter who they were. "—the trouble with you is that you don't use your head." And that was funny, too.

But bit by bit he had got the knack of it, though at first it seemed he never would. He had made a lot of things: gauges, mandrels, clamps, parts for the machines; and toward the end he had made a vase for Madge, with gracefully tapered sides and fluted moldings, accurate in its dimensions to a thousandth of an inch. Few things in his life had given him a sense of greater satisfaction. At the end of the session, when the vase had been completed and was standing on the bench, his classmates stopped to look and to compliment him on it.

Even the instructor had nodded curt approval. It had been a thrilling moment.

He had made something for Hath. He hadn't written Hath what he was doing, keeping it a secret to surprise him; thinking that when his school was finished, he would go to San Antonio for a visit with his son. And he had made these pieces to take with him when he went— a pair of dice, the edges nicely cambered, the spots precisely punched and smooth as velvet. He had labored long hours on the job, draw-filing and polishing the steel till the texture was like glass, and coating it with lacquer to keep it free of rust. He had finished them at last, close now to the end of his four hundred hours. And then one day—

It was in October and he was in the garden, raking up the leaves, when a plane came diving from the sky, directly at the house. It zoomed away and came sailing back again, circling round and round, so close that he could see the pilot waving to him. And suddenly he knew that it was Hath, for Hath had written he would come some day, dropping down out of the sky.

"Madge!" he called, but she had gone to her Red Cross class or something. "Oh, Cassie!" But he didn't wait; he ran to the garage and got the car and went racing out to Wyatt Field.

And it was Hath—Hath in uniform, with his silver wings and his lieutenant's bars, straight and hard and brown, standing by his plane, directing the mechanics. And then he'd seen his father, and had come running to him like a little boy.

Three hours they had had—

"The radio," Hath said, when they were in the car. "And it'll take three hours to repair it."

"You mean that something's broken?"

"Well—" Hath grinned, "—just between us two, I pulled a wire out of it."

"Oh—" He smiled, but he didn't understand.

"I was bound to stop and see you, and it was my only chance. Because I'm on my way—"

"On your way?" He caught his breath. "You mean—"

Hath nodded, driving the car with a careless sure hand. "I'm through with school, Father."

"Oh—" For a little while neither of them spoke. "And Nat?" he asked.

Nat was on a transport plane, Hath said. She would stay close to him as long as it was possible; and then she would go back to the town in Massachusetts where they'd lived and worked together.

"She could come and live with us, Hath."

"I know that, Father." He explained that they had talked it over. Later perhaps she would come to Wyattville, but now she felt she would be nearer to him in the East; and there were things to occupy her mind: old associations and work that she could do.

"Yes, I see," he said. He didn't urge it. They were passing Beaton's woods; he suggested driving in. Hath shook his head. He didn't want to see the place abandoned and neglected. Anyway, he'd seen it from the air. It looked quite small, he said—the park and house, like toys that children play with. And he added with a smile that everything looked small if you got up high enough.

"Yes," he said, "I guess so."

Hath turned in at the cemetery and stood for a few minutes beside his mother's grave. They didn't talk. The cemetery had been a peaceful place, out in the country, but now a housing project had grown up around it—blocks of cheap, modernistic bungalows. The grounds looked neglected and run down. No time, in these days, to attend upon the dead. His eyes strayed to the Wyatt mausoleum: ugly and ornate, and getting very shabby. Old Henry wouldn't like that. His own lot was well kept: the box hedge carefully trimmed, the grass cut short and clean of weeds, the headstones still new looking. There were four of them, room for two more. He had never thought he would be buried there, but now he didn't know; he wasn't sure of it.

They drove through Shanty Town: dirty, ugly streets, with squalid shops and third-rate movie theaters, decrepit looking cars parked against the curbing, children playing in the gutters, girls in slacks and sweaters looking back over their shoulders at boys in uniform. The swale down which he'd coasted to the levee, was a busy thoroughfare. He said—

"Perhaps you'll see old Mitch."

"Yes, Father."

"If you should, give him my love."

"I will."

"I've never heard from him, but I don't suppose he can still be angry at me."

"Angry?" Hath laughed. "Mitch is never angry, Father—except at everything."

"Yes, I know." And he laughed, too.

They drove around the Square. It hadn't changed much. The town had spread around it, leaving it alone—like an island in the sea. The old brick house with its crazy cupola and the iron fence around it; the fence was red with rust. There were benches in the Square and soldiers sitting on them, cadets from Wyatt Field. It was a pleasant day, Indian summer weather, the trees aflame with color.

He ran up the path, into the house, calling: "Cassie!—Madge— Hath is here.—It's Hath."

Three hours—

He could not remember much about them. Dozens of questions rising to your lips, which you didn't want to ask, didn't want to waste the time. Conversation starting, changing into something else; and it was hard to keep your mind on what was being said, so intent with watching—looking at your son, being proud and being frightened. Hath hadn't told them much: he had piloted big bombers, but he liked the swift pursuit ships best, P-40s and the Lockheeds, in which you were alone, whose wings became your own.—Yes, he remembered that.

When the time was almost spent he had suddenly thought of the present he had made to give his son; and he had got his toolbox from the hall and unwrapped the little pieces from a bit of oily cloth.

"Why, Father—" Hath turned them in his hands. "—they're beautiful. A pair of silver dice—"

"No, steel."

"Oh, steel.—That's something new. Where did you pick them up?"

"I made them, Hath."

"You made them?—*What?*"

"Yes—" And he explained about the factory and the school—the four hundred hours that were drawing to an end, feeling a little foolish and embarrassed, not quite understanding the expression in Hath's eyes.

"Why?" Hath said at last. "*Why* did you do it, Father?"

"Why?" He was fumbling with his toolbox, putting things away. "I don't know, Hath." And then he looked up, smiling. "Maybe for my soul's sake."

"Yes, I see." Hath laughed, but there was a catch in it. And he said lightly, "The dice my father made should be lucky ones for me."

"I hope so, Hath."

"We'll see—" He clicked them in his hand and rolled them on the floor. "Well yes, of course," he said, "a seven, naturally." And he quickly picked them up—so quickly that his father had no chance to see the spots.

He had wondered at the time if it really was a seven.

Three hours; that was all—

And they were back again at Wyatt Field; the plane standing ready on the line, its motors idling, blocks beneath the wheels, mechanics standing by to pull them out, the final minutes ticking off to nothing. And then—

"Father—"

"Yes, Hath?"

"There's one thing that I haven't told you yet—"

"What, Hath?" It was hard to hear with the motors running. He came closer to his son, looking up into his face.

"Nat is going to have a baby."

"Oh, a baby, Hath—"

"In the spring—in May perhaps."

"Yes, Hath."

"And if it's a boy, as we're sure that it will be, his name is to be Sam."

"Thank you, Hath." Hot tears in his eyes.

"And you'll look after them?"

"Yes, I'll look after them."

Hath kissed him. The mechanics didn't look surprised, didn't seem to think that it was funny. He swung into the cockpit, looking back. "Good-by," he called.

"Good luck, Hath."

The plane was gone, taxiing swiftly to the far end of the runway, wheeling into the wind, roaring for a moment, streaking past, his son's hand waving to him.

"Good-by—good-by—" Warm with pride and cold with fear.

The plane seemed to rise straight into the air, came sweeping back to dip its wings high above the field— "Good-by," it said. And then it sped away, a pin point in the eastern sky, then nothing.

The last time he had seen his son—or ever was to see him.

It seemed to him now that he had known it then, that there was no other end to it—as of a thing so advanced upon its course that it could not be checked, nor the ends of it be altered—like a design whose final lines, or threads, must be completed—

He heard the front door close; heard Madge calling Cassie, excit-

« 411 »

edly, he thought; heard her coming up the stairs, rather quickly for a woman of her age; then footsteps in the hall.

"Come in," he said before she had a chance to knock.

"Why, Sam—" She stood in the doorway, breathless from her haste, a letter in her hand. "You're up and dressed—"

"I'm well again."

"That's fine—" She was really out of breath and he shook his finger at her:

"You've no business running up the stairs like a four-year-old." He pointed to the letter. "What's that you've got?"

"From Nat—"

"Yeh, what?"

"She's coming, Sam."

"Oh!" His pulses stirred.

"Next week. Just think of that. Monday morning they'll be here." She scanned the letter, paraphrasing bits of it: "she has her reservation —it was awfully hard to get; she thinks it's safe to travel with the baby now. He's six weeks old—"

"That's not very old," he said.

"Well, she thinks he's old enough. And he's so strong and healthy—"

He nodded, not listening to the letter: details of an infant's life.— Madge had been there when the child was born. She had gone to stay with Nat when the time was getting close, and had taken her to Boston where she could be sure of the best of care. It was too late then to take a chance on the trip to Wyattville. Madge had been away a month, writing to him daily, voluminous reports—*communiqués* he called them.

She turned the page. " 'Little Sam and I send our love to Father Sam.' " Her voice was tremulous and her eyes were moist with tears. "Sam, dear, it's so wonderful. Just think of having a baby in the house —a baby that belongs to us."

"Yes, Madge."

"God *does* hear our prayers, Sam."

"Now and then—" He smiled.

"But wait; that isn't all—" She was looking in the envelope.

"No? What?"

"His picture, Sam." She held out a little snapshot. "A picture of your grandson."

"Well now—" He took it eagerly.

"You see?" She leaned over his shoulder. "I told you, Sam—"

"Told me what?"

"That he looked like Hath."

"Like Hath?" He laughed.— A tiny, chubby baby with a very blank expression, not resembling anyone.— "Nonsense, Madge. All babies look alike."

"Oh no, that isn't true, Sam. He looked like his father the day that he was born; I saw it instantly." She got the picture from the dresser and put it in his hand. "Now you look at them together and you'll see."

"Yeh—" He studied them: perhaps there might be something—the shape of the head, around the eyes and mouth; certainly the baby didn't look like Nat. "Well, maybe—" he admitted.

"Of course," she said triumphantly. "Now turn it over, Sam. See what Nat wrote."

He turned it. On the back was written: "Sam Braden II, born in Boston, May 3rd, 1943." He nodded, repeating to himself— "Sam Braden second—"

"I like the sound of it," Madge said, "the *second* at the end; it seems to sort of finish it."

"Yeh, finish it—" He tucked the snapshot in the leather frame with the picture of his son, and he got up from his chair and put the picture back in its place upon the dresser. "I think I'll go downstairs," he said, "and sit out on the porch."

"Yes, why don't you, Sam. It's such a lovely day." She was turning back the bedclothes, tidying things.

He went down slowly, his hand upon the stair rail, across the cool, dark hall with its fanlight of colored glass, across the living room, spacious and high ceilinged, with its flowered carpet whose design time had almost effaced, with the plaster curlicues where the chandeliers had been—a comfortable room, neat as a pin, sunlight filtering softly through the porch vines. In a corner of the room there was an alcove which, in years gone by, had been called the *den*—one of those oriental nooks, invented in the eighties or the nineties, screened with a bead curtain, furnished with a divan and teakwood taborets and hanging Moorish lamps, where Elliott and Daphne had their after dinner coffee and gentlemen could smoke cigars and cigarettes. As a child it had intrigued his fancy, whisking him away to the Arabian Nights. He would see himself in robe and turban, brandishing a scimitar; and Eileen, his favorite wife, or sometimes just a slave girl, but with bracelets on her arms and adoration in her eyes. He would defend her or order her beheaded, as the case might be. It would not have surprised him in the least if a genie had come forth out of a bottle.

The erstwhile *cozy corner* was his office now, contained his desk and files, and the padlocked ledger wherein was written the history of his life.

He went out on the porch and sat down in the cushioned chair which had been his father's, looking across the garden to the Bentley house. The sun was high, already past its zenith; the day was fine. He drew deep breaths, thinking how good it was to be outdoors again. The corn had grown inches while he was in bed, and there was some weeding to be done. Thinking of a child playing in the yard, picking out a tree with a low, straight branch which would sustain a swing. He smiled: that would come later.

Clang—bang— They were hammering again. They had knocked off for lunch and now they were resuming. It was louder out here on the porch. He turned his head but he couldn't see through the honeysuckle vine.

Madge came out, chattering: she would not be home for lunch, a meeting at the Red Cross, and then there was a *drive* about tin cans; she might not get back until late afternoon; would he be lonely?

"Don't you worry about me."

"Well—" She went on talking: something about the ration books and the butcher not having any meat. He couldn't hear her through the noise and he said abruptly—

"Have you any idea what they're doing over there?"

"Doing?—over where?"

"That racket. Don't you hear it?"

"Oh, you mean the fence?" And suddenly she looked confused.

"Why yes—" He eyed her, puzzled by her manner. "What's it all about?"

"Well—" Madge hesitated. "—you see, she's giving it—"

"Who?—giving what?"

"The iron fence—Eileen—"

"Oh!" He nodded.

"To the government, Sam—to melt it up for scrap."

"I see."

"And—" Again she hesitated.

"And what?"

"And the house—she's giving that."

"Yeh?" He smiled. "To be melted up for scrap?"

« 414 »

"Of course not. Don't be silly. It's for the USO—a clubhouse for the soldiers."

"Oh—" He turned the matter in his mind. "Well, I can't think of any better use for it."

"No." Madge fussed around, picking withered blossoms from the honeysuckle vine. "Everybody thinks it's very generous of her." Suddenly she turned to face him. "I might as well tell you now as any time—"

"Tell me what?"

"She's here."

"*Here?*—in Wyattville, you mean?" The past began to stir, and he felt with his fingers for the moisture in his hands.

"Yes," Madge said, "at the hotel. She came a week ago, just after you were taken sick. I didn't tell you because I thought it might annoy you. But I don't suppose it matters any more?"

"No, of course—" He laughed. But it still mattered, even now—pricking remnants of it.

"Susie Bentley gave a tea, about the USO; that's where I met her." He nodded.

"It's amazing how she's kept her looks. Her hair is white, but I think it's even prettier; and her face looks just the same, hardly a wrinkle in it; she's kept her figure, too. And her clothes—" Madge sighed. "She asked about you."

"Did she?" Feeling something in him wince.

"She was very cordial, Sam. She didn't seem the least bit silent or reserved—not cold, the way I always thought she was. She said she was so sorry you were ill, as if she really meant it."

"Yeh?"

"I think she's changed—"

He shrugged.

"We talked for quite a while. She spoke about her son; he's a major in the Air Force. It seems that he and Hath were friends. I didn't know that, Sam; did you?"

"Yes, I knew it, Madge." Wishing that she hadn't mentioned it, hanging on her words.

"Oh! Well—" She went on picking dead things from the vine. "He's been in England, but she was expecting him to come home on a furlough, just for a few days—"

"Coming *here*, you mean?"

« 415 »

"She didn't say. I suppose he would come here if she were still here, Sam."

He nodded. The palms of his hands were wet and he rubbed them on his knees.

"I saw her on the street this morning—" She gathered up the faded blossoms in a scrap of paper. "—and a young man in uniform walking at her side. I wasn't close to them—"

He didn't speak.

"I thought I ought to tell you—"

"Why not?" He shrugged impatiently.

"Because of Hath and—everything."

"Nonsense!" But it wasn't nonsense. Old wounds, old bitterness—

"I've got to run," she said, "or I'll be late." She paused at the door, fumbling with the latch. "Oh yes—"

He waited, eyes on the garden, determined not to help her.

"Eileen thought you might like to contribute something to the USO. They have to make repairs and alterations to the house, and she wants to have a tennis court."

"Oh, a tennis court!" He laughed, tight lipped with irritation. That tennis court she'd wanted nearly fifty years ago, that Old Henry hadn't wanted.

"I told her that I'd ask you."

"Certainly," he said. "Find out what she wants and I'll draw a check to you, and you can give it to her."

"Oh, thank you, Sam. I'd love to do it."

He didn't answer.

"You'll be all right? You won't be lonely, Sam?"

"I'll be all right."

She went into the house. He heard her speak to Cassie; heard the front door close.

Clang—bang— Hammers striking iron. He sat with his feet cocked on the porch rail, thinking about things he didn't want to think: old memories of injury and defeat, things to which it seemed there would never be an end. The two of them—

Cassie brought his luncheon on a tray—a substantial looking meal such as he'd been having since he started on the swing shift at the factory, commencing work at four o'clock in the afternoon and finishing at midnight. He had asked for the swingshift and he liked it: half daylight and half dark, breaking the monotony, and disposing of the evenings which he dreaded. He said, deciding suddenly—

"I wish you'd pack my lunch box, Cassie."

"Your lunch box?" She looked startled.

"I think I'll go to work this afternoon."

"But you just got out of bed. You ought to take it easy for a day or two."

"I'm all right."

"Did you tell your sister?"

He shook his head.

"I don't think she'd like it."

He didn't answer that.

"She didn't order anything for sandwiches."

"I'm not particular."

"Well—" She went back in the house.

He was finishing his lunch when he heard the telephone, and heard her answer it. She came to the door, speaking through the screen.

"You're wanted on the phone."

"Yeh? Who?"

"Major Wyatt—"

"What?" He jerked around, thinking that he hadn't understood, that he was hearing an echo in his brain; and there was the noise across the Square.

"Major Wyatt," she repeated. "That's what he said."

"Asking for *me?*"

"Yes, you he asked for."

"Are you sure, Cassie?"

"Yes," she said indifferently and went back from the door.

He got up heavily and went into the house, across the living room, into the hall. The telephone receiver was hanging from the instrument. He took out his handkerchief and wiped his hands before he picked it up.

"Hello—" he said.

"Mr. Braden?"

"Yes."

"This is Neill Wyatt—" A voice out of the grave—pleasant, gracious, careless. He could hardly hear above the beating of his heart, the confusion of his thoughts. "I've been here for a day or two, visiting my mother. I have to leave tonight and I didn't want to go without communicating with you. I hope I haven't bothered you. We heard you had been ill—"

« 417 »

"I'm all right now," he said.

"Oh, I'm glad of that, sir. Well, you see, your son and I were close friends, Mr. Braden—first when we were youngsters in a school in Switzerland, and afterwards at Harvard. But of course you know all that—"

"Yes, I know—"

"But I don't believe you know that I was with him, sir—well, that is, that I was there when he lost his life."

"No, I didn't know—"

"No, sir, of course. I meant to write, and then I found that I'd be coming home, and I thought perhaps I'd have a chance to tell you. I've talked it over with my mother, and she thought I ought to do so, that you'd like to hear about it from someone who was there—"

"Yes. Yes, I would—"

"If I could call by and see you, Mr. Braden—"

"Yes, please. When could you come?"

"Say, in half an hour, sir, if that would be convenient."

"Yes, convenient," he repeated. "Thank you very much."

He hung the receiver back, leaning against the wall, waiting for his pulses to subside, struggling to clear the tumult in his mind—a tangled mixture of the present and the past, the living and the dead; thinking of Elliott, standing with his back against a table on which there was a vase of tall white flowers, surrounded by reporters shooting questions at him—ugly, brutal questions, and the flash bulbs popping— "There will be other Wyatts," he had said, smiling at them calmly, being sure of it and himself. And he had been right: no end to it or them, and the dead ones coming back out of their graves.

He could hear Cassie singing softly in the kitchen, crooning to herself the way the negroes did—melancholy dissonance, disturbing and depressing to those whose skins were white, who could not detach themselves and serenely contemplate the mysterious agony of life.—He went into the living room, pausing uncertainly in the center of it, considering what to do with half an hour. And then he turned abruptly and went into his office—the alcove in the corner of the room. The back of it was curved in a bow window, once covered up with oriental draperies but open now to the sunlight and the air, whence could be seen the sidewalk and the path leading to the door. Sitting at his desk he would see him coming—this boy named Neill, who had Neill Wyatt's voice.

Besides his flattop desk there were two chairs, and a shelf of books and files which, after the fire, he had brought in from the old house. He had not been out there since; he had no concern about it. He felt that the old house would take care of itself as it had always done. He had tried more than once to put this feeling into words, saying that the old house had a life of its own, independent of puny human matters; that it was possessed of a *reality* which was its own protection. But it wasn't very clear.

He sat down at the desk—the padlocked ledger in its place on the corner of it; some letters, accumulated in the week that he had been ill. He thumbed them over: bills, deposit slips from banks in Chicago and New York, a note from Dr. Goldsmith—two lines reduced to formula which he knew by heart: "Miss Braden is quite well and seems contented. There is no change in her condition." He filed it in a file marked "Nelly." There were dozens of these notes, neatly clipped together, one for every month, twelve for every year.

He slit the business envelopes with a paper knife, sorting out the items of deposit, adding up the figures on a scrap of paper. Quite a lot of them would gather in a week; they wanted looking after every day. He unlocked the ledger with a tiny key which was fastened to his watch chain, leafing through the pages of it— "Description" of investment, in a cabalistic line— "Date" of acquisition— "Cost" what he had paid— "Market" as of the last inventory date—and the figures, columns of them, pages of them. From time to time the bank would take the book away and bring it up to date, eliminating items with red ink lines drawn through them—items that matured or were called or liquidated, and substituting new ones; *adding* new ones, too, for the list was always growing, month by month and year by year: income piling up and crying for investment; even with the taxes there was always something left, and now there wasn't anything to spend your money for—and nothing that you wanted, nothing you could buy.

He uncapped his fountain pen and began methodically to make the entries, on pages titled "Income." But his thought strayed away behind the figures—

He had been sitting here on that afternoon three months ago—a wintry, blustery day in March, writing to his son—Captain Braden now, for Hath had been promoted. He was writing of the fire, already three months past, though he'd written of it fully long ago. But now he had something else to add, a conclusion he had reached, which was difficult to state, but he would try: that Glencoe had been destroyed because it had no purpose, because it wasn't *real*—a house of cards on quicksand. And he thought Hath must have meant something of this sort when he said that it was "finished—finished in the world," though at the time he had taken the remark in a quite literal sense. But now he seemed to see that much more was involved: that Hath had not been speaking of the house and acres, but of a way of life, an attitude of mind, a set of values.

He repeated in the letter something else that Hath had said—or rather, Nat had said it, suggesting the reason that he must go to war: "For my soul's sake," that was it. He had been a little vague about it then, but he thought that now he'd begun to understand; and that this had application to Glencoe and the fire—indeed, to almost everything that had happened in his life, that he had done or failed to do, and the motives which had prompted him. It was, he wrote, as if he saw his life reduced to entries in a ledger; and there was an asset column titled "For My Soul's Sake," and the page beneath it blank— no, not entirely blank; that was hardly fair. But there was very little written on it. And the figures on this page were the measure of one's wealth—one's *real* wealth.

He did not mean, he said, to accuse himself uniquely, for it was his generation which must be indicted; he, himself, was no more than a reflection of the world in which he'd lived, not atypical at all. He could only be convicted of having realized the fruit which his fellow men had coveted, of being a winner in a race in which, as it turned out, there were not any winners, since there were not any stakes—no *real* reward for winning; but only the winners had a chance to find that out. He would plead guilty to success—the very same in pursuit of which most people lived and died, never knowing that the stars at which they grasped were fireflies and marsh lights. And success had this advantage: once in your hand you could examine it and appraise its actual value—a benefit denied to less successful men.

"Values," he wrote, "that's where we have been wrong: bad accounting methods, confusing liabilities with assets; the books are in a mess. But I think that it is changing—not just for the duration, as many people say. And I believe in you, Hath—all you fine young men who must suffer for our faults, who must fight and win a war which you had no part in making, and who must remake a world which we have wrecked—I believe that you will not repeat the old mistakes."

He had written that, when, glancing up, he saw through the window in the dusk, the figure of a man coming up the walk, stepping carefully, slipping on the ice—a man of middle age in a worn overcoat, with, a cap with flaps pulled over his ears, and mittens on his hands, and a yellow envelope.

He watched him absently, recognizing him as the man who ran the Western Union office. Grogan was his name. Sometimes, sending off a wire, he had paused to chat with him, exchanging stories of their early railroad days.—Grogan coming up the walk—coming to the door.

And then suddenly he *knew*. He thought his heart stopped beating, but he was not surprised; he felt as he had felt that night when Madge had waked him to tell him that Glencoe was on fire—as if he were expecting it, had known that there could be no other outcome to it. He got up quickly, hurrying to the door, walking in a dream, feeling he had left himself sitting in the chair. He did not want the man to ring the bell, did not want Madge or Cassie to have any share in this.

He was in time, waiting at the door. If he had needed any other evidence, it was in Grogan's face and his averted eyes. The man said mumblingly, holding out the message—

"I didn't want to phone this, Mr. Braden. I thought I better bring it—"

"Thanks—" He took the telegram.

"I'm sorry, Mr. Braden—" And Grogan turned away, glad to be gone, walking carefully down the path, slipping on the ice.

He closed the door and opened the message, which he had no need to do, for he knew what it would say and he hardly read the words. Then Madge was in the hall, asking what it was, seeing the answer in his face. He handed her the wire.

"Oh, Sam—"

"Yeh—" He went past her into the living room. "Atonement—" he said, as if he were explaining something to himself— "Atonement—"

"Atonement?" She came and put her hand upon his arm. "What do you mean, Sam?"

He didn't answer. She shook his arm to recall him to his senses, crying out in loving kindness—

"Atonement? And for *what*?—Oh, Sam!—You who have been everything to everyone—always—all your life—"

He looked at her and saw that she would never understand. He went back to the desk and read again the letter he'd been writing, and tore it up.

People had been kind—yes, very kind. Mitch had written to him, a hasty scrawl, not saying much; but there were blots, as if the ink had run, as if tears had fallen on it. Perhaps they had been tears out of a bottle, but they would be no less *real* for that. Old Mitch—

Clang—bang—That old iron fence had been anchored there to stay; they'd been hammering all day long and they hadn't got it down.

He made the final entry, neat figures in the ledger; and he closed the book and snapped the lock and put it back on the corner of the desk. He'd been watching through the window, watching all the time from the corner of his eye. And now he saw a boy in uniform coming along the sidewalk, looking at the house—a boy like Hath, not like Hath at all, yet like him—a young man in a summer uniform, clean and trim and smart, with a strip of colored ribbons on his tunic, and silver wings, and the golden maple leaves—walking briskly, like a soldier, but jauntily, too,—straight and hard and brown, like Hath, and not like Hath—looking like his father, the image of his father, except that he had his mother's hair, blond hair—brushed straight back, no doubt, underneath his cap which was cocked a little to one side—and if he were swimming, he would have a way to twitch his head, flinging back his hair out of his eyes.—Neill Wyatt coming up the walk—coming to the door.

He got up quickly, hurrying to the hall, not wanting the bell to ring, not wanting Cassie there. His hands were wet again and his heart was pounding. He opened the door and stood waiting on the threshold.

"Mr. Braden?"—Neill Wyatt's voice, Neill Wyatt's face; but he had his mother's eyes—blue eyes, steady, smiling. He was not come in mourning, asserting obvious grief, as a stupid person might. Jaunty was the word, but not the kind of jauntiness which could give offense—careless, easy, gracious, sure of himself.

"Yes—" They shook hands.

"I'm glad to meet you, sir. I've been looking forward to it. You see, I've always felt as though we were related—" There was a humorous twinkle in his eye. "—you having once been married to my mother."

He smiled. It wasn't an impertinence, as it might have been if someone else had said it.

"Funny we've never met before, sir."

"Well, we have," he said.

"Really, Mr. Braden?"

"Yeh—" He pointed. "Right out there on the sidewalk. You were riding a velocipede."

"A velocipede?" Neill Wyatt laughed, and his laugh was like his father's. "I don't remember that, sir. I've only been here once before, when I was a little chap of four or five."

"Twenty years ago," he said, "about that, I should say. You were looking at my car and I said I'd sell it to you. You said you'd like to buy it but you hadn't any money, and I suggested that we make a trade: the car for the velocipede."

"What did I say to that, sir?"

"You said—" He smiled, remembering. "You said, 'I don't think my mother'd like it.'"

"Did I?" The young man was amused. "I must tell my mother that."

"Yeh—" He nodded. "I didn't know you then, know who you were, but afterwards—" He stopped. "But come in, Major Wyatt—" He led the way into the living room. "Your father lived here when he was a boy. The family used to come in the summertime—"

"Yes, I know, sir. My mother told me. She pointed out the house the other day."

"Oh, did she?" He went on talking, outwardly quite calm, but his nerves were like taut wire. He was postponing an ordeal which he was uncertain he could face, hoping his emotion would subside. He said, motioning toward the porch, "They used to sit out there, drinking lemonade. Your mother came over here a lot. There was a hammock in the corner of the garden—"

The young man nodded pleasantly. "I suppose you knew my father very well?"

"Oh yes, I knew your father—"

"My mother and my Uncle Wayne say I look like him. Do you think so, sir?"

He looked and looked away. "Yes—" he said, speaking as if he intended to say more, and his visitor waited, but he added nothing.

"I never saw my father. He was killed before—"

"Yes, I know—" He changed the subject. "They used to go out driving in a dogcart with red wheels—and a team of horses. Quite a thing in a little country town—"

Neill Wyatt laughed. "I can imagine."

"They didn't care what anybody thought. But please—" He turned back into the room, going toward the alcove.

"Comfortable old house, sir."

"Yes, comfortable—" He moved a chair across the desk from his.

"This is my office. It was a sort of cozy corner when your father lived here—oriental things and Moorish lamps. But sit down, Major Wyatt—"

"Thank you, sir." There was a silence.

"A cigarette?" He offered the box and struck a match, but it went out.

"Don't bother, sir." The young man struck one for himself, speaking through the smoke of his cigarette, neither solemnly nor casually: "My mother asked me to express her deepest sympathy."

"Thank you," he said and added in a moment, "Thank her for me." Again there was a pause. He waited, drumming softly with his fingers on the desk.

"I hardly know how to begin, sir?"

He didn't speak and presently the boy went on.

Hath had been his closest friend, he said—first in that school in Switzerland, and then three years at Harvard, and ever since. He was the older by a year or two—by eighteen months, to be exact; and so he'd always been a bit ahead of Hath—could win from him at tennis, four sets out of five, unimportant things like that. But Hath was the better student and got the better marks. He never would have thought that Hath would make a flyer, but that only went to show how far wrong you could be, for, as it turned out, Hath could fly circles round him. He had been among the best. "Yes, the very best," he said. "I don't know if you knew that, Mr. Braden?"

He shook his head.

"No, of course, he'd never tell you." But that, he said, had been the fact: what the fellows in his outfit thought about him, from the C. O. down—that he was among the best. If there was a job to do that wanted guts and brains, they'd pick Hath Braden for it. He paused and tapped the ash from his cigarette. Hath was a fighter pilot and he'd been with the bombers; their airdromes were widely separated. They never saw each other except when they managed to wangle leave together—or sometimes in the sky, if the outfit Hath was with happened to be over them, acting as their convoy. He'd know it if the radio began to talk in German somebody shouting, "Achtung!" and a lot of guttural words. Hath did it for a joke. It would scare the bomber crews out of their wits, making them believe they'd got their wave lengths crossed, or that a Jerry had sneaked right in among them. The C. O. raised Cain about it, but Hath would do it now and then, out of earshot of the field. And when he heard that warning "Achtung!" in his ear, he could be pretty sure Hath wasn't far away.

And then, as like as not, when they were out of danger of attack, Hath would come diving down, shooting by the bomber as if it had been tied, leaning out to wave. And he'd have a fleeting glimpse of the markings on the nose: a pair of painted dice—a four spot and a trey. "Lucky Seven" was the name he had given to his ship. "But of course you know that, sir?"

He nodded.

"And I suppose you know that underneath the dice there were six swastikas—the six that he'd shot down?"

He nodded. He had stopped drumming on the desk and his fingers were clasped tight upon the edge of it.

"But perhaps you don't know, sir, that there should have been three more—the three that cost his life?"

"No—" He shook his head.

"Nine was his total, sir—and the last three, three to one. He'll be decorated for it when they get around to it: the Flying Cross perhaps; it ought to be the best they have to give. And some day I presume you'll get a full report in military language."

He nodded.

"But I can tell you, sir, and I'm sure that there's no one better qualified to do so, for I was there and saw it." The young man paused to light another cigarette, holding it between his thumb and finger, gesturing with it gracefully, as his father would have done.

The week before, he said, they had both got leave and had gone up to London to spend their holiday, having quite a time of it, taking in the shows, being gay and lazy. The last night they were there a man named Mitch Ballou, the father of Hath's wife, had taken them to dinner. They had gone to the Savoy and had dined extremely well and had quite a bit to drink—champagne in fact. Mitch had been good company; toward the end he had been a little drunk, but he had been amusing and the evening most successful. And then the check had come and Mitch had captured it, though Hath had tried to take it. No doubt it was a whopper, for Mitch had looked aghast; possibly he didn't have the money in his pocket, but he'd hung onto the check, protesting that the party was on him. And Hath had gotten out his dice, as he was sure to do when there was a question of who would pay a bill, or a dispute, or anything—"The dice you gave him, sir. He always had them handy in his pocket."

« 425 »

"Did he?"

"Oh yes!" The young man smiled. "He'd roll them out on a table or a bar on the slightest provocation, or on none at all; and if anyone admired them, as people often did, he'd always say, 'My father made them for me—made them with his hands.' He was very proud of you, sir."

"Proud of me?—You really think he was?"

"I know he was. He thought the world of you, sir. But—" He laughed apologetically. "—silly of me telling you a thing like that, because of course you know it."

"Yes—" He nodded slowly.

"Funny, too—" Neill Wyatt cocked his head, looking more than ever like his father. "—because in school and college I didn't have the idea he was very close to you. But lately he was always talking of you—the kind of things you'd want your son to say about you. It used to make me wish I had a father of my own. Well then—" He went back to his story.

Hath had gotten out his dice, insisting that they gamble for the dinner check; and Mitch had agreed to that, and they had rolled the dice and Hath had lost—that is, he'd won the check, remarking as he put the dice back in his pocket: they'd been lucky in the air, not so lucky on the ground.

They had parted on the pavement in front of the Savoy, for they were to leave on different trains, from different stations. It was a drizzly night. He had stood at the curb, waiting for a taxi, watching Hath go hurrying down the street, looking back and waving, calling, "I'll be seeing you." And the next time he had seen him—

It was a day in March—dirty, muggy weather, but the sun breaking through a little now and then. His squadron had been ordered on a bombing mission—targets in Holland: factories, bridges, railroad yards, and a munitions dump which had been assigned to him. They had taken off in the afternoon when the sun—what sun there was—would be behind them, flying high above the Channel, with an escort of fighters in the clouds above them; but at the time he hadn't known what outfit it was.

They had kept in close formation to a dispersal point, and then peeled off to their respective tasks, which were all close together, or comparatively so: two or three to this job, and two or three to that, or sometimes only one, as it had been in his case. They had come down through the overcast and found it fairly clear as they approached the ground. And they had picked their target without much difficulty, encountering little flak, and surprised and pleased that it should be so easy.

The bomb doors had been opened and they had made a pass, flying low to drop their eggs where it seemed they couldn't miss. There had been more flak then, but not enough to bother. But though it appeared they must have hit their target, still, aside from the explosions of their bombs, the effect was not at all what they'd expected. And so he had decided to make another pass at an even lower altitude, and drop another batch in a slightly different place.

And this, as it turned out, was a mistake, for the damage they'd expected had only been delayed; the disaster was preparing. And this probably explained why the flak was unalarming—that the ground crews were not taking any chances and were getting out of reach as quickly as they could, not wanting to be slaughtered with their own projectiles. However that might be, they had come in again on this second try and were directly over it, when the whole thing had gone up in a terrific blast—flame and smoke and sound—

The young man shook his head, smiling reminiscently. "I can't describe it, sir. The truth is that I don't remember much about it. But if you can imagine what it would be like on top of a volcano when it was erupting?"

He nodded. His fingernails were white, pressing on the desk.

"I was certain we were done for." And it had been nearly that: one man was dead—the gunner in the blister, and the blister blown flat; two more were badly hurt; and the rest of them banged up and their wits knocked out of them. The ship a limping wreck, riddled like a sieve: one motor was washed out and one was staggering; oil lines cut, spraying oil on everything—you couldn't read the instruments; controls all out of gear; the radio was smashed—they could hear but couldn't send.

Bail out and crash the ship had been his first idea, but this would have been fatal to the wounded men, and so he had determined to keep going while he could. They had thrown overboard everything that could be lifted—including, in their haste and dazed confusion, all their ammunition except the belts already in the guns, two of which were jammed and useless; and this had enabled them to gain a little altitude. But the ship remained completely unmaneuverable, with scarcely flying speed to keep it from a stall, wallowing like a tanker in a heavy sea.

His co-pilot was unconscious, hanging in his belt; the navigator badly hurt and unable to assist him. He had steered a compass course, guessing at the drift since there was no one to figure it, heading through the dusk at murky orange streaks which marked the setting sun, praying for the darkness, expecting every moment to be spotted from the air or from the ground, which in either case seemed fatal since they could not fight nor run.

Minutes ticked away. And then, with the Channel still far off, he had made out a pin point in the western sky—a pin point growing bigger every second, to a dime, then to a dollar, coming like a comet, diving toward him like a hawk. An enemy patrol: he had no doubt about it, nor any of the outcome. The young man paused, rolling his cigarette between his thumb and finger— "Not a pleasant situation to be in, sir."

He nodded, his heart caught in a vise, for he sensed now what was coming.

The young man went on, not dramatically at all—lightly, but not flippantly. He had warned his gunners to stand by, telling them to hold their fire until they were certain of it, seeing nothing else to do but to do the best they could and be shot down in the end. The plane was pretty close now, but still too far away to be sure what it was, with the sunset in his eyes. And then—

"Achtung!" A voice out of the sky into his ear. And he knew that it was Hath. And the Lockheed diving at him like a Stuka in a flood of German words, missing him by meters, zooming up to loop around him.

"Yeh?" he said, and he let loose of the desk, leaning across it with his elbows on it. "You mean, Major Wyatt, that he'd come back for *you?*"

"Yes sir, for me. He'd come back alone—to find me if he could."

"Yes.—Yes, I see." He leaned back in his chair, swinging it a little to look out of the window—an afternoon in June, lawn and flowers in the Square, children playing underneath the trees, graveled paths and benches, girls and soldiers strolling—not seeing what he looked at and not hearing very well what the young man was saying, which no longer seemed important—seeing instead a small boy on a log raft in the river, treading the rolling logs as if he didn't know that they were dangerous—or didn't care about it; hearing him say, stuttering a little, the way he'd do when he was excited. "You—you—you all right, Sam?"

« 428 »

But the young man went on talking: Hath had told him—flashing by and off again, away a mile or two, climbing like a rocket, diving back, playing like a porpoise, in and out and all round—finding he could hear and could answer with his wings, answer yes or no— "You all right, Neill?" he'd asked. And he had dipped, "Okay." Then Hath had told him: his outfit had been convoy to the bombers. They'd met no opposition, everything had been routine, running like a watch, and he'd thought they'd all come safely out of it. But coming back, just before they reached the Channel, he had heard the bombers talking to each other, and had learned that Neill was missing, though none of them could say they had seen the ship, shot down. But one reported that he had seen the plane close to the ground, and had seen it disappear in a sheet of flame and smoke from which he had not observed it to emerge. "Not so good," Hath said. "But I thought I'd come back and have a look around." And that's what he had done: once safe above the Channel he had left his outfit, which he had a right to do since he was in command, though perhaps they wouldn't like it on the ground. Anyway, he had come back.

They had gone on together through the darkening sky: the trim pursuit ship loafing at half throttle, and the straining, lumbering derelict, with the dead man in the blister, and the badly wounded fellows lying tangled in the wreckage, the co-pilot still unconscious and sagging in his belt; for though it seemed a lifetime had elapsed since the disaster, it was really no more than a few minutes. Hath had kept on talking to him, intending no doubt to bolster his morale which wasn't very high—questioning him about the damage: was the landing gear all right?—and the flaps?—and this and that? And kidding him a little, guessing what had happened, poking fun at bombers which couldn't get away from their own exploding bombs.

They could see the coast line now and his hope began to rise, for there seemed a decent chance they would not be intercepted, and if the ship kept flying he might yet bring her home. And then, when safety appeared to be at hand, within reasonable expectancy—

The young man shrugged and smiled. "But that's the way it goes, sir." He pointed with his cigarette. "Dropping down out of a cloud— one, two, three of them—hovering for a moment, then coming on like shots—enemy fighters, sir. They'd spotted us at last, in the final shred of daylight."

"Yeh—" He swung his chair back to the desk, his attention coming with it, tensely riveted again.

And Hath had laughed. "I'll get you through," he said. "You keep that old tub going." He'd dipped his wings to show he understood, and he had warned his gunners, but knowing they could be of little help. He had revved his limping motors to the limit they would take, his eyes glued to his instruments, his whole attention centered on his job. And for the rest, he could not say there was much that he had seen, but it must be pieced together from fragmentary observations of himself and of his crew, an uncertain reconstruction of what had taken place in that fleeting bedlam of confusion—the darkness and the tracers, and the four ships changing places, whipping round each other —and all in the twinkling of an eye, a matter of split seconds.

The enemy, he thought, had done the natural thing, had performed the proper tactic in the situation as it appeared to them, not knowing that the bomber was a helpless, battered wreck which they could dispose of at their leisure. They had delegated one to hold the escort off while the others closed in on the bomber from the rear, diving straight at their objective with an interval between them. But Hath had dodged an issue with the ship assigned to him, diving sharply from its onslaught and coming back from underneath on the tail of the first one closing in upon the bomber; and, taken unaware, it had gone down in his first burst of fire. "One," he had shouted; and he had gone on through, diving this time beneath the belly of the bomber, zooming up ahead of it, wheeling to come back, catching the second one almost head on. And again, the enemy, intent upon his target, was taken unaware; and the ship went down, spinning like a corkscrew. "Two," Hath shouted.

"By God, sir—" Neill Wyatt stood up suddenly, leaning with his hands upon the desk, stammering just a little with excitement. "It—it was magnificent."

He nodded.

"But it couldn't last forever, sir—not a horseshoe nor a seven." The third had got him, but he had got it, too, for it had gone down in flames. He couldn't say exactly how it happened: the combat was too fast to follow with the eye and the tracers were like sparks beaten from an anvil. None of them could afterwards describe it. "Achtung!" Hath had cried when he was hit—or it had been then, he thought, and then some German words trailing into silence. He'd thought that Hath was fooling, if he'd thought at all about it; and then, not hearing him, that his radio was out or that his own had quit; not suspecting he was hurt, for the plane had gone on flying—was still in level flight and apparently uninjured when the battle had been won and the last of the enemy had vanished. But then it seemed to falter, yawing and skidding as if it went unguided—the four spot and the trey nosing up and down. And then at last it fell, not spinning, not on fire, dropping gently like a leaf, slipping off on one wing, steadying for a moment, and slipping off again—like a ship without a pilot. At the end it turned nose down and dove into the sea.

"That's what happened, sir." The young man pressed out his cigarette in the ash tray on the desk. "I thought you'd want to know just how it was."

He nodded.

"I think he was dead while he was flying—when I no longer heard him speaking to me. That's the way he would have wanted it."

He nodded. It was somewhere in his mind that he had heard the story long ago, that no detail of it was new or unexpected, that it could not have been different or had any other end—that something long unfinished, had been at last completed.

"I owe my life to Hath, sir—six of us do." Neill Wyatt wasn't being solemn or emotional: there wasn't any alteration in his manner, any quaver in his voice; but his eyes were very earnest, convincingly sincere. "I'd like to think I'd have done the same for him. I hope I would, sir."

"Yes," he said, "I am sure that you would." And he was sure of it. Neither of them spoke again. After a moment he got up and walked with the young man to the door, and when they were outside it on the step—

"Thank you very much," he said, holding out his hand. "Thank you, Major Wyatt."

"I wish—" Neill Wyatt hesitated. "I wish you'd call me Neill, sir."

"Why yes—" He smiled. "Good-by, Neill, and—good luck."

"The same to you, sir." The young man brought his hand up in salute and went briskly down the path.

He turned back into the house, closing the door behind him, and there was Cassie standing by the stairs in the dimly lighted hall, with something in her hand—as if she were waiting for him.

"It's your lunch," she said.

"Oh yes—" It took him a moment to come back.

"If you're going to work, it's time for you to start."

"Yes, so it is." He took the lunch box from her. "Thank you, Cassie. He thought that she was looking at him curiously, and he turned back to the door, picking up his hat. "Yes," he said, "I'd better start."

He cut across the Square—that was the shortest way: across the Square, through Shanty Town, down the winding swale, now a busy thoroughfare—the old way of his childhood. He had time enough; he needn't hurry. A pleasant afternoon, children playing on the grass, girls and soldiers strolling, men like himself with lunch boxes like his underneath their arms. He came to the center of the Square where the paths all intersected, and suddenly he stopped, staring through a vista in the trees.

There was the old brick house with its crazy cupola, but the iron fence was gone, whisked away and vanished—not a trace of it remained. The old house looked familiar and strangely unfamiliar, like a person caught undressed—not imposing in the least, certainly not formidable, but exactly what it was and always had been: an old brick house with a crazy cupola. Funny what a difference an iron fence could make. He laughed softly to himself. Nobody to keep in and nobody to keep out—not any more. Fences coming down—

"Hi, Sam!"

He looked around and recognized a fellow that he knew, an acquaintance in the factory, whose lathe was next to his—a good machinist, too,—a man about his age, a little younger maybe. The man caught up with him.

"I missed you, Sam," he said. "You been sick or something?"

"Yeh, sick—" He smiled. "I'm all right now."

They walked along together—